The Girl Who Cried Wolf

Robert Ferrigno

Other books by Robert Ferrigno

The Horse Latitudes
Cheshire Moon
Dead Man's Dance
Dead Silent
Heartbreaker
Flinch
Scavenger Hunt
The Wake-Up
Prayers for the Assassin
Sins of the Assassin
Heart of the Assassin

Visit Robert online at www.robertferrigno.com

In memory of my good friend, Steve Plesa.

Like any good musician, he left in the middle of the night for a better gig.

DiMedici Press

PROLOGUE

GLENN PUMPED AWAY on the swing, rusty chains creaking as he watched the last of the sunbathers lazing on their towels, legs crossed, bodies tangled. Music drifted from cars in the parking lot. Little kids played tag with the crashing waves, foam tickling their bare feet as they dashed out of reach, squealing. He swung higher now, pulling himself straight into the clear blue sky, leaving the earth behind. The setting sun hung just above the horizon, the Pacific streaked with red and purple and gold. Toxic as far as the eye could see. If he thought about it too hard his head would explode.

Eli rinsed off under the shower at the edge of the beach. A short, muscular surf rat in knee-length jams, he was an amped-up nineteen-year old with crackling blue eyes and sun-bleached dreads. He turned off the shower, shook out his hair, and sauntered over to the swing set. "Tree's *still* not back? You think something's wrong?"

"*Everything's* wrong."

"Lighten up, you know what I mean." Eli cranked off one-handed pull-ups on the chinning bar, biceps popping. "You think he got caught?"

Glenn kept swinging, higher and higher. While he had spent the last half hour watching for cop cars through the 25cent-a-minute tourist binoculars, thinking about everything that could go wrong, Eli had romped in the surf with a stray dog like they were blood brothers, innocent and mindless and free. Fucking idiot.

Glenn could see the housing development on the bluffs overlooking South Laguna, three-story behemoths rising from the orange dirt— Golden Sky Estates, prices reduced to $3.5 million and half of them already sold. Fourteen houses in various stages of completion, the workman gone for the day. It had taken eight years of legal battles before the developers won the right to build on the bluffs, eight years and the developers finally got their way by giving a few acres of salt marsh to the nature weenies as a permanent bird sanctuary. Big whoop. A seagull drifted overhead, oblivious to the filth in the air, the heavy metals in the fish it ate. Lucky bird not to know what was killing him. Glenn felt his cells under assault with every breath he took.

The winds blew up from the south, straight off the San Onofre nuke plant, scrambling Glenn's DNA, singeing his bone marrow. If he ever wanted to breed, which he *didn't*, he'd probably father some two-headed retard. The richies ready to move into Golden Sky Estates wouldn't have to worry—they'd have bottled water and HEPA air filters, they'd pop iodine capsules to prevent radiation sickness, and spend whatever it took to eat certified organic. If you had money, the rest of the world could fuck off and die. Must be nice. Glenn was determined to find out just how nice. Cleo was going to help him. Girl had opened his *eyes*. Pointed out the line in the sand, and what happened to people with the courage to step over it. Not that Glenn needed much encouragement.

"Southern California rules," said Eli, doing slow rotations on the monkey bars in the dusk. "Swimming in the ocean…you can't beat it."

"I hope you kept your mouth closed. You're going to swallow a condom out there someday."

Eli winced. "Yeah…I forget how dirty it is," he said, his pectorals flat as salad plates, twitching now. "I seen all kinds of tar balls and fish in the water floating belly up, and this one kid had a dead crab stuck on top of his sand castle."

Glenn closed his eyes as he gripped the swing chains, pumping higher and higher. He didn't give a shit about crabs or fish or little kids and their sand castles. He let his head fall back, swinging slowly, his long hair trailing across the sand, and he imagined his hair writing words in a foreign language, storm warnings no one but he could read. It was hard being the smartest one. He was twenty-nine, taller than Eli, smooth muscled, sleek and powerful—with his olive skin and good looks he could have probably been a male model. A real charmer in baggy cream-colored shorts and a well-worn HARVARD polo shirt. He probably could have gotten in to that fancyass school too if his grades were better or he hadn't blown off the SATs or his old man hadn't been such a loser. Screw it. The polo shirt was as good as a diploma anyway. Besides, after today—

"I *thought* that was you."

Glenn opened his eyes. Saw two girls looking down at him, teenagers in string bikinis, salt crusted on their tanned bellies. He pushed his sunglasses back onto his forehead.

"I saw you at the Eco-Summit last year in Santa Cruz," said the redhead. "You and the cutie pie on the chinning bar. There was an old guy too. You gave a seminar on free-climbing...so we could hang banners off bridges to save the forest and the Gulf and all the rest of it. The three of you had a funny name...what was it?"

"Monkey Boyz. With a Z."

"Monkey Boyz, right. Fits you too." The redhead dragged a pink toe in the sand. "I thought you were really brave. Really committed."

"Sure, I remember you." Glenn looked her over. "You were the only one who got past the first story of the practice structure."

"I used to be a gymnast. Then I hit puberty."

Glenn smiled. "You hit it pretty hard too."

The redhead blushed. She had three gold hoops in her right ear, another in her belly button. Maybe another someplace else. The other girl was busy watching Eli doing rotations on the bar, giggling as he hesitated at the top, toes pointed toward the sky, showing off for her. "Where's the other one?" said the redhead. "The geezer."

"He's not here. Just me and Eli." Glenn stood up, inches from her now. "I'm Glenn," he said softly. "*Glenn*...like a quiet place in the woods."

The redhead nodded. "Okay." She had a tiny pimple on the side of her mouth. Could be herpes. He took a step back, but she didn't seem to notice. "I guess you guys are here for the big STOP CORPORATE CRIME rally, huh?"

"That's right."

The wind lifted her hair and she pushed it back. "It's just so cool. Seems like every car on the freeway has a *Go Veggie* or an *Anarchy now!* bumper sticker."

"Yeah, blows against the empire."

3

The redhead looked confused. Her friend called to her, said her mom was there. "Maybe we could get together at after the rally tomorrow?" she hurried. "I'm working at the Humble Harvest Falafel stand."

"Cool," said Glenn.

She kissed him on the cheek. "Totally."

Glenn wiped his cheek, watched her chase after her friend. He wondered if he should clean the spot with alcohol.

"Tree just drove up," said Eli.

Glenn ambled to the pay-binoculars, digging in his pockets for change. His heart pounded as he swung the lenses toward their van.

Tree got out of the old VW camper, so tall that he had to bend almost in half to clear the door. He started towards the playground, a glum chum in his late 30s, but looking older, his long hair and beard streaked with gray. A logger before he saw the light, Tree wasn't much for talk, but he was hardcore and the man could climb. He wasn't as fast as Eli, who muscled up the tallest timber, and held the speed record for the Golden Gate, but Tree climbed effortlessly, instinctively, not even looking where he put his hands or feet. Glenn wasn't much for art galleries and poetry, but watching Tree scamper up a three hundred year old redwood at dawn was as close to beauty as he had ever seen.

Glenn turned the binoculars to the housing development on the bluffs, the half-built houses sharp as sticks. Incredible view from the mansions. Some business fuck could probably spot seals and dolphin from his Lay-Z-Boy on the patio, track gray whales going south to Baja to spawn. Ring a little silver bell and here comes Josephina or Esmeralda with a cold beer and caviar on a Ritz cracker. Houses probably came with a screening room and a bathtub deep enough to drown an elk. Glenn sensed Tree standing beside him as he watched the house through the binoculars. "You smell like the inside of an oven, big man."

"Yo, Tree!" called Eli, doing walkovers on the parallel bars. "Check this out."

"Any problem cutting the lines?" said Glenn.

"No," said Tree.

Glenn focused on a huge crow perched on a porta-potty at the edge of the bluffs. Bad decision at every level. "How long before you make the call?"

"Soon," said Tree. "Got to give the gas time to build up."

CLICK. The binoculars' time ran out, the image suddenly black. Glenn looked up, watched the horizon. The sun almost gone now, the ocean bleeding. The last of the locals packed up their things, shaking out their blankets. A doofus with a metal detector walked the dunes, head down, headphones on as he doused for nickels and class rings. "You got a quarter, Tree?"

"We should get out of here," said Tree.

"No way I'm missing the big finale," said Glenn.

Eli did slow spins on the bar.

Glenn held his hand out. Resisted the impulse to snap his fingers.

Tree hesitated, then gave him some change.

Glenn fed five minutes worth of quarters into the binoculars.

Eli straddled the bar. Squinted at the bluffs. "Uh-oh."

"What?" said Glenn.

"Car's coming," said Eli.

Glenn peered through the binoculars. A white car drove down the main street of Golden Sky. Slowed. Parked in front of the model home. Shit.

"You said there wasn't going to be anybody there," said Eli.

"Wasn't supposed to be." Glenn gently turned the focus knob, the image sharpening, so clear now that he could read the license plate number. A woman in the front seat touched up her lipstick. "Her bad luck."

"*Her?*" said Eli, still sitting on the bar.

"Bitch in a big ass, white Mercedes," said Glenn. "A real ozone killer. Gotta be a realtor." He zoomed in closer. "Tall blonde getting out...walking toward the house—"

Eli shaded his eye with one hand. "I seen her at the open house last week. Stone MILF." He glanced over at Glenn. "Shame to waste something that sweet, bro."

"What, the Girl Scout troop was full so you signed on with me and

Tree?" said Glenn. "Hike up your nutsack, Eli."

"I'm just saying...why not wait until she's gone?" said Eli.

Glenn whistled, eyes pressed against the binoculars. "She just ran out of the house. Got her hand over her mouth. Left the front door wide open, so the gas is leaking out all over now. She going to ruin everything if we let her." He looked over at Tree. "You going to make the call or not?"

Tree clutched the cell phone.

Glenn stared at him. "We're making a *statement* here, big man. No more demonstrations. No more shutting down freeways and torching Hummer dealerships. Tree? Look at me, Tree. We have to show them we're serious."

The phone trembled in Tree's hand.

Glenn went back to the binoculars. "She's in her car now. Car's zigzagging...she just ran into the curb..."

Tree punched in numbers on the phone.

Eli did a handstand on the bars.

Tree's finger crooked above the last number.

"You wait any longer there's not going to be enough gas to do the job," said Glenn. "You either get in line to gangbang Mama Earth or you do something about it."

Eli spun around the bar, faster and faster.

Tree's finger stabbed the last number.

Eli flipped up, made three rotations in the air and landed on the sand. He stuck the dismount. Threw his hands up.

The model home exploded in a blue fireball as the natural gas inside ignited. Splintered 2x4s and orange barrel-tile rained across the beach. Secondary explosions erupted from the other houses that Tree had rigged. Deafening explosions, the flames feeding off themselves now. The Mercedes rolled slowly out of the smoke, covered in fire as it tumbled off the bluffs. The car landed upside down onto the beach, tires ablaze, black smoke rolling across the sand.

Eli stared at the burning car. Slowly lowered his hands.

Glenn smiled so hard he was afraid his face was going to crack.

"I...I don't want to be here anymore," whispered Tree.

"Sure," said Glenn. "Okay."

"I want to go someplace green," said Tree.

"That's just where we're going," said Glenn. "Seattle's as green as it gets. I've got plans for us. This is just the beginning." He swung the binoculars around the beach, checked out the open-mouthed spectators. Car horns beeped. He scanned the distant jetty through the binoculars. Stopped. Focused. Not believing what he saw. Cleo looked back at him from the jetty, straight black hair catching the wind, her white dress billowing around her legs. She looked right at him. Right into his heart. Blew him a kiss. Glenn shivered as the heat from the burning Mercedes rippled across the beach like a fiery snake.

CHAPTER 1

"HOW MUCH FARTHER to Bumpkinville?" Remy Brandt steered the red Porsche with one hand, tires squealing as she sped up the narrow, winding road, outracing the headlights. Rain lashed the trees hanging over the road, sent leaves swirling in their wake.

"Almost there...and it's *Woodinville*." Grace Schearson huddled in the small back seat, her plastic raincoat crinkling with every movement. A pretty girl grown careless with her appearance, or maybe just too busy, her brown eyes tired, her nails chipped.

Mack Dupree sat in the passenger seat, one arm draped across Remy's shoulders. He stared into the night, into the houses behind low fences and hedges, their windows warm puddles of yellow light. He imagined families...kids bickering over the TV remote and spilled Cheetos, Dad working on a beer gut and Mom dying her hair in the kitchen sink. He wondered if they knew how lucky they were.

"Could you *please* slow down, Remy?" said Grace.

"Good luck with that." Mack turned toward Grace. "Plenty of room out here. Must be nice to live someplace where you could sit on the back porch in your underwear and read the Sunday paper."

The car skidded on the wet pavement. "As you can tell, I'm still working on housebreaking the boyfriend," Remy said to Grace.

Grace smiled at Mack. "Good luck with that."

Mack watched the road now, pressing a non-existent brake pedal as Remy slid the car through the turns at peak RPM, the engine screaming. He gently kneaded the back of her neck, caught her look of pleasure in the glow from the instrument panel. She was like one of those big cats in the zoo that spent their whole time pacing. Once they were released, once they got a chance to really open it up, there was no stopping them. He inhaled her perfume. He knew exactly how she felt.

"*There,*" said Grace, pointing. "Next house on the right."

The car bumped up the gravel driveway, came to a stop. Rain sizzled on the hood. The lawn was soggy and overgrown in the feeble glow of the porch light, a pink flamingo lying on its side beside an untended flowerbed. The house needed paint, one of the shutters hung crookedly, and the wooden stairs sagged.

Remy turned off the engine. "I always wondered what hillbilly heaven would look like."

Mack let Grace out.

"Watch the second step. It's rotten." Grace ran toward the front porch, the rain making pockata-pockata sounds on her raincoat.

Remy stayed behind the wheel, staring at the house. The yard. She shook her head. "Thanks for doing this tonight. I know you'd rather be on the road."

"You could be nicer to her," said Mack.

"If I wasn't a bitch Grace would think I was patronizing her. She's very proud." Remy walked toward the house. Turning up the collar of the cashmere coat was her only concession to the rain. She almost slipped on the second step, grabbed for the railing. Those high heels of hers cost a month's rent, but they gave no traction. Not that Mack was complaining. She beckoned to him at the top of the stairs. Hair to her shoulders, blonde and lean and restless. She tapped her foot now.

Mack ignored her, ignored the rain too, looking around in the darkness, checking the shadows around the house, the nearby trees, trying to get a sense of exactly where he was. Old habit. Learn the terrain. Remember your first impression. Pay attention. He listened to the rain, uncomfortable and not sure why. He climbed the stairs, stepped over the second one, and joined Remy for her entrance.

Grace circled the living room, turning on lights. A small room with cracked plaster, one of the lampshades singed from the bulb. A threadbare easy chair faced a worn brown leather sofa with a crocheted Afghan across the back. Grace finished her circuit, a little out of breath. Nerves. She had been jumpy since the moment they were introduced earlier this evening, avoiding eye contact, fiddling with her hair. She and Remy were both thirty-one, but Grace looked ten years older. Thickening through the middle, her makeup poorly applied—he didn't blame her for being jumpy.

He *did* blame her for the FREE MUMIA poster tacked on one wall, the cop killer in his sullen martyr pose. Mack hated that poster. Seemed like every frat-boy dope dealer he ever busted, every strong-arm artist he took down had that poster. Gangbangers were more dangerous, but at least they had style, preferring images of the Virgin of Guadalupe or an Aztec warrior velvet painting. One look at that Mumia poster and he wished that Remy had begged off this quickie cocktail hour. They could have been on their way back to California. She could tell Grace they'd catch up at the next reunion.

Remy surveyed the living room, hands on her hips. "Well, you can stop your pursuit of the bottom, Gracie. Mission accomplished."

Grace tossed her plastic raincoat in the corner. Let it drip onto the buckling hardwood floor. "We can't all be heiresses, that would spoil all your fun."

Remy smiled, and it was pure and genuine. "Yes...actually, it would."

Grace laughed along with her, the two of them giving each other the finger. Old friends, a million miles apart but they both treasured honesty. Appreciated its limitations, too. Grace could give as good as she got.

"I haven't seen you in so long," said Grace, "and I feel like we could just pick up where we left off. As if we're still a couple of college girls sitting in Professor Jessup's class—"

"That asshole," said Remy.

"I thought he was going to have an aneurysm when you contradicted him about the application of the Wheeler Principle," said Grace, remembering. "*Don't argue with me, young lady,*" she mimicked, "*I've been teaching fundamentals of tort law since you were in diapers.*"

"*...since you were in diapers,*" said Remy in perfect harmony.

Grace stared at her, a mix of warmth and wonder...maybe a little envy too. "You haven't changed a bit. You look just the same."

"So do you, Gracie."

"Gracie...you're the only one who ever called me that." Grace's weak smile faded. "You're wrong, though. I have changed. I'm not at all like I was then. I had such grand plans. I was going to save the world. You must feel vindicated." She looked at Mack. "I used to tell her that entertainment law was a waste of her talents, and Remy would say, if the world needed a defense attorney it was probably guilty."

"I was teasing," said Remy. "You were so serious, and I liked arguing with you."

"No, you were right." Grace walked into the kitchen, pulled a tray of ice cubes from the freezer. A cocktail shaker and bottles of gin and vermouth were already set out. "I've been wasting my time. And time is all we have."

"Bullshit," said Remy. "Entertainment law is all about ego and power. While I spend my time arguing over square footage of the star's trailer, last year you argued that salmon preservation case before the Ninth Circuit. So who's wasting their time?"

"It was *three* years ago that I argued before the Ninth and I lost the case," said Grace, eyeballing the booze into the shaker. "In the last alumni newsletter I saw a photo of you having lunch with Sandra Bullock."

"The food was lousy, and Sandy spilled her iced tea on me," said Remy.

"*Sandy?*" said Grace.

"Let's continue the debate the next time we get together," said Remy. "Right now the question is, *when* do we get to meet this mystery boyfriend of yours? I can't wait to take a look at the man who finally found your G-spot."

"Soon." Grace shook the cocktail shaker. "And he *wasn't* the first."

"Vasco de Gama had an easier time finding the fountain of youth," said Remy.

"It was Ponce de Leon." Mack shrugged. "For those keeping score at home."

Remy kissed him hard. "Nothing like being corrected by a state university graduate."

Mack kissed her back. Harder. "What makes you think I graduated?"

CHAPTER 2

PROTECTED BY DARKNESS, Glenn peered through the side window into the brightly lit living room. Rain dripped off his face and jacket. He couldn't make out the conversation over the sound of the rain, but the intimacy between Remy and Mack was obvious by their expression, their playful stance. Too bad. Glenn didn't like the boyfriend. Not at all. One of those walk lightly types, looking around when he got out of the car. Glenn had pressed himself into a thorn bush to avoid being seen and it had *hurt*. Glenn watched his own angry face in the window. Distracted by his reflection, he arranged his wet hair until he was pleased. It didn't take long.

CHAPTER 3

REMY SIPPED THE martini. Cocked her head. Went back for more. "Gracie, you're a hopeless do-gooder with no sense of style, but *damn,* you make an honest drink."

"A complement from her highness?" Grace fanned herself with her hand.

Mack drank half his martini, slide open the glass door to the deck. He stood in the doorway, the sound of rain filling the room.

Grace moistened her lips with the martini. "Did you *really* break a man's jaw on your first date with Remy?"

"Well...I didn't know it was our first date until after I hit him," said Mack.

"I was at the Kenya Club with the most boring studio exec in the world, which is saying something," said Remy. "Around midnight I sent Mr. VP for Development on his way, had another drink and left to get a cab. Two men who had been pestering me to dance followed me out. They evidently were under the impression that if you call a woman a cunt often enough, she'll melt in your arms." She winked at Mack. "That's when our hero stepped in."

"No wonder you fell for him," said Grace.

"It was easy," Remy said to Grace. "So many of the men I deal with professionally think the size of their penis is directly proportional to their decibel level, but Mack talked to the yahoos with the *softest* voice. Very polite. He said that there had clearly been a misunderstanding and they should go use their considerable charms on the ladies back inside. Mack gave them a chance to retreat." She grinned, showed her canines. "I'm glad they didn't take it."

"So you were in the club too?" said Grace. "You saw Remy leave?"

"I look like a dancer to you?" said Mack.

Grace nodded. "Yes."

"You're a lousy judge of men." Mack smiled. "I was at a gas station across the street when I saw her going round with her gentlemen callers."

13

"We ended up talking until dawn at this barbeque joint, Mack soaking his fists in ice water while I fed him hot links. We've been together ever since." Remy went to sit on the sprung couch but thought better of it. She finished her drink, looked at Mack, swaying. "Six months...six months, and we still bicker like newlyweds."

"Love at first sight...there's nothing like it," said Grace, flushing. She looked like she didn't know what to do with her hands. "My boyfriend and I, we're the same way. It's like riding an avalanche, being swept along, faster and faster, and even when you tell yourself to slow down, to *consider* what you're doing...you just can't stop."

Mack blinked away his blurred vision. Tried to anyway. He set down his drink on the counter. Almost missed. "I'm going to get some...some air." He stepped out onto the deck, the rain beating against his face, the coolness welcome after the warmth of the house.

"That must mean it's right, doesn't it, Remy?" said Grace, her voice throaty. "When you can't stop yourself?"

"I hate weak men," said Remy. "All those agreeable ass kissers...they all have such...such fine manners, but none of them would lift a finger to help you. Not...not if you really needed help." She started towards Mack, but her knees buckled just inside the doorway.

Mack saw her slump to the floor. He grabbed her armpits, tried to drag her onto the deck, out into the fresh air, but she was sooooo heavy...dead weight. His hands slipped away from her, and he fell backwards, his head banging against the deck. It would have been funny, but he was too tired to laugh. The front door closed. Somebody leaving...or somebody coming in. He needed to clear his head, then he could try again to move Remy. He staggered to the deck railing, his footsteps splashing in the rain, and the railing's rotten wood give way under him, Mack tumbling off. Down. Down. Down into the darkness, branches and leaves tearing at him, as he rolled end over end, bouncing off rocks, hard things, sharp things. He passed out before he stopped.

CHAPTER 4

GLENN SAW GRACE put down her drink on the glass coffee table, her hand shaking. She sensed his presence, turned and rushed to him. Embraced him in spite of his wet clothes. He pushed her back. "Where's the tough guy?"

Grace pointed toward the broken railing on the deck, her finger trembling.

Rain pattered onto the deck as Glenn walked out, carefully peeked over the edge. He saw treetops and broken branches and mud running down the slope, but he couldn't see the bottom. Couldn't hear a thing other than the rain. Dead or alive, the tough guy was down *there*, instead of where he belonged, sprawled in the living room with the rich bitch. Come morning somebody might find him, some shithead out walking the dog or a nosy citizen with nothing better to do. Glenn shook his head. Seemed like no matter how much he planned things out, he never could catch a break. Like anything that could go wrong, would go wrong.

"I'm scared," said Grace.

Glenn spit over the side, then sauntered back into the living room, his boots leaving wet spots on the hardwood. He'd have to wipe them off later. Use a paper towel and take the towel with him. He was wearing the Italian leather gloves Grace had bought for him last week. Her eyes lit up for a moment when she saw them, then she looked over at the rich bitch.

"Maybe this was a mistake," said Grace.

"Little late for that now."

"I know...I know."

Grace threw herself into his arms again, clung to him, and Glenn could barely contain his disgust and rage. Months of listening to her dumbass pet names for him, pretending to be interested in her plans for them, months of fucking her with his eyes closed, imagining she was Cleo. Impossible to do, even in the dark. No one was like Cleo. In a sane world, Glenn would get an Academy Award for fucking Grace.

"Remy's not a bad person," puffed Grace. "She's just spoiled—"

15

Glenn lightly kissed her, felt her dry lips. "None of us are bad people."

"I guess you better go down and get Mack," said Grace. "You said you wanted to take the both of them with you—"

"Yeah, I'll drag him up the hill in the dark—maybe I can break my fucking neck too while I'm at it." Glenn shook his head. "The tough guy stays where he is."

"He could be badly injured, sweetie. *Dead*, even. There's all kinds of rocks..."

"Did anybody know they were coming here?" said Glenn.

"No...I was careful—"

"You're *sure*?"

"I made it a spur of the minute invite, just like you told me. Remy...she could never say no to me." Grace swayed, clutching at him. "I'm just so scared."

Glenn kissed her earlobe. "Don't worry, baby."

"I can't help it." Grace buried her face in his chest. "I kept thinking...all night, I kept thinking, this was a mistake. That if I just *talked* to Remy, asked her to speak to her father, that maybe he would offer to help..."

Glenn eased behind her, draped his arm around her neck.

"Remy's so smart. I...I wouldn't have gotten through school without her help. Would have lost my scholarship. Brain like a legal library, that's her..." Grace breathed heavily. "She used to loan me clothes anytime I wanted. Once...once I spilled wine on this incredible Valentino sheath. Her favorite dress, cost thousands and thousands of dollars. Remy winced when she saw the stain, then lied...said she didn't like it anyway."

Glenn stroked her hair.

"I just...I just hope we're doing the right thing," sniffed Grace.

"We're saving Mama Earth." Glenn nestled his forearm against her throat. "How can that *not* be right?"

"Everything makes sense when you say it," said Grace, "but sometimes, when you're not here, I start asking myself what I'm doing—"

"I know."

16

"What happens when Mack wakes up?" said Grace. "He's going to want to know where Remy is—"

"I've already got that worked out," said Glenn.

"You never met him, sweetie. He's no quitter—"

"Shhh," said Glenn, pressing his forearm into her throat.

"Promise me...nothing bad is going to happen to her..." Grace gasped, tugged at his arm, eyelids fluttering. "Darling...you're *hurting*..."

Glenn clamped his forearm tighter against her windpipe, looking out through the open door to the deck as she thrashed. The wind was rising, the rain sheeting against the glass. Maybe the tough guy would drown down in the ravine.

Grace wheezed. Clawed at his arm, as he kept the pressure on.

"Gosh, listen to that rain," Glenn whispered. "Global warming's a motherfucker, isn't it?"

Grace struggled feebly against him.

"Try to remember the good times," said Glenn. "We had fun, didn't we?"

Grace's arms waved in the air. A ghost signaling to other ghosts.

"You remember the first time we met?" whispered Glenn. "I said, 'Hi, beautiful. I'm Glenn...like a quiet place in the woods.' You smiled and I just knew you were going to do whatever I asked. Just like Cleo said." He squeezed her tighter still, crushing her screams. "You wouldn't like Cleo, but she said you were perfect. Just. What. We. *Needed.*" He kept the pressure on her throat until long after she had gone limp.

Glenn laid Grace on the couch, the whites of her eyes red from exploded capillaries. He covered her with the afghan, turned her head away and draped her hair across her face so she appeared asleep. Eli and Tree should be here soon...no reason to let them know what he had done. Tree could probably handle it, but Eli, he still had bad dreams over his puppy getting run over when he was ten years old.

The rain drummed on the roof. Glenn wandered out onto the deck again, oblivious to the storm, and peeked over the side. Dark as God's asshole down there. Water dripped off his nose. Damned shame about the tough guy. Glenn had intended to strangle him along with Grace, strangle him while he was passed out, and them leave them both behind while Tree and Eli drove off with the rich bitch. Grace was on vacation; it would be a couple of weeks before anyone checked on her. Time enough for the deal to go down. He and Cleo had come up with a solid plan, no loose ends. Now though…whether the tough guy was dead or not, come morning, cops were going to show up asking question. Glenn was going to have to improvise before he left.

He walked back inside, feeling the deck mushy in places, slick with moss. Whole house was falling apart.

Grace's arm flopped off the sofa like a chicken wing, and the sight of it creeped Glenn out. He tucked her arm back under the afghan, then walked over and stared down at the rich girl. Made sure she was still breathing. She was the goose about to lay the golden egg. Couldn't let anything happen to her. Nice muscle tone on her. L.A. smog made his face break out, but she had smooth skin, not a blemish in sight. Probably spent enough on facials to support a poor family in Guatemala. Not that Glenn gave a rat's ass about poor families in Guatemala or anyplace else, but it put things into perspective. All things considered, it was fucking great to be rich.

Glenn grabbed the rich girl's purse, fished out her cell phone. He was tempted to take a photo of her with his boot hovering over her face, ready to stomp her out, but decided against it. The mood he was in, he couldn't trust himself to hold the pose. He snapped a photo of her lying on the hardwood floor, checked it out and nodded. It would do.

He glanced at his watch. Where was Tree and Eli? Why didn't everyone just do what they were told? Was that too fucking much to ask?

CHAPTER 5

ELI CHECKED HIS watch. They were late. Late. For a very important date. No time to say hello, goodbye...Glenn was probably already pissed off, wondering what was taking them so long. Probably blaming Eli too. That was cool. Eli didn't care what Glenn said.

Tree yelled at him to hurry up, Tree sitting high and dry in the cab of the idling 18-wheeler while rain dripped off Eli's dreads. No headlights. Tree said they couldn't chance it.

Eli fitted the jaws of the heavy bolt cutters on the lock, the heat from the big rig steaming the air, engine idling, rain sheeting down past the green warning signs on the fifty-thousand gallon tank car: BIOHAZARD and KEEP LOAD REFRIGERATED. The rain was good. It kept people in the Beacon Hill neighborhood inside their houses. Glued to their TV sets. Minding their own business. But it had slowed them down on the drive to the bus barn. Tree smoked joints the whole ride over, swiping at the condensation on the windshield, and complaining that the defrosters weren't worth shit. Eli had just looked out the window at the storm and wished he were on a beach somewhere. Tree yelled at him again and Eli squeezed the arms of the bolt cutters. Squeezed harder. The blades cut through the thick hasp of the lock, his knuckles banging together. Damn. He licked away blood, spit, then scuffed the spot on the wet concrete. Cops could do all kinds of things with spit and blood and hair, everybody knew that. A drop of blood or nose picking and they could probably find out who you were and what grade you got in Ninth Grade Geometry. Tree yelled again. Eli tucked the cut lock into a pocket and pushed open the security gate around Seattle Metro Bus Barn #51. Open Sesame Street, dude.

Tree revved the 18-wheeler, slipped it into gear and started up the winding concrete road to the bus barn, not even waiting for Eli to climb back in.

Eli shut the gate. Snapped another lock into place. Then he wiped everything down with his soggy bandana and started after the truck.

Soaked by the time he got to the double doors of the bus barn, Eli quickly cut that lock too. He slid open the doors, then jumped out of the way as Tree rolled inside.

Eli closed the doors after him. Fumbled around for the light switch. Barn #51 had been mothballed, along with a dozen other facilities scattered across the city, but the power was supposedly still on. He found the switch. Saw corrugated metal walls. Grease-stained concrete floor. Rain making like a tom-tom on the roof. With the shutters in place, the light was probably only marginally visible. In the unlikely event anyone noticed, they would likely think it was a maintenance check.

The barn had been designed to hold a dozen buses, but the tanker-truck seemed to fill it. Heaving in place at the middle of the barn, engine rumbling, exhaust thickening the air, the gigantic truck loomed over them, the pride of Chemical Waste Disposal Inc. Eli didn't even like being near it.

Tree turned off the engine. Jumped down from the cab, blinking in the fluorescents.

"Glenn didn't say we were leaving this in a residential area," said Eli.

Tree started for the side of the tank car, flipped open the control panel.

Eli walked over and stood beside Tree. The control panel didn't mean anything to him. All those dials and gauges...but Tree knew what he was doing. "Dude, we passed a playground not two blocks from here."

Tree tapped the temperature gauge with a grimy finger. The dial was in the green SAFE zone, but he made some minute adjustment to a pressure valve.

"*Tree?* Pay attention, dude."

"What do you want me to do?" said Tree.

"This thing's a time bomb. Maybe we should move it someplace where there's no people around."

Tree made another pressure check. "Glenn said to leave it here. That's what we're going to do."

"So now Glenn's the boss?" Tree's big hands balled into fists, but Eli didn't back away. "If I wanted a boss, Tree, I'd still be working at Banzai

Burrito."

Tree smiled those big flat teeth of his. "You made a real good fish burrito."

Eli blushed. "It's all in the wrist...and doubling up on the guacamole."

Tree lost his smile. Sadness spreading. Sasquatch in denim overalls, sad eyed and shaggy, cheeks pocked where his beard couldn't reach.

The rain was louder now. Lightning echoing. Heat radiated from the truck tires and the engine. The burrito stand seemed like a long time ago. Eli shivered as water dripped from his dreads, scampering down his back like a handful of salamanders. He wished they had never started this thing. They had been doing just fine before. Going to rallies. Teaching people how to climb tall timber. How to stop the chain saws from the old growth. The Monkey Boyz had made a difference. Not enough for Glenn, though. Not enough for Tree either. Eli wished just once, just *one* time, somebody would listen to him.

"Time to pick up Glenn and the debutante," said Tree. "We're already late, but that shouldn't be a problem. I seen plenty of cars we could boost on the way here."

"You're not going to move it, are you?" accused Eli. "Families, kids...you're just going to leave it in their back yard and hope for the best."

Tree thrust his hands in his pockets. "Sometimes we got to do things we don't like."

Eli knew Tree was thinking about blowing up that real estate MILF back in Laguna, the sound of it, the smell of gas and grease. Nothing had been right since Laguna.

Tree's temper had only gotten worse. Tonight, when they hijacked the truck at the rest stop...Eli thought Tree was going to tear the driver's head off. The man had never even seen it coming. Him and his co-pilot. They had stood in front of the urinal pissing like a waterfall when Tree came up behind the both of them, shouted *Alahu Akbar!* or whatever it was that Glenn had taught him. Their heads hit so hard against the restroom tile they probably cracked it. Eli almost got sick, but Tree just grabbed their keys. After Tree scooted out to the truck, Eli closed the door and slipped an *Out of Order* sign on the knob. Tree had scooted under the truck, pried something off the housing, a GPS tracker so the company always knew where it was. Tree had tossed the tracker into the back of a truck full of cattle heading East, said that had been Glenn's suggestion too. Glenn thought of everything. But he hadn't thought of how to make Eli feel good about it.

"What is it?" said Tree.

"I'm wondering what Glenn got us into." Eli felt another drop of cold water run down his back. "This thing explodes, people all over the city are going to be coughing up blood—"

"It's not going to explode."

"You don't know that."

"It's just a *threat*. In case they think they're dealing with amateurs." Tree tapped the temperature gauge again. "See? Cool as a cucumber—"

"How's it gonna stay that way with the engine off?"

Tree slid open a compartment in the control panel, exposed a couple of heavy, three-pronged electrical cords. "Give me a hand." The cords unspooled slowly as they dragged them across the floor. Tree plugged into a power outlet on a nearby pillar, screwed down the security ring. Eli did the same. A cooling fan whirled deep within the tanker. "See? Don't worry, I know big rigs."

Churches bells tolled the hour in the distance. "I liked it better when we were torching Hummer dealerships and spiking redwoods," Eli said quietly.

"So did I," said Tree.

Neither of them moved.

"We're not doing this for ourselves," Tree said finally. "It's about *more* than us. If a woman was being raped right in front of you…you'd do something about it. You wouldn't just stand around talking, you'd *do* something." Tree's eyes watered and Eli sensed his fatigue, not any physical exhaustion, but an overwhelming weariness. A weariness that festered, a weariness at the core of the rage that had dashed the driver and his co-pilot against the tiles.

"Tree...dude..." Eli hugged him. "I'm afraid of what's happening to us."

Tree accepted the embrace, returned it, wrapping his big arms around Eli. Then he disengaged and the moment was over. "Too late now."

"I know," said Eli.

"Come on," said Tree. "Otherwise we're going to spend half the night hearing about Glenn's timetable and how we messed it up."

Eli took another look at the temperature gauge, then hurried after Tree. He turned off the lights on the way out.

CHAPTER 6

FROM HER PARKED car Cleo watched Tree and Eli scamper across the grass toward the locked gate, a couple of shadows racing through the storm. The last time she had seen them was on the beach at Laguna, staring open-mouthed up at the bluffs as the waterfront mansion exploded, incinerating the realtor and her subtle blonde streaks. A hail of human hamburger and stucco on the white sand beach. Lightning flashed and Cleo saw her own reflection in the windshield. Straight black hair cut square across her forehead and hanging to her shoulders. Milk white skin, a full mouth, soft lips. A face to kill for. Beauty might only be skin deep, but that was plenty deep enough. Making that last-minute appointment with the realtor had been a calculated risk, but it was worth it. Glenn had been just as shocked as the other two when the realtor pulled up in her Mercedes, the top seller in her office, ready to meet a potential client at a moment's notice. Glenn might have called the operation off, waited until the woman left...but he hadn't. He had crossed a line, one that Cleo had drawn. He was hers now. Another lightning flash, closer this time. Yes, skin deep was more than enough.

Rain drummed on the roof of her car as Tree and Eli scaled the chain link fence, effortlessly vaulted over the razor wire and hit the ground running. There had been no need to climb the fence—they had the key to the lock—but they had climbed it anyway, for the sheer release, aloft and airborne and no looking back. Give the Monkey Boyz wings and they would fly to the moon.

Cleo kept her eyes on the bus barn as the storm raged. It was like Christmas and knowing what was inside all the brightly-wrapped packages under the tree. Fun to be one up on the world. Even better when the world didn't know about it, not until it was too late.

There had been a politician a while ago, Secretary of Agriculture or something; he had been recorded saying that all most people wanted was loose shoes, tight pussy and a warm place to shit. The Ag Secretary had lost his job, of course, but he had been right. Glenn and his dime store fantasies...a creature of impulse fooled into thinking he was a criminal mastermind. Cleo had bigger dreams, radiant dreams, and she was willing to put in the time to make them happen. That's what made her special. She sang along with the radio, some top-40 slop about two lovers willing to die for each other. Preferring to die in each other's arms than face a lifetime apart. One last kiss before the bitter end. She tapped her brick-red fingernails against the steering wheel, her laughter echoing inside the car.

CHAPTER 7

MACK BLINKED IN the sunshine, his arm around Remy, the two of them lying in the tall grass of the outfield. Remy's baseball uniform was dusty, a smear of dirt on her cheek. He smelled her sweat as he played with her hair, aroused now. "An all-lawyer's baseball team," he said, his lips brushing her ear. "That's just…wrong."

Remy moved closer. "We won, didn't we?"

"You spiked the first baseman. You could be looking at a lawsuit."

Remy kissed him. "Let him try." So close now there was nothing else. "I love you."

"I know," said Mack.

Remy smiled. "You're *supposed* to tell me you love me too."

Mack felt the warm sun on his back, the heat spreading through him. "You already know that."

"A girl likes to hear it."

Mack looked into her eyes. Looked past his reflection. Looked into *her*. "I'm sorry."

Remy's pupils dilated. Darkness growing. "For what?"

Mack could hardly breathe. "I…I can't remember, but I know…somehow I let you down."

Remy laughed. The color in her eyes changing. Rainbows in the sun. "Let me down? You could never do that. Never in a million years."

The rainbows faded. Darkness now. Mack tasted blood in his mouth. Felt spongy ground beneath him. Head throbbing, he opened his eyes and saw green everywhere. Weeds and bushes and—"Hey!"

The boy jumped back, dropped the stick in his hand. A skinny kid in shorts and a Sponge Bob t-shirt.

Mack sat up, groaned. His clothes crackled with mud. Everything hurt. He rubbed his arm where the kid had jabbed him.

"I thought you was dead." The boy looked disappointed.

Mack lay back down, too dizzy to even attempt standing. "Not for lack of trying, kid."

CHAPTER 8

IT WAS THE smell that awakened Remy. The memory of a smell. The sweet, fragrance of her grandmother's cedar chest. The one her mother and aunts had fought over. All those stocks and bonds and it was the cedar chest that the four sisters argued about. The chest was in Remy's Wilshire condo right now—every time she opened it, she smelled her mother's strength and tenacity. She inhaled one more time, opened her eyes and was surrounded by green. Every shade and variety of green. Cedar trees rising all around her, fragrant as they rustled in the breeze. She glimpsed blue sky through the dense foliage, still disoriented. She was in a park...in the woods, lying on a platform of wood planks, with the worst headache of her life. Of *anyone's* life. She turned her head.

Two men stared back at her, lounging on the floor like they were in their living room. One was an enormous, gray-haired man in overalls, his lug-sole boots resting on Remy's suitcase, his head pillowed by her Jimmy Choo bag. The other one was a muscular kid in baggy, rock climbing pants and a tank top, his blonde hair in dreads. They both wore animal snout masks. The kid waved.

Remy blinked. "Are you...real?"

The older one wearing a rhino mask didn't respond.

The kid in the fox mask laughed. "I'm Eli. He's Tree. How you feeling?"

Feeling *terrified,* foxy. Absolutely, unequivocally terrified. Remy slowly sat up, ignoring the pounding in her skull. "Get me a triple-espresso. Two sugars. And a bottle of Advil."

Eli and Tree looked at each other.

"I'm glad you finally woke up," said Eli. "I was afraid you were dead."

"How could she be dead?" said Tree. "She was talking in her sleep."

"She could have been a zombie," said Eli. "Zombies are dead and *they* talk."

Remy couldn't decide if she was lucky to have been kidnapped by idiots, or if it made the situation even more dangerous. She sat on her hands to keep them from shaking, her head throbbing so badly she couldn't think straight. "Where's Mack?"

"Who?" said Eli.

"My boyfriend," said Remy.

"The tough guy," Tree said to Eli. "That's what Glenn called him." He looked at Remy. "Glenn said he didn't make it."

Remy felt a fist squeezing her heart. "What exactly does that mean?"

"Glenn said he took a header off the deck," said Tree. "Long way down."

"Don't worry, he's probably just fine," Eli said to Remy. "All that matters is that there's just the three of us here."

Remy didn't react. In the absence of evidence to the contrary, she chose to believe that Mack was alive. If he was alive he was going to come looking for her, and if Mack came looking for her, he was going to find her. She looked around. Where *was* here? Who had this many trees on their property? Big trees too. "Where's Gracie?"

"You make a lot of demands, lady," said Tree.

"Yes, I'm sure even the most benign inquiry tests the limits of your intellect," said Remy.

"Keep it up," Tree said softly, his eyes burning through the holes in the mask.

Remy yawned. "The rhino and the fox. Interesting fashion statement."

"Well, I wanted Iron Man, but he's a capitalist," said Eli, "and the Hallmark shop had only had rhinos and foxes and hippos, and neither of us wanted to be hippos—"

"Just get me my espresso," said Remy, with a flick of her fingers. "I'm not interested in being walked through your decision loop."

"Tree says coffee's bad for your adrenals," said Eli. "I'll make you some pine needle tea if you—"

"That sounds ever so lovely, but I'm going to have to pass." Remy pressed her palms against the rough wood planking, feeling dizzy again; the platform slightly swaying, which was impossible. She kept thinking about Mack. She wanted to believe that if something had happened to him...if he were dead...she would know it, she would sense the broken connection. The last thing she remembered was being at Grace's house, drinking a martini, and then feeling woozy. She could still see Mack starting towards her, his legs wobbling. Mack helpless...*weak*. There was a first time for everything.

"It's going to be a nice day, if that helps," said Eli. "A little overcast, maybe. I bet when this is over, you're going to be saying, wow, that wasn't so bad at all. More like a vacation than anything else."

Why wasn't Gracie here? Maybe she was with Mack. All of them drugged, but only Remy taken. Remy the rich girl. Then she remembered Gracie's awkward silences last night. The suddenness of her invitation for drinks. Her darting glances toward the door. No, don't even consider it, Remy. But she had to. Her father said envy was the most toxic substance on the planet—that's why the wealthy lived behind high walls and raised pedigree politicians. Her father laughed at his own jokes, and that one was a favorite. She remembered Grace watching her stagger across the living room. Grace not surprised at Remy's loss of equilibrium. Not in the slightest. Oh Gracie, what did you *do*?

Remy rubbed her temples. The wind blowing through her hair actually hurt. She was surrounded by trees so dense it was like swimming in green, and what was a floor doing in the forest? The breeze...it seemed to be coming from *under* the planking. She must be in a treehouse. An open platform in a cedar tree, some project a carpenter had turned out for his children. No walls. Just a simple low handrail. A lawsuit waiting to happen. Some kid falls off and twists his ankle...say goodbye to the pickup truck. "Are you okay?' said Eli.

Remy dragged herself to the edge of the platform, looked over...and froze. Unable to speak. Unable to breathe. So high up. So very *very* high up. The ground a mere blur below. A chip of wood dislodged by her panic drifted down, and she watched it float for what seemed like hours, watched it until it disappeared from view.

"Don't be scared," said Eli.

Barely able to breathe, Remy scooted back from the edge. "I'm not scared."

CHAPTER 9

MACK WIPED HIS mouth. Sat on the ground, patting his pockets until he found his phone. There were deep scratches on his hands, tributaries of dried blood. Mud flaked from his hair. He dialed Remy's cell. Waited.

"You gonna throw up again?" asked the boy in the Sponge Bob t-shirt.

Mack listened to Remy's message-voice, waited for the beep. "It's me. I'm...down below. Are you there? I'm going to climb back up to the house. What *happened?*" He snapped the phone shut, looked up the hill toward the deck. A steep slope marked by rocks and bushes and small trees, one of which seemed to have been snapped off.

"Are you a hobo?" said the boy.

Mack rolled onto his hands and knees, stood carefully. The world spun but he stayed on his feet. Cue the applause. He headed up to the house.

Remy's car was gone and the sight of the empty driveway made Mack dizzy again. They had been drinking martinis last night...gotten sick...no, it wasn't the booze. They had been drugged, something hitting hard and fast. Grace's front door hung open. "Remy!" Bad idea. Yelling drove a wedge into his brain.

If you knew the way the world worked, it was the small things that really scared you. Not smoking guns. Or serrated knives edged with blood. Not the sight of a fat man strangled with an electrical cord. Those were *facts.* Immutable, clear and present. No, it was the small things...an open door that should be closed. Red silk panties plugging a sink. A baby photo stepped on by a golf shoe, the infant's toothy grin embossed with punctures. It wasn't the horrors you saw that scared you. It was the horrors you *imagined* that kept you awake at night.

His suitcase rested in the hallway, another warning sign. Somebody was smart. He walked into the living room, one hand on the wall to steady himself. "Remy!" He didn't care if it hurt. He went room to room, but there was nobody home. He had known that since he saw the empty driveway, but he had to make the effort. He flopped on the sofa and called

Remy's number again. Got the same message. Hard not to panic. He called 911 instead. Then drank a couple glasses of cold water from the sink. Glimpsed his reflection in the stainless steel fixtures. Mud man. He washed his face, dried off with a dish towel. Tried Remy again...and got a busy signal! Mack was so happy to know she was on the phone that he hung up. Hoped that she was calling him.

CHAPTER 10

REMY PRESSED HER back against the gigantic cedar, stared at Eli and Tree. She was okay as long as she didn't focus on how high up she was. Eye contact helped, but the masks reminded her of her situation. "You *have* to be the dumbest kidnappers on the planet."

"Correction," said Eli. "We're *outlaws*. It's not about money."

"Correction," said Remy, "it's *always* about the money." She looked around, but the trees were too thick to get her bearings. "You two are in luck. It's not too late get clear of the trouble coming your way—"

"We're way past that," said Tree.

"Just bring me back to civilization—"

"I *said* it's too late," said Tree.

Eli bobbed his head in agreement.

"Fine." It had been a long shot, but Remy had to try. There were plenty of other options. Still, it was hard to imagine Gracie being part of this. The phone calls had dwindled over the years, mostly just a card at Christmas and birthdays, but...Remy realized she was wearing her favorite jeans and a hooded cashmere sweater. "What happened to the clothes I was wearing last night?"

Eli blushed.

"You *undressed* me?"

"Your clothes were soaked," said Eli. "I didn't want you to catch a cold, and Tree brought your suitcase, so I just—"

"You get a good look?" said Remy.

Eli nodded. "You got a real nice body."

"Well, aren't you the gentleman." Remy looked at Tree, snapped her fingers. "My *purse?*"

"Ma'am?" Eli cleared his throat. "When you get waxed down there...does it hurt?"

"*Ma'am?*" said Remy.

Tree hefted Remy's bag. "How do they get the leather on this so soft?"

"Ask Valentino," said Remy. "It's made from placental lambs for all I know."

"Meat is murder," said Tree.

"Yes, I can sense your ethical prowess," said Remy. "My *bag*, please?"

Tree tossed Remy her bag. "Cash and credit cards haven't been touched. Like Eli said, it's not about the money."

"Can we take off the masks, Tree?" said Eli.

"No," said Tree.

"Makes my face itch," said Eli.

Remy rooted in her purse.

"What's prowess mean?" said Eli.

Remy opened a vial, dry-swallowed four Midol. "What do you want from me?"

"Nothing," said Eli. "Heck, what do you think we are?"

"Nothing from *you*," said Tree. "That's what he meant."

"Right," said Eli. "Glenn said it's your father who's the moneybags. What did that one magazine call him, Tree?"

"The Invisible Man of Wall Street," said Tree.

"No, that other magazine," said Eli.

"The Buccaneer of Bonds," said Tree.

"It means he's like a pirate on an ocean of money and we're bringing him to justice," said Eli. "It's going to cost the buccaneer *bigtime* to bail you out. We each got a special charity. Me, I want ten million donated to the Surfriders Coalition so they can clean up Santa Monica Bay. Glenn wants ten million dollars for the Green Turtle Conservancy, cause they're way endangered after what that oil rig done to the Gulf. Tree, he's got the best one of all. He wants your Dad to deed over the old growth forest he owns in Oregon to Wild Wilderness Inc...what's so funny?"

Remy wiped her eyes. "I'm trying to imagine my father writing a check to save me."

Tree and Eli exchanged glances.

"I have to pee," said Remy.

Eli handed her an empty two-pound coffee can.

Remy hefted the can. "You better be kidding."

The Girl Who Cried Wolf

"It's no big deal," said Eli. "Julia Butterfly Hill lived for over a year high up in a California redwood named Luna—"

The coffee can bounced off Eli's head.

Remy smiled at the sound of the can falling through the branches.

CHAPTER 11

GLENN RODE PAST a total Betty on the bike path overlooking Elliot Bay, a shapely blonde with a firm ass and gel-impact trainers. Too much makeup but her knotted tank top exposing some fine abs. Probably a paralegal at one of the nearby corporate hives. Hickory, Dickery and Doc. Probably pulled down more than Grace did, and Grace was a full-on lawyer. That's where all that pro-bono gets you. Grace *had* been a full-on lawyer. He had to keep reminding himself she was dead. She looked like she was sleeping when he tucked her in on the couch last night, covered her with the afghan. Waited around almost an hour for Tree and Eli to show, Glenn half expecting Grace to suddenly sit up. Like maybe she wasn't totally strangled. Just knocked out. Like that sex game they played once in a while. But no, she was stone cold Steve Austin dead.

Fucking Eli actually knocked on the front door when they got there. Like, why not just announce yourself with a marching band? Glenn had let them in. Told them what to do, as usual. Eli had glanced at Grace, lowered his voice as though she might wake up, but Tree...he *knew*. Tree gave Glenn this look, all sad and disappointed, which was pretty much becoming Tree's default setting. Fuck him. Glenn shook his head. He didn't like thinking about Grace, not on such a pretty day. If the Buddhists were right he was going to be working off some heavy-duty karma in a future life. Emphasis on the future though. Right now...

He gently applied the brakes of his stunt BMX bike, did a 180-wheelie so he faced the paralegal, rolling slowly backwards. He smiled, but she pretended to be more interested in her pace. Nice try, babe. He did a spin, ignoring *her*, then pedaled on while a couple of bleary-eyed winos watched from a grassy knoll, their buzz courtesy of the tourists at the nearby Pike Place Market.

Putt-putt-putt from behind, as some gearhead zipped alongside on a motorized scooter, eyes forward like the king of the road. Glenn stood up on the pedals, passed him and the gearhead leaned on the accelerator, engine sputtering. Glenn kept pace, sweat slick on his forehead, the gearhead squatting on the scooter like he was at Warp-9. The two of them whipped around a curve, dodged a woman pushing a stroller, the woman shouting something lost in their tailwind. The gearhead edged closer, flipped Glenn off and Glenn reached out, twisted the finger. Howling now, the gearhead lost his grip on the handlebars, the scooter wobbling. Glenn took his hands off the handlebars and looked back over his shoulders, saw the gearhead tumbling into the bushes. The Betty saw it too, but she was too far behind for him to see her expression. He pedaled on, enjoying the view as the gearhead limped to the side of the path. Problem presents itself. Problem fucking solved. Glenn's philosophy of life.

He rode on, one-handed. Whipped out the rich bitch's cell from his pocket and put in the battery. He flipped it open with a thumb, wished that the Betty could check out the state-of-the-art camera phone. Time enough for that later maybe. Cleo said to use the phone only when he in motion—on a bus, in a car...on skates—because the cops could triangulate the signal, might even nail him if given enough time.

No chance of that, officer. Glenn had business to attend to. First off, presenting the bill for crimes against nature, and pocketing ten million dollars for himself. A little something for Glenn. A one-way ticket to the glory days. Like he always said, think of a quiet place in the woods...with a solar-powered mansion overlooking a private lake and a forty-foot sailboat tied to the dock. Eli and Tree might be happy with the simple life, but Glenn had outgrown it. No more yurts and hammocks, no more homemade beer and rough-spun sweaters that itched. Glenn wanted a plasma screen TV, and a heated swimming pool. He wanted to fly first class and drive a Ferrari to Burning Man. With Cleo at his side. If she quit telling him what to do all the time. She was going to have to work on that if she wanted to stay with him.

Kidnapping the rich girl would change everything, but it had been a tough sell to the other Monkey Boyz. Saving the old growth had finally won Tree over. Remy's father had fifty thousand acres and there was talk he was selling it to a Chinese furniture company. If you looked at it right, Remy's robber baron father had kidnapped that old growth, so they were just ransoming one for the other. That's what Glenn told them anyway. Once Tree agreed, Eli went along, like always.

Glenn pedaled past a city worker spraying poison on encroaching blackberry vines. Gave him plenty of room, holding his breath as he rolled past. Guy should have been wearing a Haz-Mat suit instead of coveralls. Can you spell *toxic,* pal? Say goodbye to your liver, your kidneys, your DNA itself. Glenn wouldn't trade places with that poor bastard for another six inches of dick.

Convincing Tree and Eli to steal the tanker truck full of chemicals...now *that* had taken some serious talking. Hard to blame them. Heck, Glenn didn't want to go anywhere near the thing either, but Cleo had told him it was like an insurance policy. If Mr. Brandt tried to weasel out of paying what he owed, they'd threaten to blow the tank and tell Geraldo or some other TV fuck why they had done it. Mr. B would get the blame. Probably get sued too. Cleo said people got money for spilling hot coffee on themselves or falling off stepladders. Mr. Brandt wouldn't take the chance. He'd pay. Tree and Eli didn't know anything about Cleo, which was just as well. They looked up to Glenn. Best not to confuse them with where he got his brainstorms.

Girl was one surprise after another. Always there with a suggestion or to point out some little thing he had overlooked. Fucked like a panther too. In a way, this whole kidnapping thing was because of something Cleo said. One day after they made love, she sat up, mentioned how weird it was that after all the tree sits and trashing those Starbucks and Nike stores, that nothing had really changed. Except Glenn was getting older and his mom's VW needed tires. Just an idle comment with her hand wrapped around his johnson, but it had made Glenn think. That was the difference between him and most people. He paid attention. An idle comment got the wheels turning. Six months later, here they were. Done deal. Glenn had the big plans and Cleo handled the details. They were a good match.

Like figuring out how to get away with a kidnapping. Snatching somebody was easy, *collecting,* that was the hard part, but Glenn had cracked the code. A kidnapping always failed during the ransom delivery. Drop off the bag of gold at the mini-mart. Leave the cash in a dumpster on

Spring Street. Yeah, and bring handcuffs too. That was the beauty of Glenn's plan. No ransom was ever delivered. Not to them. Mr. Brandt's old-growth forest got deeded over to the Wilderness Alliance. The Surfriders Society collected Eli's share. Glenn's ten million dollar payday would be deposited electronically into the Green Turtle Conservancy account with a single keystroke. Untouched by human hands. Until Glenn scooped it up a few weeks later and took a bubble bath in hundred dollar bills.

There was a rise to the path, and Glenn used it pull off a perfect tail-whip, supporting his full weight on the handlebars and spinning the bike under him, flying free. On the second full rotation his rear wheel just missed a breeder pushing twins in a double stroller. He laughed at the expression on her face, raced on.

Glenn had set up the Green Turtle Conservancy a couple years ago, installed himself as President under a phony name. A few ads in free papers around the country had brought in a steady stream of donations. Although not nearly as much as he had hoped. Not enough to save any turtles, anyway, which was no big deal, really, because turtles carried all kinds of diseases and parasites. Soon as Mr. Brandt deposited the money into the Green Turtle account, it would be automatically transferred to another other account in the Cayman Islands, and then another and another. By the time the cops realized what had happened, Glenn would be lounging poolside in Costa Rica or Brazil or Switzerland, someplace with clean air and no extradition treaty. Glenn was so smart he scared himself sometimes.

Eli and Tree had no clue what he was up to, but then, they weren't really tempted by the modern world. Eli lived in an endless summer fantasy of big waves and white sand beaches, Tree...Tree was a clear-cutter who found Gaia, a mountain man who knew explosives and how to drive big rigs. It had taken longer to drag the other two Monkey Boyz into the plan, than it was to convince Grace. He just had to use his soft voice on her. His soft voice and his soft hand. With Tree and Eli...he just had to keep repeating that nobody gets hurt. Nobody gets caught. All property is theft. He must have said it a hundred times. You think they would have learned to trust him by now.

The rich girl's cell phone address book gave Glenn a little jolt when he first accessed it. Fifty names logged and daddy was number 48. Her power Pilates instructor and accountant were ranked higher than daddy dearest. Sushi-Grotto *reservations* was evidently more important, but it was all good. When Glenn talked to daddy, when he laid out the situation, the wallet would open wide. Like they said, blood was thicker than water.

Glenn zipped past a couple of fat walkers yammering about the sale at R.E.I.; he was about to straighten them out when somebody picked up at Daddy's private line.

"Yes?"

Not hello, like any normal person, but Yes? Like, what do you *want*? Slight British accent too. Perfect.

"*Yes?*" the voice repeated, annoyed now.

"You see the number I'm calling from?" said Glenn. "You got caller ID, right?"

Hesitation. Then..."I recognize Miss Brandt's number, yes."

Miss Brandt? "You're not her father?"

"I'm Martin, Mr. Brandt's executive assistant. To whom am I speaking?"

"None of your business, Jeeves. Tell Mr. Got-bucks to get his ass to the phone."

"Sir. Kindly state the nature of your call."

"Kindly *what?*" Glenn stared at the phone. "Put him on, dickwad."

"Sir, Mr. Brandt is not available. If you or Miss Brandt would like to make an appointment—"

"Yeah, I know the drill. Brandt's a fucking man of mystery. No photos. No interviews, but you tell him, Jeeves, you tell him his daughter's in trouble."

"If Miss Brandt is in trouble, perhaps you should contact the authorities."

"The authorities can't help here, you dumb son of a bitch."

Silence. Which was fine. Let Jeeves digest that. Glenn eyeballed the girls in their summer dresses sitting on the grass, their faces tilted up to the sun. He heard Jeeves clear his throat.

"With whom am I speaking?"

"Just let me talk to Brandt. Pronto."

"*Pronto?* Oh my, that's certainly an inducement to action."

"Just let me talk to him, asshole."

"I'm afraid that's impossible. Mr. Brandt is on a spiritual retreat—"

"You're shitting me."

"No sir, I most assuredly am not. He finds these retreats clarify his thinking, and make him more effective. No phones, no internet, no carrier pigeon. Total isolation. I don't even know exactly where he is, but I can assure you, Mr. Brandt is completely out of reach."

"Nobody's out of reach, Jeeves. This is the fucking space age."

"Sir, I couldn't contact Mr. Brandt if there was a thousand point drop in the Dow."

Glenn leaned on his brakes, skidded onto the dead grass at the edge of Steinbrueck Park. Head pounding, he tried to calm himself by watching a commuter ferry crawl across the water on the way from Bainbridge Island; the ferry burned 240 gallons of diesel an hour and was filled with drivers in Priuses. Nice carbon-neutrality there, assholes. He took a deep breath. "Look...maybe this will help." He sent Jeeves the photo he had taken last night, the one of Remy lying on the floor at Grace's, eyes half-closed. He waited but there was no response from the other end of the line. "*Well?* You see it?"

"Indeed."

"*Well?*"

"Beg pardon?"

Glenn resisted the urge to throw the phone against the nearest tree. "Okay. Pay *attention*. If you had to guess...how long until Brandt checks in with you?"

"Mr. Brandt does not check in with me or anyone else."

"Make a guess."

"Ah...two weeks—"

"Two *weeks?*"

"It's a guess, sir, as you requested."

"You don't seem to get it, motherfucker. This is life and death. Remy is in deep shit."

Jeeves sighed. "Miss Brandt is *always* in deep shit, sir, and it's *always* life and death."

Dead air from New York City. Jeeves had fucking hung up on him. Glenn stared at the phone, finally switched it off. Stunned. Embarrassed too, which was ridiculous. He removed the SIM card from the phone like Cleo told him, his hand shaking. *Unavailable?* The possibility had never occurred to him. Sure, this Brandt fuck was like the phantom, but Glenn had called him on his private number. Did the rich girl have to wait in line for her own father? Jeeves had said Brandt would be available in two weeks, but that might be a guess. Jeeves was just an errand boy waiting for the phone to ring.

What was Glenn supposed to do now? Tree and Eli couldn't babysit the rich girl for that long, not without Glenn there to keep them on track. It was such a simple plan: Glenn calls Brandt, sends a photo of daddy's girl, then Brandt punches in a series of electronic money transfers and case closed. Brandt could take those millions out of petty cash from what Glenn read about him. Deal should have closed in two hours. Now he was expected to wait two *weeks?*

Glenn stood with his hands on his hips, seething. He could see a sleek, mahogany yacht tacking across Puget Sound, white sails unfurled in the morning sun. The people in the yacht already had their loot, but Glenn was supposed to wait for Mr. Brandt to call his office to collect him. He squinted at the sailboat and wanted to shot flaming arrows into it, burn it to the water line and toss a concrete block to the survivors. Sink or swim—

"Hi." Glenn turned.

The Betty stood there, face flushed. No makeup, none needed. Her green eyes teased him as she pulled her right leg behind her back, stretching her hamstrings. "Nice day, huh?"

"Ask me next week," said Glenn as he peddled off down the path, weaving through a group of joggers, so close he grazed them. Their curses lingered behind him as he rode on, faster and faster, oblivious.

CHAPTER 12

"YOU GOT TO go *again?*" said Eli.

Remy glared at him.

"Sorry," said Eli, voice echoing behind the fox mask. "Fine by me."

"Glad it meets with your approval." Remy stepped away from the saddle-sling they had used to haul her up and down the giant cedar. "I'd hate to inconvenience you two."

They had just finished a walk of the area around the giant cedar. One trail led to an creek about thirty yards from the base of the cedar, the icy waters providing their drinking supply as well as storage for cans of beer and a bottle of cold duck Eli was saving to celebrate the ransom being paid. Tree pointed out huckleberry and blackberry bushes on the tour, while Eli warned her about thistles and poison ivy. The hot spring was farther away, but Remy had pled fatigue and they returned to the base of the giant cedar.

"I'm *waiting*," said Remy.

"You take her," said Tree. "I'm going up top."

Remy watched Tree scamper up the cedar free hand. He wore heavy hiking boots, climbing as easily as if he were barefoot. Eli wore lightweight skateboarding sneakers with a checkerboard pattern. Hard for her to tell which of them was faster. She looked at Eli.

Eli picked up a small spade from beside the cedar, offered it to Remy. "You need this?"

"A gracious suggestion, but no." Remy waited until he was close, rested one hand on Eli's shoulder for support. "I'm a little rubbery."

"Still probably got that knockout dope in you," said Eli, walking beside her.

Remy adjusted Eli's fox mask. "The way you and Tree climbed down the cedar you should be wearing monkey masks."

Eli cocked his head. "Wow. You must got psychic powers or something." He looked up. "You hear that, Tree? She said we should be wearing *monkey* masks." No response.

"What are you talking about?" said Remy.

"It's a secret." Eli turned an invisible key, locking his mouth. He led them down one of them many narrow trails. "Wait until I tell Tree you got this spooky thing going. He's into white magic. Talking to ghosts and spirits. Dude says he sees elves and hobbits sometimes."

"Not you, though."

"I'm into the ocean." Eli stopped in a tiny clearing surrounded by dense underbrush. He flung his arms around, made the sound of crashing waves. "Big Blue."

"How *did* you learn to move like that?"

"Me and Glenn done a lot of Parkour. You know what that is?"

"Death wish ballet."

Eli smiled. "I got that."

Remy chose a particularly thick section of bushes. She walked behind them until she was out of sight. "May I have some privacy?"

Eli turned his back.

"*More* privacy."

Eli walked away a short distance, turned his back. "Don't worry, Glenn's got it all worked out. You'll be back home in a few days. You can have all the baths and shampoos you want. Probably won't be able to see nearly as many stars though. Too much light in the city."

Remy slipped deeper into the underbrush, her white tennis shoes scratched and dirty. Pine needles crunched underfoot. Gnats buzzed around her ears, darted into her nostrils. Chipmunks stared at her as she crept past, tiny fingers held in front of their chests. A jay screamed from a low branch, made her jump, and she almost stepped on a huge tiger-striped slug, shiny with mucous. The thought of tromping on the disgusting thing...*God,* she hated nature.

"We're going to have some good times, trust me," called Eli, talking to the bush where she had originally been. "Tree's a gourmet cook and I carved a flute. You won't be bored out here, trust me."

"Yes, it's going to be an endless concert under the stars. A carnival of wonders."

"Well, I don't know about a carnival," said Eli.

The Girl Who Cried Wolf

Remy watched him through the bushes. If Grace could see her now...maybe that was part of Grace's rationale for this idiocy. Bring Remy down to earth. Grind her nose in reality. Payback for those late night college arguments about the rainforest and corporate greed and all the rest of it. She still found it hard to believe that Grace could have resented her so much. They hadn't been close for years, but they had been friends once. Now Remy was in the middle of nowhere worrying about heat-seeking ticks carrying Rocky Mountain spotted fever, and Grace was probably in Seattle repeating her cover story to the police, and trying out her quivery voice on Mack. Well, the police might buy her story, but good luck fooling Mack.

"I'm still not very good with the flute," said Eli, "but, I wrote some songs. Maybe tonight, if you don't have anything better to do...maybe I'll play you some."

"Does Grace really think she's going to get away with this?" said Remy.

"The lawyer?" Eli still had his back turned toward her. "She's not part of this. She was in the same shape you were last night."

"Eli...tell me the truth."

"I am. She was crashed on the couch. Totally zonked."

Hard to know whether to believe him. Or if he knew the truth. "When do I get to meet Glenn? Is he the mysterious boyfriend Grace talked about?"

"Glenn's not mysterious." Eli had a boyish laugh. "You'll like him. All the girls do."

Remy nodded. Of course. Girls like Gracie in particular. "I can't pee with you so close."

"Sure," said Eli, walking away. "I got the same problem myself. I have to go at the movie theater, I miss half the movie waiting for the men's room to empty out." He slipped through the bushes, barely touching them, talking over his shoulder. Raising his voice to be heard. "It's not fair either. They only sell those monster size sodas that you'd have to be a camel to hold in." He looked back. "This far enough?"

"A little farther." Remy slipped from behind the tree, careful where she placed her feet so as not to make a sound. "Hang on, though. This could take a while." She took a deep breath and started off, walking rapidly at first, then sprinting.

CHAPTER 13

"WHAT'S TAKING HOBBS so long?" Mack paced the deck, the rotted wood groaning underfoot. Dried mud flaked off with every step. He checked his watch. "Forty minutes is plenty of time to check my bone fides."

"You in a hurry? Too bad, because Hobbs isn't." Officer Farwell sniffed, a tall, skinny patrolman, his uniform laundry-pressed, one hand resting on the butt of his sidearm. He hugged the deck near the house where the wood was most solid. One of those by the book cops who considered it a perfect career if they never had to fire their weapon in the line of duty. "Maybe they do it different down in L.A., but me, I never seen Hobbs break a sweat. Man's cool as—" He snapped to attention as Hobbs walked onto the deck.

"Relax, Bruce, you're going to pull a muscle." Detective Marcus Hobbs seemed to glide across the deck, a powerfully built, middle-aged black man with a fringe of gray hair around the temples. He walked over and stood beside Mack, the two of them looking over the edge of the drop-off, basking in the sun. Yellow crime scene tape marked the gap in the railing where Mack had fallen off last night. Hobbs rested on hand on the rail, a bit of a dandy with his seersucker suit and penny loafers without socks. A police like Hobbs, he would have another pair of shoes in his car, for when the scene was messy or he was going to have to cover rough terrain. Mack felt even more bedraggled next to him. Hobbs glanced over at Mack, and then went back to staring into the ravine. "Quite a drop. You're lucky you didn't break something."

"Yeah, I feel like I hit the Lotto."

"I still think you should let me take you to the ER, get some X-rays taken," said Hobbs. "You could have internal injuries."

Mack shook his head.

"Might help if you took a shower. You look like you slept in a dumpster."

"You kidding me, detective?" Mack waited in vain for an answer. "I don't want to taint the crime scene more than I already have."

"Don't let the yellow tape fool you. Bruce and you are the only people here convinced this is a crime scene. Bruce is going to be a fine detective one day, but this might not be that day."

Farwell hiked up his Sam Browne, set his baton and pistol rustling. "I didn't say it was a crime scene, sir. I just said you should come out and take a look."

"Well, here I am." Hobbs folded his hands over his small belly, looked down his nose at Farwell. "Why don't you get me my thermos before you hit the streets. Bring a cup from the kitchen for our guest here too."

Mack called Remy while Farwell left. Snapped shut his phone a few moments later, annoyed. "It was busy before. Now it's not in service again."

"Maybe she doesn't want to talk to you," said Hobbs.

"I told you, we didn't have a fight."

Hobbs showed his even white teeth.

Farwell returned with the thermos and cups, set them down hard.

"Thanks, Bruce." Hobbs waved him away, poured them coffee. "Hope you don't mind a little chicory in your coffee. My people come from New Orleans Parrish. Finest cuisine in the United States."

"Wow, that's a heartwarming family history," said Mack. "Makes me proud to be an American. Tell you what, you help me find Remy and I'll get you the recipe for my Great Aunt Tilly's almond Bundt cake."

"Help *you?* That's nice. I always wanted to be a sidekick." Hobbs blew across his coffee cup. "This boyfriend of Grace's, what can you tell me about him?"

"I don't even know his name. Remy and Grace were sorority sisters at Stanford. Roommates. They had been mostly out of touch until the reunion. Then Grace cornered her at the banquet, begged her to come here for cocktails on our way home—"

"Los Angeles."

"Right."

"City of Angels. Bet you know a lot of movie stars. You ever meet

O.J.?"

"Yeah, I got his knife stashed in my garage." Mack took a deep breath, lowered his voice. "Look, this oblique interrogation technique of yours is a real brain-dazzler, Hobbs, and I'm sure most felons confess all over themselves when you start in——"

"I like a little conversation with my coffee. No harm in that, is there?" Hobbs adjusted his trousers. "You were starting back to L.A. pretty late in the evening."

"Remy likes driving at night. Less traffic. We were going to stop along the Oregon coast after sunrise——"

"So before setting off on a rainy night, you decided to have a few drinks?" Hobbs showed his teeth again. "You two like to live dangerously."

"One drink and we were gone——"

"Not exactly." Hobbs sipped his coffee. "One drink and *she* was gone. You got left behind, didn't you?"

Mack moved closer, mud slaking off his clothes. "I got left behind, but it wasn't Remy who left me. She was the one who was *taken*."

Hobbs plucked a microscopic bit of dust off his suit. "I ran your history. L.A. said you used to be a knockabout copper before you tossed in your resignation. A good man when it hits the fan, that's what they said. They also said it seemed to hit the fan *all* the time when you were around."

"Captain Mendoza said that?"

"You want to know the truth about a man, you don't ask his boss. You ask his partner." Hobbs' calm brown eyes were flecked with sunlight. "So...how exactly does a busted out cop hook up with a rich girl anyway?"

"Prayer."

Maybe I should start going to church." Hobbs plucked a coffee ground from his tongue, flicked it over the railing. "Not just rich, beautiful too. I ran her through the system while I was at it. Woman even looks good on her driver's license. You must be one handsome devil after somebody takes a scrub brush to you."

"You going to take a scrub brush to me, Hobbs?" Mack said quietly.

"Yeah, L.A. said you had a temper. I can see that straight off. An excitable boy, that's what you are, a five-dollar firecracker with a short fuse. I guess I best be careful."

Mack didn't take the bait.

"Were you bodyguarding the lady?" said Hobbs. "I heard you got a job with some upscale security outfit, Executive Protection. Is that how you met her?"

"No."

"I was just thinking, if she needed a bodyguard...maybe that's how she came up missing."

"I told you, we didn't meet on the job," said Mack.

Hobbs looked off into the trees. "Did you really bodyguard Nelson Mandela when he was in L.A. last time?"

Mack didn't answer.

"Nelson Mandela. Father of his country. And there you were, right beside him for three days, that's what they told me." Hobbs shook his head. "What I wouldn't give to have been there."

"I'll get you his autograph, just help me find Remy."

"I can't do anything until 72 hours after a missing persons report is filed," said Hobbs. "Not without evidence of a crime being committed. You know that."

"I know Remy was kidnapped last night."

"Was Grace kidnapped too? Or was she part of the setup?" Hobbs stood with his hands in his pockets now, rocking. "I always thought she was a low-rent lefty lawyer, but perhaps she was a criminal mastermind on the side."

"We were *drugged*. In L.A. we call that an indicator of criminal intent."

Hobbs moistened his fingertip, riffed through an invisible notebook. Paused. Pretended to read. "Last night while drunk or impaired, you fell off the deck and knocked yourself out. This morning the womenfolk are gone."

"Womenfolk?"

"No blood, no sign of a struggle, no ransom demand. Just her fancy car gone, and your suitcase sitting all by its lonesome in the middle of the living room." Hobbs shut the invisible notebook. His face placid. "Around here, we call that a kiss-off."

Mack laughed. "If Remy was going to leave me, she would have walked down the hill, kicked me a couple of times in the head to get my attention, and given me a last look at what I'd be missing."

"She's feisty, is she?"

"That's one way of putting it."

Hobbs looked past Mack. "I had a girl wake me up in the middle of the night one time, standing there with a pot of bubbling grits. Said if I ever cheated on her she was going to give me a facial I'd never forget. Now, that girl loved me raw, but I took my house key back the next morning." He shook his head. "Man needs his beauty sleep."

"You've got your priorities wrong, Hobbs. A girl like that...sleep with one eye open if you have to, but you don't let her go."

Hobbs adjusted the knot in his necktie, still staring off into the trees. "Got to admit, there's been plenty of nights I'd have agreed with you." He turned to Mack. "Does Remy have one of those Lo-Jack systems in her car? We could trace—"

Mack shook his head. "She thinks monitoring is an electronic leash."

"A free spirit. Still, might be nice to have a leash on her right about now."

"Remy was kidnapped, Hobbs. I'm going to find her, with or without your help."

"Yes, I expect you are." Hobbs emptied his coffee over the side of the rotting deck, careful not to get too close to the edge. "How about you shower up and change your clothes, and I'll take you out for steak and eggs? I know a place. Nothing's so bad that a good meal won't help."

Mack's stomach rumbled. "I need to rent a car and check into a motel."

"Sure. You want to file a missing persons report? Might as well start the 72 hour clock."

"I changed my mind."

Hobbs cocked his head. "You don't want to file a report?"

"No."

"I thought...you said she's been kidnapped."

"She *has* been kidnapped."

"What are you up to, hotshot?" said Hobbs.

CHAPTER 14

REMY DODGED THROUGH the forest, running flat out, branches slapping at her face, pine needles crunching underfoot. A glance behind her and she plunged forward down the narrow trail, almost lost her footing.

There was a sudden movement in the bushes and Remy cried out, reared back. A brown rat-like thing dashed away and she started running again.

Faster now, round and round, following one trail and then another, too many trails to keep track of, but she didn't care. Her chest burned, her legs ached, but she kept running. Ten years since she had run cross-country at Stanford, but she ran on the beach at home every day.

She saw a swatch of yellow flowers through the trees. Freedom bouquet. Remy pumped her arms, long legs stretching out...

Eli stepped out from behind a tree, Mr. Fox waving a happy greeting.

Remy crashed into him, the two of them tumbling onto the trail. She tried to get up but he pinned her arms.

"What are you *doing?*" said Eli. "You're going to hurt yourself."

"Get...get away from me." Remy kneed him, pulled almost free when he grabbed her again. She slapped him hard, his mask slipping as she twisted away from him.

Tree grabbed her. She hadn't even seen him. He threw her over his shoulder, started walking back down the path. "A million trails through these woods," he muttered, "and not more than two or three lead the way out, but you, Miss America, of *course* you think you're going to pick the right one. The sun always shines on a girl like you, doesn't it?"

"Wait up," called Eli.

"I'll pay you a hundred thousand dollars...whatever you want." Remy kicked and struggled, but Tree ignored the blows, carrying her as easily as if she were made of feathers. "I won't...I won't press charges, just let me—"

"Where did you think you were going?" said Tree. "There's no road signs out here. No marked trails. No helpful park ranger with a Smokey the Bear cap." He held her at arm's length, looked into her eyes. "Trust me on this, lady, not everything in these woods is your friend. You best remember—"

Remy tore at his hair, accidentally breaking the elastic that held the mask in place. She watched the mask fall onto the ground.

Tree slung her back over his shoulder. "Feel better?" He stepped on the mask and kept walking, not even breathing hard. "Happy now?"

Eli scooped up the mask and hurried alongside them, his own mask pushed back on his head. He looked even younger than Remy had imagined. He winked at her. "She…she didn't mean nothing, Tree. She just wanted some exercise."

Tree grunted, not breaking stride.

"Be nice to her," said Eli. "Can't blame her for trying."

Draped across Tree's shoulder, Remy bounced with every step he took. From her position she could probably break Tree's eardrum with one hard smack, or poke him in the eyes…but like he had said, there were no signs out here, no directions, and he was so big…no telling what he would do if he were in real pain. She put her arms around his neck, casually looked around, trying to get her bearings as Tree increased his pace.

CHAPTER 15

"YOU UNDERSTAND THIS is illegal, don't you?" said Hobbs.

Mack listened; phone pressed against his ear, then wrote down a number. He read it back to Stevie on the other end of the line. "That's the only call made from her phone in the last twelve hours? You're *sure?*"

Hobbs poured syrup onto a stack of blueberry pancakes, syrup streaming over the sides.

"Yeah, I bow before your technical wizardry," said Mack. "Just let me know if Remy's phone is used again and where the call originated." He sipped his coffee, winced. "And monitor all of her credit cards. Grace's too, okay? I want to know the moment they're used."

"That's good, now we can add federal, state and local charges to the mix," said Hobbs, dabbing his lips with a napkin. "A trifecta of misdemeanors and Class 2 felonies. You want me to just pretend you're having a hypothetical conversation with a hypothetical hacker?"

"Pull up Grace's phone calls for the last three months, and see if there's a pattern of calls to any one number," Mack said to Stevie. "Focus on late-night calls, pillow talk calls and then get back to me. Yeah, I know it's a big deal, and yes, you're the only one outside the Black Circle of Doom who could...okay, the *only* one who could do it, and no, we're *not* even."

"Nice friends you have," said Hobbs as Mack ended the call. "You pull a thorn out of his paw or something?"

"More like a harpoon." Mack tried the number in New York City that Stevie had given him. He listened to it ring. "Somebody called her father's private line from downtown Seattle a few hours ago," he said, still listening.

"Maybe it was Remy calling home, telling her daddy what a bad man you are," said Hobbs.

"You don't believe that."

"Well, let's just say I'm agnostic on the matter. This friend of yours...Stevie, was he able to tell where the call was made from?"

The phone kept ringing. "Downtown Seattle."

Hobbs raised an eyebrow. "Not much help."

"Yeah, Stevie's got skills, but, unfortunately, whoever was using Remy's phone was in motion for the duration of the call, so...that's that."

The gray-haired waitress stopped by, slopped coffee into their cups and shuffled off. Das Pancake Haus had lousy food and indifferent service, but it was cheap, the portions huge, and for added entertainment, 8x10s of ancient TV cops and PIs laminated the booths: Jim Rockford, Matlock, Magnum P.I., Sipowicz and that guy from *The Wire*...Detective McNulty. The Elephant's graveyard of lawmen, sponsored by Metamucil and Dentu-creme. It was packed with senior citizens and construction workers in suspenders and work boots. Hobbs said it was his favorite restaurant.

Mack waited for voicemail to kick in, but it just kept ringing. He put his phone away. Hobbs had taken him to a motel to clean up before breakfast; Mack had showered and shaved but he still could smell mud in his nostrils, and his battered ribs ached with every breath.

"I see why you didn't bother writing up a missing persons report," said Hobbs. "Why wait 72 hours for the police when you can get started now?"

"Devil finds work for idle hands," said Mack, cutting into his fried eggs with the edge of his fork. "I'm just trying to keep out of trouble."

"Try harder," said Hobbs, splashing still more syrup to his pancakes. "You let me know if dad got hit up for ransom. I'll take it straight to the FBI."

Mack shook his head. "FBI doesn't have anybody as good as Stevie on the payroll. Besides, Feds need warrants and probable cause and mother-may-I?"

"Police need those things too. Called the Constitution."

"I'm not a cop anymore, remember?" Mack felt Columbo, TJ Hooker and the rest of the laminated lawmen watching him from the walls of the booth. "I just do what the situation demands."

"Nice to be a free agent," said Hobbs. "No Miranda, no forms to fill out—"

"I haven't got time for paperwork. Neither does Remy." A shim of eggwhite hung from the tines of Mack's fork, the edges dark and crispy. "You ever work with the FBI, Hobbs?"

"Once. And it's Marcus."

"A real thrill, wasn't it?"

Hobbs nodded. "They acted like I got my badge in a box of Crackerjacks."

"You know what their success rate is for kidnapping? Not busting the kidnappers, they're good at that, but guess how often the vic comes home alive and well? Come on, take a guess."

Hobbs jabbed at his cakes.

"Thirty-eight percent. They don't publicize it, but that's what it is."

"What makes you think you and a small town cop could do any better?"

"You're a small town cop but you're not small time, any idiot could see that. Me, I've got my own set of skills, but I'm a stranger in town. I need you, Marcus."

"My captain doesn't look kindly on his detectives freelancing," said Hobbs.

"I'm not asking you to do anything that violates regs," said Mack. "You can have the bust, I just want Remy back. Besides, you *know* you want to work the case."

Hobbs didn't respond, his face impassive.

Mack called Remy's father again. Still no answer.

"Why don't you put that away and enjoy your breakfast?" Hobbs chewed carefully, as though expecting to hit something hard and sharp. He blotted his mouth with the napkin.

"Does the cook have a problem cracking eggs?"

Hobbs leaned forward slightly. "You get some shell in your cakes? I've told Blanche to be careful—"

"Lucky guess."

"I don't think luck had anything to do with it," said Hobbs.

The waitress shuffled back to their table. "Everything okay?" She peered at the scratches on Mack's face. "I guess you're going to tell me I should see what the other guy looks like."

"I *am* the other guy," said Mack.

The waitress sniffed. "You got an honest one here, Marcus. Better watch yourself."

"Always do," called Marcus as she moved on. He loosened his belt, sighed and Mack glimpsed the handgun clipped on his hip.

"Nice piece…357 snubby. Department okay with that?"

Hobbs rearranged his jacket. "The other detectives prefer a 9mm, but I don't trust those things. Give me a revolver anytime."

"And the short barrel doesn't bang against your hip bone."

"That's right."

"So, what do you know about Grace Schearson?" said Mack.

"You don't quit, do you?"

"Just making conversation," said Mack.

Hobbs snorted. "Grace is your basic liberal activist. Pardon me, *Progressive.* Save the whales. No Nukes. No blood for oil. Money for schools, not for bombs." He smiled. "Hard to argue with that last one."

"She do any criminal work? Maybe got up close and personal with some badass—"

"Strictly consumer and environmental law." Hobbs sucked at a tooth. "Except once…couple years back. She was an expert witness for this hippy girl set a few hundred minks free from a farm in Snohomish. Something about mink farming was same thing as slavery, so the woman was justified under the Geneva Convention." He picked at his teeth with a fingernail. "Judge didn't buy that argument and the girl drew three to five. I wouldn't call her a badass though. She forgave the judge when the sentence was pronounced. Said there was no such thing as a prison except the ones we build for ourselves."

"You remember the defendant's name?"

"No, but it shouldn't be hard to find. Why would you think Grace was involved?"

"I don't think anything," said Mack. "All I know is that Grace was pushing for us to stop by her house on the way out of town. She was the one who mixed the martinis—"

"You going to eat those?" Hobbs pointed at Mack's untouched stack of pancakes, transferred them to his plate before Mack could respond. "I don't know...most of these progressive types are just talk and puppet shows," he said, sopping up syrup with a fork full of pancake. "Even the ones who go beyond talk tend to stick to property crimes."

"Maybe somebody decided to branch out," said Mack.

"Still no evidence of that," said Hobbs.

Mack pushed aside his plate, the food mostly untouched.

"You didn't like your steak?"

"Is that what it is? I thought somebody lost one of their Nikes."

Hobbs sawed away at his own steak.

"So, you going to help me, Marcus? One cop to another."

"You said you're not a cop anymore. Make up your mind." Hobbs touched the photo of a slender, intense black man on the wall. "You ever see this show? *Homicide, Life on the Street*. Best cop show ever. Even better than The Wire."

"Andre Braugher."

"Andre Braugher," agreed Hobbs, impressed. "Detective Frank Pembleton."

"Man never raised his voice," said Mack, "but he could extract a confession from a stone." He shook his head. "Last time I saw Andre Braugher on TV he had gone to fat and was in some crappy show about three guys having mid-life crises."

"Guy from *Raymond* starred in it," said Hobbs. "Got cancelled after the second season."

Mack shrugged. "Time to make a decision."

"I don't know about you." Hobbs gaze steadied on him and held. "I like things that add up. Things you can get to the bottom of. I like people like that too. No surprises."

"Hey, Marcus, I'm safe as milk."

"I've got high cholesterol. Milk could kill me."

"Anything going to kill you, it's those pancakes and steak." Mack spread his hands wide. "Come on, you going to help me or not?"

"You already know my answer." Hobbs carefully poured pancake syrup into a teaspoon, his eyes never leaving Mack. "I don't know how, but you do."

"Guys like us have to make snap judgments all the time. I knew I could trust you to do the right thing."

"Guys like *us*, huh?" Hobbs swallowed the syrup, set the spoon down. "I can't do anything officially."

"Fuck officially."

"Fuck officially." Hobbs shook his head. "My mama would have washed your mouth out with soap."

"My mama was the same way. I learned to like the taste of Lifebouy."

"I guess that settles it." Hobbs nodded. "Okay. Haven't had a partner in a long time."

"Not like we're going steady or anything, Marcus. Don't get your hopes up."

Hobbs patted Mack's shoulder, almost pushed him through the seat of the booth. "This is going to be fun."

Mack grabbed the bill off the table. Hobbs didn't stop him.

CHAPTER 16

THE FAINT CREAKING sounded like the sloop Remy and her father took out at the Cape, the eighteen footer with the Sumatran mahogany planking you couldn't buy anymore. The *Jezebel*. The slapping sound of *Jezebel* as she slipped through the waves was comforting though, the sound of speed and expertise. This sound…was different, the reality of her situation intruding, nagging at her.

She lay on a wooden platform high above the earth, the wood planks creaking and groaning in the wind. Dampness rolled through her, the night filled with the scent of the forest. She blindly reached out a hand, touched the rope railing that ran along the perimeter of the platform and hung on. An illusion of safety. A camouflage tarp stretched over part of the platform, flapped in the breeze like a sail, but with her eyes closed she was back on the Jezebel, bouncing across the waves. The problem was she couldn't keep her eyes closed forever. That was no solution. Let the others keep their eyes closed, Remy, that's not for us, her father would have said. Wide awake and unafraid, that's who *we* are. That's how we get what we want while others nurse themselves on idle dreams and fantasies. Remy opened her eyes, looked up into a sea of stars.

"Did you have a nice rest?" said Eli.

Remy turned.

Eli sat cross-legged nearby, wearing a blue down vest in the cool night air. "It's kind of nice not wearing the mask." He toyed with his dreads, laid one across his upper lip, giving himself a moustache.

Remy sat up, scratched the mosquito bite on her arm.

In the middle of the platform, Tree slowly stirred a pot of lentils simmering on a butane backpacking stove, watching her through the steam. Tree's long hair half-covered his face, his beard a gray bramble, a mountain man in grimy overalls and a blue flannel shirt. The flames from the cook stove reflected in his eyes, made his gaze terrible and angry, but Remy didn't turn away, watching him too, until he was lost in the haze.

"There's supposed to be a meteor shower tonight." Eli pointed to the sky. "Northeast quadrant. Should peak around three a.m. Not much cloud cover. If you want, I'll wake you up so you can see."

"Don't bother," said Remy, making a note of where the northeast was. She had never had much sense of direction. Never needed to. Until now.

"It's no bother." One of Eli's ears was swollen and his cheek scratched from where she had fought him. "Just so you know, we're not mad at you for running away. Heck, here you are, stuck in the middle of the forest with two complete strangers. Heck, we could be a couple of psychos for all you know."

"Yes, imagine that," said Remy.

Tree scooped dinner onto three aluminum plates. He added a handful of fresh picked greens, slid it over to her. Then he pulled a hunting knife from the sheath on his hip, cut thick slices off a loaf of dark bread and laid them onto her plate.

Remy pushed the plate back to him.

"You've got to eat something," said Eli, wolfing down his food. "That's oragainic rice and dried cherries and watercress and mint and..."

Tree scraped her plate into his own. Started eating.

"You need to eat," said Eli, chewing with his mouth open.

"What I *need* is a suite at the Four Seasons, a warm bath and a double-scotch," said Remy, shivering. "You ready to deliver that?"

Eli unzipped his down vest, placed it around her shoulders. He was bare-chested now, a silver barbell piercing his right nipple as he bent back over his plate, eating with his fingers.

Remy almost shrugged off the vest, but it was warm from his body, and she was cold. Taking the vest was a sign of weakness, she knew that, and she couldn't afford weakness, not ever, but particularly not now. Against her judgment, she snuggled deeper into the warmth, zipped it up. The vest smelled of cedar...and of Eli. She would give it back as soon as she stopped shivering.

"Better, huh?" Eli set down his empty plate, licked his fingers. "It gets cold in the middle of the night if you're not used to it, but we've got a sleeping bag for you. All the comforts." He sat on his haunches, happily bobbing his head, his ropey muscles gleaming in the moonlight. He caught her looking. "Don't worry. Nothing's gonna happen to you."

"Something has *already* happened to me," said Remy.

Eli blushed. "You know what I mean."

The silence stretched itself out and Remy listened to the wind and things skittering in the trees. Listened to the steady scraping of Tree's fork on the plate. A light sound. The big man a slow and deliberate eater. An owl screeched and Remy jumped.

"People do things they don't want to once in a while," said Eli. "They do bad things so that good things can happen. *Better* things."

"Try telling that to my boyfriend when he shows up," said Remy.

"No offense, but he's going to have a hard time finding us," said Eli.

"You don't know my boyfriend."

"I bet he's nice and everything," said Eli, "but it's not like he can just put up flyers with your picture on light poles or—"

"Mack is a security consultant. He'll find me—"

"Like those guys who put alarms in houses?" said Eli. "My grandma got one of those electronic systems. You know, 'I've fallen and I can't get up,'" he sing-songed.

"He doesn't wire houses, you jackass, he's a bodyguard. He *protects* people," said Remy.

"Wow," said Eli, genuinely impressed. "A bodyguard. That's pretty cool, huh, Tree?"

Tree kept chewing.

"If you're worried cause now you seen our faces, it's no big deal. Not like we're worried about pictures of us on America's Most Wanted," said Eli. "Tree is going all Jeremiah Johnson when this is over, no electricity, no people, totally off the grid. Me, I'm bailing for someplace with great waves. No tourists, no titty bars. Someplace where I can live off the land and just surf."

Remy looked at Tree but he continued to chew as though he were alone on the platform.

"The masks were Glenn's idea," said Eli. "Well, actually, he wanted us to keep you blindfolded, but that seemed too hardcore, so we settled on masks."

"I thought the masks were stupid," said Tree.

"He did," agreed Eli. "It was my idea. I thought the masks would make things more like a party...so you wouldn't be scared. Glenn didn't care either way, he just wanted to make sure you stayed put, and me and Tree were cool with that. We told Glenn, whatever it takes, dude, long as nobody else gets killed."

The *else* registered with Remy. She felt the word like a ice cube in her stomach, but she didn't react. She held out her hand. "Give me my phone."

"Glenn took it," said Eli.

"Give me *your* phone, then." Remy snapped her fingers. "I want to speak to Grace."

Eli shook his head. "You want to talk to Grace, you got to go through Glenn."

"Fine," said Remy, "then let me speak to *Glenn,* who seems to be in charge of everything."

"Uno," said Eli, raising one finger, "Glenn's not in charge of everything. Dos," another finger went up, "cell phones don't work here, so forget talking to anybody. Tresamundo," the third finger went up, "Glenn will show up when he's got news about the ransom. You can talk to him then." He grinned. "For now, you can always talk to me and Tree."

"Scintillating," said Remy.

Eli looked confused, but Tree's eyes blazed.

"Wait until you see the sunrise tomorrow," said Eli. "You're gonna be stoked we brought you here." He waved at the hammocks he had strung from the nearby branches. "You can just lie around and watch it all happen. It's like being at the center of the universe. God himself doesn't have a better view. Go on, try it."

Remy lay back on the platform. looking up. Stars *everywhere.* More stars than she had ever seen. The night sky a vast bowl, infinitely deep, and she felt herself shrinking...growing smaller and smaller. She sat back up, heart pounding. Somebody like her could go crazy feeling that small.

"Beautiful, huh?" said Eli. "You could learn something from this. I mean, not to brag or anything, but you might be surprised." He reached into the pocket of his jeans, brought forth a fat joint. "It's like that old movie...what's the name of it, Tree?"

"Avatar," said Tree.

"Yeah, this could be like Avatar for you," said Eli. "You come from like a different world, some air-conditioned machine world, all corporate and valet parking, and now you're part of nature and everything changes." He fired up the joint with a butane lighter. A signal flare in the darkness. "After a while, you like...you like *get* it, like totally get it, and you never want to leave." He took a deep drag, offered it.

"Where's my 3-D glasses?" said Remy.

"You don't need glasses here," said Eli, "that's the best part."

"She's messing with you," said Tree. "That's what she does."

"Oh." Eli held out the joint.

Remy shook her head.

"You sure?" said Eli. "Tree grew it himself."

"The earth grew it," grunted Tree. "I just helped."

Silence again as Eli and Tree passed the joint back and forth between them. Silence on the platform anyway. The woods were a cacophony of sounds. Squirrel sounds. Bird sounds, chirps and coos. The swoop of wings and small screams. A chorus of coyotes howling and answering. Remy wasn't sure if the sounds were louder now or if she was learning to listen. To separate the individual noises. A branch cracked in the distance and she wondered what kind of drama was playing out all around her. Life and death probably and not a camera or a cop in sight. She moved farther from the edge. Tree noticed, allowed himself a smile and she hated him for it.

Eli exhaled a thick plume of smoke. "What kind of a name is Remy anyway?"

"A rich girl's name," said Tree.

"Is your father's first name *really* Worthington?" said Eli. "Glenn said—"

"A trust fund name," said Tree. "Like the millionaire in *Gilligan's Island*." Smoke trickled from his nostrils as he stared at her. "Thurston

64

Howell the third."

"Rich folks...what are you people *thinking* when you name your kids?" said Eli.

"I find it ironic that two dimwits named Eli and Tree are critiquing my family's choice of names," said Remy. "Eli sounds like some toothless hillbilly who sodomizes the plow horse when his sister is unavailable. And Tree...how *fucking* Age of Aquarius can you get? Check your calendar, the hippies are living on Metamucil and social security."

"The woods are a sacred place," Tree said, "so I don't appreciate the profanity."

"I don't appreciate you kidnapping me," snapped Remy.

"What's wrong with the name Eli? That was my grandfather's name," Eli said, the joint smoldering between his fingers. "And 'scuse me, but I think we already gone over that kidnapping thing." He took another hit, his voice croaky as he held it in. "You obviously never heard of Patty Hearst. You want an education, talk to Tree. He filled me in on all kinds of stuff I never heard of before."

Remy had an allergy headache that threatened to burst her skull. "Do either of you have anything to drink? Something alcoholic?"

"I got a bottle of chocolate schnapps put away for special occasions," said Eli.

"How old are you?" said Remy. "Twelve?"

Eli winced, the quickly stood up, not meeting her eyes. He seemed to step into space, stepped right off the platform, dropping out of sight.

"Don't feel too proud of yourself," said Tree, smoke trickling from his nostrils. "It's easy to hurt Eli's feelings. Particularly when he likes you, which he *does*."

"What about you?" said Remy.

"You couldn't hurt my feelings with a crowbar and a twenty year grudge." Tree tapped the joint out, tested it on his tongue to make sure, then tucked it into his pocket. "You know...you're not as smart as you think. And we're not as dumb. That kind of mistake could get you in trouble."

"I love the idea of you giving me advice. Next you'll be passing on stock tips—"

Tree pushed her backwards. Remy screamed as she started to fall off the platform, but Tree grabbed her hand. He stood over her, letting her dangle in the air, his face expressionless in the moonlight.

Remy kept her mouth shut. Angry at herself for screaming.

"Look around, lady," said Tree. "Take a good hard look and see where you are. I already done things I'm ashamed of. Things I never believed I'd do, but I done them. One more added to the tally ain't going to make any difference."

Remy held on to him, felt his calloused grip.

"Tree?" Eli's voice echoed from far below. "Everything okay, dude?"

Tree watched her.

Remy yawned. Still hanging on to him.

"Tree?"

"Everything's fine, Eli," said Tree, his eyes still on Remy. He lifted her back onto the platform with a flick of his wrist.

Remy rolled onto her stomach, breathing hard. As Tree turned away, her hand darted out and palmed Eli's butane lighter.

CHAPTER 17

CLEO STOOD NAKED on the rusty fire escape landing, eyes half-closed, skin white as frost in the faint moonlight. The cool breeze hardened her nipples. Glenn's studio apartment in Belltown faced a low-income housing building across the alley, and many of them were still up, their TVs on—it made the building look like it had a hundred flickering eyes. She imagined the people inside peeking through the curtains at her, wondering if she was real or a dream. Cleo stroked her downy pubic hair, breathing through her nose, imagining their eyes sliding over her.

She could see the *Basketball Wives* on a TV directly across the alley, big-titted morons jabbering about their bling and rancid dreams, American royalty, them and their mascara-plastered cousins from the *Jersey Shore*. A bald head gleamed in the moonlight as a man on a couch switched the channel, scrolled past pitchmen hawking mega-suck vacuum cleaners and ended up on Jimmy Fallon, whose queasy grin suggested he had a vibrating egg tucked in his rectum. Cleo smiled to herself. It was easy to feel superior, but soon enough she was going to prove it.

For all her distain, Snooky got $50,000 for showing up at a nightclub, and *Hardcore Pawn* drew bigger ratings than a presidential news conference. All about the eyeballs. Cleo wasn't interested in money, not really. Money wasn't her goal, it was merely a consequence of reaching her goal. Better to be famous, but for the right reasons. Crude, crass, ridiculous; those characteristics captured eyeballs for a while, but the duration was short lived and getting shorter all the time. There was always a new buffoon, a fresh slut waiting for their casting call.

"Come back to bed," Glenn called from inside the apartment.

Cleo stroked her flat belly with the backs of her nails, still watching the blinking building from the fire escape.

Her plans had been smaller at first. Find a patsy, push him to commit a terrorist act, some idiotic statement against fur or whale hunts or genetically-modified crops. A flashy bust and Cleo would get a promotion, maybe a job at the D.C. bureau. She was almost embarrassed now to think of how narrow her dreams had been. It was seeing the Monkey Boyz blow up the housing project in Laguna, torching the mansions and the realtor inside them that had made her realize that there need be no limit to her ambitions with such willing tools at her disposal.

Fuck D.C. The country needed a hero. Someone they could wrap their hopes and fears around, someone willing to step up while the rest of them retreated to their couches, someone they could count on when everyone else betrayed them. If that someone was beautiful, smart and sexy—a size-2 Oprah with a good story, a backstory of being ignored until she couldn't take it anymore and had to act, had to save a city—the *children*—when the authorities couldn't or wouldn't, well that was a forever thing if a girl worked it right. TV, movies, books...politics, even. Men with lesser resumes and even more fraudulent autobiographies had been lauded and launched into the highest—

"Cleo? *Please?*"

Cleo stepped back through the open window into the bedroom. Glenn lay propped on the pillows, watching her, his long hair damp with sweat. Candles flickered in the darkened room, threw shadows across the walls. Across Cleo's pale skin. "You look pleased with yourself. She waited for him to smile. "Well *don't* be." She picked up her panties from the floor, stepped into them.

"Where are you going?" Glenn tried the grin again. "You know me, I'm just getting started."

Cleo didn't move. The shadows felt warm on her body.

"You're not still mad about the tough guy, are you?" said Glenn.

Cleo wasn't mad about anything. The tough guy living or dying was irrelevant. Mr. Brandt turning over the ransom or being AWOL, that didn't matter either. Just random events. Distractions to those easily distracted. That was the beauty of her plan. All that mattered was that she was seen as the hero, and that was totally within her control.

"The tough guy, he was just a temporary setback," said Glenn.

"Life is temporary," said Cleo. "Fuckups are forever."

"Hey, it's your fault, anyway," snapped Glenn. "You didn't tell me about this Mack character. You said it was just going to be Grace and her ladyship."

Cleo planted herself beside the bed, feet slightly apart, hands on her hips. "I didn't *know* he would be there, but so what? I expected you to be able to handle things."

"I did handle it. Ask Grace." Glenn looked down at the sheets. "That...that was awful, by the way. You should have heard the sounds she made." He shook his head. "Worse than drowning kittens."

Cleo paced the room, set the candles bobbing.

"Come to bed," beckoned Glenn. "I don't want to talk about this stuff anymore."

"You should have killed the boyfriend too," said Cleo. "No witnesses. No loose ends."

"He fell off the balcony before I had a chance to kill him. Like they say, shit happens." Glenn shifted in bed, the sheets sliding off one leg. He preened for her in the dim light. "Fucker probably broke his neck."

"You don't know that."

"He's either dead or in traction."

Cleo pinched out one of the candles. Then another. The solitary candle remaining bobbed wildly as she crossed back to the bed; it looked like it was bowing to her. "What about Eli and Tree? Are you sure they followed instructions? No mistakes? No fuckups? No side trips to pick up a Slurpee for Eli?"

"We've already gone over that a dozen times," said Glenn. "I told you, everything's under control. You act like you're the one running things. I told you, I got it all—"

"Did they *do* what they were supposed to?" said Cleo.

"Yeah, yeah, just I told you last night." Glenn stroked her thigh. "They parked the tanker truck just where you wanted. Not that they liked it. Eli kept going on about an elementary school nearby—"

"What exactly did you tell them?"

"Just what you told me to tell them. That we're the good guys. The truck's not going to blow. This way the media knows we could have toasted the kiddies, but didn't."

"They still don't know anything about me?"

"Why would I tell them about you?" Glenn reached for her, hooked a hand in the waistband of her panties and dragged her closer. He kissed her belly. "I wouldn't want to give you any of the credit."

Cleo played with his hair. "They left the stolen car at the rest stop?" Glenn kissed his way lower. "I *told* you...Alahu Akbar!" He giggled.

"And the tourist brochure...they left it on the floor of the car?"

"Yeah, yeah, yeah. Visit Grand Coulee Dam." Kiss. "Take the whole fucking family of retards to this American wonderland and look at all the concrete." Glenn slid her panties lower and she kicked them off. "Get a bucket of chicken and make a day of it."

"Tree took care of the—"

"GPS system, *yes*." Glenn kissed her smooth, waxed pussy. "I still think you're making this more complicated than it has to be."

Cleo eased closer to the bed. "Somebody...somebody has to keep track of all the things that could go wrong." She sighed, had to struggle to keep her train of thought as he continued to kiss her. "Right...*there*. I want to keep the FBI...the FBI busy with bigger things, in case..." His tongue darted in and out. "In case her father reports her missing."

"I'm not scared of the FBI."

"I am."

Glenn looked up at her. His face glistened in the candlelight. "The rich girl's father isn't calling in the Feds. I couldn't even get the old man's attention. He's on some kind of spiritual retreat, probably off in the jungle playing with the howler monkeys—"

"I don't believe that for a moment." Cleo rocked gently on his face "Her father is smart. He's playing hard...hard to get. Trying to take command of the situation. Trying to control the clock." She clutched his hair, twisted. "Controlling the clock is everything in this game, and we *own* the clock. You make that clear. Make it crystal clear to him."

"How...how am I supposed to do that?" gasped Glenn. "It can't even talk to him."

"No...he just...just can't hear you." Cleo tore at Glenn's hair with both hands, made him cry out. "So what you've got to do...is turn up the volume." She threw her head back, grinding against his mouth. Her shadow was huge now as she rocked. "Give him a deadline. Today is Monday. He's got until Friday to pay up. So first thing tomorrow...the very first thing...you do whatever you have to..." She groaned, threw her head back. "...but you *get*...Daddy's...attention."

CHAPTER 18

THREE A.M. AND some TV huckster with patchy hair plugs leaned against a Mercedes SL, promising to teach anyone how to make a fortune in real estate in their spare time. Mack switched channels, settled on guy in a robe covered in gold braid, Bishop somebody, offering green prayer clothes that attracted money.

Mack couldn't sleep. His body ached from the fall from the deck, his mind filled with thoughts of Remy. Telepathy was definitely bullshit, because he kept reaching out to her, trying without any hint of success to picture where she was. The motel mattress sagged slightly in the middle, and the oh-God-oh-God-oh-God couple in the next room weren't helping things either. He picked up his phone and called Mr. Brandt again. It was almost morning in New York City, as good a time as any to have his call ignored.

"Yes?"

Mack sat up in bed, almost dropping the phone. He grabbed the remote, muted the TV as the Bishop waved the prayer cloth, his smile showing Mack his grills. "Mr. Brandt?"

"This is...Martin, Mr. Brandt's executive assistant. To whom am I speaking?"

"I'm Mack Armitage. I'm——"

"How did you get this number?"

"I'm a close...a very close friend of Remy's. I have to speak with Mr. Brandt."

"I'm afraid that's out of the question, sir."

"Remy's in danger——"

"Yes, Mr. ...Armitage, the other gentleman conveyed that quite clearly, but that doesn't allow me to bend space and time."

"That other gentleman kidnapped Remy." Mack picked up the half empty bottle of beer beside the bed, took a drink. "Please, Martin, I have to speak with Mr. Brandt."

"Well, your manners are better than the other gentleman's, but I'm afraid I have to give you the same answer I gave him. Mr. Brandt is on retreat in Costa Rica. Totally unreachable—"

"There has to be some way to contact him."

"If I could contact him, that wouldn't be much of a retreat, now would it?"

Mack felt his face heat. "The man who called, did he say he was with Remy?"

"He was using her phone. Seemed rather proud of that too, for some reason."

"Did he demand a ransom?"

"No…not exactly."

"Not exactly? He called you twice in ten minutes—"

"There was no ransom demand, just some nonsense about the Earth being in peril." Another weary sigh. "The Earth is evidently *hurtin'* and he had come to collect."

"He was mad at Mr. Brandt for some sort of environmental offense?"

"I have no idea. Perhaps he thought Mr. Brandt was a major stockholder in British Petroleum. I really have business to attend to, sir."

"Don't hang up, please. Martin…have you in ever been in love?"

"Beg pardon?"

"*Love*, Martin. Someone who frustrates you. Pisses you off on a daily basis, but you open your eyes in the morning and see them sleeping beside you, and you can't move because it might be a dream and you don't want to wake up. Have you ever felt like that about anyone? Because that's how I feel about Remy."

"Yes…Miss Remy…she does have that effect on men."

The couple in the next room started up again, the headboard of their bed smacking rhythmically against the wall. Mack stood up, walked over to the single chair in the room.

"You bought some time with the man who called before, but you're not going to be able to put him off for long. He's going to call back, Martin. He's going to make a ransom demand whether or not Mr. Brandt is available—"

"Sir…even if Mr. Brandt was here, I don't think he'd pay a ransom for Miss Remy."

"He wouldn't save his daughter?"

"Mr. Brandt disinherited her several years ago. It had been brewing for some time, but Miss Remy's use of the C-word in reference to the most recent Mrs. Brandt might have been the last straw."

"Martin, this is more important than Remy refusing to kiss the new trophy wife's ass."

"As I said, sir, the problems between them had been brewing for some years now. I'm afraid ransom is out of the question at this point."

Mack stared at the muted TV, trying to figure out what was gnawing at him, some vague sensation he couldn't grasp. "Then it doesn't matter if Mr. Brandt is in Costa Rica or on Mars, does it, Martin?"

"You have a very droll way of expressing yourself, but no, sir, I'm afraid it doesn't."

There was a commercial on TV for some capsule that made your dick thicker or longer. Made it look like a zeppelin from the expression on the sexy spokeswoman holding up the pills. If the Bishop was smart he'd go into partnership with the young woman, they were both in the hope and prayers business. "You keep calling Remy *Miss Remy*. What are you, some old family retainer? Like 'Gone With the Wind' or something?"

"I've known Miss Remy since she was a child," Martin said. "I think of it as much of a term of endearment as respect."

"She never mentioned you, Martin. Not once. That's odd, don't you think?"

"I couldn't say, sir."

"I can. It's odd. Remy and I spend a lot of talking, talking about everything, no boundaries, but your name never came up."

"I really have other matters to attend to——"

"Mr. Brandt, it's time to cut the crap."

"I beg your——"

"The man who hacked Remy's phone for me said your line has multiple levels of encryption. Real black ops stuff. The kind of man who goes to that kind of trouble doesn't just pass it on to his trusted assistant while he goes to commune with the spirits. If I hadn't been so tired I would have copped to it sooner."

Silence.

Mack paced the room. "Mr. Brandt, if you've started negotiations with the kidnapper you need to tell me, because that doesn't work out very often and Remy's life—"

"I haven't started negotiations," Brandt said softly, the British accent dialed down now, more Ivy League. "There will be none of that. Not for some time."

"Are you working with the FBI.?"

Brandt snorted. "Hardly."

"Then what are you doing?"

"All that I can do. Nothing."

"So...when you told the kidnapper that you were in Costa Rica—"

"I was buying Remy time."

"Time for *what?*"

"To escape...or find some way out of her predicament." Brandt sniffed. "Remy's a very resourceful woman."

"How comforting for you."

"Loss the attitude, young man," snapped Brandt.

"Why didn't you go to the FBI when you got the call?" said Mack.

"That's not really germane."

"Fuck germane, why did you leave Remy to get out of this herself."

A long silence. "I'm not really interested in contact with the federal authorities at this moment," Brandt said finally. "I'm actually doing rather my best to avoid such contact."

"Are you under indictment, or something?'

"Let's just say some public servants wish to ask me questions that I'd rather not answer."

"So you'll risk your daughter's life—"

"Remy's been kidnapped before. I'd say it was the kidnappers who should be concerned." Brandt chuckled. "You didn't know about that did you? That never came up in your long *no boundaries* chats, did it?"

Mack ground his teeth, but stayed silent.

"Pity. It's rather an interesting story. Seventeen years old, Remy is kidnapped by two men and taken to a dreary little bungalow outside of Santa Barbara. These men did landscaping work occasionally at our California house and saw easy money. They demanded a million dollars for the safe return of my daughter, which is insulting when you consider it. At any rate, Remy was walking out of the bungalow by herself when the FBI arrived. She waved. One of the men had killed the other in a jealous rage, hacked him up with a machete, then gone to Remy's day spa for a bottle of her favorite shampoo. They picked him up on his way back. He asked if he could give Remy the shampoo before they booked him. She had been missing for only three days."

"Agreed, Remy's got survival skills," said Mack. "Do you really want to count on that?"

"I don't have a choice, Mr. Armitage. There was another call from the man I first spoke with. He demanded ten million dollars to clean up Santa Monica Bay, ten million for saving turtles, and, the piece de resistance, they wanted me to deed over the Great Barry Spread, 210,000 areas of old growth timber in Oregon—"

"So we're dealing with three kidnappers."

"Yes, yes, I suspect you're right."

"They don't want any money for themselves?"

"Idealists, evidently. Where *do* they come from?" A cup clinked against a saucer at Mr. Brandt's end, probably bone china thinner than his compassion. "At any rate, I could probably raise the cash if I thought it would save my daughter, but there's no way I can give up the Spread."

"It's *trees*, Mr. Brandt. You do whatever it takes to keep Remy alive until—"

"Those trees are currently worth almost 100 million dollars, and unfortunately, I no longer own them," said Brandt. "They've been used as collateral for a rather large investment I've made in Irish bonds."

"So contact the charities and make the donations," said Mack. "The kidnappers will free Remy. Then just have the charities give them back to you once she's safe. No group would accept donations under duress—"

"That would be a public relations disaster," said Brandt. "It would show financial desperation on my part, and my investors would get very skittish. My hedge fund couldn't survive a race for the exits. You can understand my problem."

"Oh yeah, you're really under the gun. No, wait a minute, it's *Remy* who's under the gun, you're in a penthouse somewhere moving money around."

"As I said, Remy is quite resourceful—"

"I thought you were rich. The Buccaneer of Wall Street or something."

"Yes, well, the market giveth and the market taketh away." Brandt sipped his coffee or tea. "The Eurozone problems have been devastating, and I've had some reversals in the currency market this last year. Quite...painful reverses."

"Is that what the feds want to talk with you about?"

"I expect the S.E.C. and other entities have certain...reservations about some options I've exercised. Still, the Irish bonds go to auction in ten days. If that goes well, I'll have plenty of capital to reclaim the Spread and satisfy the authorities. If Remy hasn't extricated herself from this situation by then, I'll be open to discussion with the kidnappers."

"What happens if the Irish bonds tank?"

Another long sigh.

"Then it's up to you and I to save her," said Mack.

"Is it now?" said Brandt. Another chuckle, and Mack decided he didn't much like the man. "Odd that you haven't mentioned anything about *you* going to the FBI." Mack heard the swish of fabric, and imagined Brandt crossing his legs.

"The kidnappers see Remy's face on TV, and the whole circus that goes along with it, they might get spooked and kill her. I didn't want to panic them."

"Yes, I'm certain that factored into your decision," said Brandt, "but I also know a little something about you too, Mr. Armitage. Your background. Your professional accomplishments. My daughter and I have been estranged for some time now, but I'm still her father. I like to keep track of what she's up to. *Who* she's up to. That's why I took your phone call. You're a very impressive fellow, Mr. Armitage. Quite the mad molecule. Not just competent; competence is easily hired, but *determined*, no matter the consequences. That attitude can be problematic for hierarchical organizations, but you don't really care about that. I'm sure that's really why you didn't contact the FBI. You want to bring Remy back yourself. You don't trust anyone else to do it."

"Am I going to get billed for the psychoanalysis?"

"What's that slogan on the side of police cars? *To protect and serve?* From what I understand, Mr. Armitage, you're very strong on the protect aspect, but not so much into serving. I rather like that. Are you familiar with Dante?"

"Third baseman for the Red Sox?"

"Mmmmm...not quite. Dante was an Italian Renaissance poet. He wrote once that it was better to reign in hell than serve in Heaven. That sounds like something you would say."

"Sounds like something Satan would say."

Mr. Brandt's chuckle was really starting to piss Mack off. "Ah, Mr. Armitage, it appears you were jesting about your lack of a classical education. Touché, sir. If you're really worried about the Irish bond market, I suggest you find Remy before the auction. You've got ten days. That should be plenty of time for a man of your gifts."

"You're going to tell me everything this man said to you on the phone. Every word. You're going to record his next call—"

"I recorded the first two. Just as I'm recording this one too, for that matter. I'll email them to you."

"When the man calls again, give him my cell number. Tell him I'm Mr. Brandt's West Coast representative, with carte blanche to negotiate for Remy's release."

"Lovely."

Mack broke the connection. *Lovely.*

CHAPTER 19

REMY TURNED OVER, her back ached, shoulder bones grinding against each other as the hammock swayed gently. She tried not to think of how high up she was, suspended between two branches of the giant cedar tree, positioned just above the platform. A jungle hammock, Eli had called it, war surplus, totally enclosed, with a waterproof roof against the rain and sides made of mosquito netting. The light sleeping bag kept her warm enough, but the breeze blowing through the mosquito netting was cool and damp. Sounds of the forest stirring in the morning, but she kept her eyes closed. Better to maintain the illusion of normalcy. Better to pretend that she was in her condo in Brentwood, swaddled in filtered air-conditioning and French cotton sheets. Mack was banging around in the kitchen in the boxers she had bought him, making coffee and heating croissants from Café Auberge. He'd be bringing breakfast into the bedroom any moment, pinching her little toe, asking if she intended to sleep all day, his hot kisses rousing her from this woodland dream, this awful, embarrassing, *ridiculous* nightmare.

Bad enough to be kidnapped, but to be kidnapped by these idiots…Tree, laconic as a side of beef, barely keeping his rage in check. Eli, a beautiful man-child, eager as a puppy—if they had met in L.A. she would have been on the phone with every casting agent she knew, setting him up for a tryout on one of the net rom coms, the happy slacker who gets both the neighbor's wife and daughter damp or the Jeff Spicoli surf bum who inadvertently speaks the truth. As long as Eli's six-pack stayed tight, he'd have a career in Hollywood. Instead, he and Tree were looking at twenty-five to life in some federal institution, and Remy…what was she looking at?

No, she refused to let herself think about that possibility. Indignity enough being trapped here, but to die here, strangled by Tree's massive hands, her body buried under dirt and damp leaves, never to be found…Eli might hang his head, turn away, but he wouldn't stop Tree. He couldn't. She shook in her sleeping bag, shuddering. Mack would tear the world apart searching for her, but even he wouldn't be able to find her, not here. The thought that calmed her when she woke in the middle of the night, scared by sounds, scared by the sheer height of her perch, the thought that kept her together when she was shaking apart was the knowledge that Mack was looking for her. If he was alive he was coming for her. Another possibility she didn't allow herself to think about. Mack was alive and he was looking for her, and Remy...Remy was going to make it easy on him. She was going to get *herself* out of here. Not sit around like Rapunzel waiting for the handsome prince. Remy loved that Mack was coming for her, but that didn't mean she had to wait around like a good girl. She had seen the way Eli looked at her. So did Tree.

The breeze stirred and Remy rocked gently high above the ground, cool and light as a cloud, imagining all the fun she was going to have with the two of them. They had no *fucking* idea who they had kidnapped.

She ran a hand through her dirty, tangled hair, and thought of Mr. Philippe, the look on his face when she stepped into the salon. Assuming she survived long enough to stride once again down the sidewalks of Beverly Hills. Oh Gracie, what did you *do?*

Eyes still closed, she turned her head, felt the mosquito netting against her cheek. Tears leaked from her eyes, tears of anger as much as frustration and fear. No French roast in this vast, green Neverland, no fine-milled Molton Brown soap, no faint beep of traffic far below, hard chargers on their way to fame and frolic. Just the aroma of cedar and pine, the rustle of wind in the branches, and blue jays cawing in the treetops. She smiled in spite of herself. Never let them sense your fear, that was the best advice her father had ever given her. That, and never trust a portfolio-manager who acts like he doesn't want your money. The jay's screeching was louder now, insistent, a grating, feathered alarm clock. Remy yawned, opened her eyes...and saw Eli hanging upside down from a nearby branch, staring at her.

"You snore," said Eli.

Remy sat up. Her neck ached, there were spider bites on her arm, and the sight of Eli dangling in space, dreads swaying...*definitely* through the looking glass.

Eli flipped free of the branch, spun once and landed on the platform. "Tree's down below fixing breakfast. Hope you like fresh blackberries."

Remy squirmed her way out of the sleeping bag. Carefully placed her legs onto the platform. Shaky now, the sense of height overwhelming, feeling the updraft from the forest floor so far far below. She scratched a spider bite, trying to remember if the brown recluse was native to the Pacific Northwest, and if so, when her arm would turn black, and fall off. It took so much effort to maintain her spirits. Her balance. Her belief that somehow, some way she would get out of this situation. That soon she would be back in familiar surrounding with clean sheets, hot and cold running water...and Mack. Him most of all. Easy to admit now that he wasn't here to notice how much she loved him. Not that she could give in to her feelings for him.

In any negotiation...*any*...the one who revealed their desires invariably lost. Remy was a master at contracts, walking away at a moment's notice, thanking the opposing council for their time and diligence. The sound of her heels across the hardwood was music. Sometimes Remy got to the elevator before she was called back to hear the terms of surrender. Once she was actually pulling her car out of the garage when the call came on her phone. Easier to tell Tom Cruise's people no-deal than it was to tell these two knuckleheads. She had realized that last night after Eli scampered away with his feelings hurt. Tree wanted to toss her over the edge. She had seen it in his eyes. She was used to being threatened with the most vulgar profanity. Studio heads and their MBA consigliores barking about *fuckwads* and *bitches* expecting her to be intimidated, as though she had never heard the words before. People talked about Hollywood being a snake pit, a shark tank...but it was just talk. Verbal bullies with thin wrists and socks drooping around their bony ankles. Hollywood was all threats and posturing, but it wasn't real. It was different here. She could be killed and buried without anyone ever knowing where she was. Eli seemed softer...vulnerable, but all Tree needed was an excuse.

"What 'cha thinking?' said Eli.

"I'm trying to decide how to play you against Tree so I can get out of

81

here alive."

Eli blinked, uncomprehending. Finally smiled. He was bare-chested in the coolness of the morning, tanned and golden in the first light. "No, really."

She clenched her hands to stop them from trembling. Pretended to yawn. "I need coffee. I need a real toilet. I desperately need a *shower*. My hair is filthy and my face feels like it needs to have the barnacles scraped off."

"I think you look beautiful," said Eli.

Remy picked cedar needles out of her hair, then forced herself to walk to the edge of the platform. Forced herself to look over the edge. Hard to do. Easier than yesterday though. The experts always said not to look down...but, what choice did she have? If she couldn't look down and function, she had to resign herself to being hoisted up and down whenever she wanted to do anything. Resign herself to being at *their* mercy. She feared helplessness even more than falling. She plucked a piece of bark from a branch, tossed if over the side. Watched it float down.

"It helps, doesn't it?" said Eli. "Seeing the bark drift down like that...makes it seem not so high up. You learn fast."

Remy dropped a heavier chunk of bark.

From far below came Tree's voice. "Hey!"

Remy and Eli exchanged smiles. Remy wiped her hands on her jeans. "I apologize for what I said to you last night."

"What did you say? I don't remember."

"I made fun of your name. That was rude of me."

Eli nodded. "Yeah, it was, but we were teasing you too, so...no harm done." He held the harness out for her. "We'll go to the hot spring after breakfast if you want, get yourself clean. You can just relax and listen to the birds. Maybe read a book. Tree's got lots of books. I bet if you ask him—"

"I'm not on *vacation*."

"Right. Sure." Eli cleared his throat. "Gonna be a pretty day. Soon as the haze burns off."

Remy stepped away from the edge, stretched, aware that Eli was watching her every move. "What did you do with my car?"

"Glenn took it. The Porsche is way cool, by the way. I wanted to drive it, but Glenn said he and Grace were going to hide it away once she woke up."

"This Glenn...he just winds you up, doesn't he? Tells you what to do, where to go—"

"Glenn thinks big, and that's good. Me, I'm like small is beautiful, but the money from your father is going to make a difference to the planet." Eli jiggled the harness.

Remy ignored him. "Glenn better think again. No charity is going to accept the ransom money once they know where it came from."

Eli shrugged. "That thing last night about the chocolate schnapps..." He plucked some tender cedar buds, popped them in his mouth. Chewed. "Thing is...I'm not supposed to drink hard liquor cause my liver's thrashed." He looked past her. "Hepatitis C."

Remy stared. Startled by the sadness she felt for him.

"No cure for it. Slow motion death sentence, that's what they call it."

"I know what it is," Remy said gently.

Eli assumed a surf crouch, arms spread. "I grew up surfing off Santa Monica. School...you could keep it, me and the waves, that's where it was at." He pivoted his weight, crouched lower. "Storm drains used to shoot out all this stuff into the bay. Pesticides. Medical waste. Dead dogs. You name it, I saw it out there in the big blue." He twisted, arms cocked as he walked the imaginary board. "Not like I'm complaining. *Awesome* waves after a storm." He glanced at her. "That's why my share of the ransom goes to clean up the bay. So the young surfers don't get sick."

"I'm so sorry, Eli."

Eli tilted his body, doing cutbacks across the waves. "Not your fault. Well, Glenn and Tree say it kind of is cause of you being a rich bitch, no offense." He stepped off the board. Picked up the climbing harness. "Point to ponder: I'd lay off the criticism when you're talking to Tree. He's not used to being around people, especially people like you, and well...just try and be nice, okay?"

Remy moved closer. "I *am* being nice."

"Tree...he's an amazing cat. Mystical, you know? He used to be a logger, regular chainsaw maniac. Then one day in the middle of the Great Forks range, he heard the trees talking and—" Eli glanced at Remy. "I'm serious. The trees used to talk to him. That's how come he stopped logging and started working to protect Mama Earth. He could hear the trees screaming. Said it was the most terrible sound you could imagine." He patted the giant cedar. "I never hear anything from these big guys, but I respect what Tree says, because me and the ocean...we got a thing going on too." The breeze lifted his dreads. "The forest talking to him used to keep Tree steady, hold him in place, but the things we've been doing, all of us Monkey Boyz...the trees don't talk to him anymore."

"Monkey—?"

"Tree's gobbling magic mushrooms, fasting, not sleeping, you name it, but they're not saying a word. Tree's all alone now."

"He has you, Eli."

"That's what I told him." Eli looked like he was going to cry. "I'm just saying, you got to be careful around Tree, because he's really hurting, and when Tree's hurting..."

"Thank you, Eli."

"So, you'll be nice, right? I mean, even if it's not a vacation, you can still pretend. That's what I do."

"Let's just see how it goes."

"You're going to do what you want, aren't you?"

"Yes."

Eli shook his head. "Nobody listens. Glenn's just as bad." He held up the climbing sling. "Put on the harness. I'll lower you down."

Remy slipped on the harness, brushing against him as she did. "Why don't you *show* me how to climb down? You can belay me in case I fall, but I'd like to learn."

"Wow. No kidding?"

"No kidding."

Remy gasped as she swung free, but it wasn't as bad as yesterday. She grasped the next branch, saw the climbing pegs placed at intervals. Breathe, Remy, *breathe.* Her legs trembled and she stopped, pretended to enjoy the view, while she got her courage back. "Give me some slack."

Eli did as he was told.

Remy looked to where the morning sun slanted through the branches. That way was east. The wind carried the smell of pine and cedar.

"It's really something, isn't it?" called Eli, playing out the rope as he watched her progress. "If you saw things as clear as me and Tree...I bet you'd be doing just what we are. You just wouldn't need Glenn to help with the math."

Remy laughed.

"What?" said Eli.

Remy kept laughing, and she wasn't afraid now. For the first time since she woke up on the platform yesterday, she wasn't afraid.

"About the hepatitis C," said Eli. "Just...just so you know...when I take out the big dog, I always bag up."

Remy smiled. "The *big* dog?"

"You wouldn't catch anything, that's all I'm saying. You know, if you were interested."

"I'm flattered, Eli...but I'm in love."

"Maybe you could forget you were in love. Just for a little while."

Remy shook her head.

Eli nodded. "True blue, huh?"

Remy looked up at him. Looked right into his eyes. "True blue."

CHAPTER 20

GRAYSON SAW CLEO on the far edge of the outside deck of the ferry, face to the wind, serene in shorts and a gauzy sweater, black hair flying. He gobbled down the last of his breakfast ham-and-cheese croissant. Between the grease and this coming conversation, heartburn was guaranteed. If he was smart he'd chug a couple swallows from the small Maalox bottle he kept in his jacket, but if he was smart he would have never agreed to this early morning contact. He would have insisted they meet at Pioneer Square, stroll among the winos, dodging incoming pigeon shit while she told him her tale of woe. Instead she had called late last night, said she'd ride in to work with him on the ferry and hung up. Didn't even specify which ferry. She knew he always took the 6:45 from Bainbridge. Another squirt of stomach acid for that knowledge. This morning she walked onto the ferry at the Seattle terminal, rode it over to Bainbridge, and waved to him as he drove his two-year-old Volvo onto the boat. Her way of letting him know how close she was to his happy little home. A quick thirty minute ride across the Sound and she could be on his doorstep, righting the bell...waving at him through the security glass beside the door, her image distorted while Sylvie leaned in from the kitchen, asking him who it could be at this hour. Better to meet her now before Cleo escalated.

He swallowed a lump of congealed croissant. Clutched the lapels of his suit. Pushed open the heavy doors to the outer deck. The wind caught him, the stinging mist made him take a step back before pressing forward. Cleo was the only one out there in the lousy weather, the other commuters and tourists warm and toasty inside, sipping coffee and reading newspapers. The wind and beat of the engines made it impossible for them to be overheard, let alone recorded. Say what you want, Cleo had skills. He eased beside her, his back against the railing. Checked her out. What a waste of ass.

"You look fragile, John."

"Fragile?"

"Everything okay at home?"

Grayson watched the whitecaps, wishing again he had taken an antacid. "What do you want to talk about, Cleo?"

"The little woman not attending to your needs? Did she ever do that, John, or it the kind of thing that just dribbles away over the years? I'm curious."

Grayson rooted in his jacket, pulled out a baggie of bread. He scattered breadcrumbs around the deck. Seagulls wheeled overhead, swooping in.

"Must you do that?" said Cleo.

Grayson tossed a handful of crumbs high into the air, the gulls snapping them up, cawing loudly "We are obliged to share our bounty with God's creatures. Read your St. Francis of Assisi." He had only brought the breadcrumbs because Cleo hated the gulls, found them rapacious and disease ridden. Too long on the granola beat if you asked him. Occupational hazard of working undercover. You run with the dogs and after a while you develop a taste for kibble. Grayson smiled to himself. A taste for kibble. He was going to have to tell that one to Macabee and Jeffers at lunch.

"Did you read my action request?" said Cleo.

"Of course."

Cleo turned around, kept her eyes on the passenger lounge. "Well?"

Grayson scanned the water for signs of whales while she waited for his answer. The grays were running and he kept a log. Last week he had sighted a big one, a forty-footer at least. He sniffed. His allergies were kicking up. "Your rumblings about hippies planning a kidnapping—"

"Rumblings? That's what you said two years ago when I warned that there was going to be an attack on mink breeders..."

Grayson laughed. He couldn't help it.

"A month after my warning was dismissed, over a thousand mink were released."

Grayson laughed harder, wiping his eyes. "Yes, Cleo and the nation reeled."

"The Bureau didn't take that attitude when one of our undercover agents busted a group of Occupiers planning to blow up a bridge in Cleveland," said Cleo.

"The timing was different," said Grayson, serious now. "So were the optics."

"Am I buried, John?"

Grayson shrugged. "Just keep filing your reports. Perhaps after a bit more seasoning—"

"Well, that's clear enough," said Cleo. "Who was it? I know it wasn't you; I give you too much credit for that kind of pettiness. So who destroyed my career, John?"

"Let's not be melodramatic, shall we?" Grayson turned up his collar against the cold. He had no idea how Cleo stood it out here in a light jacket and shorts. Although...he lowered his gaze, taking in the view. Although he could spend many pleasant hours connecting the goose bumps along her inner thighs.

"Would you mind not eye-raping me, John?"

Grayson grimaced. "Mind your manners, agent."

Cleo glared at him.

It was as close to an apology as he was likely to get. "Your last report has been read and filed away. Along with all your previous reports and red-flagged URGENT action requests. Right now though the bureau is tracking something of higher priority—"

"The hijacked truck? Big fucking deal."

Grayson chuckled. Cleo and her dirty mouth...he missed it. "Rather more than just a hijacking."

"More...? Come on, John, don't be coy."

Grayson watched the passenger compartment. All the sleepy commuters reading their newspapers, assured that they would arrive safe and sound.

"John?"

"The hijackers left a stolen car at the rest stop where they grabbed the truck," said Grayson, teasing out the information. "Forensics didn't lift any prints...but they found a tourist brochure for the Grand Coulee Dam and...there seems to be an Islamic connection."

Cleo looked blank.

"The truck contained 80,000 gallons of anhydrous ammonia bound for the Idaho wheat fields. Anhydrous ammonia makes a great fertilizer, but it makes an even better bomb." Grayson forced himself to stop chewing his lip. Terrible habit. All the pressures of the last thirty-six hours, but still… "Anhydrous ammonia is what Timothy McVeigh used to bring down the federal building in Oklahoma City…but his load was standard issue. The load that was hijacked was concentrated. *Much* more powerful. Needs to be kept refrigerated—"

Cleo grabbed his arm. "I want to be assigned to the search team."

Grayson removed her hand. "The team has already been deployed. FBI, Homeland Security, even ATF. Full-court press, that's what D.C. wants, that's what they'll get. Alas, Cleo, I'm afraid your services are not required."

"Right. I only graduated third in my class at Quantico—"

"You might have graduated first if not for your personnel file. Quite an interesting read. You're highly intelligent, decisive and independent, but you're also impatient and pay insufficient deference to the chain of command." Grayson enjoyed the seething anger in her eyes. "You almost got bounced your second year after a negative psych report. Did you know that? Must have been a doozy. What I wouldn't give to find out what Dr. Belson uncovered. If it hadn't been for the intercession of your Command and Control officer you'd be a security guard today." He gnawed at his fingernail, spit. "I heard the C&C brass is a dyke. Pardon me, lesbian-American. She saved your ass." Grayson resumed his search for whales. "If Hoover was alive today…maybe he and the top could swap brassieres."

"Don't shut me out, John."

"Continue maintaining cover until further notice, agent."

"What about my request for additional resources on this plan to kidnap—"

"Denied. And it's a *suspected* kidnapping. No specifics. No timeline." Grayson shivered. He couldn't wait to get back to the office. He hated fieldwork and field agents, hated undercover operators most of all, hated the mess and unpredictability, the loss of perspective. Ask an op what the center of the universe was and they'd answer whatever petty assignment they were in the middle of. Senior agents knew the center of the universe was the good graces of one's superior and care and maintenance thereof. "Goodbye, Cleo."

"So basically my job is to file reports that no one reads—"

"Don't blame me. I'm merely your handler." Grayson smiled at the term. Archaic, but suggesting the true power dynamic between them. "It's chief you pissed off. In record time, I might add. Not because you're a woman, mind you. Chief works fine with women. The right kind of women. No, first week at station and you committed the one unforgivable mistake. Chief made a joke at your expense. A silly joke, I'd be the first to admit, but not only did you not have the brains to laugh, you actually turned the joke back on him." He wagged a finger at her. "No one likes a clever girl. Don't worry though, another couple of years on shit patrol and maybe he'll forgive you. Or maybe he'll retire. Until then, enjoy the incense and granola." Big grin. "Heck, you're the only one with a security clearance who doesn't have to pass a piss test."

"What if I'm *right*, John? What if I'm right and somebody important gets kidnapped?"

Grayson squinted at the waves. "Then the rest of us will have egg on our faces and you'll be able to tell us 'I told you so.'"

"No, the rest of you will take credit and I'll be stuck where I am."

Grayson looked at her. "Who do you think you're fooling?"

Cleo stiffened.

"All your detailed reports and emails...I'm sure you have copies." Grayson smiled. "If you're right you'll be able to parley your small victory into a transfer. Just don't overplay your hand. That's your weakness, Cleo. You don't know when to stop. Like this kidnapping...you may even be right about that. Some local yokel...a Detective Hobbs called in yesterday alerting us to the potential disappearance of a young woman in his jurisdiction. California girl. Comes from money but has credibility issues. The inquiry was forwarded to me. I showed it to Chief, who said we had more important concerns that a wayward debutante."

"Thanks for the heads up," said Cleo. "I could kiss you, John."

"Wildly inappropriate in a public place, and besides, I didn't do it for your benefit." Grayson's vision blurred slightly from the wind, and when things were back in focus all he could see was Cleo's face. "We've got our hands full with this missing tanker-truck. The nation has its priorities, and a wayward debutante doesn't carry the weight it once did."

"You gave me an opportunity." Cleo tugged gently on the cuff of his jacket. "I don't care why you did it, John. I only care that you did."

Grayson felt his cheeks flush. Felt his erection. He started to tell her how much he missed her, but snapped his jaws shut. Might as well as hand her a gun. Instead he gave her a jaunty wave, then walked back to the cabin, legs wide as the deck rolled under him.

CHAPTER 21

CLEO WATCHED GRAYSON stagger inside, then turned away. Faced the wind. *Am I buried, John?* Just the right amount of quaver in her voice. *Am I?* Oh, Auntie Em, whatever shall I do? The salt spray stung her cheeks, her ears ached from the cold and she wanted to laugh so badly she could hardly bear it. Poor John. He and the boss weren't going to know what hit them. Kidnapping might be small beans, but connecting the kidnapping to the theft of the tanker truck...the whole world was going to take notice. THE WOMAN WHO STOPPED THE LARGEST TERRORIST EVENT IN U.S. HISTORY. Getting off the shit list? Cleo was going to be *writing* the shit list, and there was plenty of room on it for everyone who has tried to hold her back. For the last year she documented her infiltration of the radical greens and the threat they posed. Of course, all of her recommendations had been ignored by her superiors. *Superiors.* Right.

Within an hour after saving the city, Cleo would be all over television giving the perfect interview. Cleo proud, defiant, resolute. The face of the new FBI. One of the reporters would ask about killing Glenn, and Remy would sigh, take a deep breath, and voice her regrets for having to take a human life, and then give credit to her training for allowing her to do what was necessary. She hadn't decided if she should wipe away a tear or not. Best to wait until the camera lights hit her. Keep it natural.

Grayson and the boss would be reassigned, as would Cleo, but while they would be going to Blueballs, Idaho, she'd be going to D.C. Cleo would make the rounds of the talk shows and senate hearings. She would get a book deal...a movie deal. She'd donate all the money to the widows and children of slain agents. That would be good for another round of interviews and promotions. A seagull dove in for the breadcrumbs at her feet, and she kicked it, sent it squawking. Cleo beamed in the icy wind, hair billowing around her. In ten years she'd be running the Bureau if she wanted, but she no longer wanted that. Fucking Bono was jetting around with presidents and addressing the U.N. and all he ever did was sing a few whiny ballads and bounce a scrawny African kid on his knee. No, Cleo hadn't decided what she wanted, but she knew one thing: the Bureau wasn't a big enough stage for her. Not nearly enough.

CHAPTER 22

ELI POURED A bucket of warm water over Remy's head and she howled with pleasure, shampoo streaming down her back. Rivulets ran from the flat rock where she was sitting onto the forest floor. Eli giggled, scampered over to the hot spring and scooped up another bucket. Remy closed her eyes, tilted her head back as he dumped the fresh water over her. Another bucket. And another. Until all the shampoo was rinsed out of her hair. Tiny soap bubbles covered the ground, iridescent in the sunlight streaming through the trees. Pop. Pop. Popping.

Remy basked in the sun while Eli combed out her hair. He wore orange surf jams embossed with blue kangaroos. She wore shorts and one of Tree's huge t-shirts, the wet shirt nearly transparent now.

"You're hair…it's really silky," said Eli.

"It's my shampoo," said Remy. *"Jamais Mon Amour."*

"What?"

"It's French," said Remy. Water dripped from her hair, down her back and shoulders, and she reveled in the sensation, feeling clean and calm and more determined than ever to escape. "Best shampoo in the world. Can't live without it."

"Oh…sorry." Eli held up the small bottle of *Jamais Mon Amour.* "I…I used it all. It made such nice lather. Sorry."

Remy shook out her hair, silent now.

"I got some Dr. Bronner's pine shampoo you can use," said Eli. "It's really good too."

"That's very nice of you, Eli."

Tree watched them, perched in the lowest branch of a nearby fir, lost in the foliage. He slowly stropped the blade of his hunting knife along its leather sheath, periodically checking the blade. Remy wanted to flip him off, but Eli's warning this morning had been heartfelt. She stayed silent.

Eli tied her combed hair with a length of rawhide, his fingers lingering against her neck. "You know, this will all be over soon."

"I hope so," said Remy.

"No, don't talk like that." Eli tugged gently at the loose strands of her hair that hadn't been tied. "People change out here. You wouldn't believe how fast it happens. With me it happened practically overnight. No distractions. No noise other than the forest sounds, animal sounds, wind in the trees. No *people*. Just...life. Real life away from the concrete and the freeways. A few more days out here you won't recognize yourself."

"If you say so."

"No." Eli pinned her with his eyes, his gaze so intense she had to blink. "I'm not smart, I know that. I read a book my head about explodes, but there's one or two things I'm dead sure of, and this is one of them. You come into the big woods one way, you come out different. You come out better."

"Like *Tree?*"

Eli grinned. "Well," he said, voice lowered, "you got to know when to leave."

Remy walked over to the hot spring. Carefully stepped over the smooth rocks and into the water, further now, easing in. She sat now, the warm water lapping at her throat. "Ahhhhh." The spring dropped off precipitously, a deep, warm water pool probably thirty feet across, surrounded by drooping alder. Giant cedars loomed nearby.

Eli capered beside the pool. "Come on, Tree! Take a dip!"

Tree shook his head, expressionless.

Eli strode into the pool, making a wake. He handed Remy a rusty, 8-inch railway spike. "Throw it in the water. I'll fetch it. No hands."

"You're serious?" said Remy.

"Throw it!"

Remy hefted the spike, threw it into the pool.

Eli dove after it.

"We must have spiked over a thousand trees the last few years," said Tree, still sharpening his knife, the pace quickening. "Old growth mostly. Up and down the coast. Lot of good it did."

Eli burst from the water, the spike clenched in his teeth.

Remy applauded. It was a goofball stunt, but she couldn't help herself, giddy at the uninhibited silliness of it, relieved at the summer

95

camp normalcy of this moment. The sight of Tree watching brought her back to reality.

Eli beat his chest, gave a Tarzan yell, then dropped the spike onshore.

"I know we're pretty far from civilization," said Remy. "How did you two manage to carry me and my suitcase all the way here? And at night?"

"All-terrain vehicle," said Eli, water beaded along his chest. "We just loaded you in at the trailhead and off we went. Tree drove. I ran behind. Only took about five hours."

"You ran five hours in the dark?" Remy squinted in the glare off the pool, the water sparkling. "In the rain?"

Eli shrugged.

"You'll have to give me a ride sometime," said Remy.

"Sure," said Eli.

"Isn't an ATV a violation of your pristine ecological principals?" said Remy.

"I stole it, so it don't count," said Eli.

"We ain't pristine anymore," said Tree. "It don't matter what we do."

"You still honked off about Laguna?" said Eli, water dripping from his dreads. "Come *on,* Tree, don't be so hard on yourself. Who knew it would really go off?"

"*I* knew," said Tree. "So did Glenn." He tested the edge with his thumb, drew blood. "Laguna isn't the worst of it."

"The truck? Dude—"

"Be quiet, Eli," said Tree.

Eli made a zipping movement across his lips. Laughed and dove into the pool.

Remy scooted out of the hot spring, wrung out the bottom of her t-shirt. She flopped down, skin tingling. The truck? Time enough to ask Eli about that later, for now she was content to lie on her back, looking up at the sky. She sighed, warmed to the bone. The mossy ground cushioned. Dragonflies drifted overhead, wings diaphanous in the sun. She exhaled, a long sigh floated out of her, and Remy drifted with the dragonflies, oddly content. She knew she should be angry, making plans, wondering where

Mack was, but right now, at this moment, there was just the soft light through the trees, and the humming of insects and a sense of time stretching out father than she could see. Maybe Eli was right. A few days out here and she wouldn't recognize herself.

Eli burst to the surface, spouting water. Crowed like a rooster.

Remy rose up on one elbow. Waved.

Tree slipped down from the branch, crossed over to where Remy lay and she was grateful to him. His presence put an end to the good feelings she was having, his scowl woke her from the daydream.

"You leave him alone," growled Tree.

She ignored him, allowed his dark bulk to linger at the periphery of her vision.

"He thinks you're something special, but I know better," said Tree.

Remy yawned.

A jumbo jet crossed over a hole in the tree canopy. Remy tracked the 747, one hand shading her eyes. Going east, right toward where the sun had come up this morning. The jet hadn't achieved cruising height yet, so the hot spring couldn't be too far from the airport. Departing planes had to climb over the Sound for noise abatement, then they headed wherever they were going. So she knew now they were somewhere east of the city, probably no more than thirty...maybe forty miles away. That was something. Something to hang on to.

Tree followed her gaze. "Doesn't really do you much good way up there, does it?"

Remy squinted up at him. "What makes you think I need help?"

Tree sauntered off, shaking his head.

Remy watched Eli cavorting in the hot spring. Envied him his good humor. His joy in simple sensation. He dove under, came shooting out of the water. Again and again. She saw Tree shake his head at Eli's antics. Saw Tree try to hide his own delight in the spectacle. She lazed in the warmth of the morning. Letting the minutes slide past. Half dozing, not wanting to wake up.

Eli strode out of the pool, right towards her. He grabbed her arm, started to drag her towards the hot spring, laughing as she pretended to protest. He stepped into the water...then stopped, his expression serious. He let her go.

Remy stood at the edge of the water. Wondered if there was something in the woods she should be afraid of. Something *else*.

Eli stood there. Unmoving. His expression sadder than she had ever seen him. Sunlight glistened on the water droplets running down his sleek belly.

Remy could hear it now too. Far in the distance...the faint sound of a motorcycle approaching.

CHAPTER 23

THE BREEZE LIFTED the peeling Occupy Seattle! posters on the telephone poles as Mack threaded his way through the sullen panhandlers camped on the sidewalk. A wino jiggled a Starbucks cups loaded with coins at him. Sounded like tambourines. Mack checked the address in his notebook and crossed the street.

Blue paint peeled off the two-story house in Seattle's Capitol Hill district, masking tape reinforced two cracked windows, and a life-size Uncle Sam puppet with sharpened teeth moldered on the front lawn. A sign over the door said LAW OFFICES/WGRN, PEOPLE'S RADIO, the W in WGRN tilted, either from neglect or political purpose. The so-called alternative community might be faintly ridiculous, but someone was desperate enough to kidnap Remy.

The young woman behind the desk in the entryway didn't look up, a pretty girl with a short purple Mohawk, her face in a logic textbook.

"Is this the law office where Grace Schearson works?" said Mack.

"Grace doesn't do much law these days," she said, still reading, "but she usually shows up a few minutes before her three o'clock show if you want to come back."

"Actually, I'm more interested in talking to Grace's boyfriend."

The receptionist looked up. "Old one or new one?"

"Ah...new one."

"Can't help you. Never met the new one. He's just theoretical."

"Excuse me?

The receptionist clicked her tongue stud against the back of her front teeth. "I'm not sure the new boyfriend actually exists."

"He exists."

The stud tap-danced. "I *knew* it." She gave Mack a beautiful smile. "Data points?"

"I don't have any...data points. That's why I'm here."

"Oh...yes, of course. It's just that I'm doing a paper on inductive reasoning in everyday life and I'm using Grace and her mystery boyfriend as my primary example. You do know the difference between inductive and deductive reasoning, right?"

"Doesn't everyone?"

"You'd be surprised. Anyway, I noticed a few months ago that there was a certain...tension between Grace and Avery—"

"Avery's the old boyfriend?"

"Duh. Anyway, I observed their interaction changing. Grace would look away when Avery bitched about poor recycling habits at the potlucks, then she started wearing her hair down, and a few weeks ago she asked me if it was really true about tongue studs improving oral." Clickity, clickity, clack. "Observation, observation, observation. Hypothesis: new boyfriend. Now you tell me the new boyfriend exists, that's *confirmation*. I'm going to nail an A in this course."

"Where can I find Avery?"

She pointed.

Mack started for the stairs, stopped. "Your observations about the new hair and tongue stud question...why wasn't your hypothesis that their relationship was in trouble and she was just trying goose up her love life?"

The receptionist shook her head. "When I first started working here, I went out with Avery one time. Once was enough." She sniffed, went back to her book. "Poor baby's got body issues. A tongue stud would be wasted on him."

The walls of the stairwell were as dingy as the rest of the house, plastered with posters for rallies and flyers for lost dogs and cats. WGRN-FM programming was taped at the top of the stairs: 11am-1pm, *Grow your own* with Ginny. 1pm-5pm, *Anarchy Now!* with Freddy K, 5pm-7pm, *Legal Rights, Legal Wrongs* with Grace Schearson, attorney at law.

A thickset man sat at a desk just inside the door, an angry intellectual with a soft chin. If the ponytail was supposed to distract from his male-pattern baldness, it wasn't working. He glared at Mack's leather jacket.

"Hi, I'm looking for Avery."

"Now you can die happy."

Mack offered a hand, took it back untouched. "This is kind of awkward. I'm trying to find Grace's new boyfriend, but—"

"I don't know his name," said Avery, "nor do I have any interest in knowing it."

"Then you're a very unique individual." Mack leaned forward, rested his fingertips on the desk. "You got dumped for another guy. Anyone in that position is naturally curious about his replacement. Considering Grace's politics, the new boyfriend must have been a very involved in social justice—"

"*Justice?*" Avery grimaced. "He fooled Grace but he didn't fool me." He sucked noisily at his water bottle. "Do you have any comprehension of what a moral dilemma is?"

"This place is big on philosophical questions, isn't it?"

"A moral dilemma is having to decide between ratting out an eco-hypocrite or helping a narc who wears the skin of dead animals on his back."

Mack suddenly covered Avery's hands with his own, held him down. Their faces inches apart. "My girlfriend and Grace disappeared last night, and I think loverboy was responsible," he said quietly as Avery struggled to pull himself free. "I'm not a police officer. It would be better for you if I was."

"You're *hurting* me," said Avery, squirming.

"No…not yet."

"I told you I don't *know* anything."

"Don't think of it as helping me. Think of it as helping Grace." Mack released him, but remained hovering over the desk. The timing of the release was crucial. Not too soon or the lesson was not learned. Not too late, or resentment overcame the desire to do the right thing. For all his air of superiority, Avery was reachable. A man kicked to the curb usually leaped at the chance to show his merit. Mack sat on the corner of the desk. Picked up a small ceramic bust of Mao. "Did you know that Chairman Mao was radicalized by his wife, Jiang Qing?"

"Please…be careful with that," said Avery.

Mack turned the bust upside down. Spun Mao on his head. "It's true. Jiang dominated Mao sexually. Laid such a sweet fucking on him that old

Mao couldn't think straight."

Avery watched the spinning Mao. "What Comrade Jiang did to Mao..." He swallowed. "The sex...it was a disaster for the party. Totally counter-revolutionary."

"It was probably pretty good for Mao though," said Mack.

Avery's set his mouth into a thin, straight line as the bust continued to spin.

"The way I figure it, loverboy must have done the same thing to Grace," said Mack. "Can't blame her for being swept away. Hardcore sex and hardcore commitment—"

"Commitment?" Tiny flecks of spittle dotted the desk. "Man drives a *diesel* smog-rocket. That's how committed he is."

Mack grabbed the bust of Mao before it toppled over, tossed it to Avery.

Avery bobbled the bust for a moment, clutched it. "Is...is Grace really in trouble?"

"I think she's gotten involved with some very dangerous people. You may be the only one who can help her."

"Yes...yes, I suppose I am." Avery set the bust of Mao carefully back down. "I suspected something was wrong when she bailed on the Biodiversity Rally a few months ago. Grace *lives* to fight Frankenfoods." He fingered the papers on his desk. "Suddenly, a few months ago, rallies are pointless. Ballot initiatives are pointless. She even stopped recycling. I should have known then it was over." He looked up at Mack. "If Grace is in trouble, it wasn't her fault."

"Whose fault is it?"

Avery stayed silent.

Mack leaned closer. "Who did she get herself involved with, Avery?"

Avery rocked back in his chair, getting some distance. "How much trouble is Grace in?"

"I'll know when I find loverboy."

"Are you going to do bad things to him?"

"Definitely."

Avery smiled his small, nubby teeth. "A few weeks ago I invited

Grace to a Chomsky seminar after her show. She said she wasn't feeling well, but I followed her. I saw her get into a car. "His mouth twisted. "VW diesel. Disgusting contraption. Pure Halliburton—"

"What did the driver look like?"

"It was dark. I wanted to get closer, see why he was so special, but I...I couldn't do it." Avery looked at Mack. "I'm more evolved than you. I avoid confrontations."

"Did you see the license plate?"

Avery shook his head. "It was a blue VW Rabbit. Black maybe. There was a MEAT IS MURDER bumper sticker. Which I also doubt the sincerity of."

"I'm going to give you my cell number. Ask around. If there's anybody you think I should talk to, give me a call. Maybe between the two of us, we can get Grace out of the hole she's dug herself into."

Avery's lower lip quivered. "Grace...she used to make me laugh. Silly things, but it made the day easier knowing I was going to see her that evening. I mean I always knew it had to end..." He shook his head. "She's lacto-ovo and I'm vegan. What did I expect?"

CHAPTER 24

A DIRT BIKE rolled up the trail, braked hard, sending the bike in a half-skid now, the rear wheel kicking up a rooster tail of dust. The dust cloud drifted across the clearing around the hot spring, spread across them and Remy tasted rotting wood at the back of her throat.

Waist-deep in the water, Eli coughed.

Engine still idling, the rider stayed where he was, astride the power, anonymous behind his helmet and face guard. He gave the engine a final rev, the sound bouncing off the trees, then turned off the engine. Slowly took his helmet off. Theatrical. A real drama queen, knowing they were watching. His face remained obscured behind a bandana patterned with yin-yang symbols. Had to be Glenn.

Eli turned to Remy. He looked like a little kid just told that Christmas was cancelled, and putting up a brave front. "See...you're going home already. Just like I said." He waved at the rider, his bare chest coated with dust. "Hey, Glenn. You want to take a soak?"

Glenn sauntered over. He stood on a small rise, hands on his hips. "Why isn't she blindfolded?"

"How is she supposed to walk around blindfolded?" said Eli. "She'll break her neck."

"You keep her blindfolded and tied up," said Glenn. "Isn't that what I said?"

"Yeah, you said it all right," said Eli, "don't mean it's going to happen. Tied up, 24-7? That's just cruelty, dude. I wouldn't do that to a lobster."

"If she's not blindfolded, why aren't you wearing masks?" demanded Glenn. He pointed to the bandana covering most of his face. "Like *this.*"

"We tried that," said Eli. "Didn't work out."

"Now she can ID you," said Glenn.

"Don't matter. We're going ghost when this is over, going off the grid, just like we talked about." Eli splashed water at Glenn. "Come on in, wash off the road grime."

Glenn turned to Tree. "Eli's an idiot, but I expected you to have more sense, Tree."

"Hey," said Eli.

"Blaming others is one of the five signs of a poor leader," Remy said to Glenn. "You want to hear the other four?"

"Shut up, lady," said Glenn "You're in enough trouble already."

"What's wrong?" said Tree.

Glenn approached Remy. "Where's my manners? I haven't even introduced myself. I'm Glenn." He must have smiled under the bandana. "You know, like a quiet place in the woods." He grabbed her by the hair. Dragged her over to one of the old growth cedars, as she kicked and swore. Swung her head *hard* against the trunk.

"Hey!" shouted Eli.

Remy flopped onto the ground. *Stunned.* She tried to sit up, but her arms kept shaking. She could hear Eli shouting at Glenn, and the sound of his voice hurt her head.

Glenn squatted down in front of her. Sweat cut through the sheen of dust above the bandana. His eyes...he looked so pleased with himself.

Remy blinked, fighting not to pass out.

"Don't go to sleep." Glenn slapped her across the face. Not hard. He wasn't trying to hurt her now. He just wanted to humiliate her. "Look at me."

Eli grabbed Glenn, pulled him away from Remy.

Lights danced in front of Remy's eyes. Twinkling stars...

"*Apologize* to her, dude," said Eli.

"Gosh, I'm sorry about that," Glenn said to Remy, kneeling back down beside her. "I was just trying to get you to pay attention."

Remy hung on to those cold eyes as she sat up. "Pay attention to what?" Her cheek tingled where he had struck her. "*You?*"

Glenn smiled, but it didn't warm his eyes. "We've just met, you and me, but I want you to understand that I'm a nice person. We're all nice people here. Good people. No one wants to hurt you—"

Remy laughed.

"Me and Tree and Eli...we just want to give Mother Earth a chance,"

Glenn said gently, the bandana vibrating as he talked. "Somebody's got to stand up and say, hey, you corporate pricks, you SUV greedheads, quit fucking with the planet, okay?" He poked Remy's arm. "Your Daddy has a chance to do the right thing, but he's playing hard to get. So now it's on me to make him do the right thing. Understand?"

"Oh, I understand everything I need—"

Glenn punched her in the face, the back of her head smacking the tree.

Eli threw Glenn onto the ground. "What's *wrong* with you, dude?"

Glenn stood up. Ignored Eli.

Remy's face was in the dirt. Grit in her mouth. She rolled onto her hands and knees, trembling uncontrollably, barely able to breathe. Nothing to be ashamed of, she told herself. The trembling didn't show weakness, just shock, and that was an uncontrollable reaction. Glenn had done her a favor. Her whole face throbbed, but the pain gave her clarity. Glenn might have wanted to get her father's attention, but he had gotten *hers* instead. Blood trickled from her nose but she made no attempt to wipe it away. Just breathe, Remy. Breathe and focus. Glenn was a coward and cowards loved to gloat. Where was the fun of a sucker punch if you couldn't revel in the effects? Remy half closed her eyes, waiting, feeling her heart rate slow.

"I hated doing that, but you kind of asked for it, you know?" Glenn sat beside her like they were a couple of buddies on a picnic in the woods. "I'm just glad it's over with. Violence in any form upsets me—"

"Liar." Remy licked her lips. Tasted blood.

"Harsh," said Glenn. "Very harsh."

Remy could see Eli hovering, looking embarrassed and upset. Tree stood a little ways off, expressionless. "Grace always had lousy taste in men," she said to Glenn. "You though...you're a new low even for her."

Glenn glanced at Eli. "You see? I'm *trying* to be nice to her, but she won't let me."

"Just leave her alone," said Eli.

Remy wiped at the blood running from her nose. "I want to speak with Grace."

"No way," said Glenn. "You got a negative attitude."

"What are you afraid of?" said Remy. "Let me speak to her."

Glenn took Remy's phone out of his jacket and for an instant she thought he was going to call Grace. "Smile for the birdie!" He took photos of her, one after the other. Even put a finger under her chin, tilting her head back to get the full effect of the blood. "I really hate hitting a woman, but if this is what it takes for Jeeves to realize we're serious—"

"Who's Jeeves?" said Eli.

"Some flunky says we can't talk to her daddy for two or three weeks," said Glenn, not taking his eyes off Remy, lingering on her breasts and throat.

"Two or three *weeks?*" said Tree.

"That's not so bad," said Eli. "She's not much trouble anymore. Really."

Glenn gently stroked Remy's hair and Remy allowed it. The trees surrounded them, silent witnesses.

"The French...the French have a saying," Remy whispered to Glenn.

Glenn leaned closer to hear.

Remy felt a bubble of blood inflate from her right nostril...the bubble inflating and deflating with every breath. "The French say a woman is like beefsteak. The more...the more you beat her, the more tender she becomes." The bubble popped.

Glenn patted her knee, let his hand linger. "I like that."

"I thought you would." Remy reached in her pocket as she looked into his eyes. "A man like you...you're a walking compensatory mechanism."

"What's that supposed to mean?" said Glenn.

"It means..." Remy's fingers closed around the butane lighter she had stolen from Eli. Turned the flame control to full on with her thumb. She wasn't trembling anymore. "It means, sooner or later, women always get wise to you, don't they?"

Glenn took his hand away, balled it into a fist. "Hey, lady, if you're not tender enough yet, maybe I could give you another—"

Remy flicked the lighter, fire shooting into Glenn's face. Glenn screamed, tried to pull away put she held on to him, held him in the flames until he fell backwards.

Glenn howled on the ground, beating at his smoldering eyebrows. He tore off the scorched bandana, stumbled toward the hot spring.

Birds screamed in the branches.

Tree shook his head.

Eli winked at her. Gave her the wiggling, Hawaiian hang-loose hand gesture.

Remy wiped her face, smeared blood across her cheek. She had probably made things worse but she didn't care. In fact, she felt better than at any time since she woke up in the forest.

CHAPTER 25

THE CLERK BEHIND the cash register inside the Shell station was watching a game show on TV when Mack walked up, a sour middle-aged woman with a smudged SMILES ARE FREE button on her bright orange blouse.

"You're one of the few stations in the area selling diesel," said Mack. "I'm looking—"

"The pump not working?" said the clerk, still watching the game show. "It sticks sometimes—"

"I'm looking for a blue or black VW diesel Rabbit with a *Meat is Murder* bumper sticker."

The clerk glanced at him, then went back to the TV. People onscreen were cheering wildly about something, balloons and confetti falling from the overheads.

Mack placed his business card on the counter. "You spot the VW and take down the license number, it's worth a hundred dollars."

The clerk ignored the card, turned up the sound instead.

As Mack turned to leave he saw her hand dart out, snag the card. Her eyes never left the TV.

An hour later Mack had finished cruising the parking lots of two natural food stores, a tattoo parlor and an outdoor equipment outfitter. Saw plenty of *Meat is Murder* bumper stickers, but none of them on a VW diesel. A doughy checker at Capitol Hill Organics said she thought she had seen a VW with that sticker in the lot a few weeks ago, but she didn't know who it belonged to, and the more she thought of it, she wasn't sure if she had really seen it. She said her dream therapist pegged her as overly suggestible.

Mack noticed a circle of young guys playing hackie sack on the edge of a small park and pulled over. Littered with fast food wrappers, the park was a barren stretch of dead grass and stunted trees. The guys glanced over as Mack approached, then returned to deftly kicking the hackie sack back and forth. They were fit and healthy, covered in tattoos, dressed in baggy, knee length shorts and t-shirts.

"Excuse me," said Mack. "I need a little help."

"Just a *little*, John Q?" A guy with a faded Obama t-shirt bobbled the sack from one knee to the other. Laughter all around. Great to be young and convinced the world was one great big joke, the punch line always meant for someone else. Obama guy did a half turn, batted the sack across the circle.

"I'm looking for a VW diesel—"

Obama guy spat at Mack's feet.

"Buy yourself a Prius, you'll feel better," said a guy in a No Nukes shirt.

"Get a bus-pass, John Q," said tie-dye guy, dribbling the sack from one foot to the other.

"This VW has a *Meat is Murder* bumper sticker—"

"I call bullshit," said No Nukes guy, looking around for the cameras. You punking us, John Q?"

Mack snatched the hackie sack. Then felt his phone vibrate. Checked the number. Stevie.

"Give it back, John Q.," said Obama guy.

Mack bounced the sack off Obama guy's forehead, walked away, the phone to his ear. No one followed him. "You run the credit cards?"

"I love you too," said Stevie.

"Sorry," said Mack. "It's been a lousy morning."

"It's probably not going to get any better. Grace Schearson is boring. *Voyage to the Center of the Earth* remake boring. Only one credit card and very little activity on it. A Discover card no less. Not doing her part to drive the economy at all. We're never going to bust through the recession that way. Shops mostly at J.C. Penney and the Gap…a single purchase two weeks ago from Nordstrom…looks like a dress, Most expensive thing she's bought in ages."

"Must have been the outfit she wore to the reunion."

"Ra-ra, sis boom ba. Balance paid off every month. No liens, no bankruptcies. Probably reuses her aluminum foil and measures out the toilet paper—"

"Any regular restaurants?" Mack walked towards his car. "The receipt should reflect she paid for herself and a guest."

"Checking. Checking. No...nothing jumps out at me."

"Grace didn't own a car. Did she buy gas anyplace?"

"Um...no."

"Any activity on her card or Remy's in the last few days?"

"Nada."

A garbage truck rumbled past as Mack opened the door to his car. Papers and fast food wrappers swirled around him in a whirlwind of grit. "Why don't you email me what you pulled up? Maybe I'll see something—"

"Already did it. I've got to go—"

"One more thing."

"Isn't there always?"

"Can you tap into the database for the Washington State Department of Corrections?"

CHAPTER 26

REMY SAT AGAINST the giant cedar. Her head ached, but she kept her eyes on Glenn who squatted in front of her. One of those vain, handsome men who always overestimated themselves. His happy face bandana stuffed in a pocket now. Maybe she should have just let him get away with punching her. Turn the other cheek. Maybe it would have been smarter not to antagonize him. Not see his face.

No. It was good to see what Glenn looked like. Good for him to know, for them *all* to know who she was. There was no longer any pretense of them letting her go. She had made a career of being able to assess who was the real power player in the room, and who was just the false front. Eli might smile and offer to help, but it wasn't his decision whether she lived or died. Being let go had always been a false hope, one designed to make her play the good girl who did what they told her too. That false hope was gone, and just as well. Illusions engendered weakness and Remy couldn't afford to be weak,

Eli knelt in the clearing, braiding a tiara of wild flowers while he hummed to himself. He looked up, saw her watching. Did Eli know how things had shifted in the last few minutes? Remy saw Tree standing nearby with his arms folded, a sour expression on his face. *He* knew.

"How are you feeling?" Glenn smiled at her. If would have been one of his best qualities if he hadn't been so aware of it. "We got off to a rough start. Maybe that's my fault—"

"You think?" said Remy.

Glenn rubbed the last of his eyebrows. Burnt hair drifted down and his smile faltered for a moment. "Your daddy is a busy man. Out of touch and out of reach, supposedly. I had to do something to get his attention."

"Next time..." Remy dabbed at her nose, which had started bleeding again. "Next time send him a candygram."

Eli laughed, his fingers gently twisting the flowers. "She's something, isn't she, Glenn? Toldja."

"Yeah, she's something." Glenn reached for her, then thought better of it. "I bet you're a wild ride, lady. I bet you buck a man so hard—"

"Let me talk to Grace."

"Quit asking about Grace," said Glenn.

"What did you do to her?"

Glenn slid his tongue across his lower lip. "If you're nice, maybe I'll show you."

"Did you kill her?" said Remy.

"Hey, that's not who we are," called Eli. "Tell her, Glenn."

"I'll bring you back to the city soon as daddy comes through," said Glenn. "You can talk to Grace then. You can trade stories about what a nasty boy I am."

"I don't believe you."

"That's the second time you called me a liar," Glenn said softly, his eyes like stones.

"She said her boyfriend's looking for her," said Tree. "According to her, he's some kind of hero for hire."

Glenn shivered in mock-fear. Stood up in one smooth, graceful motion. "I'll be back as soon as daddy comes through. Maybe sooner if I get bored or lonely." He hitched up his jeans. "You'll be back sleeping on silk sheets and ordering the help around before you know it, lady." He ambled over to his motorcycle and Tree followed.

Remy walked over to Eli. She watched Glenn and Tree in conversation, unable to hear what they were saying.

Tree looked over at Remy. You would have thought something hard and heavy had dropped onto his shoulders.

"It's going to be okay," said Eli. "You'll see. You and Grace will be laughing about this in a few days—"

"Grace is dead," said Remy.

"No...no, she and Glenn are tight," said Eli. "I never met her, but Glenn says—"

"She's *dead*. They're going to kill me too unless you help me."

Eli shook his head. "Don't talk like that." He gently laid the flower tiara on Remy's head. Smiled. Pleased at the effect. "Don't worry. Like Glenn says, we're the good guys."

CHAPTER 27

"YOU *GOT TO* be shitting me, Jeeves," said Glenn.

"No, sir, I am most definitely not...*shitting you,*" said Martin.

"Mack Armitage, that's the guy I'm, supposed to talk to?" Glenn raised his voice as the city bus accelerated, the peroxide grandma in the row ahead half turned, trying to listen in with her hearing aids. "Built guy but moves light? Looks like a real wiseass? Is that the Mack we're talking about?"

"I'm not a very good judge of who's a wise ass and who's not, sir. I've authorized Mr. Armitage to negotiate the release of Miss Brandt while I endeavor to contact her father."

"Made an executive decision have you, Jeeves?"

No response.

Glenn stared out the window as the bus lurched down Broadway in the late afternoon, wondering how things could have gone so bad so fast. This was supposed to be his chance to get rich and do something for the Earth. Instead, it was turning into a festival of get fucked and run around in circles. First you need an Ouija board to contact old man Brandt, then the rich girl cops a major attitude instead of being all don't-hurt-me-don't-hurt-me-*please.* He rubbed what was left of his eyebrows and smelled burnt hair. Now the tough guy turns up alive and well. What else was going to go wrong? Maybe the sun goes nova? Or the chick from the falafel stand in Port Angeles last month had herpes?

Glenn jabbed the grandma in the row ahead with his cell phone, made her turn around. Times like this, he wished he hadn't listened to Cleo. He had been eager to do something big, something important, a real statement, you know, and Cleo had suggested they grab Remy. She had read something about an alumni meeting being planned in Seattle. Way things were turning out, they would have been better blowing up the Starbucks world headquarters like Glenn first wanted to do. Course there was no real money in that, which was part of the reason he had listened to Cleo.

114

The bus lurched to a stop, people filing in and out.

"Would you like me to repeat Mr. Armitage's cell-phone number?" said Jeeves.

Glenn already had the tough guy's number; it was right there in the rich bitch's phone. He stared out the window at the passing Capitol Hill storefronts—espresso joints, Cambodian take-out and tattoo parlors. Cleo was going to flip if the tough guy was alive. He was half-tempted not to surprise her at the Gravity Lounge. She would start in, telling him he should have checked, he should have slid down the mudpile in the pouring rain and made sure the tough guy was dead. City mud was full of toxic metals and weird, mutated organisms from suburban pricks over-fertilizing their little patch of heaven. Let Glenn get his asshole eaten up by a swarm of hybrid fire ants carrying the black plague or something, Cleo didn't care, just as long as he did what she told him to. Someday—

"Sir?"

"The Mack I'm thinking about is supposed to be dead."

"Perhaps you were misinformed, sir."

"You sound like a wiseass to me too, Jeeves. I got a movie clip I want to show you that might change your tone—"

"You'll have to show your little movie clip to Mr. Armitage," said Martin. "I have a dinner engagement. Ta-ta."

Glenn listened to dead air and promised himself when he collected his Green Turtle Conservancy check, he was going to fly to New York City, fly there first-class with Cleo, and throw Jeeves off the fiftieth floor of whatever fancy office building he worked in. Ta-ta, asswipe.

CHAPTER 28

MACK SPOTTED CLEO seated in the corner booth of the Gravity Lounge, the best spot in the house, with a perfect sightline to the stage. Cleo Hutchinson. She looked just like her online photo—tall, thin, with ghostly white skin and glossy red lipstick. Her straight black hair swung against her bare shoulders as she nodded to the music, just like her namesake. At least the popular conception of her namesake. The rest of the crowd was dressed down in jeans and baggy shorts, skimpy blouses and hockey jerseys, tats and piercings on every bit of exposed skin, but Cleo wore a slinky black cocktail dress with a plunging neckline, her skin flawless and unmarked.

Avery had called Cleo the press agent for edge culture when he called this morning, said she was both trusted and lusted after. A critic for the *Edge,* a local alternative paper, Cleo knew everyone, from musicians to radical politicians, fourth-wave chefs to street punks. Avery said Mack should talk with her.

Mack worked his way over to Cleo, dodging spiked-out waiters and patrons stumbling towards the bar. A jostling crowd, all knees and elbows and spilled drinks, without excuses or thank-yous. Just as well. He was in no mood.

"Hi Cleo, we've never met—"

"Yes, and I'll have to forgo that pleasure a little longer, handsome," said Cleo, her eyes on the stage. "Drop your business card or your invitation to the CD release party and I'll get back to you."

"I don't have a band, I've got a problem. I'm Mack Armitage."

Cleo looked him over, taking her time. "Pleased to meet you, Mack." She wagged her black manicure at the other side of the booth.

A waiter appeared almost instantaneously. The overheads gleamed on his shaved head, Chinese ideograms tattooed on his temporal lobes.

"Another passion pit for me," said Cleo, holding up her half-finished drink, "and one for my new friend here." She peered at Mack as the waiter retreated. "A man with a problem. Just your bad luck I don't have any maternal instincts."

"That's okay, I've been weaned." Mack slid the photograph from him wallet to her. A snapshot of he and Remy on the beach at Baja, the two of them just out of the water, the sunset turning them golden. "This is my girlfriend, Remy."

"Lucky you." Cleo's gaze strayed to him. "Lucky her."

"Remy was kidnapped Sunday night."

Cleo flicked the photo with a fingernail. "What did she do?"

Mack shook his head. "Her father's rich. The man who contacted his office said the earth was in peril and he had come to collect."

Cleo sipped her drink.

"You don't seem surprised."

Cleo raised an eyebrow. "I was wondering when the hardcore would take it to the next level, but then again…are you sure that the Greens are behind this?" She leaned forward slightly. A tiny birthmark lay nestled between her creamy breasts. "Most progressives think the ice caps will melt before the power brokers do anything. That doesn't mean we start kidnapping every debutante with a trust fund. Otherwise Kim Kardashian would be flashing her cootchie on a milk carton instead of TV."

"Kim Kardashian evidently wasn't available. Remy was."

Cleo slowly shook her head. "I don't know—"

"Look, I don't give a shit about saving the whales or the rainforest, all I care about is saving Remy."

Cleo fanned herself with a hand. "Well, I declare," she drawled, "I do believe I'm getting moist. I've never met a real live knight of the Round Table before."

"You still haven't."

"Isn't this something the police should be handling?" said Cleo. "I'm no expert, but you seem way too emotionally involved—"

"The police are doing what they can. I'm doing the rest. No harm in that, is there?"

"You tell me," said Cleo.

"Remy was kidnapped while we were visiting Grace Schearson. Do you know Grace?"

"Slightly. A true believer with a weakness for lost causes and clunky shoes."

"She and Remy were sorority sisters," said Mack, "so maybe Remy was a target of opportunity."

"You should talk to Grace's boyfriend. He's a producer at this hippie radio station—"

"I've already talked to Avery."

"Of course. And he pointed you to me." Cleo finished her drink as the waiter approached. "You're a bad man, Mack Armitage. People who ask for help should tell the *whole* truth."

"That's setting the bar pretty high."

The waiter interrupted, laid their drinks in front of them. Passed Cleo three business cards. A couple of guys waved to her from across the room, lifted their drinks.

Mack started to speak but Cleo laid a hand on his wrist. "Hang on." She nodded at a disheveled middle-aged guy slumped onstage, gripping the microphone like he was drowning. "I like this guy."

"My father and I were at each other's throats for as long as I can remember," said the man onstage. "Every morning, from the time I was ten until I moved out, we fought over who would say 'good morning' first. Even today I look bowl of Cheerios and I want to punch somebody."

CHAPTER 29

GLENN WAS THINKING about the rich bitch's ear curled up in a cigar box when he saw Cleo sitting with the tough guy in a corner booth of the Gravity Bar. Ruined a perfect fantasy. Glenn right in the middle of imagining how great it would be to mail Mr. Brandt his daughter's ear, like, *here* pops, this is what happens when you make somebody like me wait. A very cool fantasy until he saw Cleo and the tough guy head to head. If Glenn had X-ray vision he could have seen clear through the table and checked out the dude's hardon.

"I have a half-hour wait for a table," said the hostess, "but I can seat you now at the bar."

"Yeah, fine."

Hearing from Jeeves that the tough guy was still alive was bad enough, but seeing him with Cleo...Glenn felt like the floor was spongy, like he could fall through at any moment. Reminded him of that night at Grace's, hearing her make those sounds while he squeezed the life out of her and tried to pretend he was someplace else. He was just glad he couldn't see Grace's face while he strangled her. Things like that could haunt a person. Spoil the buzz when he hit his payday.

Glenn followed the hostess to the bar. She smelled good, and normally, he would have leaned in close, making small talk, working his smile, but he was off stride, no two ways about it. Besides, his burnt-off eyebrows probably made him look like a zombie. That thing with the ear, that wasn't twisted shit like some weirdo keeping body parts of his mother in the freezer and the neighbors said he was quiet and gave out full-size Snickers bars at Halloween. Cutting off that bitch's ear, that was payback. Mother Nature didn't forgive and forget and neither did Glenn.

He ordered a wheatgrass fizz from the bartender, watching Cleo and the tough guy in the mirror behind the bar.

Glenn had only seen the tough guy that one night, the night he choked out Grace, but that had been enough. The guy had pissed off Glenn that first night, and he pissed him off now. The way he sat in the booth now, foot propped up like he owned the place. The way he smiled at Cleo. Cleo made most men nervous. She had made *Glenn* nervous the first time they met. Not this character. Glenn was tempted to saunter over, ask him if he had lost something. Ask if there was a reward for its safe return. See what the tough guy did then.

Fucker must be here looking for the rich girl. Hot on the trail. Wanting Cleo's help. Ask Cleo. That's what everybody said. You got a band? A club opening up? A demonstration that needed a parade permit? A visiting guru looking for a vegetarian potluck? You go ask Cleo. Glenn still didn't like seeing the tough guy with her. Made him want to do something about it too.

CHAPTER 30

"THIS IS ABOUT saving somebody's life, Cleo," said Mack. "Doesn't that interest you?"

"Not really." Cleo's cocktail dress rustled as she shifted in the booth, her hair sliding across her long white neck like a black tide. "Depends who they are. Oh gee, did I hurt your feelings?"

"Yeah. You want to kiss it, make it better?"

"Maybe." Cleo maintained eye contact while she sucked at her drink. "Does *she* kiss it?"

Mack tore himself away from her gaze. She had a way of speeding things up, then abruptly slowing down. One moment they were just talking, the next they were hurtling in a whole new direction. "Look, I'm just a visitor here. The man who kidnapped Remy is evidently some asshole who got fed up torching Hummers. Avery said you knew everybody. He said you could help."

The waiter delivered more tickets to upcoming performances.

Cleo nodded at two skinny musicians across the room. They waved back, eager as minnows at feeding time. "I used to work phone sex," she said to Mack, her eyes still on the musicians. "Good hours, great pay, but the best part was the ache in the voices on the other end of the line. Those two over there would do anything to get me to mention their band in my column. You're the same way. You need me so bad you can taste it."

"You want to charge me by the minute, Cleo?"

"I like hearing you say my name. Have you ever called a sex line?"

"I prefer it when women lie to my face."

"If you called me once, you'd be a regular. Once I started talking you'd burn through your paycheck to keep the meter running. I know what boys like."

"What about men?"

"No such thing. There are just boys and boys pretending to be men." Cleo finished her drink. "I'll ask around about your girlfriend, but I have to tell you, Avery was wrong about me. I don't know everyone." She cocked her head at him. "The kind of desperate character that grabbed your girlfriend. I keep my distance from those types. Too unstable. Unpredictable. They scare me."

"I doubt that. I can't imagine what it would take to scare you."

Cleo stroked the birthmark between her breasts with the back of her nails. "Well...you were the one who said you preferred women who lied to your face."

Mack stood up. He was tired. Tired of the conversation anyway. Tired of the way Cleo seemed to be enjoying his distress. Not that he was special. It was the distress she basked in, a need only she could slake. Or pretended she could. Like she said, she did great at phone sex, homing in on a caller's unspoken desires, fanning the flame of desperation.

"Going so soon?" pouted Cleo. "I thought we were having fun."

"I can only handle so much fun." Mack wrote his cell phone number on the back of one of the tickets the musicians had sent over. "Whatever you can do...whatever you can find out, I'd appreciate it."

Cleo beckoned to him. When he bent closer, she kissed him lightly. "Don't thank me until I've given you something to be grateful for."

CHAPTER 31

REMY LAY ON her back, looking up, dizzy with the raw wonder of the stars overhead. The platform underneath her gently swayed in the wind, the ropes attaching it to the cedar tree groaning rhythmically. She had to press her palms against the wooden planks to remind herself where she was, to hold herself in place so she wouldn't float off into the night. Her hammock was slung nearby but she was in no mood to sleep. Most evenings since she had first awakened in the forest had been overcast, but tonight the bowl of sky was pure black above the trees, the stars like spilt milk. She lay there looking up and felt like she was falling into the night. The only thing that would have made it even more perfect was Mack beside her.

"Beautiful, huh?" said Eli, lying where Mack should be.

"I've never...never *seen* so many stars," Remy said softly, as though by raising her voice she might shatter them.

"Not like they're making any new ones, lady," growled Tree from the other side of the platform. "You just ain't been paying attention."

"I guess you just can't see them from L.A.," said Eli.

"No, not like this," said Remy. It wasn't pollution that blocked the stars from the L.A. skies, it was the light of ten thousand office buildings and towers, of headlights and billboards drowning everything else out, nothing but people and cars and buy buy buy. Now she wondered how she could ever live without the stars, knowing that they were out there in places like this.

"See that?" said Eli, pointing. "That constellation...that one's my favorite."

Remy had to shift slightly to see where he was pointing, almost cheek-to-cheek with Eli now. "Those four bright stars there?"

"Yeah, that's Kurt Cobain," said Eli. "Those other stars, the less bright ones are his guitar and—"

"That's the constellation *Hercules*," said Tree, disgusted.

"See, the way his arms are positioned?" continued Eli, arm still pointing. "He's cranking out the power chord from *Smells Like Teen Spirit*, or maybe *Bleach*. Astronomers still aren't sure."

"It's Hercules and he's *kneeling*," insisted Tree.

"What's that…fuzzy patch in his middle?" said Sarah.

"That's Courtney Love." Eli sighed. "She broke his heart."

"That's M13," said Tree, voice rising. "It's a globular cluster of over 300,000 stars."

"I have to go along with Eli on this one," said Remy. "That's clearly Kurt Cobain." She pointed at another group of six stars. "What about that?"

"*Oh*, that's a good one," said Eli. "That's MechaGodzilla—"

"That's *Cancer*," said Tree. "Cancer the crab. Those are his two pinchers—"

"Those are MechaGodzilla's armored arms," said Eli, smiling sweetly. "You got some bum information, Tree, no offense. Cancer is a *disease*. MechaGodzilla is an awesome sick *robot*."

Tree stood up, towering over them. "The constellations are all about Greek *Mythology*." He tore at his beard in frustration. "During his twelve labors, Hercules was attacked by a giant crab. When Hercules killed the crab, the goddess Hera put it in the sky, next to Hercules' other victims, the Lion, the Serpent and Hydra."

Eli glanced up at him. "Dude, that's crazy talk. Hercules, giant crabs…they're not real. Kurt Cobain, he's on the radio. He's on YouTube. Google it. *He's* real. Same thing with MechaGodzilla. Check out Netflix, Tree, and you can watch him battle Godzilla—"

"*Enough*." Tree squeezed his temples until his knuckles were white. "I keep listening to you, Eli, I'm going to kill somebody." He vaulted over the railing of the platform, seemingly jumping off into space.

Remy raised herself up and peeked over the railing, saw Tree scurrying down the cedar branch by branch in the dim light. He was quickly lost from sight, but she could hear the whisper of branches as he continued his descent. "Tree doesn't give you the proper respect, Eli."

"Well…he's old school, that's all."

"I wonder how long you're going to let him decide everything for you, that's all."

"Tree's a good guy, and an awesome climber," said Eli, his eyes on the stars. "Got to respect that, but the man needs to get his facts straight."

Remy lay back down, settled in beside him again. "I think you're a better friend to him then he is to you."

Eli didn't answer. Just lay there beside her, the two of them looking up, drifting in the night sky, losing themselves among the stars.

No wind tonight, not even a breeze, just a taut stillness, as though the whole forest was waiting for something. A meteor streaked across the sky; Remy and Eli gasped in tandem, then laughed at themselves. She thought of Mack, Remy embarrassed now.

"How did you end up being part of this?" said Remy.

"This? We're all part of this. The moon and the stars—"

"I mean the *kidnapping*, Eli."

"Oh."

"You're not anything like Glenn and Tree."

Eli raised himself up on one elbow. "I didn't used to have any focus, no direction, just smoking weed and following the waves. Then I met Glenn." He lay back down. "I was surfing up at north slope, totally radical place, way private, only get to the beach by climbing down this sheer rock cliff on a knotted rope. I bet this local a joint of purple Kush that I could free climb to the top faster than he could using the rope." He turned his head, grinned at Remy. "I totally fried that dude, just shut him down, and Glenn came up to me afterwards, fist-bumped me, said I climbed like a righteous monkey. He helped me smoke that Kush, and we started talking, and he was like *totally* long-term planning, like 'what are you doing for Mama Earth, Eli? You on *her* side or the side of the corporate gangbangers raping her?' Once I thought about it, I was like, easy call, dude, sign me up with Mama Earth. A week or so later we hooked up with Tree. He and Glenn were already tight, they just needed a third, which was kind of cool, because nobody had ever needed me before."

"I guess my question to you, Eli," Remy said carefully, "is do you still need *them*?"

"They're family," said Eli. "Not a matter of who needs who

anymore."

"Eli...you still have a choice."

"No. No, I don't." Eli turned away from her, turned back to the sky. "When...when your dad pays the ransom, you don't have to go back," he said. "Like you said, you can't see things like this in L.A."

Remy stared at him. He had told her he was nineteen, but he looked even younger, his face smooth, not a line in it. Nothing more dangerous than innocence, she reminded herself. Too easy to forget things like that out here, easy to forget yourself in the music of a stream rushing across the rocks, or birds trilling at dawn. Every day, every moment freshly born.

"It's not really so bad here, is it?" said Eli. "I've been watching you on our walks. You move different now. You got that deep woods glide already. Happens fast, doesn't it?"

"Very fast," said Remy, not realizing she had said it out loud until she felt her lips move.

"See, you're adjusting, that's cool," said Eli, fingering one of his dreads, rolling it back and forth. "Pretty soon, it'll be like you were born here—"

"I don't *want* to get adjusted."

If Eli heard her, he didn't acknowledge it, staring up at the Milky Way as he played with his hair. "You could stay here, at least until it gets cold," he said matter of factly. "There's all kinds of things we could do. Fun stuff. There's a waterfall two days hike away that you won't believe. And fields of fall flowers, tiny blue flowers no bigger than the head of a pin and they smell like apple pie. Warm apple pie. Then, when the snow comes—"

"I can't stay here, Eli."

"No problem. I get restless too. We can head south, catch some waves in Mexico—"

"That's not what I mean. I can't stay with *you*. I can't live like this. I have another life."

"Sure." Eli rested a hand on his heart. "Sure, I know that. I was...speculating. That's the right word, isn't it? Just speculating. You've got another life. I get it."

Remy turned his head so that he was forced to face her. "I like you, Eli. You're a good person. I think if you had your way, you would have never kidnapped me."

"I'm not so good," said Eli, lowering his eyes, "not anymore."

"This wasn't your idea, I know that."

"No, it wasn't, but I couldn't let my boys down. Got to look out for each other—"

"Loyalty only goes so far," said Remy, as the wind rose, the trees rippling. The platform swayed, but she barely noticed it. "You did your best, Eli. Now it's time for you to make things right."

"Too late for that now," said Eli, voice cracking.

"No, it's not."

Eli shook his head.

"Eli..." Remy rested her hand against his cheek. "You think about it, and when you finally decide to do the right thing, you just have to look at me and nod your head, and I'll know."

"Like a secret sign?"

"Yes. *Our* secret sign."

Eli looked into her eyes. "I wish we were someplace else. Just the two of us."

"All you have to do is—"

"I'm not dumb, you know." Eli turned back to the night, his eyes shimmering in the darkness, stars reflected into them. "Everybody acts like I am, but I pay attention. I notice things. I see what you're trying to do, but it's not going to work. I don't blame you for trying to get away. You didn't ask to be here, we *took* you, so it's only right that you'd do anything you can to get home."

"Tree and Glenn are going to kill me, Eli—"

"I won't let that happen."

"You may not be able to prevent it."

"People always underestimate me. Glenn does it all the time. Even Tree does it once in a while." Eli looked at her. "You just need to remember one thing when you get scared or worried. I won't let anything bad happen to you. That's a promise."

127

Remy nodded. At that instant she actually believed him.

Eli sat up. "I just wish...I just wish you weren't trying to trick me. I wish it was just you and me someplace else, and I didn't have to worry about you running off." His voice was lower now, as though he were talking to himself. "I know places on the Mexican coast, tiny fishing villages with great waves and white sand and no tourists. You can live there for hardly any money, just sleep on the beach and teach little kids how to surf."

"That sounds nice, Eli."

Eli blinked at her, a kind of Morse code he didn't even realize he was sending. "If...if we had met on a beach, and none of this had ever happened, you might have fallen in love with me."

Remy took his hand. He resisted for an instant, then sighed and squeezed her hand back.

"I know," said Eli. "I *get* it. You already love somebody."

"That's right." She saw that her acknowledgement had wounded him.

"The tough guy," said Eli. "That's what Glenn called him."

"His name is Mack," said Remy.

"He's so lucky."

"I think you'd like him, Eli."

"No...I'd be too jealous." Eli blushed, started to get up. "We should go to sleep."

"I'm not tired," said Remy.

Eli hesitated, then sat back down beside her. He squinted at her, working something over in his head. "You...you could have lied to me. You could have said maybe if we had met on a beach somewhere, you would have seen riding the waves and maybe...maybe you would have fallen for me. You didn't, though. You told me the truth."

"I did."

"That's something, isn't it? That counts."

"Yes, the truth...it's something, Eli."

Eli lay down beside her again, the two of them looking up into the night.

"Eli...when you were talking with Tree before...you were just having fun with him about the constellations, right?"

"What am I, an idiot?"

Their soft laughter rose from the platform. Somewhere close by an owl responded, which made them laugh harder.

"I like teasing Tree, and besides, why should we call the stars what the Greeks did?" said Eli. "What did they ever do for us?"

"Other than Euclidean geometry and the fundamentals of democracy, not a damn thing."

"Exactly." Eli nestled closer to her, cheek to cheek now. "You want me to teach you some more constellations?"

CHAPTER 32

MACK BENT DOWN, reached far under Grace's bed, still thinking about Cleo. A woman who considered conversation an erogenous zone. He found dust balls and an old Kleenex under the bed, a couple of M&Ms and an *In Style* magazine that Grace was probably ashamed of anyone seeing.

"You moonlighting as a maid now? Because if you do windows, I've got work for you."

Mack banged his head under the bed, scooted out, cursing. Saw Hobbs rocking on his heels in the doorway, hands thrust in the pockets of his rumpled charcoal gray three-piece. "Why, you need help around your house? I'm a holy terror on nasty yellow buildup, but I don't do windows."

"You may end up doing six months for B and E," said Hobbs.

"You're going to have to find Grace to make the complaint." Mack ripped through the nightstand, pulling out drawers. "What are you doing here?"

"Got a call from one of the neighbors about activity at the house."

"They called *you?*"

"I made the rounds after the...disappearance. Passed out my card. People appreciate the personal touch when it comes to law enforcement."

"I'll have to remember that," said Mack, checking the back of the drawers.

"What are you looking for?"

"A snapshot of Grace and her new boyfriend..." Mack pawed through the top drawers contents: a couple of Judith Kranz paperbacks, a diaphragm and well-squeezed tube of contraceptive jelly. "A matchbook from their favorite restaurant..." He slammed the drawers shut.

"You're a romantic," chided Hobbs. "I should have known. Good cop, but a lousy detective, that's the rap on you."

"That what Lieutenant Gibson said?" Mack walked to the desk in the corner. He riffed through yellow legal pads, looking for notes scrawled in the margins, addresses or phone numbers...*something.* "Guess I better drop him off my Christmas card list."

"He said you were almost more trouble than you were worth. He also said you could have your job back anytime you want."

"Not interested."

"Not surprised." Hobbs ambled over. "Detectives are cool customers. Glorified accountants with sharp eyes and a badge. No emotional involvement, that's my motto, but you, you're a hothead...too much Tabasco in your cornflakes."

Mack kept working.

"Me, a good jigsaw puzzle and a couple of imported beers and I'm a happy fellah," said Hobbs. "You, I bet you never worked a jigsaw puzzle in your life. Late with your paperwork too, am I right? Yeah, I heard all about you. Tough on the bad guys, but tough on the good guys too."

Mack emptied the desk drawer onto the bed. "These jigsaw puzzles you're so fond of..." He thumbed through yellow legal pads. "I bet they all feature anatomically-perfect Playmates with Barbie doll smiles."

Hobbs nodded. "Jennifer Jackson. Miss March, 1965. First African-American centerfold."

Mack rifled through the contents of the desk drawer. "You pull Grace's sheet?"

"I thought your buddy Stevie could hack into anything."

"Maybe he missed something."

"There wasn't really that much to miss," said Hobbs. "Grace has a few misdemeanors. Failure to disperse. Failure to obey a lawful order. Blocking a public sidewalk. Your basic weekend protestor resume." He straightened a framed photo on the wall—Grace as a child wearing Indian princess buckskins and fringed moccasins, her face already serious and burdened. He took the photo off the wall, checked the back.

"You said you weren't going to the FBI, Marcus. That's not what I heard."

"Checking up on me, are you?"

"I like to keep up on current events."

"Well, that brotherhood of the badge stuff only goes so far," said

Hobbs. "I started worrying about how it would look if something happened to her, and—"

"You started worrying that if Remy ends up dead, your dick is in the wringer."

"You ever notice how cop metaphors are always out of date?" Hobbs went through the books on Grace's nightstand. "Dick in the wringer. There hasn't been wringer washing machines in fifty years, and yet—"

"Why did you go to the FBI?"

"I thought we could use some help."

"*Are* they helping?"

Hobbs put back a dog-eared Dean Koonz paperback. "No."

Mack threw open the doors to the closet. "How about you do an unofficial search on a VW diesel Rabbit. Blue or black. At least five years old. Got a Meat is Murder bumper sticks so that's more evidence of an eco-terrorism connection—"

"Right. *The earth is in peril and somebody is going to pay,*" said Hobbs. "You ever think that might be just to throw us off the track?"

"It's the best lead I've got."

"It's probably the only lead you've got." Hobbs shook his head. "Okay. I'll run it through Traffic, see if a diesel got ticketed in Capital Hill or Belltown, That's Granola Central."

"Probably multiple violations," said Mack. "Unpaid, too." He went through the clothes on the hangars, turning out the pockets. "The people who kidnapped Remy probably intended to grab me too, so there wasn't anyone to sound the alarm. Sheer dumb luck on my part to fall off the deck." He ran his hands along the seams of the clothes. Bent down, examined the shoes on the bottom of the closet. Mostly sensible flats, a couple pairs of dressier go-to-court heels. "Only problem is, Remy's father isn't around to hear the ransom demand." Mack hated keeping things from Hobbs, but like the detective said, the brotherhood of the badge stuff only goes so far. "Even if Brandt was available, he might not pay it. He's a Class-A bastard from what I've read."

"Maybe her father knows something you don't," Hobbs said.

Mack hefted the hiking boots, held them up to Hobbs. "Check the

132

treads, most of the shoes are well worn. These are almost new."

"Never cared for the great outdoors myself," said Hobbs. "Reminds me of Deliverance and Ned Beatty getting ramrodded by that redneck. Sooooeeeeeee."

"What did you mean about Remy's father knowing something I didn't?" said Mack.

Hobbs adjusted the knot in his necktie, uncomfortable. "I talked to somebody at the local FBI office. Feds got a stick up their ass about locals, you know how that goes, but he was willing to do some checking..."

"Spit it out, Hobbs."

"This isn't the first time Remy was supposedly kidnapped. She disappeared when she was sixteen. Her father contracted the Bureau, hired his own security crew, full electronic sweep. They found her a week later in Rio with her tennis instructor."

Mack stared at him. "Remy's not sixteen and I'm not a tennis instructor."

"I'm just telling you what I was told."

"Okay. Now we both know."

"That's not all." Hobbs rooted in one ear with a finger. "Two years later, she got kidnapped again, for real this time, with a ransom demand and everything. Five thousand dollars. You believe that? Five thousand dollars. *Cash*. The note actually said 'cash.' Just as her father is digging the ransom money out from between the cushions of the living room sofa, Remy walks in the front door. Says it was all a misunderstanding. Some high school kids she was tutoring had watched *Scarface* one too many times and duct-taped her to a chair in one kid's basement."

Mack moved closer. "How did she——?"

"Seems while the ringleader was making the ransom demand from a payphone at the nearest 7-11, Remy convinced the two knuckleheads left guarding her that the tape around her ankles was cutting off her circulation." Hobbs grinned. "*Then* she wanted a drink of water. The water he brought wasn't cold enough, so she sent him back for ice. And a clean glass. *Then* she had an itch, in a private spot, no less, so the other knucklehead untaped one of her hands so she could scratch it. Whereupon

133

she kicked him in *his* private spot, tore the tape off her other hand and ran out the basement door." Hobbs hitched his pants. "Getting away like that says a lot about her, but she refused to press charges and the kids walked, which brings us back to Rio and the tennis instructor. Some folks might conclude she's the girl who cried wolf."

"Is that what you've concluded?" said Mack. "Because if you have, what are you doing helping me?"

"Let's just say the FBI isn't about to get involved without, and I quote, 'clear and compelling evidence of a criminal act.'" Hobbs sniffed. "Me, I'm just a local yokel with time on his hands."

Mack went back to the bed, started sorting through the emptied contents of the desk. His movements rough now. Angry.

"What are you looking for?" said Hobbs.

Mack pulled a small notebook from the pile. "It's a hiking journal." Hobbs looked over his shoulder as Mack turned the pages. "I didn't connect it before...but I should have." He ran a finger down the notations. "Grace has about...fifteen hikes logged in here. All in the last three months." He looked at Hobbs. "All these years arguing for the environment, but it's only in the last three months that she gets out of the city and into the woods."

"Maybe she was trying to get in shape," said Hobbs.

Mack slipped the journal into his pocket. "Maybe she picked up a new boyfriend."

Hobbs held out his hand. "Give me the journal. That's evidence."

Mack shook his head. "You need a crime for there to be evidence. Is this a crime scene, detective?"

Hobbs had dark brown eyes, bright and a little watery around the edges. Fatigue probably, or maybe he had worked the job too long and knew how things usually turned out. He slowly put his hand down. "No...not yet."

Mack nodded. "Just so you know...I didn't have any idea about those prior incidents with Remy."

"Women...anybody says they're the weaker sex must have never met one."

"It doesn't matter what happened before. Remy wouldn't do that to me. This isn't a setup. She's really in trouble...and it's my fault."

Hobbs watched him.

"That night...Sunday night when we pulled up to Grace's house, I *knew* there was something off, something wrong. I didn't act on it. I just went inside and let it happen." Mack closed in on Hobbs. "What's the point of having good instincts if you don't act on them?"

Hobbs rested his palms on Mack's shoulders. "Can't act on every impulse. You just *can't*. They lock people up for that."

"I'd rather be locked up."

"I know." Hobbs let him go. "We'll find her. Don't you worry, we'll bring her back, safe and sound."

CHAPTER 33

GLENN WATCHED THE tough guy through the bedroom window at Grace's house. Just like old times, only this time the fucker probably wouldn't fall off the deck. Unless Glenn decided to give him a push. That would be fun. He could just imagine what Jeeves would say when Glenn called and told him he'd need a new bitch.

Glenn had been hiding in the thick bushes for twenty minutes, when a car pulled up out front, this big black cop getting out. Man didn't take two steps before Glenn knew what he was. Nobody else walks like a cop. Heavy with authority. Slow too, like they knew they didn't need to rush. Glenn about shit himself at first, thinking the cop was looking for him, but the cop just ambled inside. So there went Glenn's fantasy of seeing if the tough guy could survive two falls down the hillside.

Glenn had followed the tough guy from the Gravity Lounge. Soon as Mack got up, Glenn had whispered to a blonde at the bar, snagged a set of keys from her bag. The tough guy was driving out of the parking lot by the time Glenn beeped the blonde's remote and found her car. He almost lost the tough guy...but he didn't.

The cop and the tough guy were going back and forth like old buddies, Mack rummaging through Grace's drawers. He wasn't going find anything. He wasn't going to find Grace either. Sometimes Glenn thought about her, thought about her at the oddest times too. She hadn't been anything special, but the look in her eyes as he strangled her...that kind of things stays with a person.

Glenn leaned closer, trying to hear what they were saying and a twig snapped underfoot. The tough guy glanced towards the window, Glenn retreated back into the shadows, heart pounding as he became part of the darkness. A minute later he eased forward and the two of them were back yapping as the tough guy went through Grace's desk drawers. Fucker didn't respect privacy, not a bit.

Slowly, carefully, Glenn retreated into the bushes. Keeping low he made it back to the blonde's car that he had parked down the street. He would wait them out. Mack would have to leave sometime. Have to go *home* sometime and Glenn would be right there, a few blocks behind him all the way.

CHAPTER 34

"THERE'S NO BLUEBERRIES back in there," called Eli.

"Just a minute." Remy bent down among the trees. Through the underbrush, she could see Eli standing in the creek, his t-shirt tied around his waist, seemingly oblivious to the icy water churning around his bare shins. She hurriedly scratched her name and Mack's cell phone number on a flat piece of bark with a large, rusty nail, added HELP!

"I said there's nothing there," said Eli. "I found a ginormous patch of berries on the other side of the creek. Tons of them. We can eat as much as we want and still have plenty for dinner tonight."

Remy slipped the nail back into her jean shorts. She rolled up the sleeves of her white blouse, the fabric almost transparent. "Coming." She palmed the piece of bark, and walked out of the trees.

"Careful of the rocks," said Eli. They're slippery."

Remy took off her running shoes and stepped gingerly into the creek, feeling her way across the flat river rocks. The bubbles tickled her toes, and the rushing water made her teeth chatter even in the warmth of the early afternoon. Eli held out a hand but she ignored him, making her way halfway across. When he turned away she set the bark down in the water, watched as the current carried it rapidly downstream. That's where the people were: downstream. Fisherman and campers, swimmers and kids on inflatable rafts. If any one of them found the bark with her message on it, that's all it would take. She and Eli had walked for almost an hour to get here, taking one trail after the other. She probably couldn't find her way back to this spot, but if a search team was sent upriver to find her, one way or the other she'd make sure they knew where she was.

"You okay?" said Eli.

Remy watched the piece of bark bounce against a boulder and continue downstream. It was the third one she had launched today. She turned and smiled at Eli. "Fine."

"You look pretty when you smile," said Eli.

"You should see me when I haven't been kidnapped."

"I wish you wouldn't talk like that," pouted Eli. "I think we're making progress. You're going to be a nature girl yet."

"You never know." Remy sat down on the shore. She wiped her feet dry and slipped her shoes back on. Her toes were still gritty. "So where's the blueberry thicket?"

Eli pointed.

A half hour later they were finishing up at the blueberry patch, faces and hands stained blue, two large Ziploc bags brimming with berries beside them. A valley sloped down from where they worked, the terrain covered with scrub and yellowed mulegrass. Sun beat down through the branches of the scrawny trees around them, the air sharp and sweet with pine resin and the morning rain. Gnats floated overhead. A week ago she would have been annoyed at the insects, swatting ineffectually at them, but now...bugs seemed part of daily life. Like Eli said, you change fast out here. Proof positive of that was that Remy was actually quoting Eli as though he was an expert on something.

"What's so funny?" said Eli.

"You."

Eli licked his fingers.

Remy picked a few more blueberries, gently placed them in the empty metal pie pan. These wild berries were half the size of the organic ones as Mrs. Gooch's on Melrose, but these were much sweeter, intensely flavorful.

Eli lightly raked his nails across his bare chest, left blue streaks across his flat pectorals as he watched her work. "Most folks treat berries too rough, busting 'em all up." The ring through his left nipple gleamed in the sunlight. "You've got a light touch."

"Good to know I'm developing a marketable skill while being held hostage."

"I don't like that word."

"Hostage?" said Remy, still picking berries, trying to use the bare minimum of pressure, making a game of it. "It's the truth, isn't it?"

"Doesn't mean I have to like it."

Remy popped a blueberry into her mouth. "Then do something about it."

Eli lowered his eyes.

Remy bounced a blueberry off of Eli's forehead. "That's what I thought."

Eli puffed his cheeks up, slowly let the air out. "It wasn't supposed to turn out like this. It was like grab the rich bitch—no offense—have daddy pay off Mama Earth and then hand you back safe and sound. It was like almost too easy."

"Bad ideas always seem too easy. Just draw me a map and I'll find my way out of here. Draw me a map, that's all you have to do."

"Tree would be *so* mad. If he caught you—"

"He won't catch me."

Eli shook his head. "Tree says the woods talk to him. He'd know right away what you were up to and then it would be really bad."

"I'll take the chance."

"I won't. I don't want anything to happen to you." Eli held out a canteen that he had filled from the creek. "Truce?"

Remy took a long drink, the water so cold her teeth ached. Her friends in L.A. would be horrified to see her drink water that didn't come from a bottle. Water that wasn't imported. Might as well drink from a hose at a rural gas station, Jane...she took another drink, wiped her lips with the back of her hand. She hadn't known water could be so delicious. She stared at the back of her hands, noted her ragged cuticles. She walked back to the creek, Eli beside her, the two of them washing the stickiness off their faces and hands.

Eli cupped a drink of water, slurping it up. "Were you really a lawyer?"

Remy shook out her hair. "I still am."

"Glenn said you used to hang out with movie stars."

"It's part of the job when you do entertainment law."

"Was it fun?"

Remy didn't answer. It had always seemed like fun, but now...now it seemed like mostly laughing at jokes that weren't funny, and pretending to be interested. Faking interest in the Malibu pad designed by the latest hot architect, or admiring the specs of the next-gen Gulfstream, nodding as the star regaled her with how he had leapfrogged the waiting list. Last month...was it *really* only last month, she had actually laid in a mud-bed beside a prospective client, the two of them swaddled in an algae and lamb placenta wrap, while the three-time Oscar nominee regaled her with the life-changing benefits of her last colonic.

"Bet you never picked blueberries with those movie stars, did you?"

"No. I never did."

"Maybe you should think about another line of work." Eli shrugged, embarrassed. "Just sayin'."

"Maybe you should show me the way out of here," said Remy.

Eli shook his head.

"Help me escape and everything goes back to the way it was before." Remy put her hand on his wrist. "You, Tree, Grace...even Glenn, we all start fresh. No cops, no—"

"Too late for that."

Remy kept her hand on him. "Why?"

"It's not just you." Eli looked away. "There's other stuff."

"Like what?"

Eli stood up. "Tree said you were going to try and get inside my head."

Remy got up slowly, stretched, aware of him watching. The breeze blew across the stream, cool and clean. She saw movement in the trees on the other side of the valley, maybe a couple hundred yards away. She shaded her eyes from the sun, heart pounding. There were people there, four...no, five of them in floppy hats, bent over, pulling at the ground. Hikers maybe, or college students. "I'm...I'm going to take a little walk, Eli. Why don't you wait here—"

"It's okay, I'll come with you," said Eli.

"No offense, but I'd rather be by myself." Remy kept walking, unhurried. Eli still hadn't noticed the hikers. "I just need some time to think."

Eli shook his head again. "That's not such a good idea. You can get lost so easy out here you wouldn't believe it."

Remy nodded. "Okay. Would...would you get me a drink?"

Eli reached for the canteen hooked in his belt.

Remy patted his hand. "That water tastes like plastic. Would you mind refilling it with fresh water. Please?"

Eli sighed, started back towards the creek.

Remy waited until he was halfway there, then waved frantically at the hikers. No response. She walked towards them, slowly at first, then faster, still waving her arms. One of them looked up at her. Remy started running. "Help! I've been kidnapped!"

All of the other hikers stood up now, staring at her, their faces indistinct, dressed head to toe in dark trousers and hooded sweatshirts.

"Help!"

"Hey!" shouted Eli.

Remy kept running, the underbrush whipping against her bare legs.

The hikers backed up. They were carrying something...baskets, small baskets.

"Don't go!" shouted Remy.

"Be careful," called Eli, right behind her.

Remy ran towards the hikers, but they didn't look at her as they hurried in the opposite direction, scooting deeper into the trees. They were almost out of sight. She sprinted, gasping for breath, as much from excitement as exertion. "Don't *go*! I'm Remy Brandt! I've been kidnapped!"

The hikers disappeared into the trees.

"Stop!" called Remy, sprinting after them.

"Remy!" shouted Eli.

Remy burst through a hedge of brush, and the ground gave way beneath her. She staggered backwards, clutching at the bushes, the leaves tearing through her fingers as she slid down the embankment. She hit her head, finally came to rest near the bottom. When she opened her eyes, Eli was beside her, holding her hand.

"Thank *God,*" breathed Eli. "I was afraid you broke something."

Remy pulled her hand away, tried to sit up and doubled over.

"Take it easy," said Eli. "I think you just got the wind knocked out of you."

"Why...why didn't they stop?" said Remy.

"They were scared."

"Of you?"

"Of *us*. They're Hmong."

Remy didn't understand what he was saying.

"Hmong people," said Eli. "Mountain folk from...I forget the name of the country, but it's near Vietnam. They're real shy. They don't speak English or anything."

"They don't need to speak English." Remy carefully sat up, her head throbbing. "They'll tell people what they saw——"

"All they saw was there was a couple of crazy white people running at them, and that's nothing new," said Eli. "They're real gentle, but they have to protect their secret spots from other pickers. That's how they support their families. They were gathering exotic mushrooms when you surprised them. Real money in that. Chanterelles and matsutake caps sell for over twenty dollars a pound at Whole Foods, and cantherellis, which is this gross-looking yellow fungus, that shit goes for megabucks in Europe. Sometimes Tree bumps into Hmong people. He likes them, says they walk light in the woods."

"What do they think about him?"

"They do this when they see him." Eli pressed his palms together and bowed, backing away. "They think he's some kind of forest demon or something."

"Maybe they're right," Remy said softly.

"Why would you want to run away from me?" said Eli. "I thought we were having a good time."

Remy's eyes welled up.

"Please, don't cry."

Remy turned aside. "I'm *not* crying."

CHAPTER 35

THE UNIVERSITY GREENHOUSE was at the edge of campus, tucked away from the street noise, with a great view of the 520-bridge traffic inching across Lake Washington. A cool breeze rippled the grass, made the dandelions sway. Peaceful. Fuck that. He had been running around in circles all day. Mack pushed open the door, and stepped inside.

It was like being underwater. The late afternoon light filtering through the mossy glass was murky and green, and Mack moved slowly through the overgrown aisles, moist plants brushing his arms as he edged his way past. Condensation dripped down the walls, and he had to fight to keep from hurrying. He spotted a scrawny man in a dirty white lab coat carrying a tray of seedlings, grunting with the effort. "Professor Tanner?"

The man set the seedlings down, pushed his glasses back with a forefinger. Wisps of limp brown hair framed his face, made him look younger. Almost fetal. The lenses of his glasses were sticky with fingerprints, a Superman band-aid bracing the nosepiece.

"Your secretary said I'd find you here," said Mack. "I wanted—"

"Give me a hand with these." Tanner nodded at the trays on the benches. "I'm moving them into the east wing and my T.A. is out sick."

Mack picked up a tray, stacked another one on top. "Where do you want them?"

"This way." Tanner scuttled along the concrete floor. Now that he had Mack, he didn't bother carrying anything. The greenhouse filled with dwarf pines and fir trees, the place smelling like air freshener. Tanner indicated a bare table and Mack set the trays down. Tanner lightly touched the pine sprouts, caressed them. "They've very delicate. The light in the west wing was all-wrong. Too intense. Look how their edges are curling."

Mack peered at the sprouts. "If you say so."

Tanner sniffed, cocked his head like a parakeet. "What's your major?"

"I'm not a student. I just wanted to ask you some questions."

Tanner thrust his hands in the pockets of his grimy lab coat, puffing himself up. "If you want advice on the best way to grow blitzkrieg hydroponic pot or grafting techniques to maximize resin production...well...you can just forget it."

"I'll deal with the grief later, but that's not why I'm here," said Mack. "I was told you have connection to the local Greens."

Tanner indicated another tray. Waited until Mack had picked a couple more up. "You were misinformed."

Moisture dripped off the glass overhead, landed on the back of Mack's hand. Warm as sweat. "You were one of the featured speakers at the Take Back the Earth rally."

"So many rallies, it's hard to keep them all straight. Yes...I remember that one. Bit of a mistake." Tanner directed Mack to put the trays of seedlings next to the others. Pointed to a couple fifty-pound bags of organic compost. "I need those moved out back. I'd love to help you, but I have lumbar adhesions."

"You want me to hot wax your car too? Maybe change the oil?"

"I don't own a motor vehicle. Mass transit is the only hope for our society."

"Glad to hear there's some hope." Mack slung a bag of fertilizer over one shoulder. Hoisted the second bag onto the other, then trudged outside and laid them where the professor indicated. "What made you think the rally was a mistake?"

Tanner pulled a pack of cigarettes out of his lab coat, Lucky Strikes. Unfiltered smokes, the ultimate coffin nail. "You don't mind, do you?" He fired one up before Mack could respond. He puffed away, idly fingering one of the many brown-rimmed cigarette burns in his lab coat. "Tobacco smoke is actually good for the plants. I'm a bit of an iconoclast on that point, but I'm certain I'm right. I'm working on a monograph. Not that it will ever get published. You have no idea of the insular—"

"The rally?"

Tanner exhaled directly onto a rubber tree. "Yes, of course. It was the venom of the speakers. The angry rhetoric. All that Days of Rage nonsense. Blows against the empire, yap yap yap. I could see the direction they were heading in." Another deep drag. "The world certainly is in peril—no one with a functioning cerebral cortex could argue the point—

but that doesn't mean we have to shout ourselves hoarse—"

"The earth is in peril. Interesting phrase."

Tanner shrugged. "Bit of a cliché actually." He pulled a piece of tobacco off his teeth, flicked it into the plants. "Who did you say you were working for? Federal or state?"

"I'm...independent."

Tanner smiled. He had missed another fleck of tobacco between his incisors. "No such thing. We're all interconnected, that's one of the primary laws of biology. A tree falls in the middle of the forest, it doesn't *matter* if you hear it, you're still affected. Whether through increased erosion or the rotting tree providing a breeding colony for termites—"

"Professor...with all due respect, I don't give a shit."

Tanner looked stunned.

Mack took the cigarette out of Tanner's mouth, ground it underfoot. "I'm not a patient man under the best of circumstances, and right now I'm sleeping in a cheap motel next to the freeway, eating in my car...and I'm *scared*. I can handle the lousy food and accommodations, but I don't like being scared. This keeps up much longer, somebody's going to get hurt."

Tanner stared at Mack as though he was a new species of orchid.

"My girlfriend...the woman I love has been kidnapped by a group of environmental terrorists. Their ransom demand featured the same phrase you just used." Mack watched Tanner but the scientist didn't look concerned, as though he had been caught in a slip, but merely shook his head.

"I'm disappointed, but not surprised," said Tanner. "There is such a sense of frustration running through the movement. A sense that time is running out for the biosphere—"

"Grace Schearson is involved with the kidnapping. Do you know her?" It was a test. Avery from the radio station had told Mack that Tanner had appeared on her show several times.

"Yes...yes, I know Grace." Tanner looked shaken. "She's committed, but it's rather hard to imagine her being involved in something like that. She's an attorney—"

"Stretch your imagination, doc."

The professor blinked. "Yes...of course. Must be open to any and all possibilities when discussing the human organism. I sometimes forget that. Too much time spent among the arboreal kingdom—"

Mack handed Tanner a printout. "This is the list of speakers and sponsors for the rally. Any of these individuals or groups seem like candidates?"

Tanner went over the list carefully, lips pursed. A methodical man. Unconcerned about her personal hygiene, but he probably read the fine print in his phone bill, looking for misspellings.

"Who was it that just caught your attention?" demanded Mack.

"Oh..." Tanner looked embarrassed. Tapped the printout. "Michael Soaring Eagle. Very hard core. Have to be for a nice Jewish boy from Long Island to change his name from Michael Goldberg to that." He shook his head. "Soaring Eagle said there could be no rules of engagement in the battle for the earth. Excellent speaker. Very eloquent. Very dynamic. Soaring Eagle said rather than lie down on the tracks before the locomotive of capitalism, we should be willing to blow up the tracks and beat the engineer to death with the rails. Applause must have gone on for five minutes—"

"Where can I find this dipshit?"

Tanner sniffed. "The Arkansas Correctional Institute, as of two months ago. Sentenced for torching a chicken production facility just outside of Little Rock. Said it was no different than Auschwitz. A holocaust of beak and claw. Rather melodramatic, but still..." He cleaned his glasses with the hem of his filthy lab coat, placed them back on his nose. "Soaring Eagle should be out next year."

"Did he have any associates? Any other hard core believers?"

"Not that I know of, but I imagine he was quite popular." Tanner scratched his head, examined his finger. "I'm sorry I can't be more help."

"Did you see Grace at the rally?"

"Oh yes, she was podcasting it."

"Was she with anyone? Someone you thought might be more than a friend?"

Tanner shook his head. "I was busy leading a discussion group on sustainable backyard agriculture. '*Beyond Window Box Gardening.*' Not as flamboyant as wrecking the locomotive of capitalism, but rhetoric only goes so far. Then you have to dig your hands into the earth." His face fell. "I didn't draw much of a crowd at my lecture, and most of *them* didn't stay for the whole thing. These people at the rally, they call themselves Greens, but they don't grow anything."

"Could you give me some names, doc?"

"I don't have any names. No faces either, at least for the ones most likely to be involved in a kidnapping. The loud talkers...the broken window brigade, that's what I called them. They give themselves fanciful names and wear ski masks—"

"Then pass me on to someone who might be able to help. Someone who wasn't turned off by the bravado—"

"Is that how it works?" Tanner clapped his hands with glee, face smudged. "Is that how you found me? You follow a data chain until you discover what you're looking for?"

"It's not glamorous, but it works."

"No, that's not true. It's quite glamorous." Tanner pushed back his glasses. "It's...science." His face brightened.

Mack felt his phone vibrate.

"There *was* a band that played the rally...they weren't on the schedule but they had this one song, *Hijack the Rich.*" Tanner sniffed. "Not very good musicians, just a refrain about 'Robin Hood the Rich, make Wall Street our bitch...' Something like that. I don't remember the name of the band, but perhaps you could ask around."

Mack checked the incoming number on his phone as it vibrated again. "Remy?"

"*Remy?*" mocked Glenn, his voice a high falsetto.

Mack covered the phone. "Thanks, doc." He headed for the door.

Tanner tapped another cigarette out of the pack, waved goodbye.

"How are you doing, tough guy? This must be pretty hard on you."

"No, I just want to give you what you want and get Remy back, that's all that matters."

"Very broadminded of you. If it was me, I'd be worried about what she was up to. I'd be wondering what she'd be willing to do to keep me happy. Not that I need any leverage. I've got a way with the ladies."

Mack stepped outside. The air felt cool after the warm humidity of the greenhouse. He listened for background sounds on the phone: church bells, car horns, airplanes overhead…anything.

"What are you up to tonight, tough guy? Keeping yourself busy?"

"What's with the *tough guy?* Have we met?"

"Oh, I've seen you, but you haven't seen me."

"I'm Mack, what your name?"

"My name is Mr. Fuck You."

Mack stayed silent. He heard the faint sound of a siren on the phone, and for a moment thought he heard one at the edge of campus too. Just an echo, but he looked around anyway, expecting to see someone in the shadows watching him.

"If I can't speak to Remy, can I speak to Grace?"

"No…not right now. Soon, though."

"What do you want?" said Mack. "I'm authorized to negotiate terms——"

"You got video capability on that phone of yours?"

Mack's phone pinged and he saw Remy with her back against a big tree, dazed, blood pouring from her nose. He almost stumbled, unable to take his eyes away from the screen.

"She's a little under the weather as you can see…but almost good as new."

"Yeah…you have a way with the ladies."

"You'd be surprised." Laughter. "You got a pencil, because you might want to write this down."

Mack fought back anger, kept his voice even. "Just tell me what you want."

"Daddy has until noon next Monday——"

"That's not enough time. We don't even know where Mr. Brandt——"

"Then *find* him or the rich bitch——"

"Give us until next Friday."

"Too long. She's already getting on everybody's nerves."

"How many is everybody?"

No response.

"Look, I want to make this work for you," said Mack. "Just give me some time."

"Fine. You have until…I don't know, let's make it 2 p.m. *Thursday* to electronically transfer two ten-million dollar payments to the charities of our choice. Not a minute longer. I'll text you the details later. Brandt also has to deed over that old growth forest of his to the Save Nature in the Raw Conservancy. Probably best if we don't involve the cops or the FBI, but that's up to you. Maybe you want her dead. I could understand that. Bitch is just asking to be smacked around."

Mack stared at the image of Remy slumped against the tree. "No cops. No FBI."

"That's the spirit."

"Grace has to know the charities will never accept money under these circumstances."

"Let's find out. Besides, what's twenty million dollars to Brandt?"

This joker evidently didn't know anything about rich people. "True, but Mr. Brandt will need assurances that Remy is safe before he makes the transfers—"

"Yeah, yeah, she safe enough for now, but don't make the mistake of thinking we're peace and love flower fucks, or your girlfriend will never forgive you. You got eight days, tough guy, no excuses, no extensions. You tell Jeeves if he has to send a search team for Daddy dearest he better get started. Eight days."

"I understand."

"Plenty of rich girls in the world, all of them with invisible dollar signs on their heads. You get Remy killed, it's just going to make it easier for us to get paid the next time."

"No one wants that to happen. We just want her back safe."

"Your girlfriend said you're some kind of bodyguard. That right?"

Mack didn't answer.

"Hey, Mack, I'm not a professional or anything, but considering the situation…you must not be so good at your job, huh?"

Mack heard laughter before the connection broke.

CHAPTER 36

MACK SQUEEZED THROUGH the crowd at Jubilee Mombassa, ears ringing from the techno-funk blasting from the speakers. The crowd in their 20s and 30s, mostly white, and with enough collective facial jewelry to outfit a tribe of headhunters. He kept to the outside of the main room, got banged around by drunks and kept walking. Finally spotted Cleo at a roped-off table with a beefy redhead in a Seahawks jersey. Mack stepped over the blue velvet rope, dragged a chair over.

Cleo waved away the approaching bouncer.

"Make yourself at home, jackoff," the jock said to Mack.

"Back again?" Cleo smiled at Mack. "You remind me of a dog I had once. Cute little fellow. No matter where I was, he'd show up and shove his snout in my lady parts." She laughed. "I was just *crazy* about that dog, but nobody else could stand him."

"We need to talk," said Mack.

"Wait your turn," said the jock. "She's here to check out my brother's band."

"You see what I mean about nobody liking that dog, Mack?" Cleo finished her drink and stood up. Smoothed her black sheath.

Mack and Cleo stepped into the alley behind the club, the fire exit door closing heavily behind them. The alley smelled of urine, crystalline layers of ancient piss seeped into the mossy stones. Cleo just had on her dress, arms bare, no coat. Typical Seattle behavior. These people ignored the rain, walked around in the drizzle and mist in shorts and t-shirts, in *sandals,* for God's sake, while Mack shivered in a leather jacket and sweater. He hadn't been warm since he and Remy arrived ten days ago. Even sunny days didn't seem to drive away the chill. Their shoulders brushed as they strolled along the cobblestones—they might have been barefoot on the beach they way she acted, but he wasn't fooled.

"How *did* you find me?" said Cleo.

"Wasn't hard. I just checked the *Edge.* There were only two clubs that popped for a full-page ad. Figured you'd have to cover whatever bands were playing there."

"Nice to meet a man who understands the economics of a free paper." Cleo squeezed his arm, close enough that her breast brushed against him. "Now, what's so important, handsome?"

Mack heard the fire exit shoved open behind them, the door hitting the wall hard.

The jock lurched into the alley. He looked even bigger standing than he had sitting down, two hundred and seventy pounds of freckled nastiness. Probably had adrenal glands the size of footballs. "What's a guy have to do to get your attention, you cunt?"

"You could try setting yourself on fire," mused Cleo. "Or cutting off your dick. You *do* have a dick, don't you?"

"Oh, *that's* a good answer," Mack said to her. "That'll really defuse the situation."

A beer bottle smashed against the wall of the alley, sprayed them with glass.

The jock lowered his head and charged. Mack sidestepped at the last moment and tripped him, the beefy redhead skidding face-first on the cobblestones. The jock got to his feet, unsteady, blood pouring down his face. "You *tripped* me."

Mack made a sideways chopping movement with both hands. "Clipping," he announced. "Ten yard penalty. Repeat the down."

The jock swung at Mack. Missed. Another swing. And another. A flurry of punches, but Mack stayed just out of reach. "Stand *still!*"

"How about a truce?" said Mack. "You're a lethal weapon, I admit it."

Cleo laughed. Which didn't help. Not at all.

The jock waded in, fists flying, but this time Mack stepped *inside* his guard and kicked his feet out from under him. The jock fell backwards, cracking his skull on the cobblestones. He tried to get up, then lay back down.

Mack offered his hand, slowly pulled him up onto his feet.

The jock wiped his arm across his face. Smeared blood from ear to ear. "Lucky...lucky for you my brother's set is about to start or I'd put you in Intensive fucking Care." He spit towards Cleo. "And *you*...you

Robert Ferrigno

don't know shit about music."

Mack watched him stagger off. Another happy ending. He turned, saw Cleo holding on to a wall of the alley, her right foot raised slightly.

"I broke a heel on the cobblestones," she said, showing him the snapped-off high heel. "I think I twisted my ankle. Can you walk me home? It's not far."

Mack offered her his arm, and she limped beside him out of the alley.

Cleo's apartment building was on a shabby side street near downtown, a few blocks from the all-night cafes and Laundromat, right next door to a print shop with a taped-over front window. An elderly wino sat on the curb, sucking at a bottle in a brown bag. He stood up and bowed to Cleo, then sat back down. Music echoed through the halls as they climbed the stairs to the second floor, Cleo leaning on Mack. Most of the bulbs on the second-floor were burned out or missing—they walked through puddles of light and shadow as she led them to her apartment at the rear.

"Why don't you come in?" said Cleo as she unlocked the door. "You said you wanted to ask me a question." She kicked her shoes off and walked inside. "So, ask away. I promise not to rape you."

Mack hesitated in the doorway, then..."Deal."

She had a small, one-bedroom apartment. Living room with a kitchen overlooking the alley. Two-burner gas range. Noisy refrigerator. Tiny table with three mismatched chairs. Cracked plaster walls. Clean though. The dishcloth neatly folded over the edge of the sink. Dish rack empty. Soap dispenser free of gooey drips. A Cézanne print of a bowl of fruit, perfectly aligned. No Che. No Mumia. No *Yes We Can*!

Cleo turned her back to him. "Help me with this zipper, will you?"

"Walk you home, unzip you..." Mack unhooked her black dress. Took the zipper down a couple inches, "...the demands never end."

"You have no idea." Cleo shook her hair out, eased the zipper down a bit more. Getting comfortable. "Why don't you sit down and relax?" She walked into the tiny kitchen, and he noticed the tiny gold chain around her ankle sliding back and forth with every step. "Tea or instant coffee?"

"What? Oh...coffee." Mack watched the nape of her neck as she

153

stood at the sink running water into a copper kettle. Her top four vertebrae stood out from her slender back as she put the kettle onto the gas range.

"You were too nice to Dixon," said Cleo, taking a jar of instant and a couple of Starbucks cups out of the cupboard.

"The redheaded jock?" Mack shrugged. "Best to give a guy a chance to walk away with his dignity intact. Saves wear and tear on the knuckles."

"You could have just waved that big ol' gun of yours and scared him off." Cleo sat at the table, moved her chair closer. "I felt it when I bumped against you."

"You flash a gun, there's a risk somebody might up the ante. You'd be surprised at the people packing these days." Mack shook his head. "A gun's a last resort."

"Probably more fun to punch him out anyway," said Cleo.

"Not really."

"What's wrong with you, Mack? Don't you want to impress a girl?"

"You get off on the rough stuff?"

"Who doesn't? It's a biological imperative." Cleo looked into his eyes. "The female is always drawn to the brute who can protect her."

"You don't look like you need any protection," said Mack.

"You'd be surprised."

Mack broke eye contact. "You were at that big Take Back the Earth Seattle rally a few months ago?"

"I like your technique. You make a statement with a question mark at the end. It's harder for people to lie that way. I do the same thing in my interviews. The things people reveal..."

"A band performed..." Mack was suddenly conscious of his technique. No one had ever noted it before. "They weren't on the playlist, but they had this song, *Hijack the Rich*—"

"Bite the hand that feeds you, fight the boss that bleeds you," sang Cleo, "burn his house, steal his wife..."

"Who are they?"

"The Robin Hoods. What's the—?"

"Why didn't you tell me about them last night?"

"Lose the tone. I'm not on trial." She stared at him. "Oh…evidently I am."

"Why didn't you tell me?" said Mack.

"I didn't mention them, Mr. Paranoid, because the Robin Hoods are currently bouncing along the back roads of Scotland in a mini-van. Four junkies halfway through a two-month tour of skiffle clubs and shooting galleries. By the time they get to Glasgow, they'll be skin-popping Drano. You want their email address? I'm sure they know *exactly* where your girlfriend is."

The teakettle started whistling.

"There was no one else at the rally that got your attention? Someone caught up with the slogans? Ready to hit the barricades?"

"I see, you just zipped past the apology and on to another question." Cleo shook her head. "The rally was full of poseurs and blowhards." She stepped into the kitchen. "Cream in your coffee?"

Mack got up from the table. "I'm going to take off."

Cleo padded towards him. "Why don't you stick around?"

"It's late and you've got more clubs to go to."

"It's early and the clubs can wait. I'd don't usually get home until dawn." Cleo swayed as she walked towards him. "Come on. It doesn't have to mean anything, you know."

"Then why bother?"

"Ah, one of those noble guys." Cleo sighed. "You don't know what you're missing."

Mack opened the front door. "Sometimes it's best to maintain the mystery."

CHAPTER 37

"HEY, BABE?" GLENN said softly, just loud enough to be heard over the buzz in the Alligator Room. It was after 1 a.m., Cleo's latest stop on her circuit of clubs, dives and spoken-word hellholes.

"What happened to your face?"

"I was playing with matches." Glenn touched the remnants of his singed eyebrows. Every time he looked in the mirror he wanted to do bad things to the rich bitch. "Where's your new fuckbuddy?"

"Mack? You were at Mombasa?"

"Yeah, I saw you two at Mombasa. Saw you at the Gravity Lounge last night too. Me, I like keeping an eye on you."

"That was intensely idiotic." Cleo sipped her drink, not inviting him to sit down. "I *told* you, we can't be seen together until this is all over."

"You can see the tough guy anytime you want though, right?" Glenn sat down beside her. "I got to sneak around to get a sniff, but *he* can sit down at your table anytime he wants, take you home anytime he wants—"

"Spare me the jealousy. It's your fault he was there. It's your fault he's still alive. He's either dead or in traction, that's what you told me—"

"He *will* be when I'm done with him."

"Don't do anything stupid," said Cleo. "I know it's an effort—"

"Yeah, I'm so stupid that I found out where the tough guy's *staying.*"

Cleo's face stayed calm, but her eyes became knife points. "You followed him home?"

"He's bunking at a lousy motel on Aurora," Glenn said proudly. "Room 217."

"*Why* would you do that? It's not about him."

"Yeah? You could have fooled me."

"What's that supposed to mean?"

Glenn shrugged. "I talked to Jeeves in New York yesterday. The tough guy is handling the negotiations. So I guess it's not such a bad idea knowing where he sleeps at night."

Cleo stared at him.

"Changes things, doesn't it?"

"Why would Brandt's assistant give a job this important to a man he never met before?" Cleo looked past him, waved at someone on the other side of the room. "This isn't right. Something is very wrong."

"Rich guys like Brandt always have somebody do their dirty work." Glenn leaned over the table, grinning. "Jeeves is Brandt's bitch. Now the tough guy is *Jeeve's* bitch."

"No..." Cleo shook her head. "No, he's not."

"Don't look so worried, babe. I got it under control."

Cleo reached into her bag, took out a tube of lip gloss. Glenn could tell she was thinking things over. Over thinking it, if you asked him. She applied a sheen of gloss to her lips. "Did you give Mack a deadline to transfer the money?"

"He keeps coming around you, I may give him something else."

She smacked her lips. "Did you give him a deadline?"

"Next Friday. Noon."

"That's too long."

"That's what I gave him. Practically pissed himself with gratitude too."

Cleo put the lip gloss away. "I'm going to call Mack tomorrow morning and offer to help him out. Introduce him to some people."

"I don't think that's such a good idea."

"I doesn't matter what you think." Cleo wiggled her perfect pink toes. "He helped me home. I'll tell him I want to show my gratitude."

CHAPTER 38

HI," SAID MACK.

The young woman looked up at him. She was on her hands and knees in the middle of the baseball diamond, a bucket of pulled weeds beside her. Slender. A grad student in her early-20s. Pretty, but unconcerned about it. Dark-blonde hair in a ponytail, a happy-face scrunchie holding it in place. Pale blue Rayburn Correctional Institute jumpsuit.

"Are you Sky Friedman?" said Mack.

Sky wiped her forehead, smeared dirt. Appraising him. "You're not on my approved visitors list."

"No...I had to call in a favor to see you. I'm Mack."

Sky watched him. "You have nice eyes." She plucked a weed, tossed it into the bucket, moved on. The infield was dotted with weeds, the chalk lines wobbly, the outfield fence twelve feet high, topped with coils of razor wire. Beyond the fence, the Seattle skyline was visible in the distance.

Mack got down beside her, pulling weeds too.

"I'm not going to tell you anything," said Sky. "It's nothing personal, I really do like your eyes, but we didn't do anything wrong. I got caught, that's all."

"You fried the main operating computers of over fifty Mercedes," said Mack. "The dealership estimated the damage at over three million dollars."

"I killed computer chips. Those vehicles were killing the earth." Sky pulled weeds with both hands, humming happily. "I don't believe in violence."

Mack pulled a dandelion, tapped the dirt from the root and tossed it into the bucket.

"Don't knock away the soil," said Sky. "It spreads the seeds. We end up with more weeds than we started with." She looked back at him. "You should tell that to the men who sent you. Tell them it's a metaphor. A rough touch creates more enemies—"

"Sky…stop for a moment, please? No one sent me."

Sky stared at him. "Okay." Sweat beaded along her hairline. "The government doesn't care about those land yachts I ruined. They want to know how I toasted those computers. Dr. Hagen said they requested five copies of my doctoral dissertation, then asked him to explain it to them." She shook her head. "He couldn't, and I *wouldn't*."

Mack handed over a snapshot of he and Remy on the beach in Baja.

She took it, taking care not to get it dirty. She looked at him. "The two of you are very much in love."

"Her name is Remy. She's why I came to see you."

Sky waited, and Mack thought of the difference between her response to the photograph and Cleo's yesterday.

"Remy was kidnapped last Sunday." Mack sat back on his haunches. "Eco-terrorists are holding her for ransom—"

"That's a total violation of all our principles—"

"They said the earth is in peril and somebody was going to pay."

Sky shook her head, ponytail whipping from side to side. "You don't save the earth by hurting *people*. That's metaphysically absurd."

"Do you know anyone who might have done this?" said Mack. "Someone tired of demonstrations and sit-ins, someone grown impatient. Maybe they mocked what you were doing, called it ineffective…"

Sky shook her head.

"In any small group, there's always someone who talks a big game. He drives a golf ball longer, his work is more important—"

"Do you really think I know anyone who plays golf, Mack?"

"You know what I'm getting at. When you and your friends sat around talking about how to advance the cause—"

"Like at the tofu potluck? Sitting around with our Birkenstocks and macramé?"

Mack smiled in spite of himself. "Was there someone who needed to prove that he was more hard core than anyone else?"

"Does it *have* to be a he?"

"No, but the one I talked to was."

"I don't know anyone like that." Sky handed back the photo. "I would tell you if I knew. I didn't lie when I was arrested. I didn't lie in court. I'm here because I did the right thing, and because I told the truth about it."

"One of the men who kidnapped Remy called me last night. He's a total narcissist, all bluster and insults."

"There's a lot of anger and self-loathing out there...but most of the supposed greens try and hide it."

"This guy doesn't hide it, not the anger anyway. Not the arrogance either. Likes to talk about Remy coming onto him, trying to get a rise out of me. Does that sound like anyone you ever met?"

Sky smiled. "That describes half the men on the planet."

"No." Mack slowly shook his head. "This guy's the real thing. He convinced Grace Schearson to get involved in the kidnapping."

"I'm sorry to hear that. Grace is a good person." Sky gently plucked a weed. "A little needy, perhaps." She brushed back her hair. "I wish I could help you."

"Thanks, anyway. If you think of anything...I'll leave my number at the desk." Mack should get moving. Hobbs wanted to have lunch. Time to go...but, Mack wished he could stay here and pull weeds. Maybe sleep in the sun. Wake up and find Remy beside him, her head resting on her arm, asking him what he dreamed about. He was aware of Sky watching him, but it didn't bother him. "How...how long do you have to weed this field?"

"I don't *have* to. I want to. I don't like seeing things ignored or abused."

Mack looked around at the overgrown field. She had a long way to go.

"You carry a lot of tension in your neck, Mack."

Mack stood up. Knees cracking. "If I don't carry it, someone else will have to."

CHAPTER 39

AN EMPTY CAN of Georgia Girl cling peaches perched on a large rock, dappled by early-morning sunlight filtering through the trees. Faded wrapper on the can, Georgia Girl herself buxom as ever, forever young, but peeling slightly, an edge of the label flapping in the breeze. A jay cawed, but Georgia Girl remained serene—SMACK! The can flew off the rock, tumbled end over end in the grass.

"Score!" cheered Eli, pumping his fist.

Tree fitted another stone into a rawhide sling, while Eli raced over to replace the can, dreadlocks flying. Remy affected an air of boredom, cleaning the dirt from under her nails with a sliver of wood and wishing she had a manicure set so she could jam the nail file into Tree's neck. She didn't have a nail file though, or any idea of how to find her way out of the woods, so she contented herself with making escape plans and playing the bitch. Truth be told, it wasn't a hard role to play. She smiled as she extracted grit from under her ruined manicure. More like method acting.

"What's so funny?" said Tree, wild-eyed, garrulous now, talking to Eli, talking to himself, talking to Remy. Angry at everyone. He pulled a handful of leathery mushrooms from his pocket, ugly, bulbous things with red spots. Amanita muscaria. Magic mushrooms. Fairy toadstools. "You laughing at me?"

"No, I'm not laughing at you," said Remy, careful now.

Tree stuffed a couple mushrooms in his mouth. "I don't like being laughed at," he said, chewing with his mouth open. "I've had enough of that to last me my whole life."

Remy gave him room. Tree hadn't slept after returning to the platform last night—every time Remy woke up she could hear him muttering to himself, and this morning he had burned the oatmeal, thrown the pot onto the ground, glaring at her.

Eli raced back from setting the cans back in place. He plopped down beside her, a little out of breath, more from eagerness than exertion. "What are you thinking about?"

"David and Goliath," said Remy.

"The cartoon?" said Eli.

"It's from the Bible, Eli," said Tree.

"David used a slingshot to kill Goliath the giant," Remy explained to Eli.

Eli looked from one to the other. "I thought that was Jack and the beanstalk Mickey Mouse climbs up with Donald Duck—"

"I'm not talking about cartoons or comic books or TV shows," said Tree, whirling the sling faster and faster. "Goliath worked for the Philistines, real slash and burn types who wanted to clear-cut the whole world. Goliath was putting down a whipping on the Israelites when David stepped up. This little shepherd boy nailed Goliath with a stone from his sling"—a can of pork and beans went flying—"Game over."

Eli nudged Remy. "Is that true?"

"Sort of," said Remy.

"It's in the *Bible*, lady," growled Tree, fitting another stone into his sling.

"Listen to yourself," said Remy, unable to keep quiet. "A born-again kidnapper. You pick up any incongruity in that?"

"Just watch your mouth," said Tree, whirling the sling around his head for another shot. "That's all I'm saying."

"Or what?" said Remy.

A can of creamed corn bounced into the air, the Jolly Green Giant going end over end.

"She's just talking," said Eli. "No need to argue."

"You're sweet, Eli," said Remy. "Be careful. Tree's the boss, don't you know that?" She stretched. "Unless Glenn's around."

Tree stalked over. "You *really* think that shit will work with us?"

"Got to correct you, Remy," said Eli. "Monkey Boyz, are totally *not* into bosses. Like everybody is equal, you know? One man, one vote."

"This isn't a camping trip, Eli," said Tree, "and she's not your friend. You remember how she torched Glenn? That could have just as easily been me or you."

Eli shook his head. "Glenn was asking for it. Besides..." He nodded at

Remy, lowered his voice to Tree. "It's just a matter of time until that Stopping-Home Syndrome kicks in. Then she'll be all sweet and everything."

"I think it's going to take longer than a few days with her," said Tree, whirling the sling round and round.

"Stopping home syndrome?" said Remy. "Oh, *this* ought to be good."

"That's like...like when a person's been snatched and after a few days they start acting real nice to everybody," Eli said earnestly. "Then the ones who snatched 'em go get them pizzas and clean clothes...maybe even a bathrobe."

Remy rubbed her temples. "You're giving me a migraine. I want a valium, *stat.*"

Eli massaged her shoulders. "Tree can fix you a sage poultice—"

Remy shrugged him off. Deep breath. "Thirty years ago, bank robbers in *Stockholm,* Sweden took some customers hostage. The situation went on for days and days while the cops negotiated with the crooks. A week later, when the police finally took control, the customers actually defended the robbers. Loyalty transference. *That's* Stockholm Syndrome."

Eli did a backflip. "I beg to differ."

SMACK went another can.

Remy rubbed her temples again as Eli cartwheeled across the clearing. "I'm in the middle of nowhere arguing word definitions with Bomba the Jungle Boy."

BAM! Another can drilled into the grass. Tree stood over her, sucking pieces of magic mushroom out of his teeth. "Look lady, it don't *matter* if it's Stockholm Syndrome or Stopping-Home Syndrome. Whatever it is, you ain't got it."

"Amen," said Remy.

CHAPTER 40

CLEO SAW GRAYSON step out of the revolving door of the federal building, head straight for his favorite espresso cart on the corner. He looked beat. Too many late nights trying to find the tanker truck. Dreaming fiery dreams of the Grand Coulee Dam breached. Meltdown at the Hanford nuclear disposal site. The Kitsap Peninsula submarine base in ruins. Endless possibilities for mischief. Grayson and the task force didn't have a chance. Cleo didn't intend to set the load of anhydrous ammonia off…she didn't have to. Either way, the detonation would blast Grayson and the entire Seattle office off the map.

Striding across the sidewalk, Cleo intercepted Grayson, dropping the manila folder she had brought for the occasion. The wind caught the pages, sent them tumbling.

"You aren't supposed to be here," hissed Grayson as he bent to help.

"You're just a gentleman helping a damsel in distress," countered Cleo, beside them. Their knees brushed. "Did you get my action request?"

"I don't give a damn about your petty problems. Grayson scooped up the papers. He was getting a bald spot at the top of his head. "The chief is getting heat from D.C. that you can't believe. When he sweats, I sweat…"

"You didn't read my request," said Cleo, the two of them standing now. She straightened the retrieved papers, slipped them back into the folder. "I had contact with the missing woman's boyfriend yesterday. The California girl you spoke of—"

"Get to the point."

"Remy Brandt was kidnapped Sunday night. Same night the tanker truck was hijacked." Cleo looked into his tired eyes. "Maybe there's a connection."

"Are you *really* that desperate to be part of the strike team?" Grayson shook his head. "You're pathetic, Cleo."

Cleo tapped her foot, keeping cadence. Grayson was going to get what he deserved. They all were. Her only regret was she'd never be able to tell them what she had done.

"Let me make things simple for you," said Grayson, bits of color blooming on his sallow cheeks. "A successful kidnapping requires precise planning. Hijacking a tractor-trailer requires that same precision. *Coordinating* these two events is several degrees of difficulty beyond the stoners and food-stamp anarchists you deal with. The cop who contacted us about the kidnapping wasn't even sure a crime had been committed. No blood, no forced entry, no violence. Meanwhile, the tractor-trailer driver and his helper are still in the hospital. Disparate methodology. You remember your classes in crime classification, don't you? Disparate methodology indicates disparate suspects."

Cleo maintained eye contact.

"No pattern means no connection," said Grayson. "We're done with our morning lesson. I want you to leave now. Keep sending your action requests. Your little memos. Your helpful emails. But if you make direct contact with me again, without an express written order, you better pack some long underwear, because I'll ship you out to Amish country and you can spend your time counting the tits on the dairy cows. Am I clear?"

"Quite clear."

"Sir."

"Quite clear, *sir.*"

Grayson turned on his heel, walked on toward the espresso stand.

Cleo watched him. She didn't allow herself a smile, but she positively *throbbed* with erotic pleasure. Easy enough to ruin a man with a lie. Doing it with the truth...that was so much more fun.

CHAPTER 41

GLENN LEANED OVER the computer screen at the Helios Coffee Hut and Internet Café. The coffee hut buzzed with early-morning conversation and that light jazz shit the owner thought mellowed people out so they bought his overpriced bake goods. The waitress waved and Glenn waved back. Rachel...or Raquel, he could never remember. Birth mark on the inside of her right thigh and ticklish too, which was a lot more important that her name. Someday she would remember the wild times she had fucking a millionaire and didn't even know it. Course Glenn wasn't a millionaire at the moment...

He brought up the Green Turtle Rescue Pledge Drive site, doubleclicked.

Blink. Blink. Blink. *Current count: $84*

Glenn did this every few weeks, just to see if anybody was hitting the site, popping in some cash for the baby turtles. No change since last week. Cheap bastards. Soon though...soon, you could add seven zeroes to the total. Once Mr. Gotbucks bailed his daughter out, Glenn would electronically transfer the money to a bank account he had set up in Rio. He'd take the next flight down, flying first class all the way.

Rachel or Raquel brought him an orange-mango scone. "My treat," she said, trailing her hand across his shoulders as she left.

Blink. Blink. Blink. *Current count: $84*

If the tough guy and Mr. Brandt didn't get it together, Rachel or Raquel wouldn't be remembering fucking a millionaire, she'd be remembering fucking the eco-warrior who killed the poor little rich girl. Glenn fingered the singed stubble where his eyebrows used to be. He half-hoped the tough guy and Mr. Brandt tried to stiff him.

CHAPTER 42

"WHAT ARE YOU doing?" said Tree.

"Tying my shoelace," said Remy, kneeling by the side of the trail. A flat rock the size of a TV remote lay within reach. "Is that okay with you?"

Tree glowered at her, a bearded grizzly in worn jeans and a blue thermal undershirt. "You're the one wanted to go on a hike."

Remy palmed the spoon she had sharpened.

"I'm so *bored*," mocked Tree, hands on his hips. He looming over her in heavy, steel-toed logging boots, his dark eyes set into a nest of wrinkles. "There's nothing to *do* out here." He snapped his suspenders. "You've been living a pampered life, lady, and it ain't gonna last. The earth won't put up with it."

"How nice that the earth confides in you," said Remy.

Tree turned and walked on ahead, moving quietly in spite of his size, slipping through the branches that overhung the narrow trail without disturbing them. Even the ever-present chipmunks didn't react to his passage, just watched him go, wringing their tiny hands, the same chipmunks that scurried away from Remy with every step she took.

Remy quickly scratched her initials on the rock with sharpened end of the spoon, added Mack's phone number and the word HELP, then left it beside the path. All things considered, she'd rather brain Tree with the rock, but that wouldn't accomplish anything other than making her feel better.

She hurried after him. "Wait *up!*" Her voice sounded desperate, but she was utterly calm.

Tree snorted in disgust, kept walking.

Remy lagged slightly behind, breathing hard, as if at the limits of her endurance. Let Tree think she was weak and whiny; she had learned in Stanford moot court the advantage of underplaying your strengths, pretending confusion, then overwhelming the opposition at the last minute.

This was her first solitary walk with Tree. Usually she went off with

Eli or the both of them, but Eli had been gone when she woke up this morning, and when she asked Tree where he was, he had simply said "business," and refused to elaborate. She had watched the big man while she ate breakfast, wondering if this was the time he was going to kill her. She liked to think that Eli wouldn't let anything to happen to her, but she knew there was the possibility he would accept it as long as he didn't have to be there to watch. She had kept the sharpened spoon in her fist while she ate, determined to at least draw blood before she died, but breakfast had passed quietly.

Fight or flight. Remy didn't believe she could win a fight with Tree, but she had been preparing for escape since the moment she woke up in the giant cedar. She had kept herself busy since then. She flirted with Eli and asked Tree if they had voted to make Glenn the boss, or if he had just assumed command while they tucked their tails. She made lists, she took notes, she asked seemingly innocent questions and kept track of the answers. What was said and unsaid. Tree stayed on guard, grunting out responses, or ignoring her, but he got edgy sometimes on their outings, wordlessly steering them away from certain areas. An unspoken lapse, but it was enough to make her curious.

Unlike Tree, Eli gushed information, eager to please, and Remy kept him going, encouraging him with a shy smile or a touch on the arm. She knew all about the Monkey Boyz now, the festivals they attended, the demonstrations they participated in, the vegan potlucks and fancy squats in abandoned California subdivisions. The three of them had escalated their actions in the last two years, moving from breaking windows of corporate coffee shops, to vandalizing SUV dealerships, to torching a BP gas station. Eli had looked proud when he told her, as though they had accomplished some great victory. The people united, will never be defeated. Not even a trace of irony in his voice. Then, a few months ago they had done something in Southern California, something bad, something that made Eli turn away, tears in his eyes and refuse to talk about it.

Remy needed the lists and the notes, needed the gently probing conversations. They were about more than collecting data and searching for personal weaknesses that could be exploited; it was a way to make her think she was doing something, moving beyond the passive. Most of all it was a way to maintain control over herself...and her fears.

She considered every meal, every walk as a deposition, hoping to create one doubt that she could exploit, uncover one fact that she could use. She asked Tree if Glenn had picked their campsite, or if Tree had actually done that on his own. She teased Eli into singing along with her as they skipped down the trail, pop songs, nonsense songs, the two of them belting it out at the top of their voices. Usually Tree ignored them, hushing them only when he was tired of the noise, but twice now he had silenced them in the same part of the forest, clearly worried that they might be overheard. She also made sure that their hikes always ended in cross country runs once they left Tree behind. Eli was faster than Tree, and faster than Remy for short distances, but Remy ran five or six marathons a year. If she was ahead of Eli after the first mile, he'd never catch her. The problem was figuring out which way was civilization.

Even with Tree's occasional lapses, she still didn't have a clear sense of where she was, and getting lost out here could be deadly. There were dozens of trails, most of them hooking around on each other, leading even deeper into the forest. A green labyrinth. For the last week she had come back to camp after their hikes, excused herself and surreptitiously added to her notes at the back of the *Earth in PERIL!* paperback Tree had loaned her, brief notes about where she had been and what she had seen. The map she had started was still sketchy, but it had actual landmarks interspersed now: the waterfall, the hot springs, the massive tree that had been hit by lightning, the meadow of wildflowers, the ravine near where she had seen the Hmong mushroom pickers. Her sense of direction was still unreliable, but getting better. Hard to accurately gauge direction when the sunrise and sunset was filtered through the trees, but at least she was making educated guesses now.

"Could you slow down a little, Tree?" Remy wailed. "*Please.*"

Tree increased his pace.

Remy smiled at his broad back, tied a piece of white silk torn from her favorite teddy around a sapling. She had inked her name and Mack's phone number on the silk last night. News of her kidnapping had to be all over TV, Mack would see to that. She hurried to catch up with Tree. Still, Glenn hadn't mentioned anything about news coverage when he showed up, which was odd. From what she had seen of him, Glenn should have been bragging that everyone was talking about their heroic actions, that the seas were already rising and the earth beginning to heal…instead, nothing.

Remy shook off the thought that she might have disappeared without anyone noticing. That would have to mean that Mack was dead…or maybe he had reasons for keeping the news off TV. That was the only possibility. If Mack was alive, he was coming for her.

Mack would do his best, she knew that, but Remy wasn't going to stand around and wait to be *rescued* like one of those wispy heroines in the romance novels. She'd rescue herself. She hid a small makeup mirror in the pocket of her shorts; if she ever saw a plane flying overhead she'd be able to signal them, but there had been no planes other than the passenger jets flying in the distance. Most of the time the tree canopy prevented her from signaling even if a plane did show up. Yesterday she had actually considered starting a fire in the underbrush to draw the attention of the outside world, but the woods were damp from the rain, and, even if she were successful, there was no way of knowing if she'd survive a forest fire. No, torching the woods was a last resort, but the thought gave her a strange comfort. Nothing was off the table.

Tree turned around as the trail split.

Remy bent over, hands on her knees, hanging her head.

"You're soft," said Tree. "Too much easy living."

Remy nodded, still bent over, pretending exhaustion.

"That earthquake in Chile a couple years ago, the floods in China and the fire in Colorado burning up half the state," said Tree. "That was just a preview of coming attractions."

Remy looked up at him.

"The earth isn't going to just lie there and take it forever," said Tree. "Payback's coming and it's not going to be pretty."

"You'd like that, wouldn't you?" snapped Remy.

"Damn right," said Tree. "Cities in ruins, freeways collapsed, burning cars and fast-foot joints as far as the eye can see...I'd do the goat dance."

Remy stood up. "What about the people?"

"What about 'em?"

"What happens to them when the earth strikes back?"

"Some of you die and the rest of you learn a lesson," said Tree.

"Kids too?"

Tree looked uncomfortable for a moment, then his expression hardened. "Better they learn it when they're young."

"You mean the ones who aren't dead. The dead ones don't get to learn anything."

Tree stared at her. The forest, which a moment earlier had been raucous with the sounds of jays screeching went silent. Remy should have lowered her eyes, mumbled some excuse, but she didn't.

"You think the earth would shed a tear if the whole human race disappeared?" Tree said softly.

"I don't know about the earth," Remy said. "*I* would."

Tree turned his back on her, started walking again, double-timing it down the right hand trail.

Remy stacked three rocks atop each other on the side of the trail, another marker for her map, then followed Tree.

CHAPTER 43

"YOU NEED TO eat more," said Hobbs, waving his fork at Mack. The two of them sat in Hobbs' regular booth at the Olde Pancake Haus, Hobbs in a dark green suit that was too tight on him. "You don't clean your plate, that's your problem."

"So *that's* my problem," said Mack. "Considering the possibilities, I got off cheap."

Hobbs gnawed at a strip of thick-cut bacon. "Nothing wrong with you that couldn't be helped by more salt and sugar. That's all I'm saying. Appetite, that's the secret. You lose your appetite you might as well cash in. That's why I eat here. Pancake Haus serves breakfast 24 hours a day. Breakfast is your best food value." He stifled a belch in the palm of his hand. "Got the lab results back on those martini glasses from Grace's. Traces of GHB, just like you thought. I mentioned it to the Assistant D.A., thought he might bump it up, maybe get some more manpower assigned—"

"What did he say?"

"He said the presence of GHB didn't prove anything." Hobbs set down the coffee hard enough to clink the saucer. "Said you, Remy and Grace might have just been having a party. Swinger's ball, or something. No *probative* value, is actually what he said, which sounds a lot better than he's a lazy bastard who wants a case handed to him all wrapped up with satin ribbon and a bright red bow."

"So it's still just you and I working it," said Mack, grateful for the ADA passing on the investigation. "That's enough."

Mack cut into a stack of sourdough pancakes with his fork, chewed, not tasting a thing. The two of them were seated in the Hawaiian Eye booth, another one of those TV cop shows from the Paleolithic era that Hobbs loved. "They have a new version of Hawaiian Eye on TV, Marcus. You should check it out."

"I like the old stuff better."

Mack tapped a photo of a perky blonde in one of those old-fashioned two-piece bathing suits that showed about two inches of bare midriff. "Who's she?"

"Cricket. She was supposed to be a singer in one of the hotel lounges."

"Girls in the new version wear string bikinis." Mack pointed to a smiling Hawaiian man wearing a pineapple-print shirt. "Who's this?"

"You don't know anything about the golden age television, do you?" Hobbs shook his head. "His name was Kim. Cab driver. In every episode, these two half-ass white private eyes would have to ask Kim to help them out, either fill them in on the local crime kingpin or show them where the boyfriend of the missing college professor lived."

"So Kim was the Hawaiian Huggy Bear."

Hobbs grunted, unbuttoned the middle button of his suit. Sopped up yolk with another piece of buttered toast. "I had Farwell canvas the neighbors, hoping one of them might have gotten a glimpse of the new boyfriend." He shook his head. "Nothing."

"That's the problem with the modern world. Nobody snoops on their neighbors anymore."

Hobbs licked yolk off his lower lip. "Any more contact with the girl's father?" He slathered a triangle of toast with blueberry preserves. "I'd think the kidnappers would be making a clear ransom demand by now."

"No." said Mack. "Not yet."

"Too bad. With a clear ransom demand maybe I could pry some help from the feds."

"Like I said, nothing yet." Mack sipped his coffee. It bothered him to lie to Hobbs, but not enough to risk having the detective hand off the responsibility to the Bureau.

Hobbs watched him. "If I promised to keep things all in the family, would you tell me the truth?"

"That might do it."

Hobbs waited.

"There's been a ransom demand. They want Brandt to donate money to a couple of environmental organizations, and deed over some old growth timber he owns in Oregon."

"True believers," said Hobbs.

"They may not be above cutting themselves in for a slice," said Mack. "One of the charities, save the green turtles or something, is set up in the Cayman Islands. No financial disclosure laws, banks records are locked up tighter than the Vatican. Stevie hacked in—all he could see was there's not much money in the account, and nobody's name is on the books."

"Could be a cut-out account," said Hobbs. "Just a way station to transfer the money someplace else, or...could be that one of the prime green turtle breeding areas is the Caymans." He shrugged. "I watch the Discovery channel sometimes."

"I'd like to think it was greed," said Mack. "Greed makes people vulnerable. Altruism confuses things."

"I got a little good news," said Hobbs. "Farwell came up empty with the neighbors, but I talked to a checker at the local market yesterday. She said about a month ago Grace came in, face flushed—checker called it 'love rash.'" He started on another piece of toast. "Checker said there were pine needles in her hair. Checker asked Grace if she had been at the park and Grace just walked out."

"So Grace and loverboy went on a hike, trying to find a place to stash Remy. Big deal. We already know—"

"There's more." Hobbs sipped his coffee. "When Grace left, the checker saw a streak of dust up her back, like she was riding a dirt bike without much of a rear fender." He peered at Mack. "You don't get it, do you?"

"So they were buzzing around the woods in a dirt bike instead of hiking? Why is that important?"

"Because, city boy, you're not allowed to take a dirt bike on most of the trails in Grace's hike book."

Mack smiled. "We can narrow the search."

"That's right."

"I've get Grace's hike book out of my car," said Mack. "You can check off the sites that don't allow motorcycles."

Hobbs dabbed his mouth with a napkin. "You want to come over to my place tonight? I'll pick up some barbeque and we can watch a Mariners game."

"Baseball?"

"Not the way the Mariners play it, but it's a close as we get in this town. What do you say? Might do you some good."

"Let me get back to you. Besides, you probably need to clear it with your wife."

"Don't have a wife."

"Funny, you look married, Marcus. No offense."

"None taken."

Mack nodded. "Police work's hard on a marriage——"

"Never had a wife."

Mack detected the hint of anger. "Okay. None of my business."

"I was engaged once. Her name was Dianne. You would have liked her. Can't say if she would have liked you though." Hobbs slid Mack's plate of toast in front of himself. Carefully buttered it, taking his time. "I was fresh out of the Army and living in San Francisco. Saved up my pennies the whole five years I was in uniform to buy her a diamond. One carat, teardrop cut. Dianne loved that ring." The knife scraped back and forth across the toast. "Twelve days before our wedding…she got jacked on the way to her car. She was working late, as usual. Dianne always was an earner." The knife sounded like sandpaper, slapping back and forth across the toast. "Maybe she took too long getting the ring off, maybe it got stuck on her finger. Maybe she just flat out refused. Dianne…like I said, she dearly loved that ring."

"I'm sorry, Marcus."

"Police worked the case for a week or so, but there were plenty of other killings that summer. Victims that were more important. You know how it is. Priorities." Hobbs kept his hands busy with the knife and the toast. "So I decided to find the man who murdered Dianne myself. I wasn't a cop then, but I had been an MP in the service, and I had an…aptitude. I knew how to ask questions, how to listen. I knew when to be hard, when to be soft. Took me almost four months. Burned out the clutch on my Chevy going up and down those hills." He bit into the toast. "I found him though." He looked at Mack as he chewed.

"What happened to him?"

"Dianne...she meant the world to me. There were other women...but it was never the same after Dianne."

"You get a conviction?"

Hobbs shook his head. "Man took the easy way out. Jumped off the roof of a seven story building."

"Doesn't sound easy to me." Mack watched him. "Lucky break for you. Hard for a civilian bust to hold up in court. A good defense attorney will chop up a freelancer's evidence, attack the chain of custody. Most times the perp skates."

Hobbs nodded as though he were having a conversation with someone Mack couldn't see. "I wish you had a chance to meet Dianne—" He pulled his phone out of his jacket, listening, keeping it a few inches from his ear as it squawked away. "Slow down, Farwell." He half-closed his eyes. Finally flipped the phone shut.

"What is it?"

"Domestic gone *way* south." Hobbs stood up, tossed money on the table. "The things people do to each other. You figure it out, you let me know."

CHAPTER 44

REMY LISTENED. EYES closed. Trying to isolate sounds that would signal danger. She heard only the chattering of birds around her, the rustling of the wind in the trees. It was like a John Cage symphony, only pleasurable. She would have liked to lie here listening to the forest, but time was short. Eli had gone to gather blackberries and Tree had left without explanation. Any window of opportunity she had was rapidly closing. It would be so easy to say put. Not make trouble. Wait for Mack to arrive on a white charger. Or convince Eli to help her escape. Easy to stay with the routine of the last few days: soaks in the hot spring, long walks, lolling in the sun in one of the clearings while Eli talked surfing and Tree pontificated about global warming and deforestation and all the other ways the world was dying. Three days and she was ready to dive off the platform.

She slipped between the trees and started removing the branches hiding the ATV. She moved quickly now, pushing the ATV from the underbrush, leaning into it, feeling the strain at the backs of her legs. The ATV crunched through the grass and onto the trail. Another look around and she climbed on, heart racing. The ATV had been stolen, the ignition punched, two stripped electrical wires protruding. She flicked the wires together the way she had seen Eli do yesterday, when he took her for a ride. Nothing. She flicked the wires again. Nothing. She gently pulled the choke. Flicked the ignition wires. Again. Again. *Again.*

"What are you doing?"

Remy jumped, then flicked the wire together, more desperate than ever.

Eli emerged from the woods, lips stained with huckleberry juice like a kewpie doll.

"I'm bored," said Remy, her voice matter of fact as she worked at the ignition.

"You *crazy?* Tree catches you running off...I won't be able to stop him," whispered Eli, closer now.

"Stop me from what?" said Tree, his voice uninflected...distant.

Eli smiled as he turned. "Stop you from wanting to come, big guy." He glanced at Remy, winked. "I thought I'd show her around the meadow. Last of the wildflowers—"

"You didn't tell me anything about that," glowered Tree, eyes feverish. His work shirt was stained with sweat. One strap of his overalls hung loose. "You go off with her, she's just going to fill your head with lies."

"Ease off the shrooms, dude," said Eli. "Seriously, we're just going for a little spin. Maybe pick some flowers."

"These woods ain't our property," said Tree, glaring at Remy so close that she could see the pain in his eyes. "People...people like her...they gobble everything up."

"So we educate her," said Eli.

Tree stepped in front of the ATV. His right hand rested lightly on the hunting knife stuck in his belt, the fingers crusted with dirt. "That's one solution."

Remy shivered and her fear made her angry. She slowly raised a fist to Tree, sprung her middle finger and flipped him off.

Eli giggled. "You got to admit, Tree, the lady's got stones." He pulled a spark plug out of his pocket. Screwed it into the engine. "We wake her up to nature, she'll be a one-woman demolition team fighting the good fight. Probably turn more hard core than any of us."

Remy scooted back on the seat as Eli climbed on. She didn't take her eyes off Tree.

Eli flicked the ignition wires and the engine turned over, caught. He gave it gas. Tree stayed where he was, astride the front wheel. Eli revved the engine. "Come on. We won't be gone long. Heck, you're probably better off working your buzz by yourself."

Tree slowly...slowly stepped away from the ATV.

Remy put her arms around Eli's waist. Held on as he pulled past Tree and gently accelerated down the forest path. Neither of them said anything for minutes, just bounced along the trail, kicking up dust. Remy adjusted her grip, forced to press herself against Eli to stay in place, and the heat of him made her uncomfortable.

"Flipping off Tree, that was really mature," said Eli.

Remy leaned forward. "I'm not afraid of him." She rested her cheek against Eli's back, hanging on. The vibration of the ATV ran between them like an electrical current. She was shaking now, blinking back tears.

"It's cool," said Eli, holding it steady as they zoomed down the trail. "You don't have to be ashamed of being scared. Heck, Tree's my friend. My *best* friend. Lately though, he scares the shit out of me too."

CHAPTER 45

DEIRDRE PEERED OUT from a mass of red curls, looking from Mack to Cleo.

"It's alright," said Cleo, making contact with the ugly cow. "You can trust him."

Deirdre fingered the necklace of quartz crystals that drooped between her mammoth breasts. Unconvinced. A middle-aged woman in a flowing green robe, she watched them from behind the counter of the Mage and Magik Crystal Emporium, the small storefront awash in light. Incense smoke drifted from a brazier on a counter. Jasmine and cinnamon.

"I see violence in this one," said Deirdre, pointing at Mack. She plucked at her crystals, her face the color of custard. "Violence past, present...and future."

"All I want is to find Remy," said Mack. "I don't want trouble."

"It doesn't matter what you want, trouble is what you bring." Deirdre looked at Cleo. "Trouble for all who get close to him. And *worse* for some."

"You won't help us?" said Cleo, already knowing the answer.

Deirdre shook her head, stirred the smoke. "Go with the goddess."

"That was educational," said Mack as they got into his rental car. "In an arrogant, mystical mumbo-jumbo sort of way."

"I'm sorry," said Cleo. "Deirdre does readings for a lot of anarchist groups, I had hoped..."

Mack pulled away from the curb. "Is there anyone else we can try?"

Cleo shook her head. They had been driving around for the last two hours, talking to people Cleo knew. None of them had been able to offer names or suggestions. Just as she had planned. Mack had learned nothing other than that he could trust Cleo to try and help. Cleo had learned Mack was an ex-cop. Learned he had been getting some help from a local cop. Most importantly, she had learned that he hadn't been making much progress, which was a relief. Mack was a new player in the game, one she hadn't anticipated. Glenn and the other Monkey Boyz, Grayson and the other FBI agents, they were known quantities, predictable. Not Mack.

Cleo was no more interested in ransom than she was in saving the spotted owls or restoring the watershed. Mother Nature was going to have to look out for herself. All Cleo wanted was to rescue Remy, and save Seattle from a tanker truck full of volatile chemicals. Cleo Hutchinson, the lone undercover agent, too young and beautiful for her own good, overlooked and ignored by the Bureau, but determined to follow her instincts. A beautiful storyline. She rehearsed her press conference every night before she went to sleep.

Cleo hummed happily. Mack looked over at her, went back to driving. Interesting man, made even more interesting by his potential to cause her trouble. She considered the possibility of killing Remy in the rescue attempt. Shot by a gun Cleo would plant on Glenn. Cleo performing CPR on Remy, still stained with her blood at the press conference. No, better to have a happy ending for the cameras.

Mack slowed the car, craning his neck.

"This is the third time today you've driven past the Organic Co-op," said Remy. "Are you looking for something?"

"Yeah."

"Care to *share?*"

Mack waited as long as he could. "A dark, older model VW diesel."

Cleo shaded her eyes, pretending to look. Glad that his attention was on the parking lot. God *damn* Glenn. "Why?"

"The man I'm looking for...I think he's driving a VW diesel with a *Meat is Murder* bumper sticker."

"Shouldn't be hard to find something like that," said Cleo.

CHAPTER 46

TREE STOOD BY the side of the trail, unable to remember how long he had been standing there. His mouth tasted foul from the mushrooms, the bitterness making his tongue thick. He expected toadstools to sprout in his mouth at any moment.

The cool breeze blew through him as though he were made of spider webs. Fireflies buzzed around him, flashing lights...no, that couldn't be. It was afternoon. The fireflies were sparkles in the air, atoms and molecules dancing like stars. The stuff of life. City folk were too busy to notice, but once you learned to see, it was all around. Tree had tried to tell Glenn and Eli about the fireflies. Glenn had laughed, shaking his head. Eli said he couldn't see them, but he believed Tree. Eli *knew*. He felt the same way about the ocean. Even though it was the ocean that was killing him. No...not the ocean, but what men had *put* in the ocean. That's what was killing Eli. Men had poisoned the ocean, poisoned Eli and they would poison the forests if given the chance.

The tanker truck full of chemicals they had stolen...terrible beast. Tree had felt the awful power of the tanker truck as he drove it down I-5, felt it seeping into him through the steering wheel. Tree had been against stealing the truck, but Glenn had persisted. The city was already fouled, Glenn had argued—even if the truck sprang a leak, who would notice? Easy for him to say, but the memory of the truck in the bus barn, with only the hum of the cooling compressor holding it back...there were moments Tree regretted ever getting involved with Glenn. He should have stayed in the Trinity forest. That's where he had first heard the trees crying. His awakening, that's what he called it. He had listened to the cedars and pines and aspens for a week, each tree with a different voice, a babble of sound that had scared him, made him think he was going crazy. He asked the others on his eight-man logging crew if they heard anything, but they just said no, chief, not sure if he was serious. Then they had fired up their chainsaws.

His crew had been working deep in the Trinity, cutting a base camp out of the wilderness for additional crews and equipment to be helicoptered in. Dangerous work. Radio contact just once a day, and tenuous at that. Erratic weather conditions, sunny in the morning, but by afternoon Tree raked ice crystals out of his beard. Grizzlies and mountain lions to contend with, but the boredom after the day's work was even more dangerous. Alcohol was forbidden, but all the men managed to smuggle in a bottle or two. That caused problems. Tree broke up the fights with a glance. Or a word. A punch or two of his own if need be. What the office pukes didn't know...a good crew in spite of everything, roughnecks and proud of it, strong and profane, covered in sawdust as the trees screamed in fear and pain. Tree couldn't sleep at night with the sound, and when he finally dropped off, the dreams he had...one nightmare after another. His crew snored on, blissfully unaware of where they were and what they were doing. Anything could happen when you ignored the wild things. Accidents...or worse. One sin led to another, until you could barely remember right from wrong.

He should have stayed there after the chainsaws fell silent. Gone deeper and deeper into the woods. There was nothing to come back out for, but he had come anyway. He had stumbled onto a logging road and the first car he had seen for hours, the very first car, had stopped. Eli had thrown open the door, a joint between his lips, said *hop in, dude, we might as well be lost together.* Eli. Tree shook his head. Smiled. Things might have been different if they hadn't hooked up with Glenn. Too many big ideas in that guy's head. Well, Tree was almost done with the world now. As soon as this was over, as soon as he had saved what was left of the Trinity, he was going back and never coming out.

Tree plucked a pinecone, twisted it free and his fingers pulled pine nuts from the center. He waited until he had a mouthful before chewing, the texture gummy, the taste sweet and ripe after the mushrooms. The trees would forgive him everything once this foolishness was finished. Once the girl was back where she belonged and the forest was saved.

Tree cocked his head. Listening. The faint hum of the ATV grew steadily louder. Birds lifted from the branches, complaining. Eli should slow down. He knew better. Louder still. Chipmunks raced for cover.

The ATV burst into view. *Remy* gripped the handlebars. Smiling. Eli hung on, arms wrapped around her like they were slow dancing. The ATV hit a rise in the trail, Remy and Eli cheering as they caught air, cheering even louder as they landed with a bone-jarring thud. Remy waved to Tree as the raced past.

Dust billowed around him as they rounded a curve and disappeared. He stayed where he was, watching, until he couldn't hear them anymore.

CHAPTER 47

HIS CELL WOKE Mack up. He reached for it, still groggy. He didn't recognize the number calling.

"This you?" The voice was low.

Mack rubbed his eyes. 3:04 a.m. "You got the wrong number."

"You the guy going around town looking for somebody?" the man mumbled.

Mack sat up. "Yeah, that's me."

"I could get in trouble for talking to you."

"It'll be our little secret," said Mack.

"I know these guys...they been going on about doing shit to save the planet. Wanted me to go in with them, but I said no way. They're good guys, but...maybe they done something bad."

"Why don't we get together and talk about it?"

No response.

"What's your name?"

"Nobody can find out."

"I told you...our secret."

"You're sure?"

Mack rolled his eyes. "Where are you?"

"Maybe this was a mistake—"

"Hang on. I just want to talk."

"I need some money. I want to take a welding class."

"No problem."

"Okay. You know where Aurora Boulevard is?"

Mack could see Aurora outside the window of his second floor motel room. "I know where it is."

"What kind of car are you driving?"

"Blue...Toyota or something."

"Okay. Head north on Aurora until you pass 136th street. I'll call you back."

Mack got dressed quickly. Twenty minutes later, just as he passed

136th street, his phone rang.

"There's a construction site coming up on your right. I left the gates open for you."

Mack drove past a couple of self-service gas stations, and a country and western bar called Tight Blue Jeans, then slowed and pulled through the gates of the construction site. He turned his lights out, but left the engine running and his hand on the butt of his Glock. The site was empty and barely-lit, and though the chain link fence surrounding it showed a finished skyscraper, at the moment it was just a twelve-story latticework, a spider web of steel. He got out quickly, darted over to a stack of lumber, listening. All he heard was the distant sound of music coming from Tight Blue Jeans. His phone rang again.

"Where are you?" said Mack.

"Up here."

Mack looked up. He had to tilt his head all the back to see him, all the way on the top of the structure. The man waved and Mack waved back, a little queasy. "Come on down."

"You come up. There's an elevator. You see it?"

The elevator was a narrow cage at the corner of the building. "I don't like that idea."

"I don't know you, mister. You come here…and leave your phone on top of your car."

The elevator was a rickety contraption, enclosed only to waist level, and no door. A couple of leather straps hung from the top, so you could hang on and pray before plunging to your death. Mack looked up. The man was no longer in sight. Mack got in, held on to strap and pressed the UP button.

The elevator lurched and started to rise, creaking, metal on metal. Mack felt himself start to sweat, almost cried out when the elevator came to a sudden stop at the top.

A man with a yin-yang bandana over his face stood outside the elevator.

"You're taking this secrecy thing a little far," said Mack.

The man with the bandana turned a key in the elevator housing and walked away.

"Hey, wait!" Mack stopped just outside the elevator. There was no floor to the building, *none,* just a skeleton of beams and girders. Low-watt light bulbs strung along the outer beams bounced slightly in the wind, sending shadows across the structure. "Hey!"

The man strolled along the nearest girder.

Mack got back into the elevator, his stomach doing flip-flops. He pressed DOWN. Nothing. He pressed it again, harder. Nothing.

"You need a key to operate the elevator," called the man in the bandana. "Here!" He tossed something to Mack.

Mack made an attempt to grab it, but the throw was short and the key clattered against the girder and fell.

"Butterfingers."

Just that one word, but it was enough. The man's voice was different now. The voice of the man who had kidnapped Remy.

"Nice trick," said Mack.

"I just want to take a fucking *welding* course, sir," mocked the man in the bandana.

Mack stayed next to the elevator. There was a constant updraft from below that blew against his face, the floor a grid of girders set eight feet apart.

"You're not afraid of heights, are you, tough guy?"

Mack was.

"I hope not, because if you're not willing to walk the iron, you're going to be up here until the crew comes in tomorrow morning."

"How...does this help you?" Mack held onto an upright beam and didn't look down. "What does this accomplish?"

"I just thought we should talk to face to face for a change."

"Why *here?*"

"Great view, don't you think?"

Mack turned his head. He could see the lights of downtown to the south, shadowy islands to the west, mountains to the east. "Yeah, it's a postcard. Let's talk someplace more comfortable."

The man did a back flip on the girder, the bandana flapping. A *back flip*. Landed on the girder without even a wobble. "I'm plenty comfortable."

Mack edged out onto the girder, arms extended to his sides.

"You think you're wirewalking Niagara Falls?" The man skipped along the girder to the other side of the building. "See, this is how you do it. Look where you want to go, not where you are, and you move *fast*. No fear."

Mack walked towards the man. It felt like his throat had swollen shut.

"I hear you're going all over town, asking questions." the man said, ambling back to him, hands in his pockets. "That's not in your job description. You just supposed to be Brandt's representative. So *represent*, motherfucker."

Mack tried to talk, but couldn't.

The man took a running start and jumped to the next girder, made the eight-foot leap easily. He walked toward Mack until they were directly opposite each other.

"Why don't...?" Mack's feet wobbled, arms waving.

"Careful...careful."

Mack regained his balance, his clothes clammy with sweat. "Why don't you take off the bandana so I can see what you look like?"

"I wouldn't want you to get jealous about how pretty I am."

Mack felt like throwing up. The wind stirred, shadows from the light bulbs sliding over the girders. He could hear music coming from the country and western bar, and imagined people kicking up their heels and swinging each other round and round. Mack couldn't seem to...catch...his breath.

The man jumped off his girder and onto Mack's, lightly ran his hand along Mack's hair and leaped back from where he had come.

Mack watched him, amazed, still feeling the man's touch on his scalp.

"Come and join me, tough guy. It's not that far. If we were on the ground you wouldn't think twice about it."

"We...we're not on the ground."

"This is your big chance." The man beckoned with his fingertips, which made the gesture even more insulting somehow. "You've been looking for me all over town, well, here I am."

Mack stared at the gap between them.

"You just going to let me walk away? You know I'm going to tell the rich girl all about it. *Hey, baby, I gave the tough guy his shot, and he fucking froze.*"

Mack pulled out his gun.

The man in the bandana laughed. "We both know you're not going to shoot me."

As he started to put the gun away, the man jumped from his girder again and onto Mack's, lightly slapped him on the face and walked away.

The man was counting coup like some Sioux warrior. It would have been easier for him to just push Mack over the side; this was more difficult, more dominant. The man spread his arms wide, let his head flop back, standing just a few feet away from Mack.

Mack slowly moved towards the man, his own shadow shaky and enormous.

The man did a sudden series of back flips that brought him to the end of the girder. If there had been a balance-beam Olympic judge he would have scored it a 9.6.

Mack just stared. He hated the man for what he had done to Remy, would have gladly killed him if it would do any good, any good at all, but he had to admit...what he was doing up here was beautiful. Mack admired him his grace...and his courage. He still wished he could get him on the ground. That's all it would take.

The man ran flat out towards Mack, at the last minute sliding as though heading into home plate, and Mack panicked, toppled off. He grabbed on with one arm, swinging in space, gasping, tears in his eyes. He clutched the steel with his fingers, the surface of the girder cold and gritty, then threw a leg over the top and slowly pulled himself up.

The man in the bandana stood there.

Mack lay on his belly, utterly exhausted, head pounding. He felt the girder tremble slightly as the man jumped on it, legs thrusting in and out like a ballet dancer.

Mack straddled the girder, wrapped his arms around it. Music drifted through the night like fog from the country and western bar, someone sawing away on a fiddle, faster and faster, and Mack just wanted it to slow down, wanted all of it to slow down. The wind kicked up, the shadows shifting faster now, keeping time with the music.

The man pirouetted, tapped Mack on the head and danced away. "Tag, you're it. You'll *always* be it."

"Why make this so personal? You'll get everything you want…soon…soon as I get in contact with Mr. Brandt."

The man did a handstand on the girder. "Maybe I'd rather deal with Jeeves."

"Jeeves? Oh…" Mack looked back at the elevator. He'd just have to get there and wait. Wait until the construction crew came at dawn. Arms outstretched, Mack walked toward the elevator, one foot in front of the other.

The man waited just in front of Mack. He held his hands out. "Aren't you going to arrest me, tough guy?"

"Let's go down and settle this," said Mack. "Just you and I. Personal, the way you like it. No gun, no anything. Just us."

The man kicked at his head.

Mack dodged the blow, teetered and fell. This time he grabbed for the girder and missed. Mack barely had time to scream before he hit the girder on the floor below, his head and shoulder slamming against the steel. He caught himself as he rolled off and hung on.

A moment later the man in the bandana dropped down lightly beside him. "Nice scream. Help me, Obi-wan Kenobi!" He laughed, went to one knee, close enough that Mack could see his eyes. "That was intense, huh?"

Mack clung to the girder, shivering.

"You never forget your first fall. It's even better than your first taste of pussy."

Mack tried to get up, but his shoulder was numb.

"You're no fun, tough guy, and you're not that tough. You remember that." The man in the bandana, leaped off the girder.

Mack watched him catch the girder on the floor below with both hands, swing himself around it to lessen his momentum, then drop down to the one below. Mack hung his head over the side, watching as the man did it again and again without any hesitation or wasted energy, using the girders like gymnastic bars until he landed on his feet on the concrete foundation.

The man looked up at him. Waved.

Mack kept his eyes on the girder in front of him as he slowly scooted forward. It took him ten minutes to get to the end, where the beams formed a right angle and he had more to hang on to. The man in the bandana was long gone now. He checked his watch. Just a few more hours. The music from the club wafted on the breeze as he waited for morning.

CHAPTER 48

"DON'T YOU WISH everything could stay just like this?" said Eli.

Remy was dimly aware of Eli's voice as she daydreamed beside the huckleberry bushes. She lay on her back at the edge of the meadow, head pillowed on her arms. A necklace of wild flowers looped around her neck, pink and yellow and blue petals. Eli wore a matching strand. The ATV left back on the trail, the two of them alone in the wild silence of the meadow A pair of red-tailed hawks floated above, waiting for a rabbit or squirrel to get comfortable, to forget all the infinite directions death could snatch them from. The sun played peek-a-boo behind the clouds, but she could sense the cold coming.

"I mean, it wouldn't be the worst thing in the world, right?" Eli leaned his head on his elbow, his face only inches from hers. "Living off the land. No cops, no bosses. In tune with it all, you know?" He tickled her face with a flower. "This is my favorite spot in the forest. At sunset the deer come out to graze. They get so close...it's like TV."

Remy worked her fingers into the warm earth. All the ripe woody smells of the forest mingled with the scent of fresh grass. It *was* beautiful.

Eli plucked huckleberry blossoms from the bushes around them, held the pale white flower to her lips. "Taste," he said. "Taste it."

Remy's tongue darted out, lapped the single golden drop on the tip of the stem. She smiled. Lapped another of the bell-shaped blossoms. Like honey...the most delicate honey, the stuff the worker bees saved for the queen.

Eli brought more blossoms to her lips. Then to his. Both of them savoring the sweetness until their mouths glowed.

Remy lay with her eyes closed, warmed by the sun.

"This is something, isn't it?" said Eli.

Remy drifted. More relaxed than she could remember. All sense of time lost...memories fading in the heat. She could have been here forever, part of the forest...

"Being here with me...it's not so bad, is it?"

Remy felt the hum of bees around her and it was like music.

"I mean...it's not like you're a prisoner," said Eli. "Not really."

Remy opened her eyes. Saw him hovering over her. She remembered everything now.

"I know places...places in Mexico, little villages along the coast..." Eli stuck a flower in his hair. "Sun and sand and clear, blue water, fruit hanging off the trees...as close to heaven as you can get and not be dead."

"Why don't we go there?" Remy said lazily.

Eli grinned. "Deal." He gave her a quick kiss.

Remy stood up. "Let's go."

"Now?" Eli looked up at her, shading his eyes with one hand. "What about Tree?"

"Tree can take care of himself."

"No...I couldn't leave Tree to deal with Glenn. Besides...we can't go until your dad comes through with the ransom." Eli tugged at her hand. "Once he pays off Mother Nature, you and I will head south and never come back."

Remy kissed him. "I don't want to wait."

Eli pulled back from her. Shook his head. "I'm not stupid, you know. People always think I am...but, I'm not."

"I don't think you're stupid."

"I learned how to drive an 18-wheeler just by watching Tree that one night. Glenn thinks he's so smart, but he don't even know how to double clutch—"

"Take me out of here, Eli. They're not going to let me go, no matter what my father does. They're going to kill me."

"No one's going to kill you." Eli's bright blue eyes shimmered in the sunshine. "That's a promise. Cross my heart."

Remy sat back down. Half turned away from him.

"Maybe when this is all over...if you still want to give it a try, I'll show you that little Mexican village I was talking about before. I'll teach you how to surf. I bet you'd be really good too."

Remy didn't answer.

"Are you thinking about your boyfriend?"

"Yes."

"Oh." Eli offered her the joint again, but she didn't take it. He shrugged. "It's not like I'm asking you to choose between him and me."

"Glad to hear it."

"Don't be like that." Eli pinched the joint out, dabbed the hot end with spit. "I'm just saying that things might not be the same between the two of you when you get back. You're different now."

"Not that different."

"It happens fast for some people...so fast you wouldn't believe it." Eli gently took her hand. Caressed her dirt-crusted nails. "Look at you. Here you are digging into the earth. Enjoying it. When you first got here, no way you would have done something like that. A few days, that's all it's taken you to see things the way they really are. Tree's surprised, but not me. I could tell you were special. Some people, you could put them out here for a year and they'd still scream when they saw a spider or bitch about not being able to plug in their hair curler." He kissed her hand. "Not you, though. You took right to it."

"I make the best of things."

Eli stared at her with his soft, deep eyes.

"It doesn't have anything to do with you, Eli."

Eli looked away.

"This...this 18-wheeler you talked about. Was that the truck that made Tree so upset at the hot spring?"

"I'm not supposed to talk about it."

"Tree's not here." Remy played with his dreads. "Did you steal a logging truck?"

"Not even close. You're ice cold."

"Did you run over someone with the truck?"

"Still cold."

"An 18-wheeler...that's a big truck. Was it something you were hauling?"

"Hot. Surface of the sun hot."

"What was in the truck?"

"Tree...he beat up the two guys from the truck. Just wailed on them.

We wore our masks, but we didn't even need them, he hit them so fast. I told him to go easy, but Tree, he's got a temper."

"Eli? What was in the truck?"

"Something really *really* bad."

"A bomb?"

Eli shook his head. "Tree...he knows how to use dynamite and stuff from when he was a logger, but what was in the truck...it scared him. Scared me too." He patted her arm. "No need to worry, though. We left it back in the city."

"You left...something dangerous in the *city?*"

"Wasn't my idea. Wasn't Tree's either."

"Where did——?"

Eli jumped up. "Time to go."

"Eli? Where did you leave the truck?"

"We can take the long way back," said Eli, ignoring her. "Give you a chance to see some different scenery."

"Good." Remy knew when to stop asking questions. Time enough to return to the subject later, when Eli wasn't so on guard. "I want to drive the ATV again."

"Sure." Eli smiled. "Maybe when this is over, I'll teach you how to drive an 18-wheeler."

CHAPTER 49

MACK CUT ACROSS two lanes of traffic, horns blaring on all sides as he pulled into the parking lot of Capital Hill Organics. His shoulder still ached from his fall last night. The fall was bad, the humiliation was worse. He parked across from the dark blue VW diesel Rabbit he had spotted driving past. Finding Remy, and finding the guy in the yin-yang bandana was the best way to deal with the shame. He got out of his car, excited now, making sure not to hurry. Shoppers rolled out of the store, pushing carts that clattered on the asphalt, but he ignored them. He bent down beside the VW, lifted up the corner of the drooping bumper sticker. Heart pounding. Looked like someone had tried to peel it off.

MILK IS MURDER.

Milk? Avery said the VW has a Meat Is Murder bumper sticker. Avery also said it was night and he couldn't see it very well.

"What are you doing to my car?" A pregnant woman pushed her shopping cart closer, aiming right for him. Her red hair bristled around her face. "I asked you a question, mister." A baby in her backpack peeked over her shoulder, listening.

Mack smiled. "I rear-ended you a couple weeks ago, but you never put in a claim."

"You trying to pull something?" demanded the woman.

"Just clearing my karma. A man was driving—"

"Only man in my life is Cobain here," said the woman. The baby gurgled behind her, waved at Mack.

Mack waved back. "You sure you didn't loan your car to somebody?" He wandered toward the driver's door, peeked in. The back seat was filled with cloth diapers and toys.

"Maybe you hit the son-of-a-bitch who stole it last month." The woman pointed to the cracked dash, bare wires sprouting.

"Maybe. You were lucky to get it back."

"Yeah, like there's a big market for these old diesels." The woman opened the door, and Mack helped her load groceries into the back seat.

"I'm embarrassed driving the piece of shit, but Cobain's father said it was all I was getting for child support." She pushed her hair back, deftly slipped the backpack off. The baby solemnly watched Mack at she squeezed him into the car seat.

"Was there anything new in the car when you got it back? Something the thief might have left behind?"

"Like a couple pounds of cocaine?" The woman got into the car. "That kind of thing happens to other people. Some people get ripped off and find coke or cash in the car when it gets dumped." She turned the key in the rigged ignition, the engine grinding, trying to turn over. "Me…I find used condoms squashed on the floor mat and a couple of half-eaten veggie burgers."

The baby suddenly started squalling, an undulating howl like a British police siren.

CHAPTER 50

"WOW, LADY," GASPED Eli, "you're fast."

Remy stayed bent over, hands on her knees, breathing steadily, the back of her neck cool and damp. Her side ached, her lungs burned, but she kept a grim smile on her face.

"Tree? Am I lying?" Eli wiped his nose. "She's amazing, right?"

Tree sat down heavily on a boulder beside the path, his face flushed and sweaty. "Yeah." He eyed Remy, not even trying to hide his suspicion. "A couple days ago she could hardly keep up, now look at her."

"Told you, Tree," bubbled Eli. "This healthy living is going to turn her right around."

"We should start back, it's going to be dark soon."

The golden dusk filtered through the trees, diaphanous as a dream, gnats floating in the golden air. Jays cawed overhead, raucously staking out territory. Remy could hear chipmunks skittering in the underbrush, turned and saw one of them sitting on a log, cheeks stuffed, masticating wildly as it stared back at her. She had never realized how ravenous nature was until she came here. She caught herself. *Came* here. Yeah, like it was an excursion, a stay at a holistic spa.

They had set out on a run about an hour ago, making major elevation gains as they switchbacked up and down the terrain. Every time Tree or Eli suggested they stop, Remy had mocked them, increasing her speed and they had been forced to keep up. She was trying to wear them down, put them in their places, but she also wanted to get a sense of what things were like far from their home base at the cedar tree. Maybe even see the lights of civilization from the high ground. The forest thinned out a little, but all she could see were trees and more trees stretching out through the growing darkness.

A gunshot echoed. Another. Another.

"Tree?" said Eli.

"Hey!" Remy sprinted down the trail toward the sound of the gunshots. "Hey!"

Robert Ferrigno

More gunshots, closer, rapid fire now.

"*Hey!* I'm here!"

Eli scooped Remy off her feet as she slipped on loose gravel, dragged her towards the brush lining the trail. She kicked and scratched him until he loosened his grip for an instant. She jumped up, but Tree grabbed her by the hair, jerked her back down, pulling her deeper into the hedges as she cursed and kicked at him.

A low rumbling sound undulated through the trees.

Remy clawed at Tree, but he smacked her with the back of his hand, hit her so hard she almost threw up.

"Tree, *dude*, that is unnecessary."

"Shut up, Eli." Tree sat behind her on the ground, and wrapped his arms and legs around her, pinning her with his bulk and his steamy heat. He held her down with one arm, covered her mouth with his other hand, his palm rough against her lips. "You make a sound," he said in her ear. "One word, just one word, I'm going to snap your neck. I don't care about the ransom anymore. I am *done* with this nonsense."

Remy panted, trying to breathe through her nose.

Eli sat beside them, took her hand.

Remy jerked free of Eli.

"Go ahead, try biting me," said Tree, reading her mind. "See what happens."

The rumbling in the distance got louder, but there was another sound, even closer…she thought it was a horse clomping down the trail, but then, through the foliage, Remy saw a white-tail deer staggering towards them. The deer bled from multiple gunshot wounds, blood leaking down its dappled brown flanks.

Tree moaned, and you would have thought he was the one who had been shot.

"Poachers," hissed Eli.

The deer stumbled, fell to its knees, then rose slowly, legs bent, trying to maintain its balance. It stood there, wild eyed, just up the trail from where they were hiding.

The rumbling was a roar now, the sound of a large engine revving.

The deer lowered its head, exhausted. Blood dripped off its black nose into the dust.

A battered Harley screeched to a stop down the trail, its headlight freezing the deer. An unshaven man in jeans and camouflage jacket got off. He unslung the AK-47 off his back.

"Tree?" whispered Eli. "Don't you do *anything*."

Remy felt Trees fingers tighten involuntarily over her mouth.

"I mean it, Tree. You're just going to get somebody killed."

The man approached the deer lackadaisically, a hulking tub of guts, his shadow rolling across the trail. Lank brown hair obscured his face. His jeans were filthy, the camouflage jacket crusted with dirt, his bootlaces untied. His hands gripping the semi-automatic rifle were scratched raw, covered with sores. He took a short, running start and kicked the deer in the ribs, knocked it to the ground. "You fucking *bitch*. Thought you'd get away from me?"

Remy heard Tree growl softly in her ear.

The man pointed the AK-47 at the downed deer. The deer looked up at him, wide-eyed in the headlight beam. The man unloaded the rifle into the deer's chest, and the sound seemed to reverberate in Remy's lungs like the tolling of church bells. A mist of blood hung in the air for a moment as the deer twitched. Then the man shot her in the eye and she lay still.

Remy lowered her head, and part of her was aware that it was the same movement that the deer had made at the end, when there was no place to run and nothing to do but wait for death. *No.* She lifted her head. No. She stared at the man through the screen of brush, kept her eyes on him as he casually draped the rifle across his shoulders and walked back to the motorcycle. He was whistling.

A few moments later the man walked the motorcycle to the dead deer. He hooked a chain around its neck, then attached the chain to the back of the motorcycle and got on. He revved the engine, put it in gear and slowly let the clutch out. The Harley groaned, barely budging the deer. The man gave the motorcycle more throttle, still more, the tires sending up dirt and pebbles as he took off, dragging the deer carcass behind him.

Remy watched the deer's body bump along behind the Harley until it disappeared down the trail.

Tree released his grip on her. Slowly stood up. She could feel the rage seething inside him.

Eli stayed sprawled in the weeds, shaking his head back and forth.

Remy walked over to where the deer had been murdered. She touched the toe of her running shoes into the blood puddled on the trail, then looked off to where the man on the motorcycle had gone. She could barely hear the sound of the engine now as the darkness closed in.

CHAPTER 51

"HOW'S YOUR HEAD, tough guy?" Glenn sat in the passenger seat of Cleo's car as she drove, his feet up on the dash, watching the stars through the sunroof. "You took a really hard hit last night. I was worried about you."

Silence on the line.

"You there?"

"What's going on?" said Mack.

"Hickery dickery dock, mouse ran up the clock. You talk to Papa Bear yet?"

"Not yet, but don't worry, you'll get paid," said Mack.

"Just four more days. No excuses after that. Daddy might as well be on Mars for all I care."

"Can I speak to Remy?"

"You know, I think the little lady's developing a taste for me. She makes these sounds—"

"Let me talk to her."

"I don't think she wants to talk with you. I told her what happened last night and she kinda...well she kinda looked disappointed. Like she lost respect for you, or something. Can't blame her. You should have seen your face when you slipped off the girder...I about pissed myself laughing."

"We should have a play date again sometime," said Mack.

"Yeah, tough guy, maybe this time you could bring a parachute—"

Cleo grabbed the phone. Turned it off.

"Hey!" shouted Glenn.

"You talk too much," said Cleo, eyes on the road, the freeway nearly empty this late at night. "What's this about Mack falling off a girder?"

"We had a little adventure on the monkey bars last night. I took him up to the high iron."

"You *confronted* him?" Cleo said quietly.

"You should have seen him, babe, hanging on for dear life, teeth chattering he was so scared."

"I can't believe how stupid you are sometimes."

"Hey, I wore my lucky bandana, and used a stolen phone, so relax."

"The idea is to keep a low profile," said Remy. "No direct contact. I thought we were clear about that."

"Tell that to yourself," snapped Glenn. "You're the one who likes getting up close and personal with him. Me, I know what I'm doing."

"Like with the VW? Did you know what you were doing there?"

"Big deal." Glenn waggled his fingers. "Give me back the phone."

"Do you know who the Son of Sam is?" Cleo put her blinker on, took the Beacon Hill exit. Harborview County Hospital sat at the very top of the hill, an old deco-style trauma center that was a real meat locker on Saturday nights. "Son of Sam was a serial killer in New York City." She pulled over to let an ambulance scream past. "He would walk up to young couples sitting in parked cars, and shoot the girl in the head with a .44 magnum. He killed six girls over the course of a year, all of them with long, brown hair. He wrote letters to the paper, signed them Son of Sam. Panicked the whole town. Headlines every day and girls getting their hair cut short just in case. The cops couldn't stop him. They had no idea who he was…until some low-level uniform checked parking tickets given out around the times of the murders and a car registered to David Berkowitz came up. *He* was the Son of Sam"

"Your point being?"

"My point is that even little mistakes can trip us up. You confronting Mack could have been a disaster—"

"A disaster? I fucking *owned* him."

"It was a mistake. Just like you picking up Grace in your mother's VW was a mistake. You leaving the VW in a garage that I signed for, that was another mistake—"

"You're paranoid, babe. You haven't lived there in—"

"My *name* is on the lease. You knew the combination of my lock and felt comfortable enough to use it. That's considered a causal link. Get it? The VW ties you to Grace, and the VW in my garage ties you to me."

"You give the cops too much credit. Besides, it will all be over soon."

Glenn beckoned. "Now, give me my damned phone."

Cleo tossed him the phone and kept driving. Turned left at the boarded up Quick-Gas station, headed deeper into the old neighborhood. No streetlights here. She passed the alley where the garage was located, circling.

"This is bogus," complained Glenn, "it's not like anybody's watching some ratty ass garage."

Cleo ignored him. Moron had no sense at all. She had been walking him through the whole thing step by step for the last year, making sure she stayed invisible. Until today. She almost choked when Mack said he was looking for a diesel VW with a *Meat is Murder* bumper sticker.

She had told Glenn a dozen times to never make contact with Grace any way that could be traced. Strictly pay-phone calls. No visits to the radio station. No dates in public places. Wear a hooded sweatshirt with the hood up unless you were alone with her. Impress upon Grace how important secrecy was. That part Grace understood immediately. She got off on it. Hurried encounters in stolen cars and late-night visits were dangerous and exciting to her. A woman with a very limited imagination for what constituted excitement. Just like Glenn had a limited grasp of what constituted intelligence. Picking Grace up in his mother's car? He told Cleo he had been in a hurry, and it was just that one time, and he had been too busy to take the bus. Excuses, excuses, and it got worse. When Cleo asked him tonight where the VW was, he told her not to worry, *babe*, it was safe in the garage. She only wished she could kill him twice.

CHAPTER 52

"YEAH, TOUGH GUY, maybe this time you could bring a parachute—"

Mack listened to the dead air, rested his head against the back of the chair. The motel room was lit only by the TV, sound off. It made a lousy nightlight, but it suited the lousy motel. A motel where the TV was bolted to the dresser and the glasses in the bathroom were plastic, and you do *not* look under the bed. A stakeout motel. He should call Hobbs and tell him about the phone call. Tell him about the first one too. Maybe tell him about his fun on the girders last night. Instead he called Stevie, who picked up before the first ring had finished.

"Hey, Mack."

Wherever Stevie was, there was no background noise. None. He could have been in a bomb shelter inside a mountain of lead or a soundproof booth from one of the old quiz shows. Leave it to a master snoop to make certain his location wasn't compromised.

"I got another call—"

"I know."

"You know?"

Stevie sniffed. "I set things up so I get alerted whenever Remy's phone is in use, whether it calls you or anyone else."

"And?"

"Nothing." Stevie blew his nose. "Nothing on the one he used to call you on last night either. He's careful, this guy. Removes the battery when it's not in use, removes it as soon as he's done talking."

"Does he call anyone else?"

"Just you and Brandt, and he's always moving. No way to pinpoint his location."

"What about me. Can you pinpoint my location?"

"Of course," Stevie sniffed again. "You really should check into a better motel."

"I'm moving out tomorrow."

"Good. Those places are bacteria magnets. Bedbugs too—"

Mack hung up. He rubbed his eyes in the TV glow, suddenly itching. He was moving out tomorrow. When he had come back from the construction site this morning, he found a pair of lacy white panties tied around the door of his room, a crude heart drawn on them in red lipstick. It didn't matter whether they were Remy's or not, the man in the bandana had found out where he lived. Mack had decided to stay another night, just in case the son of a bitch tried to push his luck even more. He hadn't though, so Mack was moving.

Onscreen, the talk show host mugged for the camera. Shots of the audience, mouths wide, applauding on cue. Camera homed in on a couple of hot girls, and the girls seeing themselves on the monitor, waved to the folks back home.

Mack stared at the ceiling. Time was running out to find Remy. Five days. Maybe when they reached the deadline, Brandt would give the kidnappers what they wanted. No father would let his daughter die if he had the money to save her. He tried not to think of the possibility that Brandt might *not* actually have the money to save her. The air in the motel room felt as heavy as his heart.

Mack got up and walked into the bathroom. A shower and a shave and he'd be ready to start making the rounds, asking questions. He turned on the water in the shower, and undressed. By the time he looked in the mirror over the sink, his reflection was hidden in the steam.

CHAPTER 53

CLEO STAYED INSIDE the car while Glenn worked the combination lock on the garage door. Three rickety garages, side by side, their rusted locks as much a matter of faith as security. The houses across the alley stayed dark. Sounds of late night TV drifted on the breeze, but she ignored it. She needed to get the VW Rabbit out of her garage. The FBI had no interest in the kidnapping now, but once she busted it open there had to be no loose ends and a direct connection between her and Glenn was definitely a loose end. One thing she had learned, never give some bored reporter an excuse to start digging. No telling what they might turn up.

"There," said Glenn, sliding the garage door open as though it were some magnificent achievement.

The VW diesel squatted in the tiny space. She had rented the garage when she lived in the neighborhood, kept her car there while she lived in a single room for a year, making a name for herself, establishing her street cred. That's where she had met Glenn, who crashed in the basement in between climbing demonstrations with the other Monkey Boyz. She hadn't thought about the space after she moved to Belltown. Forgotten about it until Glenn told her he left his mother's car inside. He didn't think she would mind. Not like you were using it. Share and share alike, right?

"Wait." Cleo slid down in the seat, out of view.

Glenn moved into the shadows of the garage.

The sound louder now. Louder. A kid on a skateboard rolled down the alley, the kid lost in the tunes on his iPod. He glanced into the garage, not slowing, rolled past the overflowing trashcans, the broken washing machine rusting away.

Cleo waited until he disappeared. "Hurry up."

Glenn got behind the wheel. Turned the key. The glow light on the dash went on, then off. He cranked the engine. Nothing. He beat on the steering wheel. Tried it again.

Cleo drove forward, closer to the VW. Grabbed jumper cables from the back seat of her car, and popped the hood. Tossed the cables to Glenn.

Glenn grinned. "You think of everything, babe."

Cleo watched him hook the cables from her battery to the VWs. Not everything, asshole. She revved the engine as Glenn scooted back inside the VW.

The VW's engine turned over. Died. Turned over. Died. Glenn cursed. Screamed at the car as he tried it again and again, the engine dying each time. He grabbed the headrest off the passenger seat, flailed at the dash with it.

Cleo imagined Glenn with a bullet in his face. The back of his head blown out in chunks. She revved her engine higher.

Glenn ground the starter...the finally engine *caught*. He fed it fuel, increased the RPMs, charging the battery as filthy black smoke poured out the tailpipe, filling the garage. He gave her the thumbs-up. Coughing as he disconnected the jumper cables. Ran over to her car and threw them into the back seat.

She kept her headlights off, ready to leave. A light had come on in one of the nearby houses. It might be someone taking a late night piss, or someone curious about the commotion in the alley.

Glenn drove the VW forward, had barely inched it over the threshold of the garage when he put it in neutral. Got out and went to the back. More curses. He sauntered over. "Back tire's flat. My mother and her fucking cheap retreads."

"Do you have a *spare?*" said Cleo.

Glenn shook his head. "No jack either."

"You never considered the possibility you might *need* them?"

"I like to stay positive, babe." Glenn leaned half in the window. "You ask me, the flat tire is kind of a sign that we should never have come here."

"We've got to move it—"

"Relax," said Glenn. "My old lady's car is fine just where it is, for now anyway."

Cleo didn't argue. There was no point when he got like this. She watched him back the car into the garage, lock it and get back into her car, taking his time. Posing. Not much longer, Cleo, she told herself. Soon this would all be over. No more Glenn. No more field reports to men who didn't read them, men who laughed at her when she left the room. She drove down the alley. Waiting for Glenn to say something, and knowing it would be something remarkably stupid. Just a matter of time.

"Don't be mad," said Glenn.

"Okay, just for you."

"I mean it," said Glenn. "The flat tire's not your fault. Probably all kinds of nails and glass in the garage. You probably should have swept it out when you left...but, it's no big deal. I'm not blaming you." He kissed her on the neck, right under the ear...the sensitive spot that always made her tremble. "Where to now? I've got some ideas—"

"Do you still have that extra detonator that Tree made?"

"It's at my place. We didn't need all of them in Laguna, so—"

"Let's go get it," said Cleo, accelerating.

"Cool." Glenn put one foot up on the dash, posing. "We gonna blow up something?"

CHAPTER 54

SKY FRIEDMAN SAT atop the pitcher's mound of the Rayburn Correctional Institute baseball field. Legs crossed in a full-lotus facing the sunrise, back slightly arched, her eyes half closed. The field immaculate, not a weed in the infield, the chalk lines protractor-straight. The outfield fence was topped with razor wire, but Sky's expression remained serene and sweet, the face of bliss in the morning light. Must be nice. Her eyelids fluttered as Mack sat facing her. "You're up early," she said.

"Look who's talking."

"Sun salutations allow me to orient myself for the day." Sky's hair drifted across her flawless skin. "You should try it."

"I might just do that."

Her eyes were wide now. "I'm serious."

"I'm not."

"You have a fresh bruise on the side of your face."

"You left a message on my phone. Said you wanted to talk."

"I wasn't expecting you until later," said Sky. "Visiting hours aren't until 11. They're pretty strict about that."

"Fresh donuts and fresh coffee for the duty officer...the secrets of my success."

"The man you were looking for, the one who kidnapped Remy..."

Mack leaned closer.

Sky rocked gently, her hands resting palm-up on her knees. "Most of the men in the movement are quite...gentle. Not weak, but not at all arrogant, like the man you described. Grace was intelligent. The man who seduced her, the man who was able to get her to betray her beliefs...he must have been very smooth...and very handsome." She took a deep breath, slowly let it out. "This man...I think I may have met him."

"Where?"

"A party at Evergreen last year. Evergreen is the university in Olympia." Sky kept rocking. "Finals were over and there was a party at the state park. Homemade beer, drums, bonfire, dancing. At one point I saw

210

this man watching me. Sexy beast, but too aware of it, if you know what I mean. He sauntered over, put his hands on my waist...which was fine, then he looked oh so deeply into my eyes and crooned, 'Hi pretty lady, my name is Glenn...like a quiet place in the woods.' I started laughing. I mean, *please*. But the look on his face when I laughed, the anger and negativity..." Her head jerked, as though trying to rid herself of the image.

"What did he look like?"

"Sandy hair...athletic body. Reminded me a little of the cute guy in those *Twilight* movies. The one with the great abs."

"And you didn't run away with him, offer to have his babies?"

Sky shook her head. "He had dead eyes."

"Glenn. *Like a quiet place in the woods*," they said in unison. Smiling.

"Who invited him to the party?" said Mack.

"It wasn't that kind of party."

Mack stood up. "Anything I can do for you, just say the word. When do you get out?"

Sky laughed and it was clear and bright as a waterfall. "Oh, Mack, I've never been *in*."

CHAPTER 55

HOBBS WAVED FROM the merry go round at the Green Lake street fair, the detective seated in a white plastic swan, surrounded by little kids belted into garishly painted horses that went up and down. Hobbs waved again. Man wouldn't give up. When the ride ended, Mack waited for Hobbs to get off, but the detective stayed put, beckoning now, and after a moment's hesitation, Mack hopped the low fence. Some skinny kid yelled NO CUTS but Mack ignored him, joined Hobbs in the swan.

A mass of new kids raced onto the ride, mounting their favorite steeds. The merry go round started up again. *Puff the Magic Dragon* burbled from the calliope, as the horses went up and down.

Hobbs offered his bag of popcorn. "I already finished the cotton candy. That's what happens when you're late."

"My loss," said Mack, declining the popcorn. He looked around at the carnival, masses of people thronged the food stalls and carnival rides that were scattered around the west end of the lake. A guy dressed like a court jester wandered past playing some medieval ballad on a flute—it would have worked better if he hadn't been wearing orange Crocs with the tights. "Interesting place you picked for us to have a conversation."

"I needed cheering up."

Mack looked at him. "You catch a doozie?"

"Caught it and closed it," Hobbs said quietly, as the kids squealed around them, standing up in the stirrups of the carousel horses, playing ride 'em, cowboy. "Wasn't hard. She regretted it as soon as she did it." He shook his head. "I'll never understand husbands and wives. You'd think there was no such thing as divorce the way some folks behave."

"Sorry, Marcus."

"Yeah...me too."

Hobbs had set up the meet, but he didn't seem interested in talking. Mack didn't mind. He went along for the ride, waiting for Hobbs to get unstuck from whatever was holding him back. It was the best way. When Mack had caught a bad one he'd head for the beach. Lose himself in the sand castles and music from a hundred blankets, Frisbees and runners along the tide line. He'd buy an ice cream cone, let it melt down his hand while he listened to people having fun. He didn't forget the bad ones. Nothing could do that, but the beach allowed him to compress a rough case, tuck it away in a corner of his mind where he wouldn't keep tripping over it.

Riding the swan was goofy and easy and soothing. Kids and their moms. Young mothers dressed in Seattle chic—bright Gore-Tex jackets and tight jeans, pearls and diamond tennis bracelets and short, casual cuts. Hardly any make up. Off the rack lips and cheeks and noses and boobs. Natural. In LA you paid for fake and paid even more for natural.

The ride slowed, then stopped. Kids complained, begged for it to go on longer. Just a little longer. Mack knew just how they felt. Hoped they had better luck than he did. The kids reluctantly filed out the exit chute, led by their pretty moms. Mack looked over at Hobbs, but Hobbs stayed put.

"Haven't gotten anywhere with Remy's Porsche," said Hobbs, watching a kid in an oversized Raiders jersey, the kid bent over his black stallion like a jockey, making whipping motions with his bare hand. "I ran some older diesel VW Rabbits through the DMV. Got a hundred and seventy-three hits—"

"That's a dry hole," said Mack. "Loverboy might have stolen the VW for his big date with Grace and ditched it later." A new load of kids filed in, climbed aboard their mounts and the ride started again. *Puff the Magic Dragon* again. Mack had hated that song for twenty years. "Besides, there's just the two of us. We haven't got time to run down a hundred seventy-three cars."

"Not even with your buddy Stevie helping?"

Mack shrugged. "Turns out it's not just meat that's murder. Milk is murder too."

Hobbs watched Mach, uncomprehending as the white swan carried them round and round.

"I got a lead from Sky Friedman this morning," said Mack. "Grace's boyfriend, she thinks his name is Glenn. No last name."

Hobbs nodded. "That helps. I'll pass it on to Farwell too. He wants to help—"

"I owe you an apology," said Mack.

Hobbs raised an eyebrow, one hand resting on the swan's wing.

"You've been going the distance for me, Marcus. I'm grateful, but I've been keeping things from you."

"I'm shocked. Trusting fellow like you playing his cards close to his chest…there goes my faith in humanity." They made another revolution in silence, before Hobbs finally spoke. "You going to tell me or do I have to say the secret word?"

Mack pulled out the photo he had printed from the cell phone clip. He held on to the photo, reluctant to give it up, then handed it to Hobbs.

Hobbs held the photo gingerly—Remy leaning against the tree, blood trickling from her nose. "When did you get this?"

"Yesterday."

Hobbs looked over at him, then went back to the photo. "Should have told me. This Glenn, he's upping the ante—"

"I know."

"You don't have to do it all by yourself."

"No, I've got you, Marcus."

Marcus stared at Remy's battered face.

"They gave me until tomorrow, but I think I can push the deadline back."

"Tomorrow? That's cutting it close." Hobbs tapped the photo. "What your girl is going through…you think she can hang on?"

"She's not tied up. They may regret that."

They both jumped as the kids squealed, then laughed at themselves.

"This Glenn…when you run the name past your contacts, you might mention that he fancies himself one suave motherfucker," said Mack. "Supposed to resemble the kid in the *Twilight* movies."

"Never saw them."

"An Abercrombie and Fitch vampire."

Hobbs handed the photo back. "That's one bigass tree she's leaning against."

Mack held the photo, surprised. "*Shit.* I was too busy looking at Remy."

"I live in an apartment. Can't grow anything but mildew on my shower stall. Trees impress me—"

"It's *huge.* Can't be too many trees like that." Mack looked at Hobbs. "Leaving Remy untied might not have been the only mistake they made."

Hobbs nodded. "What I said that first day...about you not having what it took to be a detective. I take that back." He stretched his arms across the white swan. "You have to keep an emotional distance to survive in this job, but a man with a personal interest...there's nothing he can't accomplish."

"I should have showed you the photo sooner."

"Yeah, you should have."

"I know a guy who might help ID this tree," said Mack, staring at the photo. "Maybe narrow the search."

The merry go round spun along, *Puff the Magic Dragon* playing over and over, and Mack felt lightheaded. Felt free with Hobbs. Side by side in that big white plastic swan. Two of a kind.

"How are you holding up?" said Hobbs.

"Fine."

"You don't look fine."

"Then why'd you ask me?"

"I'm an old cop, full of old cop tricks. Can't help myself."

"I'm *fine,*" said Mack.

"Man says he's fine, he's fine." Hobbs swayed to the music, glanced over at Mack. "Did you really bodyguard Nelson Mandela?"

Mack nodded. "He's an old man now, a little stooped, but his voice...it's like a lion, Marcus. It goes right through you. You hear it and you want to be a better person. Stronger...braver."

"I've got two nuts," said Hobbs. "Right or left, I'd give either one of them just to shake his hand."

A boy in a cowboy hat turned around on his horse and aimed his finger at them.

Hobbs clutched his chest, slumped against Mack.

CHAPTER 56

REMY LOOKED UP at the surrounding Douglas firs as she and Eli trooped along the trail, Eli pumping his arms like a drum major. At least he had finally stopped singing *hi ho, hi ho, it's off to work we go.* She slowed her pace, staring higher and higher, the tops of the trees lost in the foliage. More shades of green than she had ever imagined. She checked around, listening, but didn't see Tree. It didn't mean anything. If he didn't want to be seen, or heard…without even being aware of it, she moved closer to Eli.

"It's okay," said Eli.

"I *know* it's okay, I don't need you to tell me."

"Just saying…Tree's got other business to tend to."

"Who is he kidnapping now?"

"Ha-ha." Eli glanced around. "FYI, I didn't tell Tree about you running after the Hmong pickers."

"FYI, I don't care."

"I want Tree to like you."

"Good luck with that."

"I've been telling him how much you're taking to things here, how you're really getting in touch with nature and stuff."

Remy wanted to laugh, but Eli looked so serious that she didn't have the heart.

"If Tree likes you even a little…it might help."

"You mean he might not kill me when Glenn tells him to."

"I'm not going to let anybody hurt you," said Eli. "It's just…better if Tree don't know you tried to run off." He pointed to the thumb-sized pegs zigzagging up the trunk of a gigantic fir. "Come on. Let's get started."

Remy's neck ached from leaning back so far. "You better be kidding."

"You're the one said she wanted a climbing lesson." Eli looped a thin rope around her waist. "Well, class is in session." He sprang onto the trunk of the tree, free climbing. Not using the pegs, the toes of his shoes pressed into the bark, fingertips barely grazing the surface as he ascended, the belt trailing behind.

"Maybe…" Remy followed his rapid progress, tilting her head back farther and farther. "Maybe we could do this another time."

Eli made chicken clucking sounds.

Remy took a deep breath. Lifted her foot up and placed her toe on the lowest peg. Reaching…grabbed a peg between her thumb and forefinger. Her face brushed against the rough bark, literally hugging the tree.

"Keep your body back a little," called Eli, scampering higher, playing out rope. "You get better leverage."

Remy stepped onto the next peg. Pulled herself up. Her knees trembled.

"Keep your eyes up," said Eli. "And *breathe*."

Remy kept climbing. And climbing. Black gnats buzzed around her. Flew into her nose. She blew them out. Kept climbing. Feeling the rhythm now, she increased her pace slightly…and fell. Screaming.

Eli cinched the rope, stopped her fall.

Remy dangled in space. Swung closer to the trunk and held on. "I want…I want to go down. I want to go down now."

"No."

"What do you mean, no? I want to go *down*."

"You haven't been anyplace yet," Eli said amiably. "Why would you want to go down?"

"So I don't die."

Eli laughed. "There's another peg near your right foot. Little bit more. More. That's it. Okay, try it again. Good. Now feel around directly over your head. You got it."

Remy resumed climbing. Her legs ached. And wobbled. Her fingers raw from gripping the pegs. She slipped three or four more times, each time worse than the last, hanging in space like a piñata while Eli directed her motions. She didn't ask to go down though. Not after that first fall. She kept climbing. Finally pulled herself up onto the branch where Eli was perched, waiting for her.

"Nice, huh?" Eli nodded at the view. "No gnats either."

"They must be afraid of heights."

Eli pondered it for a moment, then smiled.

Remy straddled the limb, sat there, hanging on tight a hundred feet above the ground, higher than many of the trees, She could see a river in the distance, curled like a discarded ribbon, and mountains capped with snow. Contrails in the sky, dirty and gray, and higher still a jetliner inching its way to other places, other worlds.

Families inside the plane were eating lunch with miniature, tea party utensils, elbow to elbow. A father taking his daughter along on a business trip pointed out the window to the forest far below. He'd try to remember the names of trees, get confused between deciduous and conifer and start making it up, or shift into a lecture about the geological history of the Pacific Northwest, a quality time discourse on glaciers and moraines, while the little girl looked down, no longer listening, thinking instead of grizzly bears and mountain lions, and Little Red Riding Hood running for her life. No one in the plane knew Remy's name or that she was missing. No one knew she was down in the woods, watching them disappear. Not even Mack. If he knew he would be here. And he wasn't. There was just her...and the Monkey Boyz.

"Tree and me used to train Ruckus people out here." Eli chewed a fresh pine needle. City folks mostly, with big ideas about climbing electrical pylons and shorting out the gird. Bringing Babylon to its knees, that's what they used to say. Babylon." He spat, watched it fall...fall...fall. Looked at her. "None of them made it even halfway this high."

Remy nodded, embarrassed. It was one of the nicest compliments she had ever received.

CHAPTER 57

PROFESSOR TANNER'S OFFICE at the university was even more overgrown than the greenhouse and just as disorganized. Ferns sprouted beside the file cabinets, trays of pine sprouts basked in the windows, papers and books rose from every flat surface. Tanner himself wore mud-streaked khakis, an untucked wool shirt and lug-sole hiking boots. Mack barely noticed. At the moment, he and Tanner sat in front of the 21-inch flat screen monitor, the two of them staring at the photo of Remy downloaded from the cell phone.

"I told you...I don't recall anyone named Glenn at a rally," said Tanner, still looking at the monitor.

"You're sure?"

"I'm sure about this." Tanner tapped the screen with a grimy forefinger. "*Thuja plicata*...commonly known as the Western Red Cedar. A very large one. *Very* large, even for old growth——"

"So, it's rare?"

"No...*Thuja plicata* is quite common in the Pacific Northwest, but not one this size. Oh my, no." He reached for a scientific ruler, laid it against the screen. "Look at the width of the striations on the trunk, the *spread*." He clucked happily to himself. "Even extrapolating for the lack of definitive size markers...this tree is easily...two hundred feet tall."

Mack hated to spoil Tanner's fun by reminding him of why he was there. The professor had barely glanced at Remy slumped in the foreground, more interested in the bark of the tree, and the silvery-blue needles on the ground. "Doc? Where would I find a cedar tree this size? Probably not more than a few hours' drive from the city..."

"There are probably a dozen old growth areas within a hundred mile radius, most of them shrinking, under threat of development or worse, *harvesting* by the timber companies..." Tanner stopped. Peered at the screen.

Mack slumped, rubbed his forehead, giving in to exhaustion for a moment. A dozen? He only had four days before the ransom deadline.

Even if he got it postponed…a dozen tracts of forest was too much terrain to cover. He reached into his jacket, pulled the hike-journal he had taken from Grace's house. Riffled through the pages.

"Interesting." Tanner zoomed in on the bark above Remy's head.

"What?" said Mack, looking up from the journal.

Tanner zoomed in closer still. A slightly-fuzzy dot lay between the ridges of the bark. He adjusted the monitor and the dot got sharper.

"Doc? What are we looking at?"

"Callidiellum rufipenne." Tanner nodded. "Yes…*definitely* a Japanese horned beetle."

"Meaning?"

Tanner moved the curser around the screen. Zoomed in on different areas.

"Doc?"

"Another beetle in the upper quadrant…" Tanner clicked his teeth together. "Increased loss of needles for the cedar. Stunted cones—"

"Doc! Why should I give a shit?"

"I don't think it's necessary to be rude." Tanner pursed his lips. "You should give a shit, because there's only one old growth forest within a hundred miles that has a horned beetle infestation." He looked at Mack. Sniffed again. "The Hannah-Magriff Watershed."

Mack stared at the journal. The Hannah-Magriff Watershed was one of the hikes Grace had listed. He squeezed Tanner's shoulder, relaxed his grip at the man winced. "You have classes tomorrow morning, doc?"

"I have Conifer Ontology 301 at 8 a.m. and then—"

"Cancel it. Cancel the rest of the day too. First thing tomorrow, the two of us are going to take a tour of this watershed of yours."

CHAPTER 58

BIRDS SKITTERED AROUND Remy and Eli, squawking, annoyed at something.

Remy kept her eyes on the river in distance, and the snowy mountains beyond the river. Anyplace but down. Her arms ached from hanging on to the tree. "The ransom...are you really giving it all away? Don't you and Tree have *any* interest in money?"

Eli stood on the next branch, feet splayed, hands on his hips. Perfectly balanced. It made her dizzy. "Is that so hard to believe?"

"Yes." Remy laughed. "Yes, it is."

Eli tucked out of his dreads under his nose, gave himself a moustache. Made her smile. "Money is stupid...but when your dad comes through we'll probably be kind of famous. Glenn's gonna post the whole thing on the net. Inspire other people. Money doesn't count to us, but I got to admit..." He glanced around as though a squirrel might overhear them. "I *was* kind of hoping to have a song written about me. U2 or Green Day, maybe Pearl Jam." He looked at her. "How cool would that be? Girls driving along the beach, listening to the radio...thinking about me." He blushed. "Maybe it's silly, but—"

"No, not at all."

"Thanks. I haven't even told that to Tree or Glenn."

"Your secret is safe."

Eli nodded. "So I guess Friday's the big day, huh? You'll be leaving...and me and Tree and going back home. Maybe you'll hear that song someday, you and the boyfriend riding down PCH, you'll hear it and you'll think about me and the good times we had."

"Maybe."

"I know it's not been all good times." Eli tore a needle off the branch, sniffed it. "That was pretty awful what happened yesterday, huh?"

"That hunter killing the deer, or Tree threatening to snap my neck if I made a sound?"

"Don't take everything so personally," said Eli. "Not like Tree really did it."

"But he would have. If I had called out to the hunter, he would have killed me, right?"

Eli nodded. "You kind of piss him off. And that wasn't no hunter, that was a butcher."

A cool breeze rippled through the forest and Remy clung even tighter to the tree. "Would you have let him kill me?"

Eli's legs rode the swaying branch as though he was surfing. "I knew you wouldn't yell at that guy. You're smart. Anybody can see that."

"But if I *had* called out to him," persisted Remy. "If I was more desperate than smart, then what?"

"Nobody's going to kill you. The real estate lady was enough. More than enough."

"Tree killed a woman?"

"In Laguna." Eli looked past her. "It was an accident—"

"I *read* about that," said Remy, remembering now. "It was all over TV six months ago. Somebody blew up an oceanfront housing development..."

"It was an accident. That lady wasn't supposed to be there—"

"It was no accident. Somebody rigged the gas lines, then called the realtor and arranged an appointment." Remy shivered. "They never found out who made the call."

"No, Tree...he wouldn't do something like that on purpose."

"What about Glenn?"

"It just *happened*. Wasn't nobody's fault." Eli looked like he was about to cry. "What kind of people you think we are?"

"Eli...I want to go back down now."

"Sure." Eli quickly swung himself into position, pointed to the peg she needed to put her foot on. He watched her take the first tentative step. "You got it."

Remy stayed focus on the next peg, and the next.

"Tree...he says being out here brings us closer to God," said Eli, keeping up with her, "but I don't think he's talking about some Sunday School kind of God. Not a God who forgives you for stuff. More like a

PMS Mother Nature God that says leave the fucking trees and wild animals alone or I'll flood the world and drown every one of you dumb bastards."

Remy kept moving, had to force herself not to hurry. "What about you, Eli?"

"Me? I like trees and animals well enough, but I don't really believe in Mother Nature," said Eli. "Don't tell Tree."

"I'm surprised——"

"There's a fish lives in South American rivers, a tiny skinny fish that swims up the dicks of native guys wading in the river——"

"It's called a candiru," said Remy.

"Whatever. So this little fish wiggles right up the hole in a guy's dick, and that's bad enough, okay, but this…what's it called?"

"Candiru."

"Well, this candiru has little spines all over its body that point backwards, so if a guy tries to pull it out of his dick, the spines pop out and it gets stuck in there." Eli winced. "If Mother Nature made something like that candiru, she'd have to be a fucking maniac."

"So, what do you believe in?"

"Me?" Eli grinned. "I believe in big waves."

"Big waves? That's it?"

"Big waves are all about…connectedness. That's a word, right? Connectedness. A wave starts out as a volcanic hiccup in the middle of the Pacific and rolls up on Zuma or Trestles or the cove south of Manzanita, giving surfers a free ride. All of us part of the same cycle, the same rhythm."

"You're pretty far from the ocean right now."

Eli nodded. "I know."

"Maybe you and I could leave here, leave right now and go someplace warm and sunny."

Eli shook his head. "Tree told me you'd say something like that. "He said you'd say it but you wouldn't mean it. Now you said it. Kind of hurts my feelings, if you really want to know."

Remy looked up at him. "You're right, Eli. I didn't mean it."

"No?"

"No. I just wanted you to take me back to civilization."

Eli sighed, the air escaping from him. He turned his head. "I almost wished you'd stuck with the lie. I might have believed it after a while, when...when I was by myself."

"I don't want to lie to you, Eli. I just want you to get me out of here before something happens to me that you can't stop."

CHAPTER 59

MACK PEERED DOWN, face an inch away from the cool Plexiglas bubble of the helicopter's windscreen. Tanner said something...but the noise of the rotors was too loud. Mack inclined his head toward the professor.

"Seventy thousand acres," shouted Tanner. "Hannah-Magriff is a treasure. Pristine wilderness. Cedar, fir, aspen, pine. Three hundred varieties of moss, although that's not my area of interest." He glanced at Mack. "Of course, that doesn't really help you, does it? Finding a small group in the reserve, particularly when they don't want to be found...well, I don't envy you."

Mack didn't take his eyes off the landscape below, trying not to think about the passage of time, the seconds, then minutes, then hours ticking away, and each one bringing Remy closer to her noon Friday deadline. Try not to think about it...mission fail.

"Still, you have to admit, the view is amazing from up here," said Tanner. "If the reserve wasn't part of Seattle's reservoir system it would be crisscrossed with logging roads and summer homes for Microsoft millionaires."

Mack kept watch on the trees as the pilot kept the same, steady pace, trying to see something that indicated human presence. A campfire. A reflection. A marker. A neon sign flashing REMY HERE wouldn't hurt either. There was nothing, though, just a dense green canopy broken by small clearings and a river running down from the mountains. It might be beautiful to the professor, but right now, all those trees were just an obstacle. "How can you see anything?"

"Don't stare," said Tanner. "Just let your eyes slide over the terrain. I learned that doing a forest census last year. The less you focus, the more clear things become. Counter-intuitive but valid." He glanced at Mack. "Better?"

Mack nodded.

"Only use the binoculars when you've spotted something," said

Tanner. "Otherwise your eyes lose all depth perception."

Mack set aside the binoculars.

"Beautiful, isn't it?" said Tanner. "No hunting in the Hannah-Magriff. No camping either, although day hikes are permitted in the outer areas. Not encouraged though. No sanitary facilities provided. No phones or electricity. Just mixed old growth and the full range of predators and prey in perfect balance. Garden of Eden." He sniffed. "Except for the Callidiellum rufipenne."

"We have to go back soon to refuel," barked the pilot over the headphones, expression unreadable behind his reflective sunglasses. "You want to book another flight tomorrow?"

"I'm booking another flight *today*. I'm your only client until further notice," said Mack. "We'll keep coming back until it's too dark to see tonight, and then it's back again at first light tomorrow." At $500 an hour, his credit cards could keep the helicopter in the air for...for as long as it took to find Remy.

"It's your money, chief," said the pilot. "Might have to hit you with a surcharge, though. That kind of schedule means my mechanic's got to work nights—"

Mack pointed. "What's that?"

Tanner leaned over him, looking.

"Check that out," Mack shouted to the pilot. He put a hand out to steady himself as the chopper steeply banked toward the river, skimming over the treetops, the engine louder now.

Tanner shaded his eyes with a hand, leaned over—practically in Mack's lap.

The helicopter paralleled the river, suddenly tilted and Mack's stomach lurched. It didn't seem to bother Tanner. Mack tapped the pilot on the shoulder, pointed and the helicopter hovered over the river. The rotors rippled the surface, sent waves lapping against the shore. A burned-out camper trailer lay on its side on the left bank, windows shattered. Brown vegetation ringed the site, the trees nearby stunted and dead.

Mack had a sinking feeling in his stomach.

"Old meth lab." Tanner pointed. "See there? In the brush? Discarded fifty-gallon drums. Acetone. Ethyl Chloride. Red phosphorous. Hydrochloric acid. All of it highly toxic. Cookers come in for a few weeks, brew up a few hundred pounds and move on. That camper fire…they must have messed up the recipe or maybe their propane tank blew. Bad chemistry, no matter how you look at it."

Closer now. Close enough that the helicopter skids caught spray churned up by the blades. Close enough that Mack could see rotting fish littering the banks, their skeletons translucent in the sun. Hundreds of bones…the world as an X-ray. An old lab. The cookers long gone. Still, the thought of Remy out here…

"That's the only downside of the Hannah-Magriff being off limits," said Tanner. "You get all kinds of lowlifes up here and nobody to tell them to get out."

"The law only applies to the law-abiding," said Mack.

"What?" said Tanner.

Mack shook his head.

"Time to go, gents," said the pilot, veering off at full throttle, sending them tumbling in their seats as he skimmed over the treetops.

"There's someone you might speak with," grunted Tanner, pulling himself up. Straightening. "Amazing girl. Former student of mine. First rate intellect. Highly erotic. Very…very sexualized." His mouth twitched. Maybe it was a smile. "But impatient. I kept telling her, science is slow, but she was easily frustrated. As impatient as you in her own way. She writes for the local alternative weekly—"

"Cleo? I've already spoken to her. She showed me around, did what she could, but she wasn't much help. She said she keeps her distance from the violent types."

Tanner watched the trees below, lost in his own thoughts. "Since when?"

CHAPTER 60

A FOX SCURRIED across the path, startled at the approach of the ATV. Its muzzle matted with red.

Remy slowed the ATV, the sound of the idling engine echoing in the forest. "Did you see that?"

Ravens screeched at them from the nearby branches.

"Eli?"

Eli slid off the ATV and walked into the brush where fox had come from.

Remy was tempted to drive off. Tempted to take her chances finding a way out of the woods, but it was getting late. It would be dark soon, and she still didn't know where they were. So many trails and switchbacks, so many wrong turns. She had until Friday, that's what Tree had told her earlier this morning when he came back from wherever he went on the ATV. Someplace where he could use a phone, evidently, because if Glenn was in the area there was no way he wouldn't stop by to smack Remy around. She was almost disappointed. Would have been nice to see how his singed eyebrows were doing. Friday noon. Not much time, but time enough.

Eli ducked under overhanging branches, peering at something in the brush, then bent down, pushing his way deeper. Ravens flew above him, beat at his head with their wings. "Stay there," he called, barely visible now.

Remy turned the engine of the ATV off. Then followed Eli into the thicket.

"I told you to stay put," said Eli.

"Since when do I listen to..." Remy's voice trailed off as she saw what was lying in the brush, half-covered in leaves. Saw what it had been. The ravens were louder now. They sounded excited. Triumphant somehow.

Eli looked like he was going to throw up.

Remy gently elbowed Eli aside.

"Let's get out of here," said Eli.

"It's him," Remy said softly.

"You...you don't know that."

The man's blubbery face was half-gone, cheeks gnawed to the bone, eyes and nose devoured, all the soft spots. It didn't matter, Remy recognized him. So did Eli.

A patch of scalp hung from a thorn bush. The man's bare ribs showed, white and splintered, his big belly in shreds. Blood streaked the shiny green leaves. Remy knelt down beside the body. She had done ride-alongs with the California Highway Patrol when she was in law school. She had seen head-ons and roll-overs at freeway speed, rear end collisions where the gas tank exploded. This was bad, but she had seen a lot worse.

"Let's *go,*" said Eli.

Remy plucked at the dead man's dirty jeans. The same filthy camouflage jacket. 'Harris' read the stitched nametag on the jacket. He stank so bad it burned her nostrils. His hands were curled, the nails yellowed and filthy. One of his boots was missing, the other one unlaced. She used a small branch to turn the man's head. The back of his skull had been caved in, matted hair black with clotted blood.

"Don't touch him. This is *disgusting,* dude."

Remy moved the brush aside. She saw the AK-47 rifle sticking out of the bushes deeper in the thicket. She carefully scooted closer, pulled it free. The semi-automatic rifle was broken, the barrel dented where someone had beaten the hunter to death with it. The poacher that they had seen massacring the deer. She worked her way back out to Eli, tossed the useless rifle at his feet.

"I don't want it," said Eli. "Poacher got what he had coming to him. Grizzly killed him before the poacher made the bear into a rug. That's justice."

"It wasn't a bear that killed him. Bear might have been gnawing on him, but—"

"Fine. It was a wolf or mountain lion."

"It was Tree."

"No—"

"We both know who killed him, Eli."

Eli stared at the body. "Tree says poachers are the same as rapists," he said finally. "Hit and run and strip the earth bare. They just as soon kill a doe as a buck, kill the babies too."

"When Tree came back to camp yesterday, his overalls were stained. I thought it was blackberries or something, but now...now I know that it was blood."

Eli kicked leaves over the body, leaves and twigs, a cascade of forest clutter, but there weren't enough leaves in the forest to cover what was lying there.

"Tree is a murderer, Eli."

"So...so what? Man was a poacher. He had it coming."

"Think of the rage it took to do this, Eli. The absolute, uncontrolled rage." A raven landed nearby, cocked its head, but Remy didn't take her eyes off of Eli. "Do you think the kind of man who did this would be able to stop himself from killing me if he thought it was necessary? If he thought he had to? Or if Glenn told him to?"

"Tree wouldn't hurt you. He knows...he knows how I feel about you."

"He won't be able to stop himself, Eli."

"Tree...he respects my limits."

"Eli," Remy said gently. "Eli? Look at me. If you really believed that, you wouldn't be afraid to look at me."

Eli cleared his throat, kept his face down.

"Eli...you stole a truck filled with something awful. You kidnapped me. God only know what Glenn did to Grace, and now, look what Tree did to—"

"It wasn't supposed to turn out like this. We just wanted to get somebody's attention, make them stop—"

"You made things worse." Remy took his hand. "Eli, we have to get out of here. You have to show me the way."

Eli shook his head.

"I know Tree's your friend—"

"If you know he's my friend, then you know I'm not going to turn on him." Eli's eyes were so clear and blue that she could see right to the bottom of him. "Maybe Tree's going through some bad times—you ever think of that? Or maybe he told this poacher to go home and the fucker turned his gun on him. That's self defense. Tree's got a right to protect himself. Nothing wrong with that."

"Eli…"

They both turned at the faint WHOMP-WHOMP of a helicopter.

Remy craned her neck, trying to locate it. With one hand she fumbled in her pocket, came up with the small make-up mirror she had put there for just this kind of occasion.

Eli pointed at the silvery speck retreating in the distance. "Wow, *somebody's* in a big hurry."

Remy stepped into the sunshine, frantically flashing the mirror at the helicopter.

Eli saw what she was doing and snatched it out of her hand. "You don't play fair," he said, hurling the mirror into the brush. He stalked toward the ATV. "I'm leaving. You want to come, hop aboard. You want to stay out here…rock on."

Remy stared at the helicopter until it disappeared then ran after Eli.

CHAPTER 61

MACK WAS SITTING in the snack bar of the tiny Snohomish airport, watching the helicopter pilot and the professor eat their lunches, when his phone rang. He glanced at the number. Took a deep breath. Glenn. Whether or not that was really his name, that's how Mack mentally referred to him. It made him think he was making progress.

"Hey tough guy—"

"Is Remy okay?"

"Until Friday, noon, she's just fine and dandy. Real pretty hair, and she smells good in all the right places."

Mack felt his jaw clench. "I talked to Mr. Brandt."

Silence for a moment. "Well, it's about time."

"He's agreed to everything you've asked for—"

"Good."

"He just wants to speak with his daughter—"

"I could probably arrange that."

"And he needs a little more time."

"Ain't gonna happen."

"It's not like he can just push a button and—"

"Sure he can. He's fucking rich."

"He's not even in the country yet. He's flying back now. There's all kinds of legalities involved in making charitable donations of that size, and the land transfer that you want presents a whole new set of challenges—"

"Fine. Tell Mr. Gotbucks to take a few extra days to turn over the old growth, but the twenty million dollars goes out on time and on schedule."

The pilot stood up, brushed crumbs off his lap. The professor did the same.

"We'll need to talk to Remy first," said Mack, "make sure she hasn't been harmed."

Laughter. "Oh, I did her no harm, tough guy, she enjoyed every minute of it. You can ask her yourself. Just get me my money."

"I want to get you your money," said Mack. "Just try and understand my situation—" He heard dead air and was pleased. *My* money. Another mistake by Glenn. No way was this asshole going to kill Remy when he thought he was this close to a big payday. *His* big payday. No matter what Glenn said, Mack had bought Remy a little more time.

"Report says a storm's on the way," said the professor, "so I think I'm going to pass on the afternoon festivities."

"Can we still go out?" Mack said to the pilot.

"As long as you still got money, chief," said the pilot.

Mack was already in the air when he got a brainstorm, one of those good ideas he should have had sooner. He could beat himself up later, once Remy was back. Flying around all over the forest was better than nothing, but there was just too much terrain to cover. Basic rule of any search: when you're looking for a needle in a haystack, the best thing you can do is minimize the size of the haystack. Remy was smart. She might have tried to help him do just that.

CHAPTER 62

CLEO SLIPPED INTO bus barn #51, exhilarated, like walking inside a bank vault after hours. It was almost midnight, this part of Seattle tucked neatly in their beds, minding their own business. Even if anyone was up, she would have been nearly invisible walking across the property in her black sweats with the hood up.

The shutters of the bus barn were shut tight, but she kept the lights on low anyway. She walked slowly around the truck, letting her imagination run free. She gazed at the red BIOHAZARD sign on the truck, then pulled on a pair of rubber gloves.

She went over to the power socket and started unscrewing the safety rings from the plugs. Slowly at first, then faster, the gloves slipping in her haste. Even with the safety rings removed, it took both hands to pull the cables out. She stood there, listening as the cooling fans within the tanker slowed...slowed...then stopped. There was only silence in the bus barn now. Cleo smiled.

CHAPTER 63

THE TRADING POST was a wooden shack just off the blacktop, with a lone gas pump out front and a hand-painted sign proclaiming NO CREDIT CARDS NO CHECKS. Two men sat on the porch of the Trading Post playing cribbage, using a large electrical spool as a table. One was a beefy local in jeans and checked flannel shirt, one boot propped on the porch railing, the other a skinny coot in a wheelchair, a cigarette bobbing in the corner of his mouth.

Across the road the forest stretched out seemingly forever, an impenetrable expanse of tall trees. A trailhead into the Hannah-Magriff reserve was just down the road, one of the last entrances to the southeastern part of the preserve, the part closest to Seattle on the geologic survey map anyway. There were seventeen trailheads on the map, most of them served by a gas station/general store catering to day hikers. Mack had been already been to fifteen of them without success.

It was almost dark now, and he was starting to think his brainstorm yesterday at the airport had been a bust. In their conversation last week, Mr. Brandt told him that Remy had been kidnapped as a teenager, escaping after sending one of her kidnappers to the market for her special, imported shampoo. He had hoped she had tried the same tactic on these knuckleheads. Now he wondered if he might have been better off looking for her from the air.

The two men stopped their game as Mack pulled his car onto the gravel, watching as he got out.

"Morning," said Mack.

The beefy local spit chewing tobacco off the porch. He had a regular gristly-brown pyramid of chaw built up in the dirt.

"Taking a break right now," said the man in the wheelchair, watching his friend shuffle the cards. "Come back in a half hour."

"You must not need the business," said Mack.

The man in the wheelchair shifted the cigarette to the opposite corner of his mouth without using his hands. "Mister, I don't need shit."

"Except maybe a little luck, Haskell," said the local. "I'm kicking your ass."

"Just a temporary setback, Carl." Haskell swiveled his chair slightly and Mack saw the revolver in his lap.

Haskell noticed. "You got a problem with the Second Amendment, mister?"

"The Second's my favorite one," said Mack. "Without it, the rest are just promises."

"You're smarter than you look," said Haskell.

"I better be or I'm fucked forever," said Mack.

Haskell smiled, his teeth the color of filberts.

Carl spit again, slowly dealt out six cards. The deck was old and soggy, with a picture of an Indian maiden on the back.

Haskell picked up his cards, grimaced. "You cheating again?"

"How else am I going to win?" said Carl.

"Do you carry shampoo and toiletries inside?" said Mack.

"Told you, I'm on a break," said Haskell.

"Maybe he's deaf," said Carl. "One of them lip readers."

"I don't want to buy anything, I'm just asking if anybody has come in looking for fancy shampoo in the last couple of weeks," said Mack.

Haskell threw two cards away and Carl did the same.

"It's important," said Mack.

"We carry Prell...and Prell," said Haskell, not looking at Mack.

Mack stepped onto the porch. "No, sir, I understand, but did anyone come in wanting to buy another brand?"

"People got all kinds of requests," said Haskell, dragging deep on his cigarette. "Suburban farts with new hiking boots wanting to know if I carry vitamin water and imported beer..."

"Remember that guy pulled up in that electric car last month?" said Carl. "Told you smoking inside your own store was illegal—"

"Hang on now, Carl," said Haskell, waving his friend silent. "I do remember something like that. What's the name of this shampoo, mister?"

"I don't know," said Mack, trying not to show his excitement. "Something...French."

"There you go," said Haskell, "that's just what this young punk said. He'd couldn't remember the name either. Just said it was something French. He walked out with a tube of Prell, just like everybody else."

Mack pulled a chair over to the electrical spool table. "Can I sit down?"

"Looks like you already started," Haskell said coolly.

Mack decided to stay standing. "What did this young guy look like?"

"Looked like a faggot," said Haskell.

"Real faggot," agreed Carl.

"Can you be more specific?"

"He had a baby face and this long hair...with all the braids like some Jamaican, but he was white," said Haskell. "Go figure."

"Called Haskell *dude*," said Carl.

"A white guy with dreadlocks?" said Mack.

"Dreadlocks," said Haskell. "That's what hair like that's called?"

"*Dude,*" snickered Carl. "You should have seen your face, Haskell."

"Was he by himself?" said Mack.

Haskell swiveled his wheelchair slightly. "What's this about, mister?"

"He ran off with my wife," said Mack. "I think they're camped out in the reserve. She's partial to this French shampoo."

"I guess he's not much of a faggot, Haskell," snickered Carl.

"You ain't the first that happened to, mister," said Haskell, nodding at Mack.

"Was he alone?" said Mack.

"Yup. Drove up on an ATV," said Haskell.

"There's a trailer park a few miles from here," started Mack. "Maybe—"

"He didn't come from no trailer park," said Haskell. "I know everybody in there and there's nobody like him at the Rambling Rose. He come from the reserve."

"You have an ATV or something like that I could rent?" said Mack.

"If you're thinking of going in there after the wife, you best think twice, mister," said Haskell.

"Twice and twice again," said Carl.

"There's more trails in the reserve than you can count," said Haskell. "Fellah like you...ten minutes off the highway, you're not going to know where the hell you are."

Carl spit tobacco. "There's folks in the reserve you don't want to mess with either."

"You want my advice," said Haskell, "I'd let the whore stay with the punk. Plenty of pussy in the world."

"I'll remember that." Mack wrote his cell phone number on their scorepad. "Give me a call if the kid with the dreadlocks shows up again."

Haskell glanced at the phone number. "This is God's country—no cell phone signals here."

"Amen to that," said Carl.

"You must have a landline," said Mack. "You or the trailer park—"

Haskell balled up the paper and threw it on the ground. "I ain't your secretary."

"Have a nice day, Mister," said Carl, staring at his cards, the two of them lost in their game again.

Mack walked back to his car. The professor said the Reserve was seventy thousand acres. Now at least Mack knew where to focus his search. He tried his cell, but Haskell was right. No service. Soon as he got back he was going to call the helicopter pilot. Let the man know that Christmas had come early for him this year. Then he was going to call Hobbs.

Robert Ferrigno

CHAPTER 64

CLEO WORKED THE combination, snapped open the lock. Lifted the garage door, the clatter of the rollers noisy in the night. She slipped the lock into her pocket. The baggy dark-blue XXL hooded sweatshirt provided anonymity and protection from the light rain, her hair tucked back. She had shuffled onto the bus that dropped her off on Rainier Avenue, part of the crowd, the driver not even looking up.

She flicked the light switch. Nothing. Cursing now, she felt her way into the garage using the back of her hands. She never touched a smooth surface with her fingers, at least not without smearing the prints—years of training made it instinctive now. Her feet crunched on something...dead insects, shards of broken glass, Styrofoam. Her movements slightly awkward, her shoes two sizes too big. Worn-out running shoes snagged from a Salvation Army drop-off bin. She left muddy footprints in the garage...no sense making it easy for the techs. The more cautious she was, the more risks she could take. Cleo lived by that rule. She felt rust spots on the VW's trim, rough against her knuckles. She hated this car. Hated it the first time Glenn drove up in it, hated it even more now that it had become a tripwire that could bring her whole plan down.

The car in her garage was too close a link between them. Being acquainted with Glenn was part of the job. Part of her undercover role as the girl in the know. But no way could she be accused of having prior knowledge of what the Monkey Boyz were planning. The Bureau had been caught too many times aiding and abetting. Too many Senators salivated over the chance to haul some agent in front of the cameras. Parading their shock and dismay in front of their constituents. No, she needed to dump the VW. Leave it on the street somewhere. Push it over an embankment. It didn't matter. As long as it didn't have her prints on it and it wasn't directly connected to her.

On one knee now beside the flattened rear tire, a tiny pebble irritating the skin. The princess and the pea. She took the aerosol can out of her pocket, holding it with the pulled-down sleeve of her sweatshirt.

239

Shake shake shake the can. Fix-a-flat. Answer to prayers. She fitted the nozzle of the can to the tire valve, heard the compressed air and tire cement hiss as the tire slowly inflated. She unscrewed the can from the valve. Tossed it into the open window of the VW. Got into the driver's seat and slipped Glenn's key into the ignition, still using the sleeve of the sweatshirt as a glove. A couple of pumps of the gas. The engine turned over twice and started, Cleo beaming as filthy diesel smoke swirled around the car. She turned on the lights. Cried out.

A large man stood in the doorway, caught by the headlights. Hands in the pockets of his suit jacket. Casual. A large black man, the lights gleaming on his smile.

Cleo was tempted to floor it. Run him down. Flatten him and keep on driving. Something in his stance changed her mind. More than casual. *Confidence.* A man with weight and authority and a history of being one step ahead. A cop. She was sure of it.

Cleo leaned her head out the window. "Mind getting out of the way?"

The man didn't step aside. Merely made a motion for her to turn off the engine.

"If you don't move, I'm going to call 911, dawg."

The man clenched his jaw, but maintained the smile. He flipped out his ID, the detective's shield gleaning in the headlights. "I'm police, pussycat."

Cleo turned off the engine. Got out. Pushed back the hood of her sweatshirt. "Sorry, officer—"

"It's detective." The dim light from the nearby houses illuminated half his face. "Detective Marcus Hobbs."

"Cleo...Cleo Hutchinson."

"Is this your vehicle?"

Cleo stared at Hobbs. Those hooded eyes of his couldn't hide his wary intelligence. "No. It belongs to a man I used to know. Glenn. Glenn Thompson."

"That's good," said Hobbs, nodding. "I appreciate you not lying to me."

"What's going on here, detective? I'm a reporter—"

"A reporter?" Hobbs smiled. "Repairing flats part of your job description? Glenn must have been a long time subscriber."

"I'm working on a story."

"What kind of a story?" said Hobbs.

"What are *you* doing here, detective?"

"I'm just trying to find Glenn. His mother, who's the legal owner of the vehicle, said she hadn't seen him in almost a year. Motherly love is a beautiful thing. I've seen mamas wash their boy's bloody clothes Friday night, and swear on a stack of bibles Saturday morning that he was gentle as a lamb. Mrs. Thompson started out that way, until I told her the car had ten unpaid parking tickets and as the owner, she was responsible." Hobbs shook his head. "That changed her mind real fast." He nodded toward the house behind the garages. "She said the last she heard, Glenn was living at this address. Regular crash pad from what I gather." He smiled at her. "I guess Glenn squatted in the basement. All kinds of people moving in and moving out."

Cleo didn't answer. Thinking. Trying to decide.

"I walked through the basement this afternoon. Plenty of trash…but nothing connected to Glenn. Dopers inside the house didn't have anything to add to the conversation. Then I came out here to the garages. Peeked through the windows, but couldn't see anything. Jiggled the side doors. Shabby locks on these things. Oughta be a law. Nothing in garage #1. Nothing but about a thousand bottles and cans in #2. Next garage, though, I finally got lucky, because behind door #3, I found Glenn's mama's VW. Fully equipped with a *Meat is Murder* bumper sticker." He hitched up his trousers. "So tell me again, what was that story you're working on?"

"What's Glenn done?"

Hobbs brought a finger to his lips. "Shhh. It's a secret." He smiled at his little joke. "Where is he?"

Cleo knew where this was going, but she still hadn't decided. Hard to make the leap.

"Did you try to move the car last night?"

Cleo shook her head.

"Somebody did." Hobbs pointed to the front of the garage. "See those tire marks in the mud? Guess the flat tire changed their mind." He fumbled in his pocket, put something in his mouth. Held out something to here. "Lifesaver?"

Cleo shook her head.

"I've been sitting in my car at the end of the alley the last couple hours, wondering if anyone was going to show up with a spare tire or something. Had a book to read, so it wasn't too bad. Elmore Leonard. God, that man can write."

"Is Glenn in trouble?"

"Won't know that until I talk with him."

"It must be serious to justify so much of your valuable time."

"I'm off the clock, so you don't have to worry about your tax dollars." Hobbs crunched through his lifesaver and Cleo smelled cherry. "Glenn's mama said he was mixed up with some real crazies. He called her a whore once for picking plastic not paper at the grocery store. Said she was killing the planet. What kind of a man would talk like that to his own mama?"

"You'll have to read my article to find out," said Cleo.

"Man must have something powerful going for him," said Hobbs. "I mean, here you are, fetching his car for him. A real ladies' man."

It was too late. It had been too late since she saw Hobbs in the headlights.

Cleo took a breath. Lightly rested a hand on his elbow. "Well, Marcus, I guess it's time to be honest."

CHAPTER 65

TREE WAITED UNTIL after Eli had started down the giant cedar to take a piss. Waited until the faint whispering of his descent had faded. "What's wrong with Eli?"

Remy watched him from the hammock. Suspended in space. Hating the question. Remembering the horror show Tree had left in the woods. The hunter's skull crushed in a haze of blood and rage. She saw the hunter's face again, pecked clean to the bone, anonymous under the leaves. The foxes would be back by now. After the wolves and coyotes—

"I asked you about Eli." Tree's hands rested on his belt. Inches from the sheath knife. "He's all messed up—"

"Gee, I wonder why?"

Tree walked over to her. Eye level now. "He's acting funny. When I look at him he glances away. Pretends to be interested in a bird or a blackberry bush or anything other than me." His face darkened. "What did you tell him?"

"Nothing."

"You just can't tell the truth, can you? Can't even answer a simple question." Tree clawed at his beard. "It's like you're bound and determined to make me angry."

"Oh my, we can't have Tree angry."

"Something happened today. You came back from driving around and…it was like you both had a secret." Tree put one hand on the support rope for her hammock, strummed it, sent a shudder through her. "What happened out there?"

Remy clutched at the hammock, fought to speak. "Are you worried about…our secret…or *yours?*"

Tree jerked the rope, shook the hammock. His face contorted in the moonlight, pained. "You fucking him?"

Remy bounced wildly, hanging on. All she wanted…the only thing she wanted, was if he threw her off the platform…she wanted to take the son of a bitch with her.

"Are you *fucking* him?" said Tree.

"*No.*"

"I told you I didn't want you working your dirty magic on him," snarled Tree. "I don't want him mooning over you when this is over."

"What's wrong with you?" demanded Remy. "You couldn't have always been like this. If you had, Eli would never have become your friend. Is this what you wanted? Standing here, threatening a woman, pretending you're doing it all for Mother Earth. You're covered in blood, Tree. If you can't see it, I surely can."

Tree stepped back out of the moonlight. "I know that." His face was shadowed now. "You think I can't see it too?"

Remy slipped out of the hammock. Wobbly on the wooden platform.

"It...it wasn't supposed to be like this." Tree hiked up overalls. "You don't understand. You live in some concrete world, got your nose in a computer screen and your ass in a sports car. You look around now and you see *trees*. Just trees, and they all look alike to you. Just wood for your fireplaces and lumber for your mansions and it doesn't matter to you how many get cut, because they got these tree farms, neat and tidy rows of seedlings as far as the eye can see...just another crop, like corn or alfalfa. Well, a tree farm ain't a forest, and once you cut down the old growth, it's never going to be the same. *Never.*"

"You don't know me," said Remy. "You have no—"

"Old growth forest..." Tree shook his head, eyes welling with tears. "It's like walking into a cathedral...a church. Redwoods and cedars and Douglas fir hundreds of feet high, stretching up to the sky. And so quiet. You lie there at night, listening, and you can hear the *world* growing. Old growth trees were here long before the white man, and they'd be here long after we're gone, except we're *killing* them. We're killing the real forests and planting fake forests, and people like you can't tell the difference. The redwoods on your daddy's acreage are a thousand years old, and he's planning on selling them to the Chinese. Did you know that? Two hundred thousand board feet of lumber per acre. Prime lumber. I read, lady. You called me a Sasquatch first time you saw me. You meant it

244

as an insult, but I knew better. If there's anything in these woods that's close to human, I hope it has the brains to stay hid, because we got nothing to offer them. Not one blessed thing," he rasped, voice hoarse. Tree probably hadn't spoken so much in ten years.

"Tree," Remy said softly, "you didn't have to do this. If you want to save your forest—"

"I'm done talking with you." Tree wiped his eyes with the back of his hands, not caring if she saw. "Only two things that matter to me right now. Saving that parcel of old growth, and my friendship with Eli. You spoil either one of those...you ruin things for me..." He shook his head. "I wouldn't be in your shoes for all the money in the world."

CHAPTER 66

"YOU'RE FBI?" SAID Hobbs, suspicious. "Didn't know the alphabets hired such pretty agents. I'm allowed to say that, aren't I?"

"I won't tell if you won't." Cleo reached for her cell phone.

Hobbs pushed her back against the side of the garage. No warning. No hesitation.

Cleo felt the barrel of his pistol pressed under her ear. Pressed hard. Hobbs was fast and he wasn't afraid of the rough stuff. "Detective?" she said softly. "I was getting my phone."

Hobbs patted her down. Quick but thorough. No weapon, but if she had one, he would have found it. The man wasn't worried about being accused of taking liberties, grabbing a feel. Old cop motto: better judged by twelve, than carried by six. Young cops were concerned about being brought up on charges. Worried about their personnel sheet. Old cops cared about survival. Hobbs found her phone. He handed it to her, but he wasn't convinced. Good news for Cleo. Once she earned the trust of a guy like Hobbs she could ride it to the end.

Cleo dialed the private number for the Seattle FBI office. Held the phone between them so Hobbs could hear. He kept the revolver on her. .357. Some serious stopping power. When forced to act, Hobbs liked being sure. Cleo felt the same way.

You have reached the Federal Bureau of Investigation. To access your voicemail, please enter your security code.

Cleo entered her five-digit number. Heard a beep. Then entered two more numbers.

You have two messages. Grayson's voice came on, exasperated. *Cleo, I've received your emails—*

Cleo cut off the message. Looked at Hobbs.

Hobbs put the .357 away, but his sense of humor hadn't returned. "Now that we established your pedigree, maybe you'll tell me what you're doing helping a suspect in my kidnapping investigation."

Cleo walked back to the VW. Got in. Sat there in the dark. As she waited for him, she removed the battery from her cell phone.

Hobbs looked around. Uncomfortable for the first time. Finally got into the passenger's seat. He kept his distance.

"I didn't know Glenn was a suspect, and I didn't know anything about your investigation," said Cleo. "I thought I was running solo."

"I called your office about the case," snapped Hobbs. "Made my request for assistance. They didn't laugh out loud, but I got the idea."

"You got the polite version, which is more than I'm treated to," said Cleo. "I heard a rumor about a kidnapping a few days ago. I was following up on my own when I got the call from Glenn." The interior of the car smelled like wet cardboard. "You have enough on him to make an arrest?"

"He's got a couple of outstanding traffic warrants. That's all I need." He pulled out his phone. "Give me a minute."

"Sure." Cleo looked out the window. Nothing to do but hope he didn't use her name with whoever he was calling. That would be hard to work around.

"Marcus here. Call me back, youngster. I'm working on a lead. It pans out, you owe me a steak dinner at Ruth's Chris." Hobbs tucked the phone back into his jacket.

Hiding her relief, Cleo started the VW. She used her bare fingers now. Time enough to wipe things down later.

"What about my car? That's it down there. Blue Ford."

She gently revved the engine. "We'll come back for it later."

"Where we going?"

Cleo pulled out of the garage. Stopped. "Would you get the door, Marcus?"

Hobbs got out, grumbling. Closed the garage door and got back in. He had to slam the car door three times to get it to shut and it pissed him off even more. A man who needed to be told what was happening every step of the way, but also a man who could be lulled by information.

"Well, agent," said Hobbs, still annoyed, "you going to tell me where we're going now, or do you want me to clean the windows and check the oil first?"

Cleo drove down the alley, the VW lurching, belching diesel smoke.

"You said Glenn was a suspect in your investigation. I thought you'd like to meet him."

Hobbs had a beautiful smile.

Ten minutes later they were on the freeway, headed south. Cleo drove with one hand in the nine-o-clock position, kept the other in her lap. She touched nothing but the wheel and the gearshift.

Hobbs sang along to the music on the radio Nice voice too. Between that voice and that smile...he looked at her. "Why did Glenn ask you to bring him this clunker?"

"I've helped him before." Cleo let a large gasoline tanker truck cut ahead of her. A giant Molotov cocktail on wheels. The driver beeped and she waved. "He's a useful source."

"Your favorite snitch tell you he was in trouble?"

"Just said he needed the car and couldn't get to it himself." Clouds rolled in, driven by winds off the Sound. A storm running hard toward them. The air crackled with electricity, lifted the downy hair at the back of her neck. Glenn's favorite spot to kiss. "I gave him a hard time about having me run errands for him. He promised to make it up to me in his own special way."

"Thinks a lot of himself, does he?"

"God's gift."

"I hear you. Never met a violator yet who didn't think he was a special case." Hobbs glanced over at her. "Just so you know, I'm happy to share the bust—"

"Better I stay undercover. Besides, you've got the traffic warrants on him, you don't need me bigfooting it. I'll just be an innocent bystander swept up in your investigation."

"Whatever you want." Hobbs checked the freeway exit sign. "You said it was just past Auburn?"

"About a half hour past." Cleo kept her eyes on the road. "Davenport Heights."

Hobbs switched off the radio. "*Dead* Hill?"

CHAPTER 67

MACK OPENED HIS eyes, still groggy. The late night darkness in his motel room was lit only by the red digital readout on the clock radio. So much for a short nap. He sat up in bed, winced, then rolled his shoulders, stretching, pushing past the pain. He felt the fall off the girder in every bone in his body. Still heard Glenn's mocking laugh. He swung his legs off the bed, head pounding, reached for the aspirin on the nightstand. He shook four tablets into his hand, chewed them, trying not to make any sudden movements.

He picked up his phone. Listened to Hobbs' voice mail. A lead? Mack called him. Hobbs on his speed dial now. OUT OF NETWORK. Of course. He called him again. Got the same message.

Mack walked stiffly over to the window and opened the curtains. He had moved to a new motel after Glenn left the panties on his doorknob, but this one wasn't much of an improvement over the one on Aurora. He left the lights off in his room. He could see out, but no one could see in. If he had two wishes, the second one would be that Glenn knocked on his door again.

He called Mr. Brandt. He had tried him before he dozed off, but there had been no answer. He was going to call him every five minutes until daylight if he had to. Tomorrow was the deadline for the ransom payment. Remy's deadline.

"Yes, Mack."

"I'm glad to get you," said Mack. "Tomorrow's the day."

"You haven't made any progress?"

"Not enough. Getting close…but not close enough. I need you to wire half the ransom money to those two charities. Five million apiece. That'll buy us a little more time. That's all I need."

"That's not possible, Mack."

"Don't worry. They'll accept half as a sign of good faith—"

"I understand your strategy. I simply don't have the funds."

"Don't give me that. You're rich."

"Not at the moment."

"Wire them the *money*. You'll get it back. I've been working with a local cop. He called me...he called me tonight about a lead—"

"Well, there you go."

"No. No, you cheap son of a bitch—"

"Mack, do you think I would jeopardize my daughter if I had the funds?"

"I don't know, *would* you? Because it sure seems like that from here."

"My legal...situation is a bit more perilous than I revealed, I'm afraid. The great bulk of my assets have either been frozen by various federal and state agencies, or are invested in instruments which can't be readily liquidated."

"You're telling me you're broke?"

"I don't think in those terms."

"Does that include that old growth timber in Oregon?"

"Sadly, yes."

"Why didn't you tell me this before now?"

Silence.

"Brandt?"

A long sigh. "I had faith in Remy. I even had a modicum of faith in you."

"And you didn't want to advertise your situation. You didn't trust me that much."

"The financial world is particularly unkind to even the slightest rumor of weakness, Mack."

Mack stared out the window, watching the traffic. It seemed to be mostly motor homes and big rig trucks this time of night.

"I don't think you should ever dismiss Remy's survival instincts—"

"How much cash do you have?"

Silence.

Mack waited him out.

"I can wire a million dollars to these charities. A million each, which should be more than enough—"

"Ten cents on the dollar? You're going to get her killed."

Another sigh. "I'm going to have to be firm about this, Mack. I have rather more negotiating experience than you do."

Mack saw the minute column of the digital clock advance and wanted to strangle Brandt and his negotiating experience. "Fine, but hold off until just before the two p.m. deadline. I want every minute we can get."

"Of course, but I *fully* expect to get that money back. Do your job."

Mack ended the call, and sat there in the darkness, not seeing anything now but Remy's face the last time they had been together. Glenn was erratic; he might accept the down payment and grant Mack more time, or he might get insulted and use it as an excuse to kill Remy. Either way, once he saw what had been donated to his charities, he would have to tell his partners. Glenn would have to go to where Remy was. That's what mattered.

Yesterday, after he left the Trading Post, he had called Hobbs and told him he knew the general area of the Reserve where Remy was being held. Hobbs had wanted to go all D-Day—flood the area with choppers and cops, enlist every uniform from FBI to school crossing guards. Mack knew that was the kind clusterfuck guaranteed to get Remy dead, even if they were lucky enough to find her. He had a better idea.

Sometime after the 2 p.m. deadline, Glenn would be on his way to the Reserve. Somewhere on Route 221, somewhere within five miles in either direction of the Trading Post, he would veer off into one of the trails leading into the woods. Mack's idea was to stop Glenn before he made the turnoff. Glenn would be driving a motorcycle, a dirt bike, maybe a truck towing an ATV on a trailer. He'd be easy to spot on the lightly-traveled road.

First thing tomorrow morning, Mack was going to be back up in the helicopter, scanning the treetops. Meanwhile, Hobbs had agreed to stake out that stretch of 221 tomorrow afternoon with a couple of units and see who showed up. Anyone fitting the vehicular profile would be pulled over for a broken taillight or littering, whatever bullshit excuse it took for Hobbs to stop and question them. If Glenn was lucky, Mack would have already found Remy by then. If Glenn wasn't so lucky, Mack would do the questioning.

CHAPTER 68

GLENN STROLLED ALONG Fifth Avenue, checking out the high-end merchandise in the windows and grinning so hard his face felt like it was cracking. Persian carpets that cost more than the rich bitch's Porsche, designer sofas, diamonds and tigers and bears, oh my. Rain pelted him, beat against the street, but Glenn didn't care. Traffic crawled up the street towards the freeways, wage apes huddled inside after, finally on their way home to their mortgages.

Ten million dollars. Seven zeroes and the big *one*. Coming his way *Friday*. Sun'll come out tomorrow, and a barge full of money sailing into Port Glenn. Ready for unloading. Just a press of a button, that's all Mr. Brandt would have to do. Zap! You're rich, Glenn! No more sleeping in a van. Or in somebody's basement. Or in the ratty apartment he was squatting in now. No more cold showers and having to sweet talk waitresses into pocketing his bill.

Glenn did cartwheels through the puddles, his hands calloused by the grit. End over end. One way or the other, Glenn always landed on his feet. More energy than he knew what to do with. No place for a man like him in this new America, this put your fucktard shoulder to the wheel America. He ran up concrete retaining wall, did a flip, commuters watching him, faces pressed against their windows. Master of Gravity, bitches, yeah, that's who the tough guy was dealing with, and he didn't even know it.

Tomorrow the world changed. Glenn just wished he could have seen Mr. Brandt's face when the tough guy told him about his daughter. Rich prick. Probably debated whether he should pay. Maybe did a cost-benefit analysis. Money...daughter? Daughter...money? Fucker might hem and haw, but when it came time, he'd pay.

That's when the fun would really begin. Glenn would have money for a house high in the hills above Rio, with a view of the ocean and a tennis court in case he wanted to learn. Ten million dollars bought a solar powered mansion with servants' quarters. Fuck the oil companies. Maybe put in a windmill too. Yeah.

Being rich was the only way to stay safe in a toxic world. Money bought clean air and bottled water from a glacier in Antarctica free from penguin shit. Money bought ozone generators and organic produce and chelated vitamins. Cancer was for poor people and unlucky people. Cancer was for little girls who lived in the wrong housing development.

When kids started getting sick in Davenport Hills, his friend Megan's mother wanted to pack up and leave, but her father had sunk all his money into the three-bedroom rambler and wasn't about to move at a loss. Glenn and Megan had sat in the playroom, listening to her parents arguing through the floorboards. Then Megan had picked up her toy teapot and refilled his tiny china cup. It was the last time they played together at her house, Glenn's mother insisting that Megan come to their home a few miles away.

Even when Megan got that rash and the headaches, they still didn't move. Not until her mother packed them up one morning after his father went to work. Packed them up and drove them to grandma and grandpa's house. Too late, of course. Megan died three months later. Multiple organ failure, which basically meant *we don't have a fucking clue.* Glenn spent the rest of his childhood waiting for something bad to happen to him. An explosion of red welts across his back or his nuts to dry up like raisins. Nothing happened though. Glenn hadn't been sick a day in his life. Had, in fact, been radiantly healthy. It couldn't last. Even now, at this very moment, some twisty thing spiraled around in his cells, ready to sink its teeth in.

It wasn't just Davenport Hills, either, the whole country was filthy now. Rivers of sludge. Medical waste in the landfills, toxic algae in the Great Lakes, and dioxin in the chicken dinners. Carcinogenic Nation. The killing floor from sea to toxic sea. Too late to save Mother Earth. Get rich and get out, that was Glenn's philosophy of life.

He ran across the hood of a parked car, did a vaulting handstand, and kept running. His blood pounded like music. Thrash metal. Louder and louder. Ten million dollars bought a swimming pool in Rio, organic garden and super weed from Amazon headhunters, best weed in the world. Brazil...tropical paradise. No Exxon. No Starbucks. No fake cheese on the pizza or hormones in the beef. Unspoiled Brazil, land of a ten thousand orchids. That's what the National Geographic article he read called it.

With Cleo along for the ride, what could be better? Total babe. A little mouthy, maybe. A little too flirty-flirty with the tough guy. A little too quick to correct Glenn, but that could be dealt with. If not...well, she might end up dumped in Brazil. Maybe traded to a headhunter for a couple of pounds of weed. She'd better watch her step.

Laughing now, Glenn ran toward a gigantic bronze sculpture outside a bank building, some ugly, modern thing that looked like a squashed basketball. He put on a burst of speed, jumped up and somersaulted onto the other side.

CHAPTER 69

CLEO TOOK THE exit too fast, sent the VW into a skid.

Hobbs gripped the dash, steadying himself. He didn't complain though, and that impressed her. None of that *slow down, you're out of control!* crap like the flunkies at the Bureau would say. Hobbs just hung on.

Cleo steered the VW back off the shoulder, the car shimmying on the bad road. Lousy shocks. Lucky if the engine didn't blow or a wheel didn't fall off. Ruin everything. She drove slowly now, coasted the last fifty yards. Pulled under the trees near the entrance to the deserted housing development. Turned off the engine. Thunder rumbled in the sudden silence. No traffic out here. No houses other than the ones on the other side of the sagging chain link fence that sealed off Davenport Heights.

Sign on the gate: DANGER NO TRESSPASSING TOXIC CONTAMINATION.

"Hell of a place to meet your boy, Glenn," said Hobbs.

Abandoned houses beyond the gate. Landscaping long dead but the windows of the homes still intact. Vandalism wasn't worth the risk. Cleo looked at the coils of razor wire along the chain link fence and it reminded her of the bus barn—the authorities placed too much faith in fences and warning signs.

Cleo turned off the engine. Quiet night, just the wind. Even the bugs had gone silent.

"Where is he?" Hobbs sat scooted down in the seat. "I thought he'd be watching for you."

Cleo started to make some excuse, stopped as the first drops of rain spattered the windshield. It was raining harder now. Cleo was lucky. Always had been.

"Guess he doesn't like getting wet," said Hobbs.

"There's a house on the next block. Knowing Glenn, he's in the playroom off the garage, warm and dry, waiting for me to toss him the keys. Probably complain I didn't bring him a soyburger and fries."

"You've been here before?"

"Just once. That was enough."

"Staying here…isn't he worried about catching something?"

Cleo shrugged. "He said in Dead Hill there's no worry about visitors dropping in, and besides, megavitamins and colonics flush out the toxins."

"He thinks an *enema* will protect him from cancer?"

They laughed together. Sat there watching the gate, neither of them wanting to go inside. Fifteen years ago Davenport Heights had been a model planned community with freshly laid grass, smooth sidewalks, and large back yards. The rec area offered a swimming pool, baseball diamond and ping pong tables in the clubhouse. Barbeques every Friday night. A great place to raise kids. Until the kids started dying.

A chemical plant eight miles away, clear on the other side of the hill had been burying arsenic and cadmium and lead tailings for seventy years. The plant had been there long before subdivisions and freeways, long before anyone worried about toxic metals and their capacity to inch their way through the groundwater. For decades the toxic stew had spread out from the dump site, working its way downhill, permeating the soil under Davenport Heights. That was dangerous enough, but even worse, excavating the site of the subdivision had pulverized the soil, brought the poisons to the surface and sent them airborne. Kids chased each other around the yard, slid into second base. Pregnant mothers put their feet up on chaise lounges and basked in the sun. Babies played in the dirt. It took years for the poison to leach into the people. Years before someone noticed how many miscarriages there were in Davenport Heights. How many stillbirths and birth defects, strange cancers and undetermined ailments.

When the state-testing agency was finally brought in, it found levels of toxic chemicals between four and five hundred times the legal limit. The subdivision had been abandoned for six years now, but the lawsuits were still working their way through the courts, moving as slowly as the toxic plume moved through the groundwater. The site was slated for an EPA cleanup. With the budget deficit they should get to about two hundred years from now.

"This man certainly has a high opinion of himself," said Hobbs, "expecting you to come out here, middle of the night, no explanation…"

"Glenn's got his appeal." Cleo felt Hobbs watching her in the darkness. "He *does*."

The two of them got out and walked toward the gate, heads down in the rain as they splashed through the puddles. He shook the padlock and it fell off onto the pavement.

"That's a relief," said Hobbs. "I wasn't looking forward to climbing the fence."

Cleo patted him on the shoulder, felt him tense. "I'm sure you could have managed it."

Hobbs turned up his collar against the rain. "Let's get this over with. I got a friend who's anxious to talk with Glenn."

"Who's that?"

Hobbs chuckled. "Let's just say it's somebody Glenn's not going to be happy to meet."

"Mack?"

Hobbs laughed. "That rascal. He's got you bird-dogging for him too?"

Cleo nodded, pleased at Hobbs' reaction, feeling him relax. They had crossed a threshold, the two of them. "Looks like he kept us both in the dark, Marcus."

"He's something, isn't he?" said Hobbes. "Tries to act all calm, making with the wisecracks, but he's a regular five-dollar firecracker about to blow. Serve him right for us being the one to bring in Glenn." He was serious now. "Course, we still got to find Miss Brandt."

"If Glenn knows where she is, I'm sure you'll be able to get it out of him. Glenn acts tough, but if you work on his vanity, he'll brag his way into a confession."

"I'll remember that," said Hobbs.

They plodded through the empty streets of the development. Lawns stunted. Trees splintered. The families had left in a hurry. Doors of some of the houses swung open and shut in the wind. Swing sets creaked. A tricycle lay rusting on the grass.

"Place gives me the creeps," muttered Hobbs.

Cleo touched him again on the shoulder. Nodded at a house up ahead. That was the address Glenn had told her about. "That's the one. We should go around the back."

She had lied to Hobbs. Just a white lie. She *had* been to Davenport Hills once before, the night Remy was kidnapped, but she had never gone inside the house. Instead she had waited in her car outside the fence while Glenn hid Remy's Porsche with Grace's body in the trunk. He had told her everything about the house, every detail of his little adventure. Dead Hill was the perfect place to stash spot. Dump a body in even the most desolate patch of wilderness and you still had to worry about it being discovered by hikers and mountain bikers, Boy Scout troops and survivalists. Dead Hills didn't get visitors of any kind. Which was why it was also the perfect place to bring Hobbs tonight.

Hobbs moved quietly now, quickly, moved on the balls of his feet. He held his pistol along the side of his right leg. Cleo hadn't even seen him reach for it. They approached the back door of the house.

Cleo opened the unlocked door and they stepped inside. The two of them waited on the landing, listening. Nothing but the wind outside and the rattle of dead tree branches and the pounding of Cleo's heart. Hobbs heard the wind and the branches but he couldn't hear her heart. He looked around, waiting for his eyes to adjust to the dim light. Cleo tapped his arm, pointed down the steps, into the darkness of the attached garage.

Cleo went first, staying to the sides of the stairs so as not to make a sound. Hobbs did the same. When they got to the bottom of the stairs, Hobbs stepped in front of her, onto the concrete floor of the garage. He kept the .357 close to his hip, where he could control its arc of motion. The garage windows were small and high up, allowing just enough light to make the dust motes sparkle in the dim light. Cleo crunched a piece of glass underfoot, the sound echoing, and Hobbs froze.

"It's me, Glenn," called Cleo. "I brought the car."

No answer.

Hobbs looked at her, nodded. Continued. Lifting one foot. Then another. Always poised.

Cleo reached down, picked up a shard of glass off the concrete. Part of a broken champagne bottle. Glenn had wanted to celebrate after the kidnapping. Cold Duck from a 7-Eleven. Big spender. Of course, he dropped it as he got out of Remy's Porsche, the Cold Duck bubbling on the garage floor. He told her all about it when she picked him up outside the fence, Glenn pouting the whole way back to his place.

Hobbs stared at the Porsche parked in the garage. His nose wrinkled.

"I smell it too," whispered Cleo. A sickly sweet grape smell from the Cold Duck...and the other thing. She and Glenn had wrapped Grace up in a couple of large black trash bags. Used plenty of tape. The Porsche's trunk was well sealed, but the faint stink still turned her stomach.

Hobbs stood next to the trunk. He looked at her sadly, shook his head.

She nodded. Yeah, it could wait, Marcus. First things first.

"Where's the playroom?" whispered Hobbs.

Cleo right next to him. Close enough to smell his aftershave. Citrus and a hint of sandalwood. She pointed at the small door in the corner, almost invisible in the shadows. The door was set a couple steps above the floor of the garage, leading into a perfect hideout for kids. A tiny heart had been scratched onto the door. *Glenn + Megan.* Glenn had pointed it out to her the one time he had taken her here, tracing the heart with a fingernail, like it was a holy relic.

Hobbs held up a hand, indicating she should wait as he eased toward the door. Cleo ignored his hand signal, stayed right beside him, and he smiled those bright, white teeth, recognizing the futility of telling her what to do. Which made Hobbs about three levels of intelligence higher than the martinets at the Bureau. They moved toward the door together now. Hobbs slipped a small flashlight out of his jacket.

"Let me go first," Cleo said softly, her lips brushing the warm shell of his ear. She opened the door. "Glenn, honey? You here?"

No answer.

Cleo squeezed Hobbs' shoulder, ceding control of the small doorway to him. His shoulders almost filled the space. His flashlight flicked on, methodically swept the darkness. Hobbs in a slight crouch, weapon poised. Not an ounce of panic in him. The flashlight beam showed nothing in the playroom but discarded boxes, and an overturned Disney bunkbed, abandoned by a family eager to move, desperate to leave.

"Damn," said Hobbs, still looking inside.

Cleo put her hand on his shoulder, as though seeking comfort and reassurance, and Hobbs allowed it now. As he started to step aside, she slashed his carotid artery with the shard of glass from the broken Cold Duck bottle, and though she moved fast, the spray of blood hit her face, the warmth of him trickling down her cheek.

"Hey," said Hobbs, not fully understanding. Not yet. He clutched at her, then sat down heavily on the step, blood pulsing from his neck as he tried to think it through. The pistol clattered to the concrete from his numb grip. "Hey..." The flashlight fell from his other hand, rolled across the floor, the beam sending shadows across the garage.

Cleo kept her distance, watching him in the reflected light. One of her oversize running shoes was soaked with blood. She could feel it as she wiggled her toes. A couple of nights ago, she had deliberately cut herself with a piece of glass just to have an excuse to get Mack to her apartment. It wasn't a deep wound, barely more than a nick, but it had hurt more than she had expected. She watched Hobbs grind his teeth as he struggled to stay conscious and was glad he wouldn't be suffering long. Not that it wasn't his own fault for sticking his nose into her business, but she had liked the detective. A solid professional who didn't put on airs or throw his weight around. She folded her regrets into a tiny square and tucked them away in a corner of her heart. An unused corner. She had used the same mental technique all her life when faced with doing what had to be done. Very effective too. No doubts, no bad dreams.

Hobbs pressed a hand against his neck, but the blood gushed through his fingers. She could see the unspoken question in his eyes. *Why?* The only question that mattered at a time like this.

"You're too good a cop, that's why," said Cleo. "I couldn't have fooled you for long." She watched him slowly stretch his hand toward the pistol. "I never intended for this to happen. It was just your bad luck to be in the wrong place at the wrong time."

The rain beat louder on the roof. Hobbs made gurgling sounds like he was drowning.

"Would you call yourself an ambitious person?" said Cleo.

Hobbs tried to focus.

"I am. The world is rough on little people, Marcus." Cleo felt his blood at the edge of her mouth, wiped it away with her pinky. "I've worked very hard on setting up this operation. Turning Grace was complicated; figuring what it would take to make her betray her old roommate, thinking out the kind of things Glenn would have to say...the kinds of things he'd have to do. I wish there was time for me to tell you about it. I think...I think you would have appreciated all my efforts."

Hobbs blinked, struggled to keep his head upright.

Cleo glanced around the garage. "Glenn used to know a girl who lived in this house. They played together after school sometimes. Now, every time he gets a zit or a toothache, he blames it on his visits to Davenport Heights. Such a baby. If it makes you feel any better, I'm going to kill him before this is over. You have no idea what I've had to put up with." She tracked Hobbs' fingers as they grazed the pistol, tried to lift it. "Don't worry about Remy. I'm bringing her back safe and sound." She smiled at him, thinking of the tanker truck loaded with chemicals, a time bomb that she would defuse in the nick of time. "I'm going to be famous, detective. *Very* famous..."

Hobbs slumped against the steps. His hand dropped from his neck, the blood spurting onto his suitjacket.

"The trick is to know what to do with your fifteen minutes of fame."

Hobbs said something.

"What?" Cleo leaned closer. "What do you want to say?"

Hobbs moistened his lips. Beckoned.

Cleo stayed where she was. Slowly shook her head. "Like I said, you're too good a cop. I'm just going to stay here with you until——" She JUMPED as Hobbs' phone beeped.

Hobbs slapped his phone out, flipped it open.

"*Hey, Marcus, it's me,*" said Mack. "*Sorry I...*"

Hobbs tried to speak, managed a moist cough.

"*Hobbs?*"

Cleo grabbed the phone away from the detective, but it was slippery with blood, popping out of her grip and onto the garage floor.

"Can... hear me? It's Mack. Sorry I missed...call..."

Cleo turned the phone off. Tore out the battery, wanting to smash the phone to pieces. There wasn't supposed to be cell phone service in this area, but there was. Phantom reception, impossible to pinpoint, but once Hobbs turned up missing, his people might track him to the general vicinity. A twenty or thirty mile area, maybe even larger, but Cleo hated uncertainty. Not after all she had gone through.

Hobbs clawed at the floor of the garage, his nails scraping across the concrete. The bib of blood down his shirt was an apron now, spreading out farther and farther. He was looking at his phone in her hand and the sight seemed to keep him going.

"Don't get your hopes up, detective," said Cleo, her voice too loud, echoing. "It's a loose end, but I can fix it." She reached down and picked up his .357.

Hobbs exhaled. A balloon with a slow leak. He stared straight ahead now, and whatever he was looking at, Cleo didn't want to see for a thousand years.

CHAPTER 70

"WIND'S KICKING UP," said Eli, his dreads flapping around his head like Medusa. Stars blinked through the foliage around them. "Maybe we should go below...set up a tent along the fallen fir. Good protection—"

"This is just the beginning," said Tree as the wind tore through him. "Wait until you see the storm that's coming our way."

"I'm worried about the one here and now, dude."

Tree slowly shook his head. Stayed where he was, legs crossed, his back against the giant cedar. Right where they needed to pass to start down the trunk. He sliced another section off one of the magic mushrooms with his knife. He had been working through the mushrooms all evening, barely speaking since his conversation with Remy, his eyes sunk so deep into his skull now they were almost invisible.

"Let's go down," Remy said to Eli, knees bent to maintain her balance. The platform groaned underneath her feet. The hammocks spun wildly in the wind. The sleeping bags soaked now. "Come on, we don't need his permission."

"Tree, you can stay here if you want," said Eli. "We're going to adjourn to ground zero."

Tree shook his head.

"Just move a little bit," said Eli. "With all the wind, she's going to need help getting down—"

"Nobody's going down," said Tree. "There's...things down there tonight. Things that will tear the meat from your bones." He sliced another sliver of mushroom, nibbled it off the tip of his knife. "I seen 'em a while ago, slipping through the brush. Hiding along the trails. Horrible things, worse than ghosts...goblins with yellow fangs and eyes like smoke, just waiting for one of us to make a move. You go down there, you're going to die. They'll tear you apart and eat your soul. I can't let that happen, Eli. Not to you."

"So we'll stick together," said Eli. "The three of us will take care of each other, like always. Just come on down with us—"

"We stay *here*," said Tree. "All of us. We stay here where it's safe."

Rain started now, the wind pelting them with the icy spray. The branches bent in the storm, needles bristling. Cold air rushed up from the forest floor, swirling around them.

"We stay here we're going to blow away," said Remy, teeth chattering.

Tree shook his head.

"Move out of the way," demanded Remy, trying not to show her fear.

Tree chewed as he watched her, long hair flying. Bits of leaves and food were trapped in his rain-soaked beard, his pocked face livid in the storm.

"*Move*," said Remy.

"Come on, Tree," said Eli. "What's the big deal?"

Tree chewed the mushroom, oblivious to the high winds buffeting them. "We never had goblins this close until *she* came. They were out there. I could see them sometimes. Even seen the mess they left behind, but they stayed far away." A large branch tore away from a nearby tree, tumbled through the night. He didn't react. "Now that *she's* here...it's like they're not afraid anymore." He peered at Eli, rain dripping off his nose. "Maybe she's calling them. You ever think of that?"

"Tree...dude, as your friend and all..." Eli licked his lips, rested a hand on Tree's arm. "Maybe you should cut back on the shrooms. Just take a breather until Remy goes home. Then we can both get ripped. You and me, we'll stay high for a week."

Tree shook his head. "Without the shrooms I might not see the things."

"*Exactly*," said Eli. "That's exactly what I'm saying."

"If I can't see them, then they can sneak up on us," said Tree.

"If I'm causing the problem, just let me go," said Remy, squinting in the storm. Lightning flashed, a strobe that momentarily froze them, then the thunder crashed overhead, almost knocked her over. "Let me *go*," she said, shouting to be heard over the reverberations of the thunder. "Let me go and all your problems will be solved."

"You ruined everything," Tree said to Remy. Rain trickling from his beard as he stood there, legs braced, his fury elemental and enduring, strictly Old Testament. "I should have buried you in the woods the first time you ran away, but I was afraid of what would grow. Afraid you'd come back stronger. Now...now, it's too late."

"Come on, Remy." Eli started to walk past Tree, when Tree suddenly stood up, jerked Eli around.

Tree pressed the tip of his knife into the underside of Eli's jaw. "She's put pieces of herself inside of you, Eli. Little knots of hair she stuck in your food. That's how she gets you to do things. I can cut the pieces out, but you'd have to be real quiet. Not make a move." A drop of blood formed along Eli's jaw. Hung quivering in the wind. Fell. "Can you do that? Can you be really *really* quiet?"

"Tree," whispered Eli. "*Dude.*"

Remy shivered, unable to help, uncertain how Tree would react if she tried.

"If I cut the pieces out of you, everything will be like it was before," said Tree as the wind whipped the branches around them.

Eli clutched Tree's knife hand, slowly pushed it away from his throat. "It's okay." He disengaged, moved toward Remy. "It's totally okay, dude. We're going to stay here tonight, just like you want."

"You don't want me to cut her out—"

"Heck, you know me," said Eli, "I can't stay quiet. Friday, when she's gone, everything will go back to the way it was."

"I...I hope so," said Tree.

"We're safe up here, right?" said Eli. "Those things...the goblins, they can't get us here?"

"Goblins can't climb," said Tree. "They're afraid of heights."

"Good for us," said Eli.

Tree nodded. Pulled another mushroom out of his pocket, examined it in the dim light. It looked like a tiny, withered brain.

Eli and the Remy settled in at the far end of the platform, where the wood planks butted against a thick limb. Small protection, but the best they had. Eli rested against the tree, pulled Remy into his lap. Put his arms around her. Held her close. Her teeth chattered from the freezing rain, but he was warm, his arms wrapped even tighter around her now.

"You mind?" said Eli.

Remy didn't answer.

"Tree...he'll be better by morning. He'll be just fine," said Eli.

"No, he won't," said Remy.

Robert Ferrigno

CHAPTER 71

THE TILE IN the bathroom was cool against her back, Remy's eyes half closed as steam filled the shower. She had undressed Mack in the living room, the two of them silent as she led him into the bathroom. Candlelight danced on the other side of the shower curtain. Mack knelt at her feet, soaping her legs and she gave in to his touch.

"I missed you," said Remy, eyes half-closed.

Mack's strong fingers kneaded the muscles of her calves, worked their way slowly up her thighs.

Remy groaned softly as his fingers rose higher.

Mack's touch was lighter now, sliding the lather along her flat belly. He stood up.

Remy sucked in steam, her nipples stiffening as he started in on her breasts. Taking his time. Lingering. Like the song said...God bless the man with a slow hand. He stroked her slick nipples with the backs of his hands, ran his fingernails against them until she ground her teeth with pleasure. He pinched her nipples now. Pinched them harder. Almost painful and she groaned, eyes open now, seeing his face an inch from hers, eye to eye, riding her orgasm with her, drawing it out.

"I really missed you," said Remy.

Mack gently turned her around. The shower spray beating around them, needles on the flesh.

Remy spread her palms against the tile. Felt his soap her back. His hands dipped lower, soaping her hips now. Cupping her ass. She gasped, laid her face against the cool tile as he entered her, stopping halfway, allowing her to clamp down on him, tighten herself so that he was the one who cried out this time. With a groan he drove himself all the way inside her, bucking deeper as Remy braced herself against the shower stall. Mack grabbed her hair, pulled her head back, kissed her, their groans echoing against the tile. She reared back against him, worked her hips, bringing him off until he slumped against her back, slid down her legs and settled onto the floor. She turned and saw him half sitting, his head bent forward, water streaming—

Remy cried out as she awoke. Disoriented for a moment. She was wrapped in a blanket on the platform, her hair still damp from the storm last night. The forest was still. Mist floated in the air, the light shimmering. She closed her eyes, trying to recapture the dream, but it was too late.

Thursday. Her time was almost up. Tomorrow Glenn would arrive. Ready to carry her back to the city in style, ruffles and flourishes, eager to deliver her safely to a four-star hotel and Mack's loving embrace. That's what Eli said. That's what he thought too, probably. Remy knew better.

There was no one else on the platform, which was odd. Usually one of them stayed with her. With Tree, it was to guard her, make sure she didn't try and escape. Eli just liked keeping her company. Even more, Eli liked being near her. She stood up and moved silently across the wood boards of platform. Less than two weeks ago she had been afraid of heights. Less than two weeks ago she had gotten dizzy on the glass elevator ride to the top of the Space Needle. This morning…this morning, she perched high above the ground, comfortable as a sparrow. What had Eli said that first day at the hot springs? How quickly the forest changed a person. You won't even recognize yourself when you go back, that's what he had promised. Maybe.

A whisper of voices floated up from far below. Remy lay down on the platform, peeked over the edge. Through the screen of cedar boughs she saw Eli and Tree at the edge of the clearing. Arguing. Eli kept shaking his head while Tree stood with his arms crossed. Remy shifted position, head cocked, trying to hear, but they were too far away. Fine. She had eyes. She could read the signs.

Still talking, Tree put his arms on Eli's shoulders. Gently. Not a power play, more like resting his hands, a sad weariness to his action, not demand or dominance. Eli hung his head, and slowly, as though his skull weighed a thousand pounds, Eli nodded.

Remy jerked back as Tree turned, and looked up towards her. Heart pounding, Remy sat up, stared into the morning. Seeing nothing. Numb now. This is what it was like being a defendant in a capital case, an *innocent* defendant. Seeing a jury filing in to deliver a verdict. Knowing she had lost. Knowing it had been decided. She was never going back to the city. Never going to see Mack again. No telling how long the two of them had been down there arguing, but in the end, Eli had acquiesced. Ransom or no ransom, they were going to kill her.

CHAPTER 72

SUNLIGHT SLANTED THROUGH the dusty skylight in the bus barn, bounced off a girder and illuminated a single drop of moisture on top of the tanker truck. The droplet a prism of light, shimmering with the heat that hung in the air. The bus barn was stifling now, heavy with the scent of fuel oil and concrete.

A sparrow squirmed its way inside the barn through a gap in the roof, perched atop a beam. The tiny bird cocked its head at the tanker truck, taking in the intruder. The sparrow flew off the beam, fluttered over the polished surface of the tank, and touched the iridescent drop of moisture...squawking as its feet touched the blistering hot surface of the tank, the sparrow flapped back to the beam, claws curled in pain.

The drop of moisture, fiery in the sunlight, rolled down the side of the tank. Joined the thousands and tens of thousands of other drops of heat moisture that dappled the metal surface.

The sparrow clucked from its perch.

Condensation steamed the temperature gauge on the side of the truck, but the needle was clearly visible, edged almost into the red DANGER zone.

CHAPTER 73

MACK COULD SEE the watershed in the distance, lit by the morning sun, when he gave up trying to reach Hobbs on his cell. Keeping one finger in his ear to try and block the noise of the helicopter, he called the station and asked to speak to Hobbs. Officer Farwell picked up.

"Hey Farwell, I wanted to talk to Hobbs."

"What?"

"This is Mack Armitage, I wanted to speak to Hobbs."

"Detective Hobbs' shift doesn't start until noon."

Mack heard the pilot talking on his headset. "He's not picking up his phone, Farwell."

"Okay."

"It's not okay. He called me last night—"

"What?"

"He called me last night," Mack shouted over the rotors. "He said he was following up on a lead."

"When he comes...noon, I'll have...call you..."

"Did Hobbs talk to you about doing an intercept today on Route 221?"

Static.

"Farwell!"

"Yes. Two o'clock, but Hobbs...only one...can authorize..."

"I'm almost out of cell phone range. Can you make sure the intercept takes place?"

Static.

"Can you—?"

"...if Detective Hobbs said...do it, he'll..."

Mack's phone blinked out.

"Just got word from the FAA weather service." The pilot craned his neck, looking behind them. "Storm is coming in hard. We need to make this fast, chief."

The sudden acceleration pushed Mack back into his seat.

CHAPTER 74

"YOU'RE GOING TO get me in trouble." Eli screwed the sparkplug into the ATV, his eyes darting toward the underbrush. "Tree's going to shit when he finds us gone."

"Tree's not going to find out," said Remy.

"Glenn may show up too. He likes surprising people, turning up early, seeing if he catches them doing something they're not supposed to." Eli straddled the ATV, so jumpy he couldn't sit still. "Glenn hears we took off on a little jaunt—"

"Do I look scared?"

"Just so you know, Tree and me talked it all out this morning. No matter what happens with the ransom, we're letting you go."

For an instant Remy almost believed him.

Eli looked at the ground. "Don't laugh, but I'm...I'm going to really miss you."

"I'm not laughing," said Remy. That part at least was true; Eli *was* going to miss her. It wouldn't stop him from letting Glenn or Tree kill her though. "Let's go to the meadow one last time. I want to pick some wildflowers."

Eli fingered his dreads, head still down. "Nobody listens to me."

Remy raised her chin. "You wouldn't deny a girl her last wish, would you?"

Eli pressed the starter. Nothing. Adjusted the choke. He took another look at her before hitting the throttle. The engine turned, caught and he gave it more gas. "Climb on." A crow screamed and he jerked around. "Hurry *up*."

"Scoot back," said Remy.

"No way."

"I want to drive. Come on, Eli."

Eli shook his head. Revved the engine. Still looking around for Tree.

Remy held her ground.

Eli smacked the handlebars, then slid back onto the buddy seat.

Remy jumped on, hurrying now. She gave the ATV more gas, the sound of the engine echoing among the trees. She eased them onto the path, the ATV barely moving, making sure the engine wouldn't stall. Eli draped an arm around her waist, tucked his fingertips into the waistband of her jeans.

"*Hey!*"

Remy turned around, saw Tree running out into the clearing behind them.

Eli waved to Tree. "It's okay, dude. We'll be right—"

Remy accelerated, throttle wide open, sent Eli tumbling off the back of the ATV.

Eli landed hard, scrambled to his feet, laughing. "Whoa, girl! You lost me!" His smile faded as he watched Remy race down the path. He looked at Tree. "She's just having fun." He brushed dirt off his shorts. "She…she'll be right back."

Tree chased down the path after her.

Eli passed him twenty yards later, running full out, dreads flying.

CHAPTER 75

THE 18-WHEELER SEEMED to tremble in the heat of the bus barn, the molecules in its load of anhydrous ammonia stirring now. A single drop of condensation slowly slid down the truck's stainless-steel tank. Slalomed between the thousands of other drops. Landed on a minute indentation along one seam. A sloppy weld. The drop expanded. Almost overflowed the weld. The surface of the drop shimmered. Smoked. Then boiled away in the darkness.

CHAPTER 76

CLEO HEARD A hesitant knock on the door to her apartment. She checked herself in the mirror, shook out her straight black hair, and then opened the door. Glenn stood in the doorway, cheekbones stark and sexy. She kissed him, felt his nervousness, his excitement barely contained. "Come on in."

Glenn stayed where he was. "I thought you didn't want us to be seen together."

"That was then. Today I do."

Glenn took in her tight jeans, the hooded sweatshirt unzipped enough to show the black lace of her bra. He walked past her into the living room.

"Did Brandt pay up?" said Cleo.

"Not all of it, but…"

Cleo waited.

"He paid a million to clean up the bay and a million to save the green turtles."

"That's one-tenth of what you wanted. I guess Mack decided you'd take whatever crumbs he threw you."

"He left a message that he just needed a little more time—"

"And you said sure, kick me in the nuts again."

Glenn's neck flushed. "Two million dollars is a pretty nice kick in the nuts."

Cleo shook her head. "What about the old growth parcel in Oregon?"

"Well, I didn't see an announcement on the Save Nature website, but, maybe—"

"Tree's not going to like that," said Cleo.

"*I'm* not liking it," said Glenn.

"Talk is easy." Cleo draped her arms around his neck, drew him close, face to face now.

"What are you going to *do*?"

"I'm going to the woods. Going to lay a beating on her, a real beating this time. Then I'm going to send video to Brandt and tell him the price just doubled."

"Well…" Cleo kissed him, soft and slow. "…that's a start."

Glenn shrugged off his jacket. "What are you doing?" said Cleo, stepping away from him. "Why aren't you leaving to give the rich girl what she's got coming?"

"About to storm, babe. I'll go tomorrow when it clears up."

"You're afraid of a little rain?"

"A little rain? We got a fucking monsoon coming." Glenn laughed to himself. "A little rain…how about you come *with* me if you think you're so tough."

Cleo grabbed her jacket. "I'd love that."

"No, no, babe, I was just kidding."

"I wasn't."

Glenn stared at her. "Tree and Eli…they'll see you. The rich girl, she'll see you too."

"It doesn't matter, silly. We're going out to the woods and you're going to take her photo…then you're going to kill her."

Glenn looked like she had slapped him.

"You had to know this was coming," Cleo said tenderly. "She saw your face when you went there last time. Eli and Tree didn't blindfold her. They never listen. Now you're going to have to follow through and protect yourself."

"I…I don't know…"

"What's so hard about killing *her*. You didn't seem to have a problem killing Grace."

"Are you jealous, is that it?"

"Can you blame me?" Cleo pouted. "I heard the way you taunted Mack, saying how she came on to you—"

"Come on, babe, you know I was just fucking with him—"

"Then kill her."

"It…it's not that easy, killing somebody," said Glenn. "It wasn't easy watching Grace die, if you really want to know."

"I'm not expecting you to strangle her," said Cleo, walking into the kitchen. "I've got a present for you." She picked up the small paper bag she had hidden under the sink, the weight within carrying her back to the basement in the toxic subdivision.

She remembered the smell of Hobbs' citrus cologne as he had driven there, and the sight of his big hands on the wheel, the rumbling sound of his voice. A man who used his good humor as a mask to cover his sharp intentions. His eyes were the giveaway; always a few degrees cooler than the rest of him. Another time, another place, things might have turned out differently between them. He was just a local cop, but he had style, and the courtly demeanor to go along with it. Not that he was a pushover. Hobbs was the kind of old school cop who would open a door for Cleo, then slap the cuffs on her with a soft apology, maybe ask if they were too tight. But the cuffs would stay on. She had been lucky that night. She had always been lucky.

Cleo handed Glenn the paper bag, watched as he reached into the bag and pulled out Hobbs' .357, a short-barreled Colt Python with shock-cushion grips, heavy enough to beat a man to death with if you ran out of bullets. Glenn's hand trembled as he hefted the weapon from her. "Wow." He practiced his quick draw, pretending to whip from the hip pocket of his jeans. "This fucker's a cannon." He flipped open the cylinder with a snap. "Geez, Cleo, it's *loaded*."

"Course it is. A gun's like a man. Neither are any use unless they're cocked and locked." Glenn stared at the weapon. Probably trying to see its reflection in the blued steel. "You feel brave enough now?" said Cleo. "If you need help with the rich girl I can do her for you."

Glenn looked up at her. "You always surprise me, babe."

Remy slid her hand down the front of his jeans, her nails going clickety-clack on the teeth of the zipper. "You haven't seen anything yet."

"Have...have we got time——?"

"No, not now," said Cleo. "If you're a good boy, maybe we'll do it in the rain."

Glenn grinned. "I'm going to hold you to that."

"You need to find me a helmet," said Cleo. "I'd hate to get stopped for a ticket."

CHAPTER 77

REMY SLOWED AS the trail branched. *Again.* She had had taken a left at the first fork after ditching Eli. Left. Right. Left. Left. Right. Now which way? The engine idled roughly. She had driving around for almost two hours now and was running low on gas. Enough to get her out probably...if she could just find the right path. Keep calm, Remy. No need to hurry. Eli and Tree were far behind. She had her wallet, its cash and credit cards intact. Help would be available at even the most remote outpost of civilization, so take your time and make the right choice. Right or left. Faint tire tracks on both sides of the trail, so that was no indicator. She drank from a plastic water bottle. Sediment at the bottom. She drained it anyway, wiped grains of sand off her tongue.

She idled the ATV at the fork in the trail, trying to decide which way to go. She had done her best to memorize the trails she and Eli had taken on their runs, but they all started to look the same now. She hoped to return to the place where they had found the dead poacher. She shook her head, remembering the blood-caked face, the awful anonymity of the dead. She needed to go back to where Tree had dumped the body, see where that path led, maybe follow the tire tracks of the motorcycle. She thought she knew the way, but now she wasn't sure.

She took the right fork, gunned the engine, not wanting to give herself a chance to second-guess the decision. The ATV bottomed on a dip in the narrow rail, one wheel spinning before it caught. She sprayed dirt, hanging on as she raced away.

Fifty yards later the trail gave out, ending in an impenetrable wall of brush. Remy carefully maneuvered the ATV, turning it around. She drove back the way she had come. Bump, bump, bump over the uneven trail. Remy's jaw set. She almost convinced herself she wasn't afraid.

CHAPTER 78

"I DON'T KNOW why we have to do this now," said Glenn, voice muffled behind his motorcycle helmet. "Get your fucking priorities straight."

"Just pull over," said Cleo. "Sometimes you just have to trust me."

Glenn did as he was told. He usually did when it was Cleo doing the telling. He kept the engine of the motorcycle running, undoubtedly considering it a small victory.

Cleo hopped off the back of the motorcycle, put her helmet under one arm and shook out her hair. She sauntered over to where Roberto sat alone at his usual outdoor table at the Dahlia Lounge. The approaching storm didn't seem to trouble him. Probably thought all he had to was flash his press ID and the clouds would dissolve. As the main correspondent for the local NBC affiliate, Roberto had a fat expense account and a regular schedule. It was what Cleo was counting on.

Roberto looked surprised and happy to see her, greedily accepted her dual air kisses. He smelled of Paco Raban and the rosebud tuna rolls the restaurant featured this month.

"Lovely as usual, Cleo," murmured Roberto, sodomizing her with his liquid-brown eyes. He was short and stocky, elegant in a tailored black suit, his long, black hair slicked back into a pompadour. He disgusted Cleo but the camera loved him.

Cleo brought her lips to his ears, close enough to see the pores in his brown cheeks. "You have to do something for me."

"Anything." Robert crossed his legs, rested a hand on her tight jeans.

"It's important," hissed Cleo. "Keep smiling."

"Smiling?"

"I'm being watched...just do it." Cleo watched the practiced smile spread across his broad face.

"What*ever* have you gotten yourself into?" said Roberto, more amused than concerned.

"A tanker truck full of chemicals was hijacked nine days ago—"

"Yes, I heard something about—"

"I know where it is."

Robert's eyes opened wide.

"Keep smiling. Nod your head."

Roberto did as he was told. "Am I...am I in any danger talking to you?"

"We both are."

Roberto moistened his lips, eyes darting around. He stopped on the motorcycle revving at the curb down the block. "Is that him?"

"Keep smiling," said Cleo. "We're having a good time. That's it." She laughed, patted him on the wrist. "The hijacked tanker is overheating...ready to explode at any time. When it does...a toxic cloud is going to billow across the city. Thousands of people may be killed."

"Terrorism." Roberto looked like he was already reading the teleprompter for his breaking news report. "Terrorism comes to the Emerald City." A thin sheen of sweat appeared on his upper lip. "This truck...is it nearby?"

"Look, I don't have a phone...they took it," said Cleo. "So, as soon as I leave, call the information into the FBI. Tell them they have to act immediately."

Roberto's smile was back and this time it was utterly sincere. The biggest scoop he had ever gotten and Cleo had dumped it into his lap. He dabbed his upper lip with his napkin. "And where...where exactly is this truck full of nastiness?"

Cleo told him.

"You're sure? This isn't pillowtalk from one of those jerkoffs at the *Stranger*, is it?" Roberto saw the look in her eye. "Sorry." He smoothed one of his sideburns with a thumb. "So, how did you find out about it, Cleo?"

Glenn beeped the horn on the motorcycle, his face invisible behind the helmet's facemask.

"I have to go." Cleo picked up his iced latte, scooped out an ice cube and popped it in her mouth. "We can talk about it later."

"I want an exclusive interview with you when this is over," said Roberto. "All the details, the whole story. This is plenty big enough for both of us."

Cleo chomped on the ice cube, a shard of ice shooting onto the table, skittering across the tablecloth. "Oh, Roberto, you're such a gentleman."

"You be careful," Robert called after her. "It looks like it's going to storm."

CHAPTER 79

TREE AND ELI ran along the trail, running easily, long loping strides. Tree ran slightly ahead, more attuned to the faint tracks the ATV made in the dirt—he slowed...stopped. The two of them panting, soaked with sweat. Tree squatted, pointed at the tracks. "See where she's doubled back on herself? She's lost."

Eli shook his head. "I'm scared. No telling what could happen to her out here."

Tree raked a hand through his beard. "This whole thing...I wish we never let Glenn talk us into it. Man could talk the birds out of the sky."

"She said she wanted to go to the meadow one last time," said Eli.

Tree looked past him. "I can't put it all on Glenn. I blame myself too. I just took one little step after another and the next thing I know we're walking off a cliff." The creases in his face deepened. "I can still see that woman in Laguna...that real estate lady burning up like a flare. Still see that big white car of hers rolling off the hillside onto the beach. Fire everywhere...I still see it when I close my eyes. Used to sleep like a baby, but not anymore." He shook his head. "I should have never left the redwoods. I should have stayed where I was."

"I just wanted to be with her alone one last time," said Eli.

"You should have stayed put too," growled Tree, "'stead of handing over the ATV to her. What were you thinking?"

"We'll find her," said Eli.

"That we will," said Tree. "This time, Glenn shows up, we'll deal with him direct. We tell him we took a vote. The girl goes free. Two against one. Then Glenn heads off his way, and we bring the girl out to Gold Bar. Take her to the Union 76 gas station, let her call her people. You and me got our own plans."

"She said she wanted to pick some wild flowers," said Eli. "I thought maybe...when we were out there, she might change her mind about me."

"She's already decided," said Tree. "A little more time with you ain't going to make any difference. What do you think this is, Swiss Family

Robinson?"

Eli blushed. "That time we were at the meadow, her and me...I think she was considering it."

Tree snorted.

"You weren't there," said Eli. "You didn't see her face. The way she smiled. Two of us lying in the sun, smelling the sweet grass. She...she played with my hair. Said she was surprised how soft it was. She's got a feeling for me. She just needed a little more time."

"A feeling for you ain't enough, Eli," Tree said gently. "Not for a woman like that."

"I...I just had some hopes, that's all. Nothing wrong with that."

Tree squeezed his shoulder. "Let's go find her before she gets herself killed. We'll drop her off somewhere safe, then you and me will go to Seattle and drive that load of chemical hell someplace where it can't hurt nobody. We'll clean up our mess best we can."

"I want to be the one to tell Glenn what we did," said Eli, straightening. "I'll tell him we're not listening to him anymore either."

CHAPTER 80

CLEO LEANED AGAINST the gas pump, blocking Glenn's view of the interior of the Shell station. From her vantage point she could see the clerk hunched over the counter, intently watching the television. Roberto moved fast. Cleo knew he would. It had been less than an hour since she talked to him at the Dahlia Lounge and here he was doing a live standup outside the fence surrounding the busbarn wearing a yellow haz-mat suit. The area was ringed with crime-scene tape, uniformed officers and real haz-mat workers hurrying in and out of the busbarn. She thought she saw Grayson stride past in an FBI slicker, ignoring Robert's calls for an interview. He must be so pissed.

"What's so funny, babe?" said Glenn, pumping gas into the tank of the motorcycle.

Cleo ignored him. Cleo's photograph from her Facebook page appeared onscreen directly over Roberto's shoulder. A chiron appeared at the bottom of the screen: *The woman who saved a city.* Cleo felt herself tearing up. Roberto was clearly boosting his own reporting and the exclusive interview with her afterwards, but still...everything she had worked so hard for was coming to fruition.

Glenn put the hose back onto the pump, screwed the cap onto the gas tank. "I'm going to get some snacks."

Cleo took his arm. Too quickly. "What's wrong?" said Glenn.

"Let's go," she said. "We've got business to attend to. Snacks can wait."

"Yeah...that shit's full of chemicals anyway. I was just testing you." Glenn got back onto the motorcycle. Started the engine.

Cleo hopped on behind him, put her arms around his waist. "On Donner! On Blitzen!"

"What the fuck you talking about?" said Glenn.

"Go!"

Glenn peeled out, left a patch on the concrete as they hurtled down the road.

CHAPTER 81

SQUAWK FROM THE radio as the helicopter arced over the trees. "That's affirmative," the pilot said into his headset. He turned to Mack. "Gotta go, chief."

"You still have over a half tank of gas."

"FAA just sent out a storm alert. I got to take her home."

"It's not so bad——"

The pilot eased the stick to the right, the chopper starting back towards Seattle. "When you get your pilot's license and your own bird, you get to make the decisions."

Mack laid a hand on his shoulder. "Put me down."

"This ain't a pogo stick, chief."

"Put me down and go back to base. You can pick me up tomorrow. Me and Remy."

"You don't want to spend the night here. Particularly with a storm coming up."

Mack checked his watch. Almost 3 p.m. If Glenn wasn't satisfied with the ransom down payment he would be on his way to where Remy was being held. Mack knew the general area she was being held in. They had made four sweeps over this section today without spotting anything. The forest canopy made it hard to see much from the air, but he might have more luck on foot. He had to try.

In the distance Mack could see the Trading Post. He picked up the binoculars. Focused. A police car was parked behind the general store with a perfect view of the road running alongside the reserve. Woodinville PD. Must be Farwell. Hobbs was probably in an unmarked car a few miles away. Evidently the lead last night hadn't panned out. Hobbs had come through anyway. Mack almost felt bad for thinking something had happened to him. Lack of faith.

"What are you going to do, chief?"

"Drop me off along the river. It'll be easier for me to get around that way."

"Okey-doke."

Mack watched the shadow of the helicopter racing over the treetops, felt like he was melting into the vast green below.

"I got a small survival kit you can borrow," said the pilot. "Rain poncho, fire starter, water bottle and a compass. Might even have a couple of granola bars."

"How much?"

"I'm not a man to take advantage," said the pilot. The helicopter hovered over the riverbanks, slowly settled down, the blades rippling the water. "You just pay me whatever you think is fair...then double it."

CHAPTER 82

GLENN LEANED OVER the handlebars of the borrowed motorcycle as he raced down the two-lane road, trees on both sides, the engine screaming like a swarm of hornets. Hardly any traffic for the last half-hour, everybody hunkered down because of the weather alert. Even the hawks had taken shelter. He felt Cleo's arms around his waist, mirroring his posture, pressed so close against him he could feel her stiff nipples through his windproof nylon jacket. Behind them the sky was darkening by the moment, the storm running south from Alaska, building up strength. It felt like the air was being pulled past them towards the thunderheads, pulled like some tidal wave that sucked all the water off the shoreline before crashing back with ten times more. No rain. Not yet. Give it a couple hours....

The road was rougher now, the blacktop cracked, so that the handlebar vibrated in his grip as he tried to hold it steady. It didn't matter. Nothing mattered except that Glenn was rich and on his way to being a lot richer. That million dollars that Brandt had deposited in the Green Turtle project was all Glenn's. And it was just the beginning. Daddy would pay the rest of the cash soon enough. Glenn would send him another photo of Remy tomorrow. Pay it all up, pops. Consider it child support.

Glenn smiled behind the faceplate of his helmet. By the time Brandt transferred the other millions, Remy would be long dead and Glenn would be even richer. Being rich was the only way to stay safe in a toxic world. Money bought clean air and bottled water from an Antarctic glacier. Money bought ozone generators and organic produce and chelated vitamins. Cancer was for poor people and unlucky people. Cancer was for little girls who lived in the wrong housing development.

Cleo leaned forward, pressed her helmet against his. "Where do you usually enter the watershed?"

"About ten miles ahead," shouted Glenn. "Just past this general store."

"Take another route."

"Don't tell me what to do," said Glenn, accelerating. If Cleo wasn't careful, when this was over she was going to end up with the big gun in her mouth and Glenn playing Russian roulette.

"I *mean* it, Glenn," said Cleo.

Glenn drove on.

"You need to vary your pattern." Cleo squeezed him even tighter. "Like climbing...you can't keeping taking the same route up or you make mistakes."

Glenn hunched forward. "I was going to do that anyway. There's another turn off just ahead. It'll take us another half hour on the trails..."

Cleo patted his helmet. "Good idea."

Glenn slowed seeing the sign: HANNAH-MAGRITTE WATERSHED. NO OVERNIGHT CAMPING. NO OPEN FIRES. He checked his rearview. Not a car in sight. He veered of the road and through the narrow gap in the brush and into the trees. Branches whipped across his visor, potholes threatened to overturn the bike, but he was so happy he wanted to do back flips. The gun was in the inside pocket of his jacket. Every bounce in the trail banged the gun against his six-pack, a pleasant reminder of what he was going to do with it when he got to the big cedar. He accelerated, shot through a puddle, mud flying as Cleo hung on.

CHAPTER 83

THE ATV DIED at the top of the ridge and Remy coasted down to the bottom, cursing. Sweat cut furrows through the dust on her face as she unscrewed the gas cap and looked inside the tank. She flung the cap into the brush, cursed some more, then pushed the ATV in after it. She tried to cover the ATV's hiding place with branches, but quickly gave up on that idea. Tree and Eli would spot it in a second.

She listened, half expecting the two of them to round the next bend, but there were only the forest sounds of birds and breeze, of squirrels scampering from one branch to another. She pulled the large screwdriver out of her back pocket. She had found it lodged under the seat of the ATV a half hour ago. You might have thought it was a holy relic for the comfort it gave her. Comfort and joy. She wrapped a fist around the hard plastic handle. No way would she allow herself to be taken back. She had made herself a promise this morning. A solemn promise. No matter what, she didn't go quietly. She didn't go back. They'd have to kill her first.

Two weeks ago she had found a spider in the hotel bathroom and released it outside—today she was contemplating stabbing Tree in the eye with a screwdriver. Driving it into his brain. Tree…or Eli. Whatever it took. She saw her reflection in the flat blade of the screwdriver and barely recognized herself.

She started down the trail at a trot, a pace that she could keep for hours if she had to. The only question she had was if she was going in the right direction, a direction that would bring her to a road, a ranger station, a campsite.

Fifteen minutes later, she spotted a wisp of smoke through a break in the trees and cried out with joy, tears welling up in her eyes. Had to be a campfire. Hunters or hikers or a boy scout troop working on merit badges, it didn't matter as long as it was someone other than Tree or Eli or Glenn. She worked her way through the trees, right to the edge of an embankment. There was a river down there! A tendril of smoke drifted above the water, carried from someplace out of sight. Someplace close.

She started down the slope, off-trail now, half-running through bushes and brambles as she headed down the embankment. She slipped two or three times on loose dirt and stones, landed hard once, but got up, increasing her pace now.

A flurry of brown birds flew out of the underbrush, wings beating, panicked, and Remy jerked back for an instant, remembering the startled ravens that had risen up from feasting on the body of the poacher. She ran faster, panting. Her arms were scratched and scraped, her face covered in dust, but she kept moving, focused on the river and the smoke. Once she got there…once she got down there, nothing was going to stop her.

CHAPTER 84

REMY SQUEEZED THROUGH the brush along the slope, stumbling as she got closer to the river. She was exhausted now, stickers in her hair, her skin shredded by blackberry bushes, but she was free, that was all that mattered. The river was shallow here, dotted with rocks, the riverbanks more stones than sand. She took a step. Stopped and stepped back. She was shaking now. Right in front of her, a bear trap was staked out half-hidden in the brush, jagged jaws wide. A *bear* trap? After all she had been through, it wasn't just how close she had come to stepping on it, but the sight of the thing itself unnerved her. Poachers who massacred deer with automatic rifles. Nature lovers who beat poachers to death with their own weapons. Bear traps waiting beside clear, mountain rivers for the unwary man or beast....

She looped around the bear trap, careful now as she made her way down to the river. She knelt down, splashed water on her face, let it trickle down the back of her neck. Downriver she spotted a rusted camper shell on the shore, a truck parked nearby, hood up. A man bent over the engine of the truck. Remy ran towards him. All fatigue gone now. Sprinting full out. She shouted, her voice a raspy croak lost in the wind. The man kept working, too far away to hear.

She heard music as she got closer. A boombox on the roof blaring away. Ugly music. Grunts and screams and raw guitar. The music made her slow her steps, cautious now. Another change in her in the last couple weeks; she was attuned to all manner of signs and signals now, registering subtleties she would have ignored before. Fight or flight—she truly understood that imperative now, not as a slogan in a biology book, but as a primal instinct. The riverside was dotted with debris: derelict appliances, plastic water bottles, rusty 55-gallon drums, soggy sleeping bags. She quietly circled around the 4x4 pickup, trying to get a better look at the man working on it. His face hidden, skinny arms covered in tattoos. So much ink his skin appeared blue. The man slammed the hood of the truck shut. Turned. Made eye contact with her.

Remy backed away.

The mechanic's face was a skull. Cheeks sunk. Teeth missing. He looked her over, his eyes bulging, lit by a feral intelligence, He wiped his hands on a greasy rag, tucked it into his back pocket and walked toward her. "Well, lookee here. Where did you come from, sweetheart?"

Remy whirled. Ran right into the arms of another man. Another skeleton. Younger, his eyes vacant, the skin around the sockets raw.

The mechanic laughed. "I don't think she likes you, Deek."

Deek nuzzled Remy, holding her tight. He stank of body odor and a sharp, chemical stink, the same smell that had emanated from the body of the poacher she and Eli had found.

"I know, Charles," said Deek, "but that's just because she hasn't seen my good side yet."

Remy kicked him, but he just tightened his grip.

CHAPTER 85

ELI SPOTTED THE ATV in the weeds, half covered in branches. "Tree!"

Tree bent down beside the trail. Fingered a bent twig, the inside still green from the fresh break. He pointed off-trail where Remy had first started down the slope. He stood up.

"Don't be mad at her," said Eli.

Tree ran into the brush.

"I *mean* it, Tree!" said Eli, following him.

CHAPTER 86

THE MECHANIC—CHARLES the other one had called him—approached Remy, a jangle of bones and gristle. His jeans hung off his scrawny frame, a belt knotted around his waist. *Microsoft Development Group* was stitched on the breast pocket of his grimy, short-sleeved shirt. "You out here all alone, sweetheart? Or did you wander away from mommy and daddy?"

Deek cawed, arms still around Remy.

"You're making a big mistake...Charles." Remy edged her fingers toward the back pocket of her jeans. Slowly slid the screwdriver up. "The rest of my camping party will be here any minute."

Charles rubbed her cheek with his thumb. Gave her a painful pinch. "Liar."

Remy shifted her shoulders, managed to pull the screwdriver out of her back pocket.

"Hang on to her." Charles started toward a large tent, pants drooping, the dirty waistband of his white briefs exposed. "Tall Paul isn't going to believe what just washed up."

Deek sniffed Remy's hair. "I call first dibs—"

Remy stabbed him in the face with the screwdriver. Ran toward the woods as Deek howled behind her. Remy heard footsteps, increased her speed. An abandoned refrigerator lay on the rocks. Animals hides were loosely stretched out on racks: a fox with a sad tail flapping in the breeze, a golden lynx, a deer hide pocked with bullet holes. She almost made it into the trees when she slipped on a rotting fish and fell, banging her knee. Someone grabbed her hair, jerked her to her feet and Remy struck out again with the screwdriver.

Charles snarled, fell backwards, the screwdriver sticking out of his thigh.

Remy started running again, but Deek tackled her. He sat on her chest, holding her down, huffing and puffing. Breath leaked out of the screwdriver hole in his cheek as he punched her. She clawed back at him, fearless, tearing furrows down his face. Deek cocked his fist.

"No!" Charles hobbled over. Smacked Deek across the head. "Ignoramus."

"She *hurt* me!" squealed Deek, still astride her.

Charles kept his eyes locked on Remy as he slowly pulled the screwdriver out of his leg. He didn't even blink. "Don't be in such a hurry, Deek." He threw the screwdriver into the ground, stuck it just a couple inches from Remy's head. "You need to learn the pleasure of delayed gratification."

CHAPTER 87

CLEO WATCHED GLENN rapidly descend the tall cedar tree, moving so fast he was practically falling through the rain. He landed on the ground, knees flexed. "Well?"

"Nobody's home," said Glenn.

"Perfect."

"They'll be back," said Glenn.

"And you know this how?"

"Where are they going to go, Cleo? Fucking need an ark to ride this out and Tree ain't Noah."

"You said the ATV was gone."

"It is." Glenn pointed. "Even with the rain, you can still see the tracks. Eli, fucking idiot, he was always doing wheelies."

"So why aren't they here?"

Glenn shrugged. "Maybe they went mushroom hunting or something and got caught in the storm. Don't worry, babe, they'll be back."

'Don't worry,' the ugliest words in the English language. Cleo wrapped her jacket around her. She was wet and freezing, her ass hurt from bouncing along the rutted trails, and the storm was knocking down branches and trees all over the forest. She should have already been on her way by now. Over and done with this nonsense. Tree and Eli and Glenn should be lying dead in the woods, a grateful Remy hanging on tight as Cleo drove the motorcycle back toward the city. Back to a hero's welcome and a sea of news cameras.

She checked her watch. No telling when the tanker truck was going to blow. A highly unstable chemical stew, that's how the literature described the load when it was not refrigerated. Remy had allowed enough time for her to get back and alert the authorities, but there was always the possibility of a lightning strike or just static electricity setting it off. So much for don't worry.

Cleo took a deep breath, watching Glenn hide the motorcycle, piling on branches until it was invisible. It was going to be fine. She had worked too hard for things to fall apart now. As soon as she and Remy got someplace with cell phone service, Cleo would call the authorities. After an "anonymous" tip to Roberto Saiz, local stringer for CBS news. Then Homeland Security, and *then* the FBI, just in case Grayson tried to steal the credit. She wouldn't have just rescued a hostage, she would have broken a ring of domestic terrorists. Saving Remy would be good for fifteen minutes of fame, but saving a city...no telling where a woman with her beauty, brains and ambition could take that. The world was a ripe fruit...all she had to do was open a hand and catch it as it fell.

CHAPTER 88

"THERE'S NO NEED for this," said Remy, her arms spread wide, as Deek wired her wrists to the tailgate of the truck.

"Uh-huh," said Deek, finishing up.

"I was kidnapped," said Remy, keeping her voice steady. "Police...FBI, all kinds of law enforcement are looking for me."

"Not out here, I bet." The hole in Deek's cheek whistled when he talked. "Nobody out here but us."

"There's a ransom for my safe return," said Remy. "All you have to do is—"

"Charles handles the money," said Deek. "He's real good with numbers. Chemistry too. You name it, he knows it."

Charles limped out of the tent with a towering, spindly man. Tall Paul—an enormous scarecrow in a black rubber apron and yellow dishwashing gloves, his hair singed off in patches. Drums of chemicals lay on their sides behind the tent, pour spouts unscrewed, the ground discolored. The wind blowing over the drums burned Remy's nose.

"She says she been kidnapped," said Deek. "Says there's a reward out for her."

"That right?" Charles turned off the boom box, and the sound of the shallow river running over the rocks was suddenly louder. He pulled a pump shotgun out of the cab of the truck. Racked the slide. "Tall Paul? Hey, what do you think?"

Tall Paul's dead eyes sucked the life out of Remy. "Bet she tastes like chicken." He peeled off the rubber gloves with a snap.

The sky darkened by the moment, black storm clouds building up higher and higher.

"Okay, boys, time for a pow-wow," said Charles.

Bent over the tailgate, Remy twisted her head so she could watch the three of them at the front of the truck. While she watched, she worked on slipping free. A few minutes later, the conference was over. Deek wore her silk jacket, capering around, awkwardly modeling it for the other two.

Charles leaned the shotgun against the front bumper, and went through her wallet, neatly stacking the contents on the hood of the truck. Tall Paul sat on a drum of acetone, his nose stuck in a plastic bag of white powder, huffing away.

"Remy Brandt,'" said Charles, reading off of her driver's license. "Never heard of you." He rubbed his leg where she had stabbed him. "You look a lot better than your photo."

Deek examined himself in the side mirror of the truck. Jabbed a finger at his cheek. "Look what you done to my *face*. I look like a fucking zombie."

"Yeah, there goes your modeling career," said Remy, "the runway is going to have to look elsewhere for America's top model."

"What's that supposed to mean?" said Deek.

"There's a big reward for my safe return," Remy said to Charles. "No questions asked. Just bring me back to—"

Charles flicked her platinum AMEX with his thumbnail "We'll certainly take that under advisement, Miss Brandt, but look around...we're not in Kansas anymore."

"How long would it take to drive me to the city?" said Remy.

"First you got to get to a road." Charles picked his teeth with a corner of the AMEX. "It's a *long* drive along the river to that road though, and the truck here...well, I'm not much of a mechanic."

"So we hike to the road, or..." Remy pointed at the motorcycle half-hidden in the brush, the same one the poacher had driven. "You could take me on that."

"Yeah, well, only room for the two of us on the bike."

Remy could see Deek listening. "You're smart, Charles, that's obvious," she said, voice lowered. "Don't waste the opportunity."

"Flattery...oh, you'll go far with that, sweetheart." Charles slipped the AMEX back into her wallet. Hitched up his pants. "Come on, Deek. Time to take a vote before the storm hits."

Still perched on the metal drum of chemicals, Tall Paul's head jerked back. He groaned, the tip of his nose dabbed with white powder. "Charles...man, you *got* to try this new batch I just cooked up." He held out the bag. "This...this is the shit, man, the righteous kill, the bust-out motherfucking nuts."

Charles took the offered bag. He shook a mound of white crystals into the palm of his hand, hoovered the crank up in one long, twisting snort. "Ahhhhhhhhhhhhhh." He looked at Tall Paul. "You're the master blaster."

Tall Paul stared up at the sky, turning small circles.

Remy stared at Charles' monogrammed silver belt buckle. JH. Not *his* initials. The belt was huge on him, so big it had to be knotted.

"You want a boost?" Charles held out the bag of crank to Remy.

Remy couldn't take her eyes off the buckle.

"I asked you a question," Charles said softly.

"No...no."

"What the *fuck* are you looking at?" A drop of mucous hung from one of Charles' nostrils, vibrating with every breath. His face twisted, rage boiling inside him.

"The belt...I'm looking at the buckle."

Charles hitched up his pants. "You like it? I took it off this moron who was part of my crew until a few days ago. Fat John. Asshole thought he was fucking Daniel Boone."

JH. The name on the dead poacher's camouflage jacket was Harris. The dead poacher who smelled like Charles and the rest of them.

"Shoot Bambi all you want, I told him," said Charles, "but keep your damned traps away from here. He wouldn't listen. Got paranoid. Talking about perimeter control. I went to take a dump a couple nights ago and about stepped on bear trap. Would have snapped my foot clear off. That was that. Went off with him the next day and beat the motherfucker's brains out." He jabbed a finger at Remy. "You think about that next time you consider going against my wishes."

Remy felt dizzy, as though she had lost something...some trinket that brought her comfort.

"You like my new belt buckle?" said Charles.

Making Tree the murderer had aligned her with Eli, given her hope that she could turn him, but Tree wasn't the most dangerous beast in the woods. If anything, he had tried to keep her safe in his own part of the forest.

"I'm *talking* to you." Charles snapped his fingers, "Hey!" A capillary in his right eye had broken, a tributary of blood winding across the white, trailing across his vision.

"Yes, it's...it's very nice," said Remy.

Charles' eyes flared. Blue as a blowtorch. "Don't patronize me, you *cunt*. I've got a Masters in computer science from Berkeley. You want me to run some algorithmic equations for you while I freight-train your ass?

CHAPTER 89

"ALL IN FAVOR?" barked Charles.

Remy jerked at the wires around her wrists.

Tall Paul, Deek and Charles all had their hands raised.

"Looks like the ayes have it." Charles looked over at her. "You want a recount, sweetheart?"

Deek unzipped his pants.

"Cut me loose," said Remy. "We'll have more fun."

"Don't worry," said Deek, "we're going to have plenty of fun."

Tall Paul snorted more meth. He fiddled with his pants under his rubber apron, unsteady, blinking in the sun.

Deek struggled to pull down Remy's jeans as Remy kicked at him.

"What's your hurry?" Remy pulled her right wrist free, but they didn't notice. Might not have cared even if they had. Her legs buckled, and she couldn't stop trembling, but there was a coolness at her core, a sense that if she could only keep them talking, things would be fine. Words were the only weapon she had now, words and her wits. "Crank makes you impotent anyway. You're going to need a splint and some Superglue to get anywhere with that pathetic noodle."

Charles turned towards the trees. Listening.

"What a loser," said Remy. "Probably handed out towels to the football team in high school, stayed late sniffing jocks. Was that your specialty, Deek?"

Deek grabbed Remy's hair, pulled her head back. "Keep talking."

"I bet you're a real charmer with the farm animals," spat Remy, bent backwards as Deek dryhumped her. "You and your thimble dick. Baaa." She forced a laugh. "Baaaaaaaaa, Does that help? Baaaaaaaaaaaaa."

Tall Paul pushed Deek aside, sent him sprawling in the dirty. "Get out of the way, *thimble dick*. Let me show you how it's done."

Remy started tugging at the wires around her left wrist, her skin slippery with sweat. A clump of her hair drifted on the breeze; it looked like the smoke that had drawn her to the camp, thinking it was a refuge from Tree and Eli. She thought of Eli and the afternoon they had spent in the meadow...the two of them alone with the wildflowers. She thought of Mack...he was probably never going to know what had happened to her.

Tall Paul shoved Deek aside.

"Hey!" said Deek. "I called first dibs."

"Sure, Paul, he called first dibs." Remy frantically tugged at the wire around her left wrist as Tall Paul hooked his fingers into her panties. "Play fair, Paul. You wouldn't want Deek to run crying to Charles." Her hand was almost free.

Charles dropped the baggie of meth. "Knock it off. I heard something."

A rock slammed into the back of Tall Paul's skull. Sounded like a board breaking. He crumpled to the ground.

"What——?" A rock hit Deek in the side. He dropped to his knees, groaning, clutching his ribs.

A rock splintered the windshield of the truck as Charles grabbed the shotgun.

Deek tried to stand. Another rock smacked him in the head, and he collapsed.

Remy pulled her other hand free. She saw Charles scuttling around the truck, the shotgun cradled in his arms. He was close enough now that she could see meth crystals caked around his nostrils.

Eli sprinted from the underbrush, zigzagging toward them.

Charles heard Eli, turned and raised the shotgun.

"Charles!" shouted Remy.

Her cry distracted Charles for a moment, and in that instant Tree stood up from the underbrush, whipped another rock at Charles with his sling.

Charles ducked, the rock zinging past his head. He turned the shotgun on Remy, snarling. He might have fired too, but another rock hit the truck right next to him. He turned, fired at Tree. Missed.

Tall Paul sat up, dazed, rubbing the back of his head, as though he had awakened from a sound sleep. He pulled a pistol out from under his apron.

Eli rushed towards her.

"Go back!" said Remy.

Tall Paul raised the gun toward Eli.

Remy saw Eli wince as though already shot, then Tree blindsided Tall Paul, knocked him off his feet.

Tall Paul shrieked as Tree picked him up, shook him like he was a dirty diaper, then threw him back down onto the rocks. Tall Paul didn't move.

Tree looked at Remy...so *pleased*. She had never seen him so happy.

A shotgun blast hit Tree in the chest, rocked him backwards but he didn't fall. Just kept looking at Remy as Charles racked the slide, advancing on him. The second blast tore through Tree's midsection, and he toppled over. He lay there, legs bent awkwardly under him, lug soles of his boots gouging at the earth.

Eli ran towards Charles, the veered away as Charles raised the shotgun.

Charles fired. Missed. Cranked the slide and fired, again and again as Eli dodged and weaved across the camp.

Remy shadowed Charles, staying just out of his visual range.

Eli tried to hide between a drum of acetone, but Charles blasted the metal drum, showered Eli with chemicals. Eli screamed.

Charles racked the slide again, aimed at Eli.

Remy lunged at him, grabbed the shotgun, the two of them wrestling for it. Charles' eyes got wider and wider as they struggled, surprised at her dogged resistance, Remy kicking at him as she tried to maintain her grip. What did he think she was going to do, stand there like a debutante, wringing her hands while waiting for the killing to stop?

Eli bent over Tree's bloody body, muttering something about the big storm coming and it was going to be so cool and Tree didn't want to miss it.

Remy and Charles stumbled across the river rocks as they fought over the shotgun, Charles cursing, their faces so close she could smell the sourness of him. Remy held on for what seemed like hours, trying to peel his fingers away, and she wondered why Charles looked so nervous. What are you scared of, Charles? Surely not this little sweetheart—

The shotgun bucked. Remy didn't hear a thing, but her ears rang and she felt her face sprayed with rain. Warm rain. No...blood. She was covered in it. She lay back on the rocks. Exhausted. Someone was crying. She looked over and saw Eli still beside Tree, begging him not to go, Eli jerking like he was being hit by electrical current.

It started raining. "Eli?" said Remy. "Eli!"

Eli looked over at her, still twitching. "Tree...he's gone."

"Eli..." Remy moistened her lips. "You have to wash off...wash off the chemical."

Eli stared at her.

"Wash...wash in the river."

Eli staggered past her toward the river, his dreads dripping down his back with ever step.

Remy shivered, teeth chattering, wondered if she should wash off too. Try and get Charles' stink off her. Later. Too tired now. She closed her eyes, drifting. Later. Wondered if this was what going in to shock was like. It was raining harder now, beating down on her, colder than the wind.

"Hey...you!" It was Deek, her red silk jacket flapping around him in the storm. One of his eyes was swollen shut. "You...you fucking whore."

Remy saw the other one too...Tall Paul on one knee, digging in the bag of crank, dredging up a handful of white powder. The wind carried the crystals away, right through his fingers...most of it anyway, but Tall Paul snorted the rest. More than enough to bring him to his feet. He might be broken after what Tree had done to him, one whole side of his face mashed, but he was moving again, animated by chemistry and hate. Night of the Living Dead. Remy laughed and it hurt. Leave it to an entertainment attorney to think in terms of bad movies. It was a long time ago, but that's what she was...what she was.

Eli sat in the river, the icy water waist high, oblivious.

Remy was on her feet now, struggling to stay upright on the rocks, buffeted by the wind and rain. Her hands were slippery with blood as she raised the shotgun, but she held on. Deek first. Then Tall Paul. She pulled the trigger. The shotgun clicked. She racked the slide, pulled the trigger again. The gun was empty.

Deek staggered towards Remy. He bent down and picked up a rock, a boulder, three or four times the size of his head.

Deek spit at her. A bloody gob that landed beside her, a broken tooth in the center. "You killed *Charles*. You blew him all apart." He lifted the boulder over his head.

Remy gave him the finger. She wanted to tell him so much more, but she was too tired. The finger was going to have to do. She heard a sound behind her...thunder?

Deek looked startled, almost lost his grip on the boulder.

Remy turned. Mack? She squinted. It really *was* Mack, halfway down the ridge above the beach, running through the underbrush towards them. He had a gun in his hand.

Deek's red silk jacket indented, gunshots echoing, blood redder than the silk spreading across his chest. He dropped the boulder. Sat down gently as a flower falling. He looked like he was trying to figure out where all the blood came from, then lay back at an uncomfortable angle on the rocks.

Tall Paul hobbled toward them now, his broken face smeared with crystal.

Mack was almost to the beach when he howled, fell face first into the underbrush, rolling now, end over end, a length of chain trailing behind him.

Remy hurried to where Mack thrashed on the ground. He had stepped in a large trap—not a bear trap, there were no jagged teeth, but the flat jaws of the trap clamped around his ankle, his boot at a bad angle. She grabbed the rusty metal stake at the end of the chain, tried to pry apart the jaws of the trap.

Mack pushed her back, grabbed the trap. "Gun," he gritted, straining to open the jaws. "Find my gun."

Remy scooted into the damp underbrush, looking for the gun. The pounding rain quickly turning the slope to mud. She glanced back, saw Mack inching the trap wider and wider, sweat running down his forehead.

306

Tall Paul was almost to them. Remy hesitated.

"*Gun,*" hissed Mack as he awkwardly pulled his foot free.

Remy pushed aside the underbrush, eyes sweeping over the ground.

Mack tried to stand, fell over, his foot useless.

Tall Pall kicked him in the side, tromped on his knee, laughing hysterically as Mack doubled into a ball, trying to protect himself.

Mack tripped Tall Paul, grabbed at the big man's hair, tearing a clump loose from his scalp. Tall Paul laughed.

Remy's hand closed around the gun in the weeds. She scrambled to where the two men were thrashing around on the ground, but was afraid to shoot.

Tall Paul grabbed Mack by the shoulders. Rain ran down his face as he slammed the back of Mack's head into the ground.

Remy splashed through the puddles, waited for the right moment and shot Tall Paul twice, but he was so wired up he barely reacted, just kept banging on Mack. She darted in, closer...too close.

Tall Paul snatched the gun from her, started to get up.

Mack flipped the chain around Tall Paul's neck and dragged him down. As Tall Paul struggled, Mack slipped the stake through the links and started twisting, tightening the chain. Flat on his back, Tall Paul flopped about, bleeding from the gunshot wounds as he reached behind him, trying to get to Mack. The veins on Mack's hands popped out as he tightened the chain, the links digging deeper and deeper into Tall Paul's neck. Desperate now, Tall Paul tore at the chain, gagging, furrowing his heels into the dirt. Mack arched his back, tightening his grip even more.

Remy stared into Tall Paul's eyes as the rusty chain twisted tighter and tighter around his throat, his sallow complexion red, then streaked with purple. He reached for her as he bucked and twisted, and all she could see was that the whites of his bulging eyes were yellowed, and that he probably had hepatitis and...and...his eyes looked like they were about to burst out of his skull.

Mack waited until Tall Paul had stopped moving, then he waited some more, before letting go of the chain. He pushed Tall Paul off of him.

Remy bent down beside Mack, tears running down her cheek. "I'm not crying," she whispered, putting her arms around him. "I'm...I'm just happy."

Mack was breathing too hard to speak.

They held each other in the rain, neither of them feeling the storm or anything else except the warmth of each other, and how long it had been since they had been together. Remy didn't know how long they stayed like that. After a while, she helped him up, Mack hanging on her, unable to put any weight on his one foot.

Eli still sat in the river, the rain beating down on him.

The two of them slowly made their way out to where Eli was, Mack using a large branch as a crutch, making tiny gasps with every step.

"Tree's gone," said Eli as they came up behind them, not turning around.

"I know," said Remy.

The river around Eli was pocked with falling rain. "I...I don't feel so good."

"You have to get out of there," said Remy. "You'll freeze to death."

"Fine by me," said Mack.

"It's not like that," Remy said to Mack.

Eli lifted his face to the rain.

"Eli, come on out," said Remy.

"Give me my gun," Mack said to her.

"Eli and Tree...they saved my life," said Remy.

"You wouldn't be here to save if they hadn't kidnapped you," said Mack.

"I should have never listened to Glenn," said Eli, teeth chattering. He stood up, walked out of the river, so cold his skin was whiter than white. He shook out his dreads, flung water all around him. "You got blood all over you," he said to Remy.

"I know."

"I'm sorry."

"It's all right."

"Give me my *fucking* gun," said Mack.

"Promise you're not going to arrest him," said Remy.

Mack stuck his hand out.

"You can barely stand up," said Remy.

"I need to bury Tree," said Eli. "I need to bury him in the woods. Then if you want...I'll take you back to the main road. I really am sorry."

"See, Mack?" said Remy. "Like I said, Eli...he's one of the good guys."

CHAPTER 90

MACK WATCHED ELI shoveling dirt onto Tree's grave, the rain coming down so hard the kid was barely visible. "I always wanted to know what one of the good guys looked like. Somehow I never expected them to look like Eli."

"Whatever happened wasn't initiated by Eli," said Remy, "It was Glenn."

"Glenn's probably got his own problems right about now. A friend of mine staked out the road into the reserve. Cop named Hobbs. Can't wait for you to meet him."

He and Remy were sheltered by a thick copse of pine trees, Remy's arm around his shoulder, the tweeker's motorcycle parked nearby. Eli had splinted Mack's ankle, but it was still throbbing and swollen. Eli had scavenged an ax and a shovel from the tweeker's supplies. He used the ax to make a travois out of branches, attached it to the motorcycle and roped Tree's body to it. Mack sat behind Eli on the motorcycle, the travois bumping along behind them with every rise and pothole. Remy walked beside them. It had taken over an hour to get to this spot on the edge of a meadow. They were soaked and tired, splattered with mud, and it was getting dark.

"How...how long has it been?" said Remy.

"Eleven days," said Mack.

"Seems longer."

"Yeah."

"I knew you'd find me," said Remy.

"Sending Eli looking for French shampoo...that was genius," said Mack.

Remy stared at Eli working away in the downpour. "I didn't know Eli did that."

"Your father told me you had done the same thing the last time—"

"You talked to my *father?*" The wind swirled wet leaves all around them. "That must have been interesting."

310

"I think Grace is dead, Remy."

Remy nodded. Wiped at her eyes.

"If it helps," said Mack, "this Glenn...I think he could talk a lot of women into just about anything."

"How are you doing?" Remy gently stroked his hair.

"I'll live." He was having double vision off and on, but he hadn't told her. Nothing to do for a concussion, nothing out here anyway. He felt Remy clinging to him, touching his arm, his leg, maintaining contact as though to reassure herself that he was really there. Mack did the same thing.

"I killed a man at the river," Remy said softly, watching the rain drip off the trees. "One of the meth cookers...Charles. I actually know his name. He was the one who killed Tree, just...blasting away with a shotgun until Tree went down. I grabbed the shotgun before he could use it on me or Eli. I tried to take it away from him...next thing I knew it went off. Practically blew his head apart. It felt like taking a shower in blood, and I...I didn't mind at all. I was glad Charles was dead, glad I killed him." She looked at Mack. "I'm a member of the ACLU. I believe in handgun control. I...I listen to NPR for God's sake..." Her smiled was crooked. "Eli...Eli said people change fast out here."

Mack held her.

Eli put the last shovel full of dirt on Tree's grave. He stood there for a few minutes, head bowed, then walked back to them.

"We're not far from the big cedar." Eli wiped his filthy hands on his jeans.

"Good," said Remy, helping Mack to his feet.

"When we get back to camp, I'll make us some dinner," said Eli, his hands twitching. "Maybe hit the hot spring. I...I don't think washing off the chemicals in the river got rid of all of them."

"That's a good idea, Eli," said Remy.

"What's a good idea?" said Eli.

Remy glanced at Mack. "The hot spring."

Eli spat. "I got...got a really bad taste in my mouth." He looked at Mack. "What's your name again?"

"Eli?" Remy took his hand. *"Eli?'*

Eli stood there looking at Mack. "It don't mean anything. Me and Remy, we're just friends."

"I know," said Mack.

"Eli," said Remy, squeezing his hand, "we should go to the hot spring."

"It...it's not far from camp," said Eli. "I'll just drop you off—"

"No, Eli," said Remy. "We should go to the hot spring *now*. See if you can sweat the toxins out."

Mack hopped over to the motorcycle. "Come on, Eli."

"You want to ride on the travois?" said Eli, walking towards him, he and Remy still holding hands. "There's...there's room now."

"Cut it loose," said Mack. "We'll make faster time without it."

The trip to the hot spring only took a half hour according to Mack's watch, but it seemed much longer. He hung on to Eli but every bump, every puddle, every rock in the trail sent a jolt of pain through his ribs. Four or five times when Eli veered the motorcycle to the side of the road to avoid a pothole, the underbrush glanced against Mack's splinted ankle and had to suck in his breath to keep from crying out. Remy ran easily just behind them, pretending not to notice. He had quietly checked the ankle while Remy watched Eli dig the grave—the flesh was swollen and purple, the imprint of the trap embroidered on his skin. Coyote trap, that's what Eli had said. Mack didn't have any special fondness for coyotes, but nothing deserved to have that thing snap on them.

"Just around the bend," said Eli, slowing down. "Here...we...are."

Remy dashed ahead of them, came to a stop on the rocks around the spring. She put her hands on her knees for a moment, then stood up. Fog rose from the hot spring as the rain beat down on it, Remy highlighted against the steamy background. She looked like some forest sprite. Tall trees loomed over the spring, sheltering it from the worst of the storm.

Eli stopped the motorcycle. "You need help getting off, dude?"

Mack stiffly got off the bike himself. His ankle on fire, he limped to the spring and lay down beside it, exhausted.

Eli put down the kickstand of the motorcycle. He grabbed a pair of orange surf jams that hung from the branch of a nearby tree and walked into the bushes. A moment later he emerged wearing just the bathing suit. He took a running start, dove into the center of the spring, came up a moment later, spouting water, howling with delight.

"I had a puppy like that once," said Mack.

Remy helped Mack take off his jacket, his shirt. She soaked his shirt in the spring, gingerly wiped him down with it, the warm water sluicing off him.

"I feel better already," shouted Eli.

Remy kept working on Mack, cleaning the grime and blood off his face, his hands, his chest, his hair.

Eli came to the edge of the spring. "How is he?"

"I'm fine," said Mack.

Eli tossed an old railroad spike onto the rocks. "Show him our trick, Remy."

Remy threw the spike into the middle of the spring.

Eli dove in after it. Came back a minute later with the spike between his teeth, barking like a seal.

"Was he like this before he got splashed with acetone?" said Mack.

"You have to admit, it is kind of cute." Remy eased into the water, washed herself clean, then stepped back onto the rocks. "I'm going to go back to the base camp. There's dry clothes and blankets and food."

"I'm coming with you," said Mack.

"You should stay here, keep off your feet."

"If you think I'm letting you go now...after everything that's happened..."

"No...I feel the same way." Remy kissed him. She looked over at Eli. "Mack and I are taking the motorcycle to the big cedar."

"Cool," said Eli.

Mack hobbled to the motorcycle. "You do know how to drive this thing, right?"

Remy got on. "How hard could it be?"

CHAPTER 91

"YOU HEAR THAT?"

Cleo rested her back against the giant cedar tree, ignoring him. Glenn was always hearing something. A half hour ago he was *sure*. Cleo thought she heard it too, but whatever it was it had given the giant cedar a wide berth, fading into the distance. All she heard now was the rain. At least it was relatively dry under the shelter of the big trees.

"They're coming from that way." Glenn pointed in the opposite direction to the path he and she had ridden in on. "Must have circled around." He cocked his head, still listening.

Cleo heard it now too. She was just grateful that things would be over soon.

"That...that's a motorcycle," said Glenn.

Cleo heard it now too. "I thought you said they rode an ATV."

Glenn took out Hobbs' .357. "I did."

CHAPTER 92

THE FRONT WHEEL of the motorcycle hit a pothole at the edge of the big cedar, and Remy lost control. She gave it more throttle, overcorrected and spilled the bike, throwing her and Mack onto the wet ground.

Mack got up first, his injured foot resting lightly in the ground while he helped her to her feet.

"Don't say it," warned Remy, more embarrassed than hurt.

Mack looked up at the giant cedar, tilting his head back so far he almost fell over. "You actually *lived* up in that thing?"

"It was scary at first, but once you get past that...it's the best view in the world."

Mack was still looking up. "How did you get up there?"

"See the rope?" Remy pointed. "You climb the pegs to the knotted rope and just keep going."

"You actually did that?"

"Had to. The elevator was broken," said Remy.

Glenn stepped out from behind the giant cedar tree, pointing a pistol at Mack. "The tough guy *and* the rich bitch." He grinned. "Who says there ain't no fucking God?"

"You got your money," said Mack. "Part of it anyway. You do anything to her you're not going to get another penny."

"Where's Tree and Eli?" said Glenn, pointing the gun at Remy now.

"They rode off on the ATV early this morning," said Remy. "I tried to follow them, but I got lost, and then...I found this motorcycle—"

"So they just *left* you?" said Glenn.

"Eli said he was tired of the rain," said Remy. "I think they're going to California...or Mexico."

"Eli and his fishing village fantasy," said Glenn. "Live on bananas and surf all day. Fucking idiot. I gave Tree more credit than that."

"What are you complaining about?" said Mack, trying to balance himself. Remy could see him hooking his thumbs in his belt loops, his right hand close to the gun in his back pocket. "More money for you this way."

"What happened to your foot, tough guy?" said Glenn, his jacket flapping around him in the wind. "You fall off another girder?"

The storm buffeted the trees, branches rattling so loudly that Remy could barely hear Glenn.

"Did he tell you about that, rich girl?" Glenn snapped a photo of her with the phone, keeping his gun centered on Mack with the other hand. "Did he tell you about the fun we had walking the iron? It's a good story. You'll get a real kick out of it."

"I...I need to sit down," said Mack, lowering himself to the ground, rain dripping down his back.

"That's *it*, tough guy?" Glenn seemed angry. "You're just going to sit down and let me shoot you? No big talk? No trying to rush me. You're a disappointment—"

"Fuck your disappointment," said Mack, lying on the ground now, barely paying attention. One hand was behind his back. "I'm tired and you're a coward."

"Look at me!" demanded Glenn.

"Can't we...?" said Remy, laughing now, doubled over, unable to control herself. If she had one wish right now, she'd wish that she had Charles' shotgun, and it was loaded. That way she wouldn't have to depend on Mack to kill Glenn. "Can't..."

"What's so funny?" demanded Glenn.

"Can't we all get along?" giggled Remy.

Mack rolled over, raised his gun.

Glenn saw the movement out of the corner of his eye.

The two of them fired almost at the same time. Remy saw Glenn's shots kick up mud around Mack's head, saw Mack fire the 9mm three times before it emptied, but the low angle was awkward. Glenn spun around, hit in the left shoulder, but he stayed on his feet.

Glenn glanced at the blood leaking through his jacket. "You *shot* me!" he screamed, seemingly more outraged than hurt. He raised the revolver.

"Glenn!" A woman in a hooded sweatshirt stepped from behind the tree. "FBI! Put down your weapon!"

Glenn looked over at her, surprised.

The woman shot Glenn twice in the chest, knocked him backwards, his gun flying. He lay quietly on the soggy ground. The woman showed a badge to Remy. "Special Agent Cleo Hutchinson, Ms. Brandt. You're safe now."

Mack stared at her. *"Cleo?"*

Cleo smiled. "Hello, Mack."

"You know each other?" said Remy.

"I've been working undercover for the last two years," said Cleo. "Mack interviewed me while he was looking for you. He had no idea who I was."

Remy walked over to Glenn. He lay twisted on the ground, face up, one eyebrow still singed from where she had torched him with the lighter a few days ago. It seemed a lot longer ago. Rain fell on his face, drops clinging to his long eyelashes like tears.

Mack slowly got to his feet. "How did you get here, Cleo?"

"I goaded Glenn into bringing me. Told him his story about kidnapping an heiress was bullshit. Glenn was clever, but his vanity made him stupid. I had no idea he was planning to kill you, or—"

"I'm not an heiress," said Remy.

"Are you wounded, Mack?" said Cleo.

"No."

"Where are the other agents?" said Remy.

"There's just me," said Cleo. "I had a rather...difficult time convincing the bureau that environmental terrorists had kidnapped you. I heard a lot of granola and Birkenstock jokes." She smiled at Remy. "You told Glenn that Eli and Tree abandoned you. Is that really true?"

"No," started Remy. "They—"

"They're dead," said Mack. "They were out hiking with Remy when they ran into a group of tweekers cooking up a fresh batch near the river. Things got ugly. The tweekers are dead, but so are Eli and Tree. You'll want to put that in your report."

"Mack heard the gunfire and showed up just in time," said Remy, backing up Mack, glad that he had decided to protect Eli from the law. "He almost died too."

Cleo bent down and picked up the revolver Glenn had dropped.

"Let me see that," said Mack.

Cleo held up the snub-nosed .357.

"I...I know that gun," said Mack, limping forward. "It belongs to a cop—"

"Yes, Glenn told me he had taken it from a police detective."

"No way he took Marcus' gun from him," said Mack.

Cleo tucked away the .357. "You knew Detective Hobbs?"

"He was my friend."

"I'm sorry," said Cleo. "Glenn said he's dead."

Mack shook his head. "I...I just don't see Glenn being able to kill Marcus."

"I never met the detective, but anyone can be killed," said Cleo. "Anyone can be killed by anyone."

"I have to sit down," said Mack. "Little...dizzy here."

Cleo and Remy helped Mack over to the big cedar, eased him against the trunk. It was dry there, just gusts of wind-blown rain. Cleo pushed her hood back, shook out her glossy black hair and squatted down beside him. "Take it easy. Rest up. We're going to have to leave shortly."

"It's getting dark," said Remy, and I don't know the way out."

"No worries." Cleo stood up, pulled a small GPS device out of her pocket. "We'll be back on the road in a couple hours. I have to contact my office as soon as we're in cell phone range. Your kidnapping was just the first stage of a terrorist attack. Glenn told me they had hijacked a truck full of volatile chemicals—"

"The truck is in a mothballed storage facility," said Remy. "Eli called it a bus barn."

"I've already notified the authorities," said Cleo. "It's under control."

"Have they found Hobbs' body?" said Mack.

"Not yet. His department probably doesn't even know he's dead. My trip out here was unplanned."

Mack kept shaking his head. "Farwell...he must have freelanced the stakeout."

"Are you alright, Ms. Brandt?" said Cleo.

"I'm fine...and it's Remy."

"How did Hobbs die?" persisted Mack. "Glenn must have told you. Bragging...that's half the fun for him."

"No need to upset yourself," said Cleo.

Mack put a hand on the ground to stop himself from falling over. "How did he die?"

Cleo hesitated. "He said he cut the detective's throat."

"Bullshit," said Mack.

"Take it easy," said Cleo.

"Don't tell me how to take it." Mack's hand clawed at the tree trunk as he pulled himself on his feet.

"Now you did it," Remy teased Cleo, trying to break the tension. "Easiest way to get Mack excited is to tell him to calm down."

Cleo smiled back at her. "I know. First time I met him, I thought, this one's a five-dollar firecracker with a short fuse."

Remy saw Mack's head jerk. Saw Cleo's mouth tighten at the same moment, as though they shared a private joke...but neither of them was smiling.

Mack reached for the extra magazine in his jacket.

"*Don't,*" said Cleo.

"Don't what?" said Mack, his fingers closing around the magazine.

"You couldn't let it go, could you?" Cleo said to him.

Cleo looked angry and Remy couldn't understand why.

"You just *had* to keep asking questions." Cleo backed away from the tree trunk, out into the driving rain. The gun in her hand...it was Hobbs' .357.

"What's going on?" said Remy.

"Tell her, Mack," said Cleo.

Mack didn't say anything.

"Somebody tell me what's going on," demanded Remy.

"Cleo killed Hobbs," Mack said, his voice weaker. "The only one who ever described me as a lit firecracker was Marcus, and now Cleo, and she said she never met him."

"That...that's it?" said Remy.

319

"No way...no way Hobbs would let Glenn get close enough to cut his throat," said Mack. "Only somebody Hobbs trusted could get that close."

"Like an FBI agent," said Remy.

"I got sloppy," said Cleo. "That's what happens when you deal with idiots on a regular basis." She centered the gun on Remy's chest, the .357 unwavering in her grip. "Turns out Glenn was a good shot after all. He killed the both of you before I could bring him down."

Remy saw Eli peering out from the underbrush behind Cleo, the railroad spike between his teeth.

"Killing us is going to dull the shine on your halo," said Mack. "You took down the kidnappers, but the hostage died." He started to laugh but his voice trailed off.

Remy glanced over at him. Mack had passed out, his head flopped at an awkward angle.

"My halo's going to be just fine," Cleo said to Remy. "Safely retrieving you was always a secondary objective."

"Why would you do this?" said Remy. "*Why?*"

"For what it's worth, Miss Brandt, I'm sorry. I genuinely am."

"You're not going to get away with it," said Remy.

"People always say things like that," said Cleo, "but it's not true. People like me get away with it all the time. People like you do too...until now."

Remy recognized the look in Cleo's eyes—it was the look of an agent who knew she had the studio over a barrel and was going to get every one of her deal points. She inched closer to the woman, the ground spongy underfoot. It wasn't going to do any good, but Remy wasn't just going to stand there and die.

Eli staggered out of the underbrush in his surf jams, unsteady.

"If you could emotionally remove yourself from the situation, I'd think you'd admire what I've done," said Cleo, raising her voice to be heard over the storm. "The planning, the timing...the ability to adapt to changing circumstances..."

"Yeah, you're an MBA with a body count," said Remy. "Very impressive."

Cleo flushed. "You should congratulate me. I'm the woman who saved a city from a toxic terrorist attack. When I get back, I'll be the biggest story in the country."

"Another fake hero," said Remy.

Cleo smiled. "Fake heroes are what this country runs on, don't you know that by now? The accidental kind aren't prepared; they stumble and stammer through their network interviews—aw shucks, I'm just regular folks, nothing special, just send me to Disneyland and I'm happy. Not me, Miss Brant. I'm what you might call a *professional* hero. Oh, the Bureau will pin some medal on my chest, but that's chump change."

Thunder crashed across the forest, rolling like a tidal wave through the trees.

Cleo jerked at the sound, but kept the pistol on Remy.

Eli crept closer through the rain, staying right behind Cleo. He hefted the railroad spike.

"It's hard to do, isn't it?" said Remy. Cleo thought she was talking to her.

"Not at all." Cleo thumbed back the hammer on the revolver. "Not even a little—" She stumbled as the railroad spike grazed the back of her head.

Cleo whirled, rubbing her head as she raised the gun at Eli.

Eli backed up, hands raised. "Whoa, time out!" He closed his eyes.

Remy grabbed the spike from the shallow puddle it had landed in, plunged the spike into the back of Cleo's neck, driving the rusty metal deep into her milk white skin.

Cleo turned, looked at Remy, surprised, the tip of the spike visible at the base of her throat. The .357 dropped from her hand.

Eli opened his eyes, stared at the two of them.

Cleo gingerly touched the tip of the spike. She looked at the blood on her fingertips, confused.

The storm was a thousand miles away. So was the forest. Remy and Cleo were wrapped in some sort of silent cocoon, standing there alone, waiting for Cleo to decide to die. It took her a while. Seemed to anyway and the decision didn't come easy. Cleo reached out and rested her cool hand on Remy's wrist, hanging on until even her own ferocious will to live wasn't enough. Cleo sighed...slipped away and fell into the mud.

Thunder shook the air, jolted Remy, momentarily deafening her. She looked at her wrist, saw raw scratches from Cleo's fingernails. She stepped over Cleo and went to help Mack.

Robert Ferrigno

EPILOGUE

Three weeks later

"HERE'S MY FATHER now," said Remy.

Mack stood, held his hand out to the white-haired gentleman approaching their table at the Peninsula in L.A.

Brandt strode like a lion in a gunmetal gray three-piece, his silvery hair cut short. "*Hello*, Mack." Brant squeezed Mack's hand, gave his daughter a peck on the cheek. "Darling." He examined Remy, taking his time. "You look...different."

"I feel different," said Remy.

"Well, I suppose that's to be expected after your recent ordeal," said Brandt.

"Don't gush, father. You'll crack your heart."

Brandt looked past her, snapped his fingers.

A waiter appeared, inclined his head toward Brandt.

"Three vodka martinis, very dry," said Brandt.

"I saw you on the business channel," Mack said to Brandt. "The Buccaneer of Wall Street, back from the brink with a 500-million-dollar profit in Irish bonds."

"The brink may be a slight overstatement, but I had definitely attracted more oversight than I'm comfortable with," said Brandt. "I knew I just needed a little time for the world to fall into its proper place."

"At your feet," said Mack.

"Don't be bitter, Mack, it betrays poor breeding." Brandt smiled his very white teeth. "Here we are, sitting quite comfortably together, and none of us the worse for wear. I would call that a happy ending."

323

"I told them not to bother asking you for any kind of ransom, Father," said Remy. "I said they'd have a better chance throwing a bake sale."

Brandt's cheeks pinked up. "Consider it a compliment, darling. I knew you'd find a way out of your predicament." He nodded at Mack. "You and your young man here."

"I'm flattered. How about you, Mack?" said Remy.

The waiter set down three martinis and Brandt picked up a glass. "A toast."

Mack left his drink untouched.

Brandt took a swallow of his martini, set the glass down. "I understand the FBI still has no leads on the last kidnapper."

"His name is Eli," said Remy.

"Indeed. Well, I'm certain his mammy and his pappy are proud of him." Brandt beamed at his little joke. "I am sorry, Mack, about the death of the police officer...I understand he was a friend of yours. Have they found the body yet?"

Mack didn't answer.

"They found him last week," said Remy. "They narrowed the search by triangulating his last cell phone signals. They finally located Detective Hobbs in the garage of an abandoned housing development. They found Grace's body there too."

"Ah yes, your former room-mate," said Brandt. "Scholarship student, what did you expect?"

Mack started to stand up, but Remy shook her head and he sat down.

"I'm being interviewed on *60 Minutes* the day after tomorrow," said Remy.

"Lovely," said Brandt. "I'll have Cook Tivo it for me."

"I can't *wait* to tell them about your clever handling of the kidnapper's demands," said Remy.

Brandt sipped his drink. "Umm...I don't think that would be advisable, Remy. People might not understand."

"I think they'd understand perfectly," said Remy.

"I know *I* understand," said Mack.

"See, Mack understands, Daddy."

Brandt tapped his martini glass with his manicure.

"I have an idea," said Remy.

Brandt kept tapping his martini glass.

"I think you should deed over the old growth forest that Tree wanted," said Remy. "I think you should give it to the National Conservation Trust. Isn't that a good idea?"

"Don't be ridiculous," said Brandt. "That forest is worth at least eighty million dollars."

"I think that's a great idea, sweetums," said Mack. "I think it's peachy keen."

Remy kissed him. "See, Daddy, Mack thinks it's a good idea too."

"You expect me to reward one of the men who *kidnapped* you?" said Brandt.

"I expect you to do whatever is in your best interest," said Remy. "If you don't deed over the forest, you're going to get so much bad press that you're going to jeopardize your mergers and acquisitions business. If you do give up a forest, you'll gain a tax deduction and a *huge* amount of good will."

"I don't *need* good will," snapped Brandt.

"*Sure* you do." Mack patted Brandt on the back, felt him flinch. "An asshole like you can never have too many friends."

Brandt glared at Mack.

"You better get started on the paperwork, Daddy. I want you to appear with me on *60 Minutes* to make the announcement."

"A toast," said Mack.

He and Remy clinked glasses as Brandt stalked off.

"You think he's really going to do it?" said Mack.

"Of course." Remy sipped her drink, watching him over the rim. "It's the smart move and smart moves are my father's specialty."

* * * * *

Esmeralda plucked a ripe mango from the tree along the bluffs, added it to the basket of bananas and guava slung from her shoulder. The warm sun brought a trickle of sweat along the nape of her neck and she shook out her thick black hair, enjoying the sensation.

Down the beach she could see her village, small boats bobbing in the Pacific as the men came in with the day's catch, their boats heavy with success. The whole village had been lucky since the muchacho dorado had arrived a couple weeks ago. The golden boy.

There he was now. In the water below the bluffs, she saw the boy called Eli crouching on his surfboard, blonde curls around his shoulders as he rode a perfect blue wave toward shore. He must have felt her gaze, because he looked up, and at that instant lost his footing, wiping out in a froth of white water. He popped up a moment later, laughing, waved to her.

Esmeralda waved back, hurried down the path to the beach to join him.